th
eighth

MAXINE MEI-FUNG CHUNG is a psychoanalytic psychotherapist. She currently works in private practice, where she champions women and girls to use and be effective with their voice, and also supports people from ethnic minorities experiencing mental-health problems. She previously worked as a creative director for ten years at Condé Nast, *The Sunday Times* and *The Times*. She lives in London with her son.

the
eighth
girl

Maxine Mei-Fung Chung

PUSHKIN VERTIGO

Pushkin Vertigo
An imprint of Pushkin Press
71–75 Shelton Street
London WC2H 9JQ

Originally published in North America in 2020 by HarperCollins

Grateful acknowledgment is made to Mark Alexander for his
translation of Du Fu's poem "The Solitary Goose"

First published by Pushkin Press in 2021
This edition published in 2021

1 3 5 7 9 8 6 4 2

ISBN 13: 978-1-78227-696-8

Offset by Tetragon, London
Printed and bound by CPI Group (UK) Ltd, Croydon, CR0 4YY

For Joe—
Of course

the eighth girl

THE VOICES COME AND GO. LIKE FLU. WEATHER. WEEKEND SHAGS. I'M unsure how long they've been here, or if they intend to stay. I want to say they're friendly.

Alive to their company I scale the scene, first noticing the cars. Then the backup, close to a mile, crawling under my feet—snaking the strip—my eyes crimping from their blaring white lights. Families escaping the city's hum, men heading home to their wives. Girls in studied dresses switching heels for flats as they drive across town, ripe for a big night out. Everyone going somewhere, doing something, meeting someone.

Not me, I tell myself.

Not me.

There is no small corner of the world I wish to claim and delight in. No one who knows the stir in my gut. The burn. All my mistakes frozen in the tight lock of my face.

I inch forward enough to feel a surge of adrenaline, part of me always knowing it would end this way: me, the Voices, balancing on the ledge at Jumpers Bridge.

I grip the railings behind me to steady my shake, urging myself to remember how I got here—why is there a key in my left hand? I, after all, am right-handed. Still, nothing unfolds, my mind turning blank like a page erased of its words.

How long have I been here, strangling the bars? White-knuckling as if on the ride of my life—a roller coaster, a ghost train—my bare arms pimpled with cold like the skin of poultry. An ache in the base of my back.

Losing time is never good. It's an expression of the insane. An indicator of how close I am to completely losing my mind. *Concentrate*, I order myself. *Focus*.

The Voices clear their throats. A rise of phlegm foaming in my mouth, now spat down at migrating cars, a cool lick of wind guiding its direction. Like all good enforcers, they seem to engulf me tonight, pointing fingers of blame, their message both hateful and threatening.

I STARE DOWN AT THE READY DARK—

Flash.

Dusk stealing me for a beat—

Flash.

AND NOT UNUSUALLY, AN IMAGE OF MY FATHER FLARES UP IN MY MIND.

He is sitting in the corner of my bedroom, his legs crossed in the high-backed wicker chair we bought from a car boot sale. When I open my eyes I notice he is wearing a black Crombie, a blue tie—the colors of bruises. His faint eyes and bristled chin payback from the night before. Floating from his left hand is a Hello Kitty balloon.

Flash.

"Happy birthday, my sweet Xiǎo Wáwa," he whispers.

"Thank you, Baba," I say, rubbing crusted sleep from my eyes. "I'm too grown-up to be your little doll anymore. But I am sweet. Sweet as kittens."

Flash.

NOT WISHING HIM TO BE THE LAST PERSON I RELIVE BEFORE LETTING go, I picture Ella instead. The two of us are sitting in her backyard wearing denim cutoffs and cotton halters, jelly shoes rubbing the soft balls of my feet. The smell of jasmine in the afternoon air. I move a pitcher of beer around the shaded table to avoid the glare of sun. A bowl of salted nuts lassoing our thirst.

Suddenly, Ella surprises me with a silver box, a matching silk bow—which I pull, very gently, its twin loops coming apart. Inside: a stunning pair of gemstone earrings.

"Green ones," she says, "to match your eyes."

The memory calms me, and for a second I favor climbing back to safety. My helplessness eased. But then a single tear escapes, acting as a reminder of what she did.

Nerves turned on, I look down again.

How could she? Cunt.

Numb, forlorn, grief drenching my empty body, I loosen my hands. The Voices whispering softly in my ear: *Jump, you fucking crybaby.*

1

Daniel Rosenstein

I WALK TOWARD MY DESK AND GAZE OUT THE OPEN WINDOW AT THE amber evening, August light spilling through a veil of drooping wisteria. I check tomorrow's diary: *Thursday 8 A.M.—Alexa Wú.*

Normally I wouldn't start so early; certainly not before nine, but I have bent rules to accommodate her. A minor allowance because she's looking for full-time work, has several job interviews lined up, and also works nights—did I have availability early morning, because she could do any day of the week if it was early? This she spoke to my answering machine, her voice trembling at the edge. I'd wondered about this. Imagining it may have been difficult for her to ask for something—the possibility that it might be refused.

My receptionist returned her call the following day, saying I had space on Tuesdays and Thursdays. That maybe she would like to come in then? She agreed; they fixed a day and time; I added Alexa to my roster of patients.

Other psychiatrists might steer away from bending their daily routine, but I have learned such gestures go a long way in the encouraging and building of relationships, am convinced that those who experience some adjustment will eventually learn to compromise.

OUTSIDE, PATIENTS ARE FIGHTING SIGNS OF FATIGUE. WITH TIGHT yawns they shuffle about, heads limp, shoulders down—their last attempt at exercise before one of the nurses will escort them back inside the ward before supper. Earlier they appeared disorganized and manic; eyes darting, movements awkward. Handicapped as much by the medication they take as the neurosis that makes the medication necessary.

Gathering on the solid timber bench, four patients decide to rest, but reluctant to engage with one another, they stare at the huge oak and surrounding island of grass. Hands cupped in their laps as if waiting for loose change.

In the distance a flock of lively blackbirds have landed, unruffled, on the copper power lines and at once appear like musical notes. Their song is enchanting until they migrate to the blushing apple trees, their chorus now moved to the shelter of leaves.

I open the top drawer of my desk and pull out a packet of M&M's, allowing myself six candied yellow peanuts with what remains of my coffee. This I take black with three sugars—a long-standing ritual that commenced shortly after I was appointed Glendown's consulting psychiatrist eight years ago. I rest my mug on the ceramic coaster; on it: a circular hand-painted picture of Aesop's fable "The Tortoise and the Hare"—a gift from a former patient. A bipolar chef who, from the tender age of eleven, fantasized about setting objects alight. On her thirteenth birthday she set fire to her mother's entire wardrobe: the smoldering Chanel kindled to a pile of ashen confetti. I like to stare at the coaster, replaying the hare's boastful behavior and foolish confidence in my mind. Moral of the story: Never sleep on the job. Especially when your pyromaniac patient has access to a lighter.

Some clinicians claim the eroticization of gift-giving is meaningful because of its connection to the libido; that often the gift represents love and affection that is not always verbalized in the room. Even Freud, in his overzealous theories, believed a child's first interest in feces develops because he considers it a gift given up upon the mother's insistence and through which he manifests his love for her. Further insights led Freud to discover this unconscious link between defecation and treasure hunting, but in this I have to wonder. Maybe sometimes a cigar is just a cigar, a gift just a gift. A poop just a poop.

Evening drawing in, my thoughts turn to supper. A sudden rise of hunger spurs me into the tidying of clinical notes, Post-it reminders, mail, and my letter opener—also a gift, from Lucas, a recovering alcoholic who every evening had a strict one-hour OCD ritual that involved elaborate checking for serial killers in the cutlery drawer. "Oh no, not the flat ones again," I would tease. And Lucas would smile, rolling his eyes, acknowledging his need for control and obsessive compulsions before tapping the sole of his oxford lace-ups eleven times.

When Clara passed away five years ago, Susannah, who rarely visits, suddenly appeared one afternoon with a corned-beef bagel, claiming she just happened to be in the area. As she looked around my office, a glint in her eye, she jokingly named it "the Museum of Shrink Memorabilia."

"Your patients are absolutely everywhere, Dad!" She cried freely. "On the desk, on the walls, over there on the shelves. They're even in the goddamn kitchenette! You know what? You should start paying *them*!"

I had belly-laughed at the time—my kind, funny daughter. Physically her mother's child, with quick, grassy-green eyes and jet-black hair. Her broad shoulders, back then, weighted down with grief. I recall smiling—the joke causing my muscles to do something other than sag—as I grieved the loss of my wife. Her death making its own demands, my own emptiness impossible to ignore.

2

Alexa Wú

I THINK I MIGHT DIE OF EXCITEMENT. SERIOUSLY. *REASON:* ELLA Collette—best friend, bona fide babe, and, as of last night, match-maker extraordinaire! Yep. Not only do I have a date, but I also have a date *for* the date. Next Saturday. Nine P.M. Hoxton.

"He couldn't take his eyes off you," Ella teases, batting her heavy lashes, mascara having left a tinge of slate above both cheeks.

Already dressed, I jump and land on my bed, straddling Ella's flat body between my thighs, head pounding from last night's vodka tonics.

"Well, he couldn't!" she yells, triumphant, defending her ribs from my tickling hands.

"Shhh," I say, tapping my head.

"Well, he couldn't," she whispers.

I blush as I always do when Ella gets like this. Am reminded of the time my *Reason* took it upon herself to fix me up with one of her former school friends, inviting him in a hurried, liquor-laced phone call to her house one Friday night. Both of us had been loose and giddy from cheap Russian wheat vodka. But this time it's different.

This time I *actually* like the guy. He's funny. And smart. Handsome, but not *too* handsome. Tall, but not giant. *And* he has a body to die for. *Swoon!*

We met last night in Hoxton after Ella insisted that another night drinking wine at home and watching repeats of *Girls* was simply not an option.

"Fancy meeting up?" she'd called and asked, making it sound more like a demand than an inquiry. "Some cute guy came into work handing out flyers for a new club—the Electra. We got to talking. I thought it might be fun. Sounds kinda different."

"Different how?" I asked.

"You know, different."

So I went. And we met. The cute guy and me. Ella introducing us while he served sleek cocktails in chilled tall-stemmed glasses. His blue eyes holding hostage every girl seated at the bar. Ella noticed my dropped jaw as soon as I clapped eyes on him, then disappeared, squeezing my hand three times—a code we both use for reassurance. *Help,* I'd mouthed at her, palms dripping, stomach in knots, before catching his smile, which I nervously threw back. Then he leaned over and kissed me hello. I looked past his shoulder, aware the club was brimming with attractive bodies and girls performing lavish burlesque on a narrow mirrored stage. One girl with long red hair and legs for days feigned intimacy with a nickel pole at the far end. Her shoulders shimmering but her gaze somewhere else as she fingered a delicate gold necklace with a small key attached. I gawped for longer than seemed right, lost in her drops and swerves, her perfect body forcing me to want to run home and never eat again. But then cute guy's gaze brought me right back, pinning me to the spot. Stirred, I felt my breath fill my entire chest.

Flash.

Snapping back from the memory, I see Ella, drenched in mischief, cupping both hands beneath her chin to form a heart.

"Alexa and Shaun, sittin' in a tree; K-I-S-S-I-N-G," she sings, looking around me at one of my many clocks. "Fuck!"

"What?" I yell, startled. Mouth dry as a bone.

She pushes me off her—"Fuck! Fuck! Shit!"—jumps up and grabs her skinny jeans off my bedroom floor.

"Why didn't you wake me?" she scolds.

"I thought you took the week off work," I say, knowing I'm not being dense.

"I did, but I'm babysitting the kid, remember? It's half term. Mum's got that temp job."

The kid, aka Grace, is Ella's younger sister. Not particularly bratty for a thirteen-year-old, but she does have a tendency to nick stuff. A month ago it was a pair of hair straighteners, a week later steampunk comics and a manga Pop! Vinyl from Forbidden Planet. A large, goateed security guard caught her with them tucked under her sweater. He didn't report her, just scared her a little, made her cry, and then called Mrs. Collette, which, if I'm honest, was probably worse than calling the police.

"We can give you a lift if you'd like?" I say, upsetting a pile of ironed clothes stacked on top of my oak dresser. "Anna's driving me to Glendown, so we can drop you on the way."

Ella relaxes.

"Okay," she purrs, knowing she looks pretty when she pouts, "that would be great. I can pick up Grace from her sleepover, then we'll walk back home."

She throws herself, belly first, back on my bed. Her perfect elbows supporting her perfect chin. It's the kind of chin that looks good in anything: mirrors, photos, cute scarves, turtlenecks. Anything. I walk toward her, pretending I'm a photographer while Ella poses, my fingers bluffing to *click, click* on a push-button, *flash, flash.*

Chin up, chin down, Ella tilts her head. Her tired eyes narrowing for effect until a final look involving her full lips sends me off balance.

I check my watch, aware I also need to get a move on.

Ella, calmed now, picks up last month's *Vogue*. "So what's his name, this new Glendown shrink?"

"Dr. Rosenstein. But he said to call him Daniel."

"I bet he did. And I bet he said you'd have to pay through the nose for the pleasure, *thank you very much*. I guess they do that, don't they—shrinks—get you to trust them, act all friendly, lure you in before *rawrrrr*—pouncing in!"

Ella's imitation of a wildcat isn't half-bad. On hands and knees she dismisses her *Vogue* and claws her fingers, opens her mouth wide, and prowls along my bed like a tiger in the savannah. She roars again.

"You're crazy!" I laugh.

Thrilled with the compliment, Ella crosses her eyes and shows me her jazz hands.

"Anyway, enough of the shrink," she says, swapping my pajama shirt for her cotton tank top, "you're clearly besotted with this Shaun guy, which probably means I'm about to lose my best friend until you get bored of him. When are you meeting up?"

"Saturday." I shrug.

"*Saturday,*" she mimics, coy and kittenish, then points at my forehead.

"What?"

"Your bangs are all wonky," she says, her hot breath blowing the fine strands of my hair.

Not convinced, I stride toward my Venetian mirror, but when faced with my reflection, yep, soon realize what she means.

"I was going for electro-pop," I say, feeling defensive and licking my three longest fingers, using them to press down on my bangs.

"Yeah? Well, it's definitely more geek than Gaga."

"Rude!"

"Just saying."

Sweeping my long brown hair to one side, I tuck the wayward strands behind both ears. Unfortunately, my right ear is unable to hold back my hair as effectively as the left because a chunk of it is missing. I am the opposite of Mr. Spock. Were I to be invited aboard the USS *Enterprise* I would have to decline. Fact. I pinch my cheeks for a flash of color and turn, noticing that Ella, now fully dressed, has borrowed my mint cashmere sweater, which I have to confess looks a zillion times more chic on her than it ever has on me. I may sound a tad envious, but that's only because I am.

"ALEXAAAA! Hurry up. I haven't got all day. You've got five minutes, young lady!"

That's my stepmother, Anna, at the bottom of the stairs screaming her pretty little lungs out, clearly vexed. Ella and I roll our eyes.

Anna pretty much raised me after my mother killed herself—pause for a feeling—there. If my young life's taught me one thing so far, it's not to skip over difficult feelings. For many years I did my best to avoid them, fearful they'd destroy me. Comfort eating, drinking, masturbating, or sometimes even cutting—the backs of my legs, often with a blunt kitchen knife. The messy butchering ordered my pain inward and took preference over letting others witness my rage, a result of my mother's sad life and lonely death. I was too vain to cut my arms and hadn't wanted to give people the opportunity to judge me, at best, or at worst, pity me, assuming I was self-loathing, which, if I'm completely honest, I was at times.

When one of your parents kills themselves you grow up believing you were never quite good enough. But you also realize there is always a way out, however many people you might hurt in the process. Selfish, I know.

When I was nineteen years old, Anna suggested I go to therapy. "I'll pay," she said, so she did and I went and it helped. For four years I talked the hind leg off a dog. I became fluent in the language of shrinkese: exploring feelings, repeating behaviors, and patterns of self-destruction. I understood why cutting felt safer than rage; masturbating less scary than intimacy; why eating kept the Body protected and that talking was curative. Back then, Anna had me down as some kind of teenage cliché—mad, moody, and depressed, and for this she blamed my father, claiming no responsibility for her part. I eventually became a bone in Anna's contention. An inconvenience and constant reminder of the man, my father, who eventually up and left. But I haven't forgotten what she did, or rather, what she didn't do. I've stored a tiny mental note in my brain should I ever need to remind myself, the resentment felt just one among many.

"Better go," I say, collecting my denim rucksack and sunglasses.

Ella smiles and leans into me. "Your dress is on back to front. Who got you dressed, Dolly?"

Checking my collar, I notice the label that ought to be at the back is right here beneath my chin. I laugh, embarrassed, circling my red dress back to its rightful place before straightening it with a gentle tug at the waist.

"Whoops." I smile.

Ella and Anna are the only people besides my previous shrink who know about my other personalities. During my third year of therapy I decided to come clean and confessed to the other people living inside me, and that was when I was given a diagnosis of DID.

Dissociative identity disorder, previously known as multiple personality disorder, is caused by many factors, including trauma in early childhood. This leads to depersonalization (*detachment from one's mind, self, or body*) or derealization (*experiences of the world as unreal*) and dissociative amnesia (*inability to remember events, periods of time, or life history, and in rare cases complete loss of identity*).

I was fearful to begin with, thinking that if I told anyone about my condition that I'd be committed or that said shrink might attempt to control, remove, or even destroy my personalities. This was not an option. After all, I was the one who created them, which meant I got to decide who went and who stayed. Not him.

Anna has less of a grasp on my condition because she chooses to live in denial and think of my personalities more like moods. The very idea of *others* living inside me freaks her out, so I guess it's just easier for her this way. Less mad.

Those who have never seen a switch of personalities in someone often expect some big dramatic physical transformation. Something like a vampire or werewolf sprouting fangs, hair, and claws. But in reality it's much more subtle. The Body doesn't change per se, just the body language. Or sometimes it's our voice or the way we dress. Occasionally, I'm told, it can be the gaze that is actually far more unnerving than anything else.

Unlike Anna, Ella can handle it—them—us. The Flock. And even though she finds it rather amusing at times, she is incredibly attuned to us all. She can usually tell when one of us has taken the Light and seized control of the Body. Take last week: Ella and I were waiting for the Tube when Dolly, not realizing we'd left home, woke up and caught sight of a moving train and completely freaked. Ella immediately noticed the switch—a childlike look of confusion, the simple in-turn of feet and wringing of hands—then put her arm around us for comfort.

"It's okay, Dolly," Ella whispered, "don't panic. It's just a train."

Most people wouldn't know what to do with so many personalities set loose in one body. That's one of the reasons we're so close, Ella and I. Even though we're very different—opposites, even—she's not once made us feel mad or bad or unlovable.

I look affectionately at my *Reason* and follow her swishing black bob down the stairs.

"What time do you have to be there, at *Daniel's*?" she asks.

"Eight," I reply.

"Remember. Just be yourself. Okay?"

"Okay."

She turns back and smiles. "You got this."

Outside, Anna greets Ella and me with a tight jaw. She crosses her tanned, slender arms and with a pinched mouth—glossed with peach—makes a disapproving sound. I attempt a smile, hoping it might smooth things over, but she simply looks away. Clearly miffed at having missed her Zumba class, she makes a point of slamming the door of her Volvo SUV—*such a drama queen*—and mutters something under her breath about thighs and bums.

"You look nice," I chime brightly, lying.

Anna checks her rearview mirror, fingers a lone blond curl, and keys the ignition.

"Yeah, thanks for the lift," Ella adds.

I clear my throat.

"Sorry you missed your class," I say sheepishly, applying three strokes of cherry ChapStick.

But Anna's glance, mean and sharp, silences us. Refusing to indulge our docile chitchat.

"You girls," she finally snaps, gripping the leather-covered steering wheel, "why do you have to drink yourselves sick? There's no need for it, getting drunk like that. It's not—"

"*Lady*like?" I finish for her. "Christ, Anna."

Silence.

"You're right, Mrs. Wú," Ella allows, kneeing me in the back of my seat, "we're no ladies. You're *such* a bad influence, Alexa!"

I eject my seat belt, and a trio of pings fills the car, alerting us that I'm no longer safe. I twist around, giving Ella the middle finger.

"Alexa!" Anna barks. "Quit fooling around."

Sniggering, Ella winks so I slap her leg, hard, making a *you wait* face before turning back to face the road. *Click.*

The three of us are quiet. Just the sound of rushing wind from the open car windows. The SUV's husky engine and Anna's *The Best of Bluegrass* all adding ambience to our stale urban road trip. Head still pounding, I lower my sunglasses to cover my eyes, the light immediately dimmed. I step inside the Body and turn to Runner. *Thanks for the hangover,* I say, voice dripping with sarcasm.

Whatevs, she snickers.

After a short drive over to Grace's sleepover, we pull into a gravel driveway. I spot a stray cat the color of marmalade licking its ass on the front lawn.

"See you later! Thanks again, Mrs. Wú," Ella calls, slamming the car door.

As she approaches the block of flats, I notice the ground floor's net curtains twitch and part—Grace appearing in between them like some kid sandwich, an eager smile to her softly freckled cheeks. On seeing her big sister—adored and envied in equal measure—Grace dashes to open the front door, the curtains flapping in her wake. She strokes her new champagne bob, an attempt to mimic Ella, and waves. Anna and I wave back, the ginger cat now on her back and enjoying the warm reach of sun on her pink belly, oblivious to the crouching tomcat staring down from the garage wall. Ears pricked and alert.

WE SWERVE INTO GLENDOWN'S VISITORS' PARKING LOT. ANNA KILLS the engine and sighs.

Resting her lean forearm on the ledge of her open window, she looks me square in the eye. "Look," she says, "you knew you had therapy this morning. It's not my responsibility to get you here and your friend back home. If you're going to make these commitments, Alexa, you need to get yourself organized."

"I didn't realize—"

"You never do. It's like you're in a goddamn dream world."

"I was just—"

Anna's French-manicured nail pokes a hole in my sentence and cuts me off. "Just what? Expecting me to chauffeur you around?"

"Hardly," I answer back. The truth is that it's actually Ella who drives me everywhere, only last night she'd fancied a drink or five.

"Maybe I need to remind you how hard I work, the sacrifices I've made."

I retreat, noting the alley-cat look in her eyes, pupils growing, irises shrinking.

"I know, I'm sorry," I say, defeated, opening the glove compartment and choosing a hard candy from a dented tin. I offer her one but she refuses.

Silence.

Anna's face settles.

"Shall I wait for you?" she asks, a softer tone to her voice now I've apologized.

"No, it's okay. I'm going to meet Ella and Grace in the West End afterward," I say, the candy rattling against my teeth, cherry sweetening our unease.

Anna checks her rearview mirror and adjusts the collar of her silk blouse.

"All right, then," she says, delighting me with a somewhat tight-lipped kiss on the cheek. I close the door, peer in, and wave. But already she is gone, is staring ahead and driving off.

3

Daniel Rosenstein

Two patients lean against Glendown's imperial oak—a bulk of a tree—deciding on a game of I Spy. The usual conundrum of finding something other than an obvious tree, flower, or patient immediately stunting their game. Charlotte, a resident for three years, gives up after her second attempt and walks away, leaving Emma stranded, more interested, it seems, by the imaginings in her head.

"They'll be here soon. Not long now," she declares, eyes wide and remote while tilting her gaze to the sky. "Isn't that right, Dr. Rosenstein?"

I smile. Not wanting to contradict or interrupt Emma's imagined world, yet knowing it's the "happy invaders" to whom she's referring. The ones she believes to be her *real* family.

The morning warm and cloudless, I wander across the lawn. The fresh air feels good in my lungs. A trace of honeysuckle paving the way across the graveled path toward Glendown—a residential hospital for what were once termed lunatics or the criminally insane. But lunatic asylums are antiquated in the leafy suburbs of North West London and are best left to the imaginations of all things gothic. The patients are neither insane nor lunatics. Rather, they are long-standing sufferers of trauma.

Taking a turn at the knee-high borders of flowering shrubs, I run my hands along the thick dwarf hedges of lavender, inhaling the scent it leaves on my fingers. Fresh cuttings have been planted in the herb garden, rosemary and chives. A project set up last year to encourage residents' outdoor activity, though I can see it would benefit from some attention, the large-leafed ivy slowly spreading across the soil.

My thoughts turn to today's patients. The attention they will need. The care. Their rising disquiet spreading like wildfire, requiring that I hold and contain, name and affirm. Be the good psychiatrist they assume me to be. I have wondered, sometimes, what might happen if I were to disappoint them, if my ethical code were to slip. My clinical standards abandoned, their good shrink turned bad, or vigilante.

I check my watch before drifting over to count the nine sash windows punched out of Glendown's walls while Nurse Veal peers down at me. Her thick arms crossed over her tight white tunic. She neither smiles nor waves, her stare as cold as a witch's tits.

From nowhere, a fat bumblebee rests and hovers, its sound much louder than you could possibly imagine for something of its size. Perfectly still, the bumblebee sails toward me, disoriented and drunk on pollen and fine weather. I wait—the bumblebee edging nearer—then swat it with the flat of my hand. When I glance up at the window, Nurse Veal is gone.

GLENDOWN'S THICK AIR HITS ME AS I ENTER ITS IMPOSING BLACK Georgian door. The earlier fresh lavender breeze snatched from my lungs and replaced with the familiar, foreboding dank scent. Walking along the squeaky corridors, my rubber-soled shoes suck on the oatmeal-colored floor—linoleum surfaced for easy cleaning of vomit, shit, or tantrum-thrown food. The canteen filled with the smell of itself. Above me, unreachably high windows have been opened: the hope that the pungent smell of cottage pie will eventually escape.

Nurse Veal has transported herself to the office box. A perfect six-by-six-foot tuck shop where every morning at seven A.M. she doles out daily meds in tiny white paper cups like Smarties. She spots me, wipes her brow, then looks away. I check my hand for any sign of the flattened bee and continue walking toward my office. Distant cries from Ward C tailing off like a fading siren.

SHE IS ALREADY THERE WHEN I ARRIVE.

On seeing me, she stands. With quick fingers she straightens her bangs, then places both of her feet together: black round-toed shoes. Scuffed and unflattering. Feeling discomfort at her standing at attention like this—a little soldier, a child of the Red Revolution—I prevent myself from speaking: *at ease.*

She is pretty and shy, with a pale, almost translucent complexion. She dodges my gaze, instead focusing on my collar like an orphan longing to be hugged. Her eyes, I observe, are jade green and flecked with gold, wide and unsure. Her shoulders hunched. Hands nervous and wringing.

"Hello. Alexa?" I inquire, glancing up at the silver waiting room clock.

"Yes. Hello."

"You're a little early," I reply, "but come in."

Boundaries, I remind myself. Keeping firm boundaries is essential for building trust. For some clinicians, the odd five minutes are neither here nor there, but experience tells me a firm framework keeps the patient safe—and the psychiatrist too. I open the door and wait for her to follow, but as I turn, she has stopped.

Captured in the heavy doorframe, she appears small for being, I assume, in her midtwenties. Her face a heart perched above a short red dress that looks like one a child no older than ten might wear. We stand in silence for a moment while she glances over her shoulder—checking for what, I am not quite sure.

She stares again at my collar.

A slight cough.

"Would you like to come in?" I ask.

"Yes, sorry," she says, tugging at the hem of her dress.

It is standard practice for the patient to lead, to initiate dialogue by opening up and discussing what is currently on his or her mind, but with new patients I tend to sidle over into the driver's seat. Getting a hold of the therapeutic reins. It can be as simple as an introduction or a question regarding their reason for seeking treatment. Occasionally, there will be tears before either question, and that's usually when I sit back, allowing the patient's feelings to breathe. There are no hard-and-fast rules, but I believe it helps to have some sense of the person before your next move. Today I wait.

Alexa finds my eyes, readjusts her dress, and stretches. Her posture now suddenly alert, upright and focused.

"I want to resume my therapy," she begins.

"You stopped?"

"He retired."

"Oh."

"I was in twice weekly for just over four years. We did some good work, I think. But then Joseph—Dr. Applebaum—retired. Moved out of London to spend more time with his family. He had grandchildren. He was old."

"I imagine that was difficult, saying goodbye."

"It was. It—"

I sense her unease, aware of her sentence breaking off. The slight drop of her chin.

"*It was*—?" I encourage.

"It was difficult. Painful. I missed him terribly."

I shift in my seat, leaning to one side. I must look like a therapy cliché: legs crossed, wry smile, head tilted in deep thought. A box of tissues resting between us.

She twirls a strand of her long brown hair, smiles, then hands me her set of forms—a requirement for all new patients and residents beginning analysis at Glendown. Scanning her answers, I quickly observe her handwriting—cursive and childlike, signaling arrested development and insecurity.

"I notice you haven't filled in the section regarding medication," I say.

A pause.

"Is there a reason for this?"

"I don't want to be labeled. Or given a diagnosis," she explains.

Furrowing my brow, I look at her quizzically and ask her to clarify.

"I don't like labels," she defends. "They pathologize."

"I see."

A less experienced psychiatrist might step in at this point, prick the air with words—fearful of quiet, of the patient's unwillingness to talk, or of not doing enough. But a shrink who rushes in to rescue forgets to listen. He forgets that this is not about him and the easing of his discomfort.

So, I sit back.

This is when all the good stuff happens. When emotions shake and feelings surface, giving the patient time to reflect and the shrink time to observe. Alexa stares at the oil painting above my head, a landscape of the English coastline.

There she lingers, a vague and involved expression on her face. Her eyes searching the jutting cliffs and circling gulls, the inky strait of Dover's shoreline foaming at the edge of its beach. We sit quietly. The clock's tick on my desk as clear as a bell. I note her comfort with silence and do nothing to disturb it. I, however, feel a surge of loneliness in my gut and wonder what she is thinking, what she is lost to, why her attention has left our therapeutic dance.

Be patient, I tell myself. *Wait.*

Eventually she looks away from the oil painting, but catching my expectant eyes, diverts her gaze south to her feet.

I clear my throat.

"Labels can pathologize," I say, revisiting her previous thoughts, "but sometimes a diagnosis can be helpful. One would be foolish, reckless even, to prescribe an aspirin for brain damage, a bandage for a broken wrist, or homeopathy for severe depression."

She scrunches her forehead.

"I fear being misunderstood," she replies, "that I'll be stuck with a label. Branded with a certain kind of madness."

"You think you are mad?"

She shrugs.

I lean forward.

She leans back.

"Madness is a state of mind," I say, "scary if given legs. Maybe you've always believed yourself mad. And now, being here is evidence, proof, right? You can't hide it anymore. People will find out. Me included. And with that fear comes shame and guilt because you also think it's your fault—that you've brought it upon yourself. Even if you can't always remember what it is you've actually done. So it's not just a case of the whole world seeing just how crazy you are, but now you're evil and destructive too. Labeled. Branded with a certain kind of madness."

She looks at me, eyes wide.

"I just don't want everyone thinking I'm nuts," she whispers.

"Everyone?"

"Well, my stepmother mainly."

I look down again at the form.

"You live with your stepmother—Anna. What's that like?"

"A drag. She still treats me like a kid."

Her breath quickens.

"She moved in after my mother killed herself and cared for me, well, me and my father—until he took off and left us. I was sixteen."

"He didn't take you with him?"

"He didn't want me."

A pause.

"Tough?" I ask.

"Pfft. I saw it coming."

"How so?"

"He got bored. I watched Anna try to win him back, but the harder she tried the more he despised her. Then he met someone else. Someone younger."

"I meant, was it tough that he didn't take you with him?"

She shrugs, dismissing my attempt to access feelings.

"Anna assumed the worst, of course. That I'd go off the rails, have a breakdown. But I was relieved when he left. Well, part of me was."

"We'll try to steer clear of assumptions here," I say. "Here we'll work with feelings, thought patterns, behaviors, and dreams. It might be difficult at times."

She shrugs again. Sits up straight and clears her throat.

"I was taking Seroquel, but it didn't agree with me," she says, pulling back her shoulders, her voice strengthening. "It made me tired and I put on weight. A nasty rash appeared on my hands."

"And now?"

"Now I take risperidone."

"How much?"

"Four milligrams, twice daily."

"That helps?"

"It seems to, but I want to reduce it. Eventually stop taking it."

"This ties into what you and the rest of the world believe is madness? That if you medicate, you are mad?"

"Something like that."

"I see."

"I also don't like the idea of being dependent on anything."

"Anything?"

"People, places, things."

"And Joseph—Dr. Applebaum, your previous therapist?"

She stares at me, defiant. "I became dependent. He retired."

I take a moment, and stare down again at her forms.

"You're a photographer?" I inquire.

"Kind of," she says. "I recently graduated. Like I said on the phone, I'm looking for work."

"In photography?"

She nods.

"What kind of photography?"

"Photojournalism."

"Interesting," I say. "Why are you drawn to that particular area?"

"I like taking photographs." She smiles. "Always have. On my thirteenth birthday my father gave me a disposable camera and I just got into it. It's been a way for me to absorb truth and beauty. It soothes me."

"How so?"

"I guess it helps me to reorient myself. I get caught up in the moment and embody what I'm looking at. There's a kind of magnification of life. A groundedness. It's like everything in my head—the noise, the disorientation, the confusion—it all fades into oblivion." She pauses. "Sorry. That sounds so pretentious."

"I don't think it does," I encourage. "Sounds like it's been important for you. Like a life raft."

She smiles.

"When I take a photograph, I know what I see is real, and considering how forgetful I am, it feels comforting. I trust it."

"How forgetful?" I ask.

"Very."

I note the in-turn of her left foot. Her slight body twisting in the chair.

Silence.

"Last week," she continues, "I was walking on Hampstead Heath. A man ran toward an elderly woman and sheltered her with his umbrella. I caught her smile on camera. It made me happy. I might have forgotten that moment if I didn't have my camera with me. Recording these small acts of kindness helps me feel better about the world. More at peace."

"Like a balm?" I suggest.

"Exactly."

"Observing the man's kindness, what did that feel like?"

"Tender. Like the world wasn't such a sad, lonely place."

Slouching now, she lets her legs relax and fall open slightly. I watch her red dress ride up her thighs. Unaware of exposing her flesh, she remains still, not caring to pull it down. I divert my eyes.

"The way I work," I say, "is much like an alliance. I ask that you show up, work hard, respect and engage with the process, and also inform reception if you can't make your session."

She nods.

"How does that sound?" I ask.

"Good. I'd like the form again, please."

Alexa digs noisily in her denim rucksack and retrieves a pen. She writes something down, then hands the form back. I notice she has completed the section regarding medication, this time in a different hand. No longer cursive and childlike as before, but rather more adult, joined and fluid—this time signaling confidence and creativity.

"Thank you," I say.

I wonder what the antipsychotics are managing: Disordered thoughts? Voices? Hallucinations? Suicide, maybe? I could ask but instead allow the process to gently unfold. First sessions are as much about building safety as they are about forensics.

Reaching over to my side table I pour myself a glass of water, noticing Alexa's mouth open and close, like a fish's. I wonder if she would like a drink but again stop myself from asking. *Let her ask,* I think. *Don't do all the work. It strips her of agency. Let her come to you.*

She swallows.

I take another sip, waiting to see if she green-lights her desire.

She smiles.

"I bet you're a glass-half-full kinda guy, right?" she says, eyes locked on the glass.

I nod. "You?"

"Same," she says, notably pleased. Her eyes diverted and glancing again at the oil painting.

"Do you think you can help me?" she asks.

"It's difficult to confirm with certainty," I say, "but as the glass might suggest: I'm hopeful."

"Uncertainty bothers me."

"I'm sure."

"Joseph used to say 'One day at a time.'"

"Wise man, your Joseph."

She smiles.

"He was never mine," she says, "but he was wise. And he cared. I'm positive of that."

Aware she hasn't afforded to ask for a glass of water, I observe her detour to the safety of Joseph, her previous attachment. The security of what is already known quenching any uncertainty with me. She must think I'd refuse her, I think, noting that small risks will be important for our work.

She gazes down at the rug between us. One of her shoes dangles on the tips of her toes. I note the smoothness of her olive legs, her nails painted blood red. For a moment I wonder about the tiny bruise on her knee, how she got it. How long it's been there. But catching my eyes on her skin, she crosses her legs and pulls down her dress. Looks me straight in the eye.

"So how long will this take?" she asks. "You know, considering I've been in therapy previously."

Silence.

"Six months? A year?"

"It depends," I say.

"On?"

"How willing you are to seek and be frank. I think twice weekly will be helpful."

She nods.

"What do you hope to gain this time around?" I ask.

She twists her mouth and stares at the ceiling.

"Confidence," she says. "I get anxious, particularly with men. I'd also like to talk about family."

"Oh?"

"It's complicated."

"Complicated how?"

"I'm not sure what 'family' means exactly. I'd like help figuring out what *I* want rather than constantly pleasing others all the time. I'm such a useless fuckup at times."

The phrase strikes me with a startling left hook, but I do not react. If it's her intention to shock me I won't take the bait.

"So codependency is an issue?" I ask, meaning it to sound like a statement.

"Yes."

"You fear abandonment?"

"I guess. I don't like to disappoint people. I fear they'll reject me."

"You wish to be a good girl?" I say.

A pause.

Narrowing her eyes, she leans forward. Her dress now barely covering her thighs.

"Occasionally, Daniel," she purrs, "it pays to be a good girl."

I note the switch in tone, her voice deeper now. Seductive.

"You've found this to work in the past? Being good?" I say.

She runs her hand through her hair.

"Certainly."

Leaning back, her torso straightens, her arms relax like two hanging pendants. Deliberately, she crosses her legs.

"At what cost, though?" I ask.

Silence. My challenge ignored.

I check the small gold clock on my desk.

"We have to end now, Alexa," I say. "I'd like you to reflect on today's session. If anything comes up, remember to bring it next time. What's your memory like?"

"I told you earlier, I'm forgetful." She laughs. "How's yours?"

I smile, her challenge and acute observation of me duly noted.

"So write it down," I suggest.

"Sure."

"It's time," I say.

We stand.

"Next Tuesday, same time?"

She agrees and dusts down her dress. Lifts her warm jade-green eyes to mine, then walks to the door.

"Thank you, Daniel," she says, turning toward me while stroking a heart-shaped necklace tied at her throat. "It was a pleasure to meet you."

I'm aware of how close we are, that I can smell her perfume. Its scent wafting up to the fine hair in my nostrils, leaving a dizzying tang of citrus. Above her plump mouth, a perfect vertical groove touched by an angel, a fiend.

"Goodbye," I say.

I close the door, sit back at my desk, and pick up the phone.

"Hello, this is Dr. Patel speaking."

"Hey, it's me."

"Daniel. How are you?"

"Good. You?"

"Exhausted, but what's new?"

"I have a new patient," I say, "a young woman. My countertransference tells me bad things have been done."

"Then listen to it," he says. "Chances are you're right."

While transference deals with feelings that the patient transfers onto the psychiatrist and is often founded on earlier relationships, countertransference is the reverse. That is: similar irrational feelings that the psychiatrist has toward the patient. Occasionally, countertransference can make the work deeply uncomfortable, sometimes impossible. Imagine, for example, a psychiatrist who was sexually abused as a child treating a pedophile, or a victim of domestic violence treating a manic abuser. But in milder form, countertransference is a psychiatrist's most reliable tool, and without doubt the most effective.

"Age?" Mohsin continues.

"Twenty-four."

"Signs of trauma?"

"Childhood trauma, if I were to take a guess. Avoids eye contact, a tendency to dissociate. I don't quite know who was here today; there was some switching. My head feels light, certainly lighter than before the session."

"Is she attractive?"

"Very."

"Mm. Family?"

"Her mother's dead. Estranged from her father. No siblings. Apparently there's a stepmother. One of her requests, however, was to address family. I suspect what she means is the loss of family."

"Sounds likely. What about her memory?"

"Useless, she says."

"A fractured self?"

"Possibly."

"So most likely compartmentalized. Maybe a false self has been necessary for protection. Boundaries will be important. Medication?"

"Antipsychotics. Four milligrams, twice daily."

"Heavy stuff. What else?"

"She filled in the standard forms, left out the part on medication, then decided, during session, to complete it. When she handed the form back it was written in a different hand. There was definitely a younger self here. But an older self left, potentially quite seductive."

"Possibly multiple personalities? DID?"

"That was my thought."

"You'll need some help with this one."

"Why else do you think I called?"

"I thought you might be missing me."

"Ha!"

"Well, don't be shy. Call if you need a second opinion."

"You may live to regret that."

"No doubt. Well good luck, and be careful."

"Of what?"

"Deception, manipulation."

"You sound concerned."

"They're not straightforward—patients with dissociative identity disorder—dangerous in the wrong conditions."

"I'll be careful. Are we still on for lunch tomorrow?"

"Sure. Usual place?"

"See you then."

I hang up; stare down at the forms, my eyes lingering over an unfinished question that I hadn't spotted earlier.

FULL NAME: *Ale–*

Strange. I take out my fountain pen and finish her answer:

–xa Wú

OUTSIDE, MORNING HAS FULLY ARRIVED. THE SKY NOW BLUE AND SOFT, a murder of crows resting on top of the rose brick wall. Staring out at the imperial oak and thick rows of lavender, I wonder if Alexa's seductress has a name. When and if she'll return.

4

Alexa Wú

HAZY FROM THE SESSION, I WALK ALONG THE TACKY OATMEAL CORRIDOR.

That wasn't so bad, I say, haranguing everyone inside.

Dolly is the only one who responds by smiling. *I want ice cream,* she insists, scooting into my side.

Later, I say, chucking her under her chin. *It's only nine o'clock.*

Dolly makes a face. The overbearing smell of cafeteria-cooked food hijacking any air that might be circulating from the open barred windows.

Stinky, she says, holding her nose.

All doors I detect open outward, making them impossible to barricade. This I learned while watching a documentary on young offenders with Anna, who has a strange fascination for anything involving the captivity of animals or human beings. Sometimes that includes me. I imagine it's got something to do with keeping me safe. To put right what she couldn't before my father left, his strong will ruling our home, Anna doing her best to protect me in her nonsword hand as the other defended us from my father's heavy blows. But she was no match for his vile temper. Was rarely quick enough for his sneaky fists.

I'm suddenly aware of a woman—heavy with unruly blond hair—staring at me from behind a water cooler. As I draw closer she lasers me with a gimlet eye but then quickly turns away, supposedly shy. Ebbing back, she squats farther behind the barrel and taps it repeatedly. Spooked, I rush for the door. Her stare unsettling and eerie, her tapping a thorny and stark reminder of my own obsessive compulsions.

Outside, my attention stays pinned on the pretty gardens and their handsome gardener as he wrestles with a large bush of white lace-capped hydrangea. I head toward Glendown's wrought-iron gates, while behind me miracle flowers and birdsong disguise what the world labels madness.

ON THE TUBE, I'M ROCKED BY THE SWAYING TRAIN AND LEAN MY HEAD back. An image of Daniel appears: red hair, broad shoulders, his blue eyes intense, his smile soft and kind.

He knows, Runner declares in my head, *he caught the switch when some of the others stepped into the Light. He can read us. He knows.*

Do you really think so? I worry it's way too early for him to know about my other personalities.

I know so, Runner replies.

ELLA AND GRACE ARE ALREADY THERE WHEN I ARRIVE. HAVE SECURED a table at the café beneath the department store where we've agreed to look but not buy. Waving as I approach, I note my borrowed mint sweater now draped over Ella's shoulders. Grace has done the same, only hers is red.

"Alexa!" My *Reason* sings through the crowd of people. A maroon beret placed on top of her neat Dorothy Parker bob. Her signature look, acquired two years ago when she started work at Jean&Co.—a clothing store for denim nuts, those who use a coat hanger to pull up zippers on the tightest of jeans.

Three hairy guys who appear to be in their late thirties look up and follow Ella with their eyes as she glides toward me. Watch her as she kisses me square on the mouth. She turns to the men, then drops the mint sweater seductively off her shoulder and smiles.

I spot a copy of Sartre's *Being and Nothingness* resting on the table, obscured by women's style magazines. Philosophy and fashion not the easiest of bedfellows, yet add a dash of art and it makes for a lively ménage à trois.

"Hey, Simone," I say.

"Hey, Bangs," Ella flirts.

I reach over and give Grace a hug. She looks up briefly from Snap-chat, a yellowing zit on the end of her nose.

"Have you ordered?" I ask.

Ella gives her beret a little tweak. "Meh." She shrugs, perching her oversize tortoiseshell sunglasses on her nose. "You order. We've had breakfast."

"And it's a rip-off," Grace dares, adding: "Five quid for a smoothie!" which is rewarded by Ella's curt grunt.

A waitress appears.

"Still deciding," I say.

She sighs only slightly, but immediately I pick up on her irritation. A curl to her plum-tinted lip.

"Snotty cow." Grace sneers at the waitress's slim back.

"Shh!" Ella curbs.

"Well, she is! Did you see the way she looked at us?"

Ella picks at delinquent pills on Grace's red sweater.

"I've been thinking," she says, Grace nudging aside her plucking hand, "I wanna get a new job."

"How come?" I ask.

"I'm broke," she speaks bluntly. "It's all right for you. You can leave Chen's when your photography career takes off. You'll be fine, and move on."

"Move on?"

"To better things."

"You're being silly, Ella."

"Pfft," she rejects with a flick of her wrist. "Anyway, did you send your portfolio in for that job you wanted?"

"Yeah, I included those portraits of you that I took on the heath. Remember?"

She rolls her eyes. "Yeah, I remember. So what now?"

"I guess I just wait and see if I get an interview. It would be so amazing to work for Jack Carrasqueiro. You know, I even based part of my college thesis on his photography."

"I'm sure you will," she says, sulking. "You'll probably get the job too. Then what will *I* do?"

Currently I work part-time in a Chinese takeaway on the Euston Road. I'd spotted the advertisement stuck down with two Band-Aids in a window veiled with a grubby curtain and several red paper lanterns while on my way to class my senior year.

Wanted: Person to work. Must be honest and able to add. Apply within.

I was both and needed some sort of income, so decided to give it a shot. My guess is that Mr. Chen took me on because I could (1) add, (2) look relatively honest (I smiled a lot), and (3) speak Mandarin.

Mr. Chen likes to cuss in his mother tongue. Finds it amusing when he hands curt customers their order calling them "greedy pig-swilling radish brains" or "stupid, ugly baboon breath" in Mandarin, all the while smiling and thanking them in pidgin English. I like Mr. Chen. He's funny. And kind. Insists that I take food home after every shift: "You too thin, you like a stick. Stick insect!" he says, the comment not helped by the nuclear oral stench that radiates from all that raw garlic he insists on chewing. And while I don't mind working at Mr. Chen's and indulging his silliness and obsessions with the Queen, it's my hope that I will eventually have a career in photography and get a job that I love. Indeed, a job that I'm *actually* good at. Also, Anna was insistent, come to think of it, that I get a "proper" job now that I've finished college. So when I saw the photographer's assistant position with Jack, I applied and hoped for the best.

"Well?" Ella snaps again, defiant. "What about *me*?"

Grace looks up.

"We both know my mum can't hold down full-time work," she starts up again, "she isn't capable. And I'm sick of having to pay the bills."

I shrug, wishing Ella would stop being such a bitch, yet knowing Mrs. Colette's depression has caused many an employer to relieve her of work in the past.

Ella lowers her voice. "So, I heard there's a job going—"

"Where?" I say.

"The Electra."

"Doing *what*, exactly?"

"Reception and bar work."

"You'd be working with Shaun?"

"He was the one who told me about it. He said he'd put in a good word with his boss."

"I don't know. I think it's a bad idea. Those kind of clubs, I've heard they treat the girls real bad and—"

46

"Listen," she interrupts, "I'd only have to work *two* nights to make what I earn at Jean&Co. in a week."

"But—"

"Two nights!" she insists. "And anyway, I've been thinking. I really want a place of my own. Somewhere small, but mine, with *my* things."

Grace suddenly looks up.

"Don't worry, you can always come stay with me."

Grace smiles.

I take Ella's hand, impressed by her ambition. The waitress returns.

"Can I get a green smoothie?" I ask.

She turns to Ella and Grace, pen midair.

"That's all," I say.

One of the three hairy guys next to us makes a sign for the bill. Noting their distraction, Ella lowers her glasses and, all of a sudden, releases an incredulous laugh for no apparent reason while curving her shoulder in their direction. The amorous performance takes me by surprise.

"Kill me now," Grace says, hiding her face in her nail-bitten hands.

The guys look over. Bemused and intrigued, I think, with Ella's outburst. I've no doubt that if Ella dropped her cool, her swag, she would still be left with pure, painless beauty, like the promises in *Vogue*. She removes her sunglasses and leans over.

"So. How'd it go with the shrink?" she whispers.

"Good," I say. "I like him."

"Is that a credential, that you *like* him?"

"Beats *not* liking him."

"Is he cute?" she teases.

"He's my shrink!"

The waitress arrives with my tall glass of goo, which I down in as few gulps as possible, knowing it's good stuff, but all the same.

Ella pulls a wretched face.

"I hope you're not gonna become one of those god-awful bores who only eats clean food and has her ass flushed every six months. What's it called? Colonic, colonic irri—"

"Irrigation," I say.

"See! You even know the name of it. *Vrai?*"

"True," I reply, holding up *Being and Nothingness*. "But I'll only stop being a god-awful bore if you leave your boyfriend Sartre at home and stop pretending to be all *française*."

"Deal. Though *hell is other people*." Ella grabs her bag. "Drink up," she says, eyeing the guys about to leave.

I finish the goo, paying careful attention to the taste of lemon and spinach. "Ready."

"Let's go," Ella sings. "Wait till you see this jacket I want. It's *divine*!"

Standing, Ella and Grace smooth their matching bobs.

"Divine," Grace echoes.

The three of us lurch onto the escalator. Impatient, Ella starts to climb while checking her slim silhouette in the panes of glass. At the third floor, we jump off, surrounded by luxury items. Ella clearly knows where she's going and makes a beeline, Grace in tow, for an industrial clothes rail suspended from the ceiling.

"Can I help you with anything?" a sales assistant asks, thrilled, I imagine, at the prospect of paying customers.

"We're just looking." Ella smiles.

The sales assistant turns on her heel. Begins to straighten a stripy mohair sweater, aligning it with a bell jar—a stuffed crow inside. Several necklaces hanging from its beak. I think a magpie would have made more sense, but still, it's an effective display. We stop at the floating clothes rail, Ella sighing with pleasure and fixing her eyes on what I imagine is *the* jacket. But just as Ella's hand reaches to pull out her little piece of heaven, another hand swoops in—

"Sorry." Both voices chime simultaneously.

For once, I'm relieved to say the synchronized voices are not mine—a tall, pretty girl with hair like butter and gold hoop earrings steps back, smiles, and then pulls her hand away.

"Gorgeous, isn't it?" She smiles.

"Yeah." Ella sighs, stroking the soft arm of the fawn leather jacket as if it were a pussycat.

"Do you have this in a size ten?" the girl shouts over her shoulder.

The sales assistant says she will check, then totters off in search of the perfect ten. Ella, however, takes the existing jacket off the rail and tests its size, sliding herself into its creamy leather arms. She strokes it again, this time with both hands.

"Stunning," I say wistfully.

"Yeah, it looks great," the girl repeats, both of us nodding and admiring its flawless fit while Ella coos and purrs. I reach around the back of the jacket's soft leather collar, my hand feeling like it's entered the pouch of a baby kangaroo, and check the price tag.

"Are you *serious*?" I squeal, causing Grace to flinch.

"What?" Ella smiles.

"That's crazy."

"But it's worth it. Don't you think?"

"No!" I say, pulling my hand away.

The girl looks at us, bemused, the sales assistant returning with the size ten draped across her arm like a giant restaurant napkin, then offers it to the girl.

"I'll take it!" the girl sings. Not bothering to try it on. Just like that. Bam.

I turn to Ella, her face now morphed into a contorted, sadder version of itself while the girl saunters off to pay. Watching her replace the jacket on its hanger, it's all I can do not to whip out my bank card right there on the spot and shout, "We'll take it!" completely emptying my savings to ease Ella's longing. I attempt a smile, but Ella simply shrugs. Her heart clearly sick.

"Why don't we look around?" I suggest, hoping the distraction might help her disappointment, but it appears Ella's sick heart is no longer in it. Instead she stays rooted to the spot. Ogling the jacket.

Grace, now bored, wanders toward a set of mannequins, all without heads, and fiddles with a leather purse diagonally draped over one of their shoulders. As I pull out a random denim skirt, folded next to the stuffed crow, I catch Ella staring at the girl and her new jacket. Longing replaced now with a pursed lip.

"Come on, let's go," Ella says, giving the jacket one final stroke. "I'm taking us all for sweet bagels. Extra cinnamon and cream."

Head thick with unease, I bend down and stare into the bell jar. The crow's trapped beady little eyes staring back, deadened and glassy. It's as if they've been watching us all along. Our every move reflected back in their icy black glare. Slowly I stand, the crow's gaze now pursuing me as I trail Ella and Grace out toward the escalator.

Following behind, I notice their pace quickening as if in search of something or someone. But as I draw closer I lurch backward. My eyes not quite believing. Ella thrusting what appears to be the fawn leather jacket deep into her bag. She nods to Grace—the two of them now streaming ahead—sleek as wind. Their focus pinned, relentless. Like thieves in the night.

5

Daniel Rosenstein

EVERY FRIDAY AT TEN A.M., I ATTEND MY WEEKLY AA MEETING IN
Angel. For eleven years I've visited the same church, or rather, the same
rec room in the same church, and sat beside other recovering alcoholics.
On occasion, even after all these years, I can still struggle if someone
looks at me the wrong way or if life feels too good. Or if someone I
love rejects or distances themselves. "Never get too comfortable or let
your guard down," an early sponsor once said to me, "not until you've
notched up some sobriety."

For an hour and a half, I sit and mostly listen. Sometimes I share.
And at the end of it I'm still surprised at how each time my spirits are
lifted. Any earlier resentments or self-preoccupation eventually set down.
The intimacy with other recovering alcoholics often providing a remedy
for my tender loneliness. Sometimes I ask myself whether they all meet at
night—for a Chinese or Indian meal, or the cinema maybe. And whether
they've simply given up asking me because I've refused so many times.
Paranoia revealing itself, I realize I'm being sensitive and let it drop.

Today I know everyone here, apart from a couple of newcomers.
Both of them young men in their twenties. Resting a bottle of water
beside my brogued foot, I wait for the chatter to settle down. Opposite me,
an old-timer, twenty years sober, who up until last year was militant

around any kind of medication, including aspirin. Then his mother died, and it was clear he needed a little help. *Once a man, twice a child.* Next to him sits a single mother of three, seven years sober. She struggles and avoids eye contact with the men in the group. Keeps her legs crossed at all times. Today she shifts awkwardly in her chair, her face flushed and swollen. A slight shake to her voice.

"This morning," she begins, "my eldest son said I preferred his sister to him. He's probably right. My mother did the absolute opposite. She hated me, preferred my brother."

Recovering addicts will often look for reasons to make sense of the monkey on our backs. Hateful mothers, violent fathers. Broken homes. And as a result, we the addicts act on that hurt, finding brief ease in all manner of habits. For some of us, the chemical condition marked by irresistible craving transforms our affliction from a defect of character into a disease, making it a hybrid of the medical and the moral. But in my journey, I believe it to be a moral issue; that is, my desire. My desire, and my struggle to control it. I look about the room, wondering about the desire within each of us—how well we do now to rein it in, like a leathered fist guiding a wild horse, dust rising from the filth beneath our feet.

WHEN I REACH KABUKI, THE MAÎTRE D' ASKS FOR A NAME.

"Rosenstein, two for one P.M.," I say, noting his slim waist, a neat snazzy waistcoat. Our usual table overlooks the miniature Zen garden, raked and pruned within an inch of its life. I enjoy our monthly Friday lunches. Unfortunately, we had to forgo it last month because Mohsin was giving a talk at the Royal College of Psychiatrists, something he is frequently asked to do and enjoys doing.

"Your guest is already here, sir." The maître d' smiles. "Please, follow me."

Trailing the maître d' past the heavy cherry silk kimono hanging at the entrance, I think about what I'll order: the shishito peppers to start, followed by salmon teriyaki. Occasionally we share some snow crab rolls or rock shrimp, but today I intend on sticking to the two courses, painfully aware of my midlife waistline and its slow expansion. Saliva rises in my mouth and I begin envisioning the Pretty Freckled Waitress who usually serves us. Perhaps she'll be here today, I think, aware of my choice of jacket, new and fitted.

Two waiters stand at opposite ends of the bar like bookends and nod politely. Between them, a flashy barman. The top of his Calvin Klein underwear showing. Fool, I curse, and then catch myself. Aware the ridiculous outburst of envy is tied up in feeling old—certainly older than my fifty-five years. Immediately I smile to myself and forgive the fool.

Scanning the crowded room for the Pretty Freckled Waitress, I hear Mohsin's voice.

"Daniel!" He waves.

I wish he wouldn't do that, shout and draw attention to himself that way. I give a small wave back in acknowledgment, still searching for the freckled one.

We embrace.

"Hey, good to see you. Nice jacket."

"Thanks, it's new," I say.

"Very smart. At a guess, one might think you're trying to impress a particular cute waitress."

"Perceptive."

"Monica will have your guts."

"Monica will never know."

The moment the words leave my lips, guilt tugs at my throat. A memory of my father and his lies still a constant source of pain.

Seated, I notice a small water fountain has been given a home in the Zen garden: a chubby Buddha made of gray stone, beaded jade necklace resting on top of his abundant tummy, rotund and satisfied. I look down and breathe in, loosening my shirt with a tug. I wonder how he can be so pleased with himself, carrying all that weight around, then look about the restaurant and see most of the guests mirroring our jolly fat friend.

Amused, Mohsin relaxes.

"How is Monica?" he asks. "You guys must be coming up to a year pretty soon."

"September fifteenth."

"Doing anything?"

"Monica's made a list. I just have to choose one."

"Romantic." He laughs. "You guys still going to swing classes?"

"We haven't been in a while," I say, a bite of grief quickly upon me.

MY CLARA LOVED TO DANCE.

In '86, I met Clara at a beneficiary fund where she was helping raise money for the far-leaning left. She happened to be on a gap year from college but instead of backpacking in Europe or getting high on some East Asian island, opted for political fund-raising instead. At twenty-three years old she wasn't green to organizing. A second-generation red-diaper baby and the daughter of parents sympathetic to the United States Communist Party, she'd been exposed to Castro from a young age, and Marx even younger. Fund-raising was second nature to Clara; excuses to not get involved were not. She was a fighter who was keen to do the right thing by the people. At night, I'd catch her reading, almost secretly and fevered, Mao's pamphlets: "Combat Liberalism," "On Protracted War," "Talks at the Yenan Forum on Literature and Art." Her strong legs tucked beneath her, a cigarette in hand. I could watch for hours, concentration pinned on important words, an occasional smile thrown my way like a bone.

The night we met she'd worn a cloud of red taffeta and matching lips.

It was love at first fight.

"Barely lukewarm" was how Clara described my relationship with politics, making it clear that were I to have any hope in hell of dating her, I would have to up my game. So I did, quickly, noisily, making sure she saw and learned of my joining the Young Communist League as commitment for a date. Six months later we moved in together; we were married the following year.

It was Mohsin who had encouraged me four years after Clara's death to start thinking about dating. Warning me of the easy pitfalls of becoming too comfortable with solitude, as he often is. At first, I'd brushed off his advice, too hurt to even consider having sex with another woman. It felt wrong somehow, disloyal. And alien.

"I'm afraid it's just a matter of time," I had been told, in a calm bedside manner. The doctor avoiding my puffy eyes. Two weeks later the cancer snatched her away.

Alone and broken, I closed her dead eyes. Covered her limp body, turned skeletal. Riddled with pain.

Crippled with powerlessness, I'd felt hateful—of the doctors; the nurses; the man cleaning the ward's pale linoleum floor that afternoon when she passed; the young woman who, while on her phone, crashed into me; the local shopkeeper who knew I was an alcoholic refusing the malt whiskey I wanted to drown my grief; the child who'd kicked a ball and laughed as I entered my front door; the front door and its awkward lock; the sound it made when it finally closed; the world; I hated the whole fucking world, and everyone and everything living in it.

Mohsin looks over his menu.

"So. How's things? The new patient—Alexa?"

I nod. "Good. I'm still digesting our first session and the information she provided in the forms. There's a lot to process."

"Did anything unusual come up?"

I think for a moment. "She's scared of balloons."

"Globophobia."

"There's a *name* for it?"

"There's a name for most things these days. What is it: thinking of them, or seeing them, or touching or popping them?"

"I'm not sure," I say, bewildered. "She wrote it in her notes."

"With most phobias, the symptoms depend on the roots of the fear."

"Well, that would be her father."

"I see."

"I'm wondering what the most effective treatment might be, considering his abandonment of her," I say.

"Boundaries and consistency."

"And if she *does have* DID?" I ask.

"Then your task is to prevent her from losing time."

"I thought you might say that."

"Otherwise she could find herself checking out and in serious danger. That said, she may be losing time already, unable to remember her actions. You mentioned her limited memory."

"That's right."

"Depending on how dissociated her mind is, the personalities can work so autonomously that the patient might not even know who's running the body. Could be that Alexa, the host, checks out too."

I nod, wondering about this. The fractured self. How one's dissociation can be so effective that it prevents a person from feeling—or remembering, even—an alternate personality taking over, what shrinks term the ANP (apparently normal personality). But as one patient, Ruby, I seem to recall, pointed out: "There's nothing 'normal' about a personality that doesn't feel. It's like having an avoidant autopilot to navigate your day."

Ruby was constantly getting fired from work. She would turn up with no recollection that she'd even been dismissed, her desk cleared, belongings packed. Then she'd receive a letter or phone call stating her violent and abusive behavior was unacceptable and she'd be terminated immediately. We later discovered the personality that was getting her fired had been created in her teens. A fierce and destructive personality that thought nothing of hurling a glass, chair, or body at the wall.

I shake off the memory. "Well, I'll let you know how things go. So, tell me, how have you been?" I ask.

Mohsin sighs.

"They're working me like a dog," he says. "I need a holiday."

"When did you last take one?"

"January. Skiing, remember?"

"I remember it was no holiday. You were exhausted when you got back."

"Cecelia, or was it Cordelia, happened to be very energetic that holiday." He stares off. A dreamy doe-eyed schoolboy in adult slacks.

"On and off the slopes if I recall," I say. "Oh, and it was Cecelia, by the way."

"Incredible mind, Cecelia."

"You kill me."

"Now *where* is that waitress of yours? I could do with a drink."

"Is she here?" I shine.

"Yes. And looking particularly lovely."

"Great. Let's order."

6

Alexa Wú

MORNING. EARLY, BY THE LOOKS OF THINGS.

Yawning, I stretch my body into an X, moving my arms up and down—a snow angel—the elasticated bedsheet crinkling. Unsettled by the less-than-perfect snow linen I roll over, lift one corner of the mattress, and pull the sheet tightly underneath, watching it ping back to a freshly fallen bed of snow. There. Better.

The blind in my bedroom has never quite reached the bottom of my window, but for some reason, I accept this irritation into my bedroom every single morning. Pathetic, really. Procrastination easier than heed. Rolling over, I grab my camera, aiming it at the slither of sunshine sneaking in beneath the blackout blind, a shard of yellow light spearing tonight's killer outfit already laid out.

Leather pants? Runner snorts. *Are you sure?*

I wonder now if they're a poor choice.

Runner makes a face. *Sweaty fanny,* she warns.

I look around my L-shaped room, photographs of strangers taped to my magnolia walls like a family of unknowns that offer comfort on drawn-out nights. A young girl in pink polka dots. An elderly man wearing a fedora. Soft curious eyes, I imagine, caring for me, smiles to affirm. Joy caught on camera like we've been to a swanky restaurant, a party, or maybe a West End show. Sometimes I talk to them. Tell them what's on my mind. Their company witnessing all manner of triumphs and struggles over the years.

I sigh at all the clutter—chaos being an unavoidable side effect of multiplicity, despite my obsessive compulsions to keep things neat and tidy. Just staring out from my bed I can see: Dolly's Soft'n Slo Squishies, colored pencils, and stuffed elephant. Oneiroi's dream catcher, rose quartz heart, and lacy bra. Runner's Zippo lighter, leather purse, mouth guard, and deck of cards. My Canon camera and last month's issue of *PhotoPlus*. A striped sweater that used to belong to Runner, now handed down to Dolly because the mohair apparently makes her itch. A red leather satchel, also Dolly's. A bong belonging to Runner currently gathering dust, and a collection of DVDs that belong to all of us ranging from *Harry Potter* to *Kill Bill*—all alphabetically arranged. There are also a dozen clocks dotted about the room—as protection against losing time—along with a heap of unironed clothes, which I imagine no one will take ownership of, therefore making them my responsibility. Were I to open my closet door, I'm sure I'd find something belonging to the Fouls. But for now we'll keep that door closed. It's just safer that way.

Handling a bunch of mail on my oak dresser, I file it away in my top drawer: a letter on top from Daniel confirming my twice-weekly therapy and his foreseeable fees. I take a moment to acknowledge the help I need to manage my disorder, my personas. That I, Alexa, am what the medical profession calls the Host, though I much prefer to think of myself as *the Nest Builder for the Flock*. Over the years, I've preserved this refuge in my mind, picturing it much like the nests you see among ancient trees. Twigs gathered and placed with moss and earth, a peppering of feathers and lint held together by saliva for added warmth and protection. Occasionally, we have to safeguard the Nest from intruders like those killer cats you see circling thick trunks of trees, claws bared and awaiting bad weather.

I used to maintain complete control of the Body, but over the years I've encouraged more spontaneity, each of my personalities now able to take the Light and use the Body to experience the world much like any other human being might. Only occasionally do I have to negotiate with everyone inside about who comes out, especially if I don't think it's safe or fitting. For example, Dolly is only nine years old, which means she can't smoke, drink alcohol, watch rude TV, or do anything that's not age appropriate. That being said (I'm making it all sound very orderly), it doesn't always work out this way. Sometimes if I'm mega-stressed (DID and stress don't fly), in denial (DID and denial cause conflict), or drink too much (DID plus booze equals disaster), I check out—what shrinks call dissociation—and that's when it can get real messy, because I have no control over what I do or memory of what I have done. When this happens, I have to rely on the Flock to take over the Body. Sometimes it works out but sometimes it doesn't; after all, we all know families don't always make the best choices on our behalf—especially those born out of trauma.

And really, the best way to describe living with multiple personalities is to say it's like taking care of a family—a very, very *large* family with me at the center—each personality in possession of different hopes, fears, desires, interests, aspirations and memories.

There's only one rule we all agree to:

No one from the real world must enter the Nest. Not ever.

By this I mean no one can get to know us all *so* well that they have more knowledge about the Flock than I do. This could result in my losing control of the Mind and the Body. After all, the Nest is our home, our sanctuary. A place to pause our racing mind. And should anyone enter from the real world, they could destroy it and everyone who lives here.

O NEIROI PROPS ME UP WITH A PILLOW.

We'll help you tidy up, she assures me.

Thanks, I say.

Our voices are toned soft in my head, medication causing it to throb. My eye sockets throb too, like someone has pressed down hard with fat thumbs. I reach for my sunglasses as if I'm some spoiled movie star. Secretly, I envy the life of an actress—her wardrobe, her ability to sleep until noon (let's face it, she'd probably have better-fitting blinds) as well as droves of admirers. Also her talent to step outside herself and assume new identities as I have, only she gets to leave hers behind after the camera stops rolling. I, on the other hand, have to carry everyone around without a break, day after day and long nights too. The responsibility of caring for everyone inside sometimes exhausting and insufferable—especially if they're not in agreement and fighting one another for control.

Take yesterday: Dolly woke up first and sprang out of bed, which, in turn, woke me up. I was still sleepy and insisted she stay in bed a while longer, but no: *Won't! I'm not tired.*

Dolly is nine years old and has been since 2003. She arrived the night my father paid his first visit—my mother having had only six months to mulch in her tan plastic urn. Dolly is the youngest of my personalities, and even though she's been with me the longest, she remains the fledgling of the Flock.

Next awake was Oneiroi, who cracked one eye open, then closed it again. Tired and somewhat cranky. She's thirty-two and is in charge of exercise and our bedtime routine, making sure we floss and moisturize in preparation for her favorite activity: dreaming. Some of the others consider her vain and airheaded, but she's kind and well meaning. Keeps us from getting too roused or ruffled.

Dolly's playing animal hospital eventually woke Runner.

Quit it, Dolly! For Christ's sake, go back to bed, she'd shouted in my head, her throat raspy and hoarse from all the Lucky Strikes she'd smoked the night before.

Won't, Dolly snapped, *Nelly needs to go to the hospital, she's broken her trunk!*

By this time everyone was awake—including the Fouls.

The Fouls arrived shortly after my mother killed herself, their voices more vile and rising over time. They insist it was my fault she jumped in front of a train, and had I not been such a selfish little bitch, she would still be alive. Calculated cruelty is just one of the Fouls' many callous qualities woven into a hideous web of cunning spite. Of all my personalities, they are the ones I welcome least and have little or no control over. I leave that to Runner.

Occasionally, a personality can even exist without the Host (me, my-"self") knowing, though this has only ever happened to me once, not long after my father left. I was sixteen years old.

It had been a cold morning bleached white with snow when I suddenly found myself reentering the Body to discover Flo—a personality I didn't know was living inside me at the time—had "accidentally" killed someone's pet guinea pig. As I stared down at the family pet, his body stiff with cold, I was confronted with the crime and reality that it was in fact *me* who had starved the poor creature to death.

I'd broken down and cried when I finally picked him up. His tiny eyes like glazed marbles, his pale nose shriveled like a macadamia nut. Before the slow killing, I believed Flo existed as a separate person from me. This is what shrinks call an amnesic barrier or a denial/

defense/survival mechanism. So in my denial, I subconsciously disavowed Flo, as if by banishing her from the Body I could relinquish the qualities I despised in her, and therefore in myself. Fearful of her potential for destruction, I forced her into exile. She became known as Flo the Outcast.

I even imagined Flo living somewhere separate from me: in a flat somewhere on the sixth floor along the west block of the neighborhood. She also had her own family: a mother, a father, and two older brothers. Flo's face was pinched, her eyes a mean icy blue, and she was ruthless, sneaky and violent, a potential killer. I didn't like her one bit—just as I hadn't liked myself very much back then.

I later learned Flo the Outcast had seized the Body, seeking revenge on a boy called Ross—a bully who had lived on my street—and had pignapped his prized pet to teach him a lesson. Then she'd hidden the guinea pig in a cardboard box in the potting shed at the back of our house. It wasn't until sometime later that the Flock confessed to also having turned a blind eye to Flo's crime. Apparently Dolly had attempted to sneak some green leftovers for the hungry hostage, but the Flock had curtailed her kindness, fearful that Flo might punish them or that I might disapprove because they hadn't intervened sooner.

Don't forget your medication. Runner points, plumping up my pillow, pulling me from the memory.

I do as I'm told, popping a blistered risperidone from its crackly foil, washing it down with a glug of last night's stale water. Runner, I've decided, is the protector of the Flock. She runs rings around the rest of us and is the only one who dares stand up to the Fouls. Runner's in her twenties and arrived when I started secondary school. I figured we might need a personality to keep us safe, someone fierce, though safety was just an idea back then. I didn't *really* know what it meant.

Sometimes I'd "forget" to take my medication on purpose, just to see what would happen. I have to say it rarely turned out well. And like I said to Daniel, this time around I'd like to reduce it gradually, sensibly, so that everyone inside is up to speed and knows what's going on. This way, I can avoid the kind of chaos that's happened in the past.

For instance, one time I stopped taking it without telling the Flock. It was anarchy. Arguments erupted about whose responsibility it was to get dressed, make the bed, perform morning ablutions, and prepare breakfast—too many cooks, I think the saying goes—and that was just the morning. A couple of hours into the day and it was time to tackle public transport and complete strangers serving coffee. Then there was college, coursework, and other students. Later still, the gym—a breeding ground for anxiety with so many half-naked bodies and fragile egos. Next, the supermarket, which was a riot waiting to happen, what with us all liking different types of food, drinks, and bathroom products. I eventually began losing time and checked out from the stress of it all, and that's when things got really messy. Dolly took the Light, seizing control of the Body, and found herself at Chen's. After a few nights of her ringing the cash register, earnings were down by five hundred pounds. Then Runner had to step in, explaining business had been dead all week and lying that a competitor had flyered discount vouchers in the Euston area.

Away from home, I, Alexa, try my best to guide the Flock about who takes the Body without being too controlling, especially at work or on nights out. For instance, Dolly obviously can't do math and Runner, unlike Oneiroi, isn't the friendliest of people, so you can imagine the tussle between those two on a night out. Sometimes the task of looking after so many personalities causes my brain to simply short-circuit, an unpleasant feeling much like some motherboard sparking and frying my skull. When this happens, I lose time, making me feel so power-less that my OCD kicks in, and that's when the relentless counting begins: of steps walked, stairs climbed, doors opened and closed, lights switched on and off (odd numbers preferred). Sometimes I even wear the same clothes three days in a row if nothing bad happened on the previous days I wore them. Then there's the hoarding, ruminations, orderliness, symmetry, and intrusive thoughts. The list is endless.

I check my bedside clock—8:05—and reach for my copy of *Doctor Zhivago* stashed under my bed like porn. I'm at the part where Anna Gromeko discovers she has pneumonia, but just as I'm settling in, four letters flash up on my phone: ELLA.

Mildly irritated, I answer after the third ring.

"Don't tell me you're lying in bed reading one of those depressing Russian novels." She scoffs.

"Yes to both. What do you want?"

"A favor."

"What?" I say.

"I know you've got a date with Shaun tonight, but will you come to the Electra with me? To meet Navid, the owner?"

A pause.

"Please?" She tests, "I handed my notice in at Jean&Co."

"But I'm working at Chen's, then—"

"Look," she persists, "you can meet Shaun after, right? Kill two birds and all that?"

There is silence, the Flock none too pleased with Ella's use of metaphor.

"Like I said, it won't be forever," she says. "I just want to earn enough money so I can move out, get my own place."

I know my answer ought to be no, but I find myself yielding. My *Reason,* such an amazing friend who walked into my life when the rest of the world walked out, my nonblood sister, loving me in a way that no one else could.

I stare out at my bedroom. Gaze fixed on a Russian doll (a gift and Ella's idea of a joke) balancing on top of my oak dresser.

Flash.

ELLA AND I ARE LYING ON MY BED.

Two scratchy white towels covering our darling breasts and soft pubic hair. I feel a slick of heat between my thighs, the cool shower having impressed a zing of lemon on our sunburned skin. Ella catches the twist on my face as I pinch my pudge of tummy flesh, measuring its crime.

"Don't," she says, placing her damp hand on top of mine, "it's lovely. And anyway, it's only men who think tummies should be flat."

I try to feel comfortable with her closeness, likening it to the times when my mother would lovingly wash and braid my hair. How, when she tied the plastic bauble, checked it wasn't too tight, had cupped my face. "There," she'd say, "perfect."

Ella turns to me and smiles. The afternoon light sparkling behind her, the bright sun a beacon of hope encapsulating all things beautiful and just.

"For you," she says, handing me the Russian doll. "Cute, right?"

My *Reason* takes a handful of her own tanned paunch and squeezes.

Flash.

And we laugh. Our friendship like a flight of birds, free and endless.

Flash.

ALEXA!"

The flashback has taken me away for a moment.

66

Tick-tock—

Lost time. Long enough, I realize, for Dolly to have reached for a coloring book and started work on a frizzy-wigged clown who is holding a trio of balloons.

I shudder. The sight of the inflated floating rubber forcing me to quickly turn the page. "I'm here," I say, "sorry. Drifted off for a second."

"Well—?"

I clear my throat. If I don't go with Ella tonight, who else will? Who else cares?

"Well. Shaun's actually working tonight, so I guess—"

"Great!" She sings, "I'll pick you up after work."

The phone rings off.

Oneiroi wraps her arms around me, trying to soothe the rising disquiet. My mouth is dry, my palms slick with sweat. I think about the stolen leather jacket. Ella's confident glide as she cut across the department store, security none the wiser. Her glee when the three of us hit the street outside.

I walk across the dim landing toward the bathroom, counting my steps, and feel myself leave the Body, my chest suddenly awkward and strained. A child walks alongside me. Black round-toed shoes. Her presence regressed and familiar. Alarmed, she looks to me, eyes wide, hands wringing. *Don't let her go,* the child says, *it's not safe.* But before I can answer, she too is gone—has disappeared back into the dark corner of my mind. The slap of a hand across my face drowning out Dolly's cries.

S EVERAL HOURS HAVE PASSED.
Tick-tock—

I check my surroundings, recognizing the bathroom's peeling gray walls. A whiff of fried chili and garlic drifting through and kindling my senses. Relieved to see the dozens of familiar cutout pictures of the Queen, I catch Mr. Chen's high-pitched voice outside.

Tick-tock—

Come along, Oneiroi says, handing back the Body, *you'd better get dressed. Date night, remember?*

Date night? Runner mocks. *Please don't ever say that out loud.*

Confused, I take the Light. The familiar sense of shrugging back into the Body not dissimilar to climbing into an old sweater, a pair of loose jeans. Oneiroi smiles and hands me my white silk blouse and leather pants.

Don't worry, she says, *you checked out for a while, but Runner worked your shift and Mr. Chen's in a good mood. You'd better get changed out of your work clothes, though, and quick; Ella's on her way.*

Although no one's watching (apart from the Queen), I cover my small breasts, currently held rather apologetically in a starter bra. My shame causing me to shudder over their being so small, and over my nipples too, like protruding acorns that never seem to go away regardless of temperature.

I drop down the toilet seat, sit, breathe in, and quickly pull up the zipper on my tight leather pants before flesh knows what I'm up to. *Ha! Tricked you, tummy bulge.*

I liken the flabby overspill to the top of a muffin, and feel a wave of disappointment that my refusal to drink anything fizzy or eat anything fat for the past week has had zero, ZERO effect. *Damn you, body gods!*

Outside, I can hear Mr. Chen laughing with some customers—a couple, I think, who order the same thing every week: *Set dinner, C1, for 2 person.* Afterward, the woman usually asks for two fortune cookies, which she snaps open right there on the spot. After reading both, she decides which one belongs to her before handing the other to a man who I assume is her husband. He rarely reads the cookie's vague prophecy, simply places the thin line of paper on the counter, showing more interest in the angled TV on the wall.

I peer out the bathroom door, the couple framed in an elongated slice of companionship and domesticity. The woman leans against the counter, occupied with the menu, her blouse a mustard yellow under a sage-green cardigan. A large fake pearl necklace clacking at her throat. She is a little younger than Anna but nowhere near as fashionable. The husband stares at the TV screen, eyes locked on some reality TV show involving spiders and a girl in a glass case. Hundreds are released; the girl screams, her body now a mass of meager black legs.

I take out my camera and aim its lens toward the couple, dialing them into focus—*click, click*—the photograph holding a moment, a secret. The woman turns to the TV and then to her husband, tilts her head back and laughs, the girl in the glass box now frantically groping around. The woman drapes her arm around her husband and watches his reaction—*click, click*—both of them voyeurs to the girl's desperation. I am seeing them not seeing themselves. I have knowledge of them that they do not have. My hands twitch, a discomfort felt in my gut, then quickly place the camera back in my rucksack.

Who's the voyeur now? Runner snickers.

S TEPPING INTO MY SUEDE ANKLE BOOTS, I CHECK MY FACE IN THE RECT-angular mirror above the sink, noting a chip in the top corner. A crack spreading to its center causing a slight disjoin to my face. I stand on my tiptoes and my face realigns—becomes whole again. I force myself to accept that the plump-faced girl with shadows cast beneath her eyes is actually me. *Me?*

I will buy Mr. Chen a new mirror, I tell myself.

Ella is waiting for me outside.

"Copycat!" she shouts, flinging open the car door and sticking her leg out. At first I haven't a clue what she's up to, but as I draw closer I realize we're wearing matching leather pants, our legs like four sticks of licorice.

"You wore them best." I laugh.

"No. *You* wore them best!" she flatters.

Climbing into the passenger seat, I kiss Ella's cheek. "You smell lovely," I say.

"You smell of egg fried rice! Glove compartment"—she points—"there's some mouth freshener in there."

I peer in the tiny dark cubicle.

"This?" I ask.

"Yep. Spray it."

"In my mouth?"

"Wherever!"

I ignore her and toss the mint mouth freshener back in the hatch, slapping it shut.

"I'm only joking—tell her, Runner—I'm only joking, aren't I?"

"Shh," I whisper, "I haven't told her where we're going."

Ella cocks her head.

"Well, get a move on," she says, "we'll be there in ten minutes."

All right, shh, I mouth.

"Don't worry," she says, "I'll have a quiet word with her. Runner secretly likes me."

"You think?" I say.

"I know!" Ella smiles.

"Hey, I've got some good news." I shine. "That job I applied for, they called me for an interview."

"Amazing. When?"

"Next week."

I watch her face disguise her insecurity, a tinge of envy detected in her eyes because I know her so well.

"Cool," she allows.

"This is great," I say, pointing at the stereo, hoping the distraction might ease any awkwardness. "Who is it?"

Ella turns up the music.

"Haim. Three sisters, Californian. Super cool, right?"

We coast through Shoreditch, music filling Ella's small Fiat Punto. I wind down my window, the bleed of acoustics escaping as the night air enters, blowing my hair—long strands sticking to my sheer lip gloss that I wipe away and tuck behind my left ear. Girls are out, in twos, threes, or more. Their sanguine arms linked as they head into Old Street's lively bars, legs bare, skirts hitched.

Crawling up to the traffic lights, Ella stops and checks her lipstick. Cleans her teeth with her tongue and gives the lemon air freshener hanging from her rearview mirror a sharp flick. She releases the clutch. The slow vocals and off-kilter percussion telling me to *let go, let go, let go*. I close my eyes, releasing a muscle or two, working the words over in my mind like the lusty bounce of a yo-yo.

Yeah, that's it, Oneiroi whispers, *chill.*

As I sense the Body ease back, my hand reaching to loosen and set free my hair, Runner steps out.

"Where are you taking us?" she snarls, eyes at half-mast.

Ella looks at me—us—sensing the switch, and presses down on the gas.

"To a sex club," she says, "so either get on board, or get back inside."

WE PARK BENEATH ONE OF THE STREETLAMPS IN HOXTON SQUARE.

Already, small groups of thirtysomethings are gathering. The neon light from Electra's overhead sign casting a haze of magenta across naked shoulders and intimate holds. Two girls pull their boyfriends in close when they catch sight of Ella, her shoulders pulled back for extra zeal. Her swaying silhouette like the night glide of a lynx.

"He said to use the back entrance," Ella says, looking past the crowd, then pulls me with her toward the rear of the club. An alley of shadows and stink.

The Electra Girls are outside smoking. I prepare inwardly for their mood—warm, dismissive—who knows? A beautiful red-haired girl reaches in her Prada clutch, retrieves a cigarette, and tilts her head to one side while her friend offers up a light. She throws her hair across her shoulder, avoiding any possibility of it going up in flames, inhales, head sliding back. The athletic brunette forces the lighter back into the pocket of her spray-on jeans, and then leans against the wall. A clear heel raised behind her. Tenderly they embrace between long drags of smoke.

Two brittle blondes, twins, join them, both with hair piled high like Mister Softee ice creams. Both younger, they smile, but not before sizing up the other two, a lightning dart from their heavily worked eyes.

"You don't have to do this," I say, turning to Ella, who squeezes my hand three times.

"It's fine, come on," she says. "We won't be here long. Promise."

A pause.

"Everyone inside okay?" she whispers, pulling me closer.

"What do you fucking think?" Runner snaps, hijacking the Body.

Ella stops and weighs up my tone.

"Sorry," I say, nudging Runner back inside, "you know Runner. Can't shut her up sometimes."

Taking me by the shoulders, my *Reason* looks me square in the eyes. "Listen up, everyone," she reassures us, "it's gonna be fine. Trust me."

Aimed at the Electra Girls, we head toward the alley. The sound of crashing bottles makes me jump and I scoot closer into Ella's side.

I suddenly remember—nerves switched on—that the redhead is the girl who was gyrating on the nickel pole on Wednesday night. Up close, I realize she is older than I first thought. A mole floating on the top of her lip, age fixed with thick makeup and tight clothes. Her eyes are wide and buzzing, a sure sign she's stoned.

"I'm here to see Navid," Ella blurts.

Sniffing out her unease, the girls smile. Seemingly pleased that they have the upper hand.

"And who are you?" one of the Softee Sisters asks.

"Ella."

"He never mentioned no Ella," she says.

"Shaun, the barman, told me to come," Ella responds. "Said Navid's looking for someone to work reception, or the bar."

The four girls look to one another and snicker. The athletic brunette adjusting her bra strap and checking her nails.

"Nice jacket," the redhead says, pawing the collar of Ella's new leather addition. "Where'd you get it?"

"It was a gift," Ella lies.

The redhead strokes the hem, nods approvingly.

"He's in the bar," she allows. "Up the stairs, then take a left."

"Thanks." Ella smiles.

Shrugging, the other three let us pass. My back bristles knowing they're watching us as we make our way up the steep flight of stairs. When I cut a glance over my shoulder, I notice the redhead still staring, her eyes fixed. Then she winks, sly as a cat. Stirred, I smile back.

A ZIGZAG OF BLACK AND WHITE TILES LEADS US INSIDE. FAUX OPULENT deco with geometric shapes, mirrors, and chrome reflecting people's moods. I hadn't spotted on Wednesday night—my eyes fixed on a certain barman—how luxurious the polished walnut and black lacquered chairs were mixed alongside satins and furs. The seats are low and streamlined, angled for comfort in single pieces rather than suites, and on top of the bar: a huge silver airplane, wings three feet wide with propellers like giant kitchen whisks.

An Asian girl with a tight puckered mouth like the arse of a cat walks toward us wearing a short black skirt, stockings, and pearls. She strokes her long anise-brown hair, a wave of cascading curls. A headband securing her bangs.

"Is that a wig?" Oneiroi whispers, seizing the Body.

Back inside, I order again, reclaiming the Body, making sure to stay strong in the Light.

The Asian girl catches her reflection in an etched mirror next to a cream velvet loveseat, clearly not happy with what she sees. Furrows a penciled brow, adjusts a curl. I smile at her, but immediately she shoots me down with war-mongering eyes and a petulant mouth. Face hard and frozen.

She turns her back to me.

"Christ," I say, "I was just being friendly."

"No such thing in here." Ella snorts.

"So where is he, this Navid?" I ask, already averse.

Ella shrugs, looks about the room, which is slowly filling with small groups of men in expensive suits smoking fat cigars. City-boy clichés.

"Not sure," she says. "I guess we should just wait here."

Perching on the oyster barstools I count the liquor bottles lined up to ease my anxiety—*eleven, twelve, thirteen*—then turn to watch another hostess with a fake chest, also Asian, delivering a bottle of champagne with a tacky sparkler emitting colored flames. The group of men cheer. She laughs, opening the heavy bottle with a flirtatious pop, then throws back her head, revealing perfect white teeth, and allows one of the men to pat her ass. She gives him a wiggle, a silk bow on her short black skirt bouncing up and down.

After pouring she stands the bottle in an ice bucket and takes a credit card. The men relax. One puffs on a cigar, making a fat smoke ring. With his palm, he drums the leather seat beside him, an invitation to join their little party. But the hostess simply smiles, points at the bar. The man feigns disappointment, his face dropping like the painted mouth of a clown, belly straining against his white nylon shirt. He slips a folded banknote in the top of the girl's stocking.

Asshole, Runner curses in my head.

She's right, I think. He is an asshole. In his mind the Electra Girls have made a choice. Empowered their bodies to do what they want with whom they want. But we all know this is bullshit. That it simply makes these cheating bastards feel better about themselves. The ones who get off on the Electra's young, prostituted bodies, telling their wives they'll be home late—that work's a bitch—and not to wait up. What do they care that each of these girls is someone's daughter? No one here needs to know that. It's distasteful. Vulgar. Spoils the fantasy. In the Electra you can leave the outside—outside. The reality makes me feel angry.

Then immediately a little sad. Were I something to taste, this club would surely spit me out.

Ella suddenly jumps up.

"Hey!" She cheers, waving at two girls, both in skintight jeans and throwing around their flesh—tanned as a coconut—like they're auditioning for a pop video. Scanning the girls, I immediately rank myself fourth in our soon-to-be-formed girl band, falling short in the breast department—as usual. I reach around the back of my bra and yank down on the clasp, then quickly pull up the straps, hoping the hoist will make my breasts more pert.

"They work at Jean&Co," Ella whispers, the girls fast approaching.

"Hey, Ella," the prettiest girl says, kissing Ella's cheek, "what are you doing here?" The other turns to me, kisses my cheek too, even though we've never met.

"Meeting the owner."

"Navid?"

"You know him?"

"Yeah, we know him," they say in sync, pushing their chests out like bloated frigates, imagining, I suspect, that the act might conjure Navid himself. "We started work here last week. No more jeans. Thank God."

The girls laugh.

"Cool," Ella says.

"Can you tell me where the bathroom is?" I interrupt.

"Over there." The prettier girl points. "Through the double doors."

I peel myself away from Ella's side. Every intention of stuffing my tiny bra with tissues.

WHEN I RETURN, THE TWO GIRLS HAVE LEFT, REPLACED NOW BY A MAN, tall and athletic, and an older woman, short and severe.

I reclaim my spot beside Ella.

"I'm Cassie," the woman says, shaking my hand.

In a place where men think it's acceptable to buy sex, the surest way to spot the madam is to look for the businesswoman north of fifty in a sharp suit and a cruel smile. She hands me a drink, bending the pink straw at its ridge. Her eyes squint tight like razor clams, working over me.

"Thanks," I say, noting the tension in Ella's awkward lean. Her smile held and fake, arms crossed against chest.

The man finally turns to me. A toothpick loosely hanging from his lip.

"I'm Navid." He smiles.

My first reaction is panic, his hand resting on the back of Ella's barstool, wet animal eyes scanning me up and down. A Tod's loafer raised to position himself closer. Too close, I think. Dressed in a navy cashmere sweater and a blaring white shirt, he stares, working the toothpick between his lips. The two girls from before slink past us, catching his eye. He tries his best to stay focused, buckles, then turns back to face Ella.

"I'm so pleased you're thinking of joining us," he says, his voice slow and soft. The depths of his eyes like pits of rich fountain ink. "You'll fit in nicely. Won't she, Cassie?"

Cassie nods.

Urgh, say the Flock.

Ella aims her body at him, dropping her hands between her thighs, energized, it seems, by his attention. Growing fat with his praise. For a moment I picture the girls I knew living on the west block of my neighborhood. A flicker of hope that one of the older boys—or their fathers—might notice them. Someone to set them free from a life of never feeling good enough. Rarely touched or held.

Cassie looks at Ella like a prize cow. A sly diamond winking on her right hand as she reaches for a handful of nuts in a bowl on the bar. She throws the nuts at the back of her throat, then leans in, her jade bangle clacking against the bar's polished chrome. Arm flab swinging like the underbelly of a spayed cat.

"We pay two-fifty a night," Cassie says, "then there's tips."

"How much?" Ella asks.

"That depends."

"On?"

"How much they like you," Navid offers. "How much you smile."

Ella smiles. "Great!" She shines, and all three of them laugh.

An outsider, I catch Shaun from the corner of my eye, now standing behind the bar.

"Back in a minute," I say.

"Sure," Navid says, "no rush."

Of course there's no rush, I say in my head. *It's not me you're interested in.*

Shaun spots me draw nearer.

"Hey," he says, winking.

"Hey." I smile back.

His arms bulge at the hem of his white short-sleeved shirt, and I note the creep of several tattoos. On his right arm: the tail of a mermaid; on the left: the heel of a monster. Monsters and mermaids.

I wonder which he prefers, Oneiroi says. *Mermaids: no fear of depth, yet a fear of shallow living? Or monsters: not under your bed but inside your head?*

Shh, I say.

I watch him shake a cocktail, arms flexing. The mermaid's tail stretching while he adds a tiny violet hibiscus to the salted rim of a glass. He slides the peach-colored cocktail over to a girl with a stink face who breaks out in a smile, revealing crooked teeth before lowering pretty eyes.

He leans over the bar and kisses me on the mouth.

Stink Face takes her drink and hurries along.

"Still on for tonight?" he asks.

"Sure," I say, thumbing Ella's meet-and-greet situation with Navid and Cassie behind me, "I'm just—"

"It's fine, go. Find me out back in half an hour."

I know I shouldn't, but I grab his neck and kiss him again, hoping people are watching. This time a tongue. A possessive act to mark down that he's my date—tonight.

Runner covers her eyes. *Eew,* she says, squirming.

ANOTHER DRINK?" NAVID ASKS AS I REJOIN THEM, CASSIE NOW TALKING to the hostess with the fake chest at the end of the bar.

"No thanks," I reply, noting the hostess fidget nervously with the hem of her short black skirt. Close to tears, she turns and points at a group of men in the far corner beneath large deco mirrors. Uplighters on either side shine down on their clammy cheeks.

"It's such a great location. How long have you been here?" Ella says, turning amorous, noting Navid's distraction.

"Will you excuse me?" He smiles, Cassie's voice now raised. He brushes his hand across Ella's knee.

Ella smiles. Flashes her teeth. Her cheeks now the color of ripe fruit, her body vibrating with pleasure.

Navid walks over to Cassie and the hostess and slams his hand on the bar. Both are silenced, their faces suddenly hushed into stillness. He leans in, taking each of their shoulders, then sends the hostess back to the group of men.

Nice, real nice, Runner says.

I watch Cassie finger her stiff black hair, a skunk stripe of alabaster chasing the contours of her skull. She nods, full of compliance. Navid then catches her unease and places a comradely hand on her arm and leaves, heading toward our two band members, with whose tanned flesh it seems he is well acquainted. They delight like idiots, broken in like shoes from his attention. The promise of something they probably don't get at home. He looks at the girls in turn, as though waiting for a kiss. When neither girl responds, he slips them something under their table, sliding his hand up their thighs.

I turn to Ella.

"I have to go now," I say.

"Okay, I'll call you tomorrow." She smiles. "Have fun with Shaun."

"So, you gonna take the job?" I ask.

"Why not?" she says, composed and breezy—drunk on the bait of Navid's touch and flattery. "He said I can start tomorrow night."

I walk toward Navid and the girls with a sense of disappointment, unlike Ella. Her decision to join the Electra now weighing heavily on my mind. That she's been fed like some starved kitten by a man capable of hurt and manipulation seems not to dwell on her mind in the slightest. But for me, her choice stinks. For me, it's the beginning of something wrong.

Runner takes the Light and taps me on the shoulder.

"You'd better watch him," she whispers. "He's cunt drunk." A discreet fore-and-middle-finger V directed at my eyes and back out at Navid. Her gaze boring into the back of his head. As she returns to the Body I notice her fingers pointing, like a gun. She blows on them, a cool shot released.

7

Daniel Rosenstein

S O, YOU SEE MY DILEMMA?" SHE SAYS.

"I do."

"First the jacket. Now the club."

A pause.

She taps the tip of her knee several times. The act, I suppose, regulating her anxiety.

"You're concerned," I say, "understandably."

Arms raised now, she removes her sweater. Tosses it in her leather purse. Underneath: a thin tank top, the simple shape of a bra. The curves of her breasts rising and falling as she catches her breath.

She sits erect now, coral mouth lightly parted, legs crossed. Both arms resting on the chair.

"Yeah, I'm concerned," she says. "There's a zillion other places she could work. And she wants me to go back there again with her tonight."

"I see. Speaking of work?"

She looks to me, her face suddenly softening. Seemingly pleased I've remembered.

"Well?" I ask.

She suddenly sits up straight, waits, grins. She is toying with me.

"I got it!" she sings. "Jack called and offered me the job. Said he loved my portfolio, and thought I did well in the interview. He thinks we'll make a great team."

"Congratulations, that's great." I smile.

"Thank you. I start next week."

"So, new job and fun date."

From lowered eyes she gazes up at me. Coy.

A pause.

"Me, a photojournalist. Who'd have thought?" She smiles.

I smile back.

"I'm so excited," she adds, leaning forward. "I've followed Jack's work for such a long time. I can't wait to assist him, you know; make a difference, help communities connect with each other. Use my photography to tell news stories that are important."

I nod, encouraging her.

"There's something about informing people. Making them aware. Mastering a scene. Arming yourself with a camera and putting yourself at a safe enough distance to understand a situation."

"This distance, it means something to you?" I ask.

"I guess so. When you place a camera between yourself and whatever you're shooting there's a certain autonomy. It can feel intimate without the fear that someone or something could engulf you."

"Interesting word, 'engulf,'" I say.

She clears her throat and throws her hands in the air. A spontaneous act.

"I guess," she offers.

I wait. Taking in her animation and zeal. Her eyes widening with optimism, the truth of what she speaks all at once infectious.

"And your date?" I finally ask, mindful to pace the session. Our work a marathon, not a sprint.

"It *was* a lot of fun." She smiles again, seemingly lost in the weekend's events: The slow walk to Smoking Goat, where she and Shaun had eaten wild yam mussels and velvet crab washed down with delicious red wine; how he'd noticed her shyness, setting her at ease with a smile; much talking; then the cab ride home; the beginnings of kisses; the morning after, when he made her pancakes swimming in butter and syrup—her favorite, apparently.

Interestingly, she skipped the part where they practiced fevered sex, but I filled in the gaps. Briefly allowed myself the youthful fantasy of their two bodies, budding and wild.

Alexa gazes at the lithograph of the woman with a long neck propped against the window and stretches her own. Her eyes eventually settling on the oil painting above my head: "One of your other patients?" She points.

"Yes," I say.

"Do you like it?" she asks. "Or did you hang it because you had no choice? After all, you don't have to look at it."

I move forward in my chair, turn and face the painting. My eyes alert to the edge of the cliffs.

"I like it," I say. "You?"

She makes a face. "Hm, not sure," she says.

"About?"

"It looks kinda cold. Unnerving."

I gesture with my hand for her to say more.

"Makes me think of all the ways I could die up there," she continues, crossing her arms.

I lean back.

"Such as?"

"Such as jumping off the cliff. My neck twisting as it hits the sea. I'd float around. Like a discarded piece of rubbish that some sandcastle kid failed to throw away. I'd drift off slowly. Head crashing against the jagged chalk before—"

She pauses.

"—before some poor dog walker eventually finds me. Screams when she sees me floating facedown. Hair matted with blood. She'd call emergency services. A stretcher arriving to carry me away."

She clears her throat.

"Then there's the boat," she continues. "I imagine myself stranded. Unable to swim. In time I'd die of dehydration, the circling gulls pecking at my eyes. A slow and painful death. Or maybe old and alone in the lighthouse, just like Virginia Woolf's. Nothing but my thoughts to drive me to despair. My hair eventually turning white with madness."

"There's that word again," I say, "'madness.'"

She looks down.

Slides one foot inward.

"There's a bridge," she says, "by Archway. Near where I live."

I nod, knowing of Jumpers Bridge. Of the many suicides commit-ted late at night.

"I go there sometimes," she says, "when I feel sad. I stare down at the traffic."

"You think about jumping?"

"Sometimes . . ."

Her sentence trails off.

I wait.

"I try to imagine what my mother was thinking before she jumped in front of the train."

I nod.

She reaches inside her leather purse, recovers her Zippo, a pack of Lucky Strikes. Looks at them, bemused.

"No smoking, I'm afraid."

She throws me a black look, hurls the flimsy cigarette pack back in her purse.

"What do you imagine?" I ask.

"How desperately lonely she must have felt. How I'd like to stab my father in the throat."

I uncross my legs, fixing both feet firmly on the ground.

"Your rage," I say. "Your notes indicated there was violence at home. That your father was incredibly controlling and unpredictable. Tyrannical."

She nods.

"He was. Toward both of us," she says, "me and my mother, then later—Anna."

With damp eyes, she looks away.

"Can you say a little more about your mother?" I ask.

"I'm angry she killed herself and left me with him. With his violence. Then there's part of me that thinks it was my fault."

"You were a child," I say gently. "You had no such power."

"*Power?* Pfft." She rolls her eyes. "Neither of us had any power. He. *He* had all the power."

"Sometimes we direct hurt toward ourselves when we feel powerless," I say. "Believing it was your fault might suggest your not wanting to face the truth of your mother's misery. How desperate she was."

She takes a tissue. Her hand wiping gently beneath her eyes.

A pause.

"Sometimes I hurt myself," she says.

I lean forward.

She leans back.

"I cut. It helps."

"How often?" I ask.

She shrugs, reaches for a glass of water. Takes a sip.

I watch her set the glass down, making a mental note that trust is emerging. During our first session she was unable to take a drink of water. Was too self-conscious. But maybe someone else is here today?

She clears her throat.

"How often?" I repeat.

"When things—you know—get too much."

"Where?"

"The backs of my legs. And my thighs."

She makes an effort to touch behind her left knee. Soft and arched. A moment when mind and body synchronize. The Body holding the score and remembering previous harm.

"We need to look at alternative ways to self-soothe," I say, "direct the anger out. Not in."

Both feet shaking just a little, she looks down, faltering.

"Sure," she says, defeated, "whatever you say. Just tell me what to do."

My ears linger over her words. The power she gives me. My counter-transference indicating she grants power and control too easily. Is this exclusive to men, I wonder, or does she do it to women too? Do her different personalities take on diverse views of power? I shiver, the stark realization that Alexa can morph and switch and shape-shift to be someone completely different from who I think she is, and I wonder which persona is now in control.

She straightens up, brushes the palms of her hands along the thighs of her jeans.

"I should have stopped Ella from stealing the jacket," she says.

I note the diversion. The switch of events. Alexa now revisiting an earlier part of the session.

"The tyranny of 'shoulds' and 'musts,'" I say.

"What do you mean?"

"Tyrannous scoldings are not helpful. It's more effective to reflect on the decision you made at the time. Then we have more hope of learning from it."

"Right, well next time I'll intervene. It was wrong. I was negligent."

"You want to punish yourself?" I say.

"Probably."

Silence.

"It's possible part of you believes you deserve to be punished," I say. "Is there a voice that tells you to harm yourself? Slice the backs of your legs?"

She looks up again at the oil painting and nods. A glaze of wet building in the corners of her eyes.

"But I imagine there is another voice telling you not to," I say, "its polar opposite."

Still staring at the painting, her eyes narrow. "I have another voice that wants me to kill myself. Should I listen to that one too?" she snaps, her gaze now turned cold.

"It's important to listen to all of the Voices," I say. "It doesn't mean you have to act on what they say. But pushing them aside only makes them stronger."

I watch her throat swallow.

"When you're ready," I say cautiously, "you could try introducing me to everyone inside."

She reaches into her purse again.

"I'm scared," she says, smoothing on lip balm.

I lean forward a little farther.

"Listening to everyone means acceptance of your whole self, Alexa. Not just cherry-picking the good parts accepted by others."

"I've always self-harmed," she says. "If I stop, I don't know where the anger will go. Who I might hurt. I might lose control."

"Control is action. And one you can change over time. Fear prevents you from accepting your feelings. But no feeling is final. They don't have to destroy you."

"But they're risky."

"True. But there's little progress without risk," I say.

She lowers her gaze.

"Can I trust you?" she says.

Sinking into my chair, I realize she's conflicted and unsure whether to commit. But I want to see how eager she is to seek and be frank—take a risk—and not overfeed her with interpretations and answers.

Her gaze returns to me slowly.

I sit up straighter and smile. "Tell me about the Voices."

She pauses, a striking expression of unknown freedom on her face. Fear and relief all at once. I watch the rise and fall of her breath. A zing of anticipation in my own chest.

"Yesterday," she begins slowly, her voice shaking at the edge, "we were all cleaning my bedroom. Only Dolly, the youngest, showed any kind of enthusiasm. The rest just mooned about, kicking their heels and complaining about wanting to be someplace else. Oneiroi fancied yoga and Runner had ideas about some kickboxing class. And the Fouls, well, they just stayed inside. They want no part in anything we do these days. None of them seem to realize how exhausted I am."

She raises her head to check my response and laughs softly. Tucks a strand of loose hair behind her right ear—a nervous tic, I tell myself, noticing half of it is missing.

"Thank you," I say. "It's good to finally meet you all."

8

Alexa Wú

THE REDHEAD DABS THE CORNERS OF HER GLOSSED MOUTH, EYES FIXED on her reflection. She calmly slides her gaze across the changing room, adjusts her dressing gown—agape—exposing bronzed and oiled legs. A wrap of fuchsia silk tied with a sloppy bow.

"Has anyone seen my eyelash curler?" she shouts, fingering her gold necklace.

The other Electra Girls shrug. Too busy with their own hair and makeup to care. Their concentration pinned on their pretty mirrored selves, Hollywood-style lightbulbs casting shadows across their powdery faces.

"What time do you finish?" I ask, catching sight of a girl, natural and slightly plump, sitting with legs tucked beneath her on an easy chair, flicking through a stale magazine.

Ella hands over her own eyelash curler and turns to me. Her mouth outlined in deep red.

"Two-ish," she says, filling in her bottom lip, "maybe three."

"Who's that?" I whisper, nodding toward the girl.

"Sylvie," she whispers, glancing toward the redhead. "They're old friends. Apparently they go way back."

I risk a look, noting Sylvie's cute style, homely and neat. A pair of pale corduroys and modest makeup enhancing pretty eyes.

"Fancy hanging out tomorrow?" I ask, turning back and noting the clench in my gut. Potential rebuff both plain and familiar.

"Sure," Ella says.

The clench is killed. Replaced now with insecurity at the sight of the redhead's mostly naked body. Ella holds on to my shoulder, steps into three-inch heels.

"What are you and Shaun doing tonight?" she asks.

"Movie," I say, "then dinner."

The redhead forces a hoop through a naked ear, sprays her body with sweet perfume rivaling the musky damp of the room. Doomed competition, I think, everywhere. Pumping like blood through veins, the very heart of this place. The Electra Girls forced to spar like sexualized gladiators, their side glances trailing each other's moves and forming some kind of pecking order. Don't they realize they're being played? That it's the men who run the show, control the game?

Most likely, Runner says, glancing at the girls, *but they're damaged, and scared. And most likely hurting.*

I suddenly remember my final-year degree show, picturing my classmate Mia Knight's face when I was awarded the Getty Emerging Talent Award.

It was presumed that well-connected Mia, with her aptitude for lighting and lip service, along with a killer ambition, would surely snatch the award. So understandably Mia was annoyed at my success, her perfect tiny turned-up nose out of joint and stuck up in the air that I'd even applied for the award, let alone won it.

"Pfft," she'd dismissed with a glare, "I'm guessing equal opportunities played a part."

"Yeah, or maybe she shagged one of the judges," her sister Nikki scoffed, rewarded by Mia's keen snort.

I accepted the award, of course, and a smile remained in my eyes long enough to catch Mia's upturned snout in the air like she was smelling freshly slung dung. The judges each shaking my shy hand, a photograph then taken of us all together.

I stared Mia dead in the eye—

Take that, Miss Piggy, I voiced in my head. *Hai-ya!*

THE DOOR SUDDENLY SWINGS OPEN.

Navid appears with a stack of chocolate boxes balanced on his palm, a light smirk on his tanned face.

"Navid!" the redhead calls, dancing toward him and winking at Sylvie, her dressing gown waterfalling from her sleek shoulders. She presses her breasts against him, kisses him on the mouth, cheek, and neck, slightly frantic. The girls turn away. Sylvie too has a noticeable look of contempt.

"For you," he says, reaching for the top box. "Not that you need them. You're sweet anyway."

Oh please, Runner says, *I think I'm gonna throw up.*

But as the redhead reaches out, Navid draws the box away. "Not too many," he warns, swatting her ass.

She rolls her eyes, rests her manicured hands on her hips, elbows bent. Navid baits some more, each time inching the chocolate box farther back. The chorus of girls giggling in the background. A gaggle of geese.

His little game is slayed when the redhead eventually snatches the chocolates out from his hand. He takes another box then and hands it to Ella.

"For our new girl." He smiles, addressing the room. "I hope you're all being friendly and helping Ella settle in?"

None of the girls answer.

"Hey!" he shouts.

The girls turn, jolting back into themselves. Stare at Ella with defiance, muttering "Sure" and "Okay," not meaning a word of it. Ella shyly takes the box in her hands, nervously fingering the cellophane corners.

"Dark chocolate," she says, looking up. "My favorite."

There is a thirsty shake to her voice.

"You're welcome," Navid says. "It's not often we have such a beautiful girl in need of chocolate."

There is something in his voice—an endless charm—that alerts me to how this will surely play out. His eyes are slow and penetrating. His hand on top of Ella's thumbs as she clutches the box of chocolates.

He will hurt her, I think. He will chew her up and spit her out.

Sylvie and I catch each other's gaze, the magazine now resting in her lap. I risk a smile, which she returns before throwing Navid a dark look.

"Come," he says, dropping his hand to cup Ella's waist, "I'll show you around."

The redhead shifts on her heel, tossing her chocolate box to the ground.

Navid turns and clears his throat.

"Pick that up," he orders.

The redhead pauses for a second and looks him square in the eye, then bends down, scoops up the box, and thrusts it across her dressing table. The other girls feign interest in their hair and makeup, sensing, I imagine, the redhead's envy. In silence, the Softee Sisters each take a box of chocolates for themselves, and as they reach over to collect their sweet bribes from Navid's palm, I note they are also wearing gold chains with small keys attached.

"You lot can share," one Softee Sister orders the other girls, cramming her own in a black leather tote where she sits.

Ella tugs at my arm to follow her and Navid. The whitewashed paint on the makeshift walls barely covering the poop-colored brown underneath. Black-and-white photographs of seminude girls, eighties Athena-style prints of fast cars, fluffy white kittens, Pammy running down the beach in her famous red one-piece. I throw my nose in the air, professional snobbery breeding judgment, dismissive and curt.

Get you, Runner mocks, *Little Miss Photojournalist.*

On the wall next to the bathroom is a list of telephone numbers: hairdressers, beauty salons, nail bars. ~~The Glitter Girls~~ nail salon scratched out and replaced with Polish Me Pretty. Beneath: a pile of well-thumbed dictionaries and a copy of *Basic English Grammar for Dummies* beside an aging cracked wicker basket filled with a variety of beauty and hygiene items. Ella reaches in the basket and greedily swipes a bottle of apple-red nail polish to match her mouth. Clenches it tight in her hand and looks back at me with a wink. I tug at her arm but she pulls away, yanking so hard my hand drops. Her thieving, like the jacket incident, instantly bothers me. *Have some pride, some self-respect,* I want to yell. But then I realize my disapproval is most likely born of the stark and painful reminder of my own needs grown from deprivation.

"Have the girls shown you where we keep all the new dresses and shoes?" Navid asks.

Ella's pace quickens. "No, they haven't." Hope rising that her deprivation will soon be soothed by greed.

I shudder, her wanting obvious and plain.

"Well, they should have," he says, his voice strong and quick. "Come, let's choose something for you to wear."

The whitewash stops when we turn the corner. I wave Ella on. The idea of witnessing Navid's lure, his grooming of her—Ella in the hold of his slick palm and seemingly thrilled—turns my stomach. I make a phone gesture with my hand. *Call you tomorrow,* I mouth.

Okay, she mouths back, happy to be plucked from the gaggle of geese.

For a moment, I loathe her girly ways.

Navid holds out his hand, forcing Ella to catch his eyes. She laughs, seemingly shy. Nevertheless, she takes it, his tug setting her off balance. His smile somewhere close to believable. I wince.

They walk ahead. *He has her now,* I say, the Flock agreeing. Dolly hides, scuttling behind Runner, who instinctively offers a protective hand, both of them watching while my *Reason* and Navid slink away— cat and cub—nearing her rite of passage. Edging toward the wardrobe of bribes to end girlhood dreams.

Growing up, I had dreams. It seemed possible they could even come true. I wasn't completely stuck on my own. I had Anna. My personalities. And school. But it was different for Ella. Sure, she had Grace, but no father, a negligent mother, and very few dreams of her own. Validation and visibility went amiss. When offered attention she's sure as hell taken it, a little too keenly sometimes. I like to think I've reassured her like some sidekick Sally. But the sad reality, I've come to comprehend, is that it's not me she wants, but the attention of men. I see it in her eyes. The longing. Her heart wounded and searching like an orphaned cub. A message signaled in the way she holds her gaze. Her keen-to-please body. The quick opening of her mouth transform- ing a look from ashamed to sexy, that speaks: *Please love me.*

Whereas Ella's desire for attention and acceptance has kept her searching for ways to be loved, I had my love for learning, which spawned a desire to find fulfilling work. I had dreams like most girls:

buy my own apartment, travel, fall in love, ride a gondola, grow apple trees, dance regularly, plant a garden bursting with tulips, and, most intensely of all, develop stellar photography skills. I thought that if I could document the lives of others, I could exist vicariously through the intimate happenings of all those around me. Some of the uglier aspects of my own life balmed by photographing happy families sprawled out on freshly mowed lawns; pretty, delicate-skinned girls at the beach in tangerine swimsuits; a child holding hands with the air as she awaits her mother's reach; a father's hell as he notices a neighbor gazing at his daughter. Moments of mingled voyeurism and intimacy. Moments of truth.

My first makeshift cardboard camera had been made from a box of Kellogg's Coco Pops, through which I viewed the world with a squinted eye. Any feelings I had, night or day, were released and displaced on wildlife and nature views I gazed at through my cardboard and plastic viewfinders. They were views that couldn't love me back, but they couldn't hurt me either. So I was grateful for them. Anything to take me away from my fantastically dire life. And then, on my sixteenth birthday my father did a decent thing, just like the time he bought me a disposable camera for my thirteenth birthday. He gave me enough money for a secondhand Japanese model, and for the first time in forever my life had a purpose.

Finally, I'm a photographer, I voiced in my head, clutching the camera box. The proud owner of a marvelous Canon EOS Kiss III. I still remember how it felt to hold and point that first camera as I peered in close on a family of thrushes, a collection of inanimate objects around the house, an abandoned shoe. It made even things that were ordinary seem like treasure. And then I happened upon my love affair with Hampstead Heath: its vast expanse of woodland and rolling hills a place to walk and think. For hours I pored over maps, climbed fences, followed dense bushes, and jumped streams, taking photographs wherever I fancied. I discovered walled gardens, lush hedgerows, and wild, expansive grasslands, all home to nature's way. The Heath, I always felt, was bristling with life, and in turn this gave me pause to consider mine.

I look back, checking my watch, wondering how long it is until Shaun finishes his shift. I use the bathroom and then wander across the hall into a tired-looking makeshift bedroom. Chubby cartoon characters have been tacked to the wall and are lined up like little friends waiting to race. In one corner is a single bed made of pine, a duvet with Dora the Explorer strewn across. A gang of stuffed animals huddled together: a tiger, a bear, and a giraffe with one ear. I touch my own ear, finger running along the edge of gristle, softened over time. Sitting down on the bed, I look at the jumble of wooden jigsaw puzzles, hardback picture books, musical plush toys, and a demented pink rabbit with a drum. All here to satisfy little girls and boys while their mothers strip upstairs.

Next to the bed is a small chest of drawers, and on it an oval mirror, a half-eaten sleeve of cheesy puffs, and a Hello Kitty night-light. Inside the drawers, I find a bottle of Nytol elixir and sleeping pills. I imagine the men above me watching their mothers and panting, mouths slack like open garage doors. The children sleeping. The Electra Girls yielding a known value later slipped into the tops of their stockings.

The redhead appears, I assume in search of Navid and Ella. She shows little interest in my presence, my looks and breasts not up to par.

No competition here, Runner says.

I watch her squat, her dressing gown draped across her naked body, humble like a child's. Her crouch is easy and youthful. Slowly she gathers the toys, placing a musical plush doll alongside the stuffed animals, and opens a picture book.

I pretend to look away, preoccupied with my phone.

Suddenly her face softens, her gaze captivated by a family of flat-faced owls. She smiles, touches the page as if it were Braille, eyes following the words. But then she catches me watching—and snaps the book closed. She stands suddenly, setting off the demented drumming rabbit. Startled, she squats again, in search of a switch. Is relieved when the rabbit's foot finally stops thumping. She looks at me, tosses the rabbit to the ground, tearful. The batteries ricocheting across the floor.

She sure likes to throw things, Oneiroi says, noting my unease.

No wonder, I say, consoled by Runner's safe arms.

Pained, the redhead steps forward. Digs her heel in the dead rabbit's chest and twists her ankle hard enough that the rabbit eventually breaks. Her lip curls with satisfaction as she walks out.

Dread upsurging, I face the wall and wait for my chest to settle.

And then something occurs to me. Who replaces the batteries? Someone is in charge of making sure the kids are offered gifts, toys—or even drugged?—while their mothers strip upstairs. Who's grooming them? Priming them to do what their mothers do? Is it Navid? Cassie?

I lean against the wall and turn to the page that roused the redhead's smile. Three owlets stare back at me. They have woken up to find their owl mother gone. Disappeared.

Where? they wonder. *Will she return?*

I look up. My motherless reflection suddenly caught in the oval mirror resting on the pine dresser. I think of how my mother—bothered by countless migraines—would still read to me in the comfort of her bed: Judy Blume, Enid Blyton, Beatrix Potter, with a dauntless surge of love, knowing closeness wasn't something she created for the reward of it. Her love was as willing and as natural as the day was long. And her mother light would surface and remain luminous and ablaze whether people liked it or not.

Flash.

I AM NINE YEARS OLD.

"Raise your arms," my father says.

I close my eyes and wait while he drops a black velveteen dress over my head. The white scalloped collar fastened with a pearl button the size of an eye.

Flash.

I look down at my patent shoes. Also black, with a complicated buckle. Their size pinching my small toes. Earlier, he'd laid the clothes on my bed like one of those paper doll dress-up sheets that you cut out and stick to a naked paper girl. With both hands I smooth down the fat cloud of velvet, enjoying the softness on my sweaty palms.

Flash.

"Be brave, Xiǎo Wáwa. No tears. Make Baba proud," he says.

My mother's coffin appears. Three fleshy stems of red amaryllis placed on top.

With damp, tired eyes I watch it disappear through ruched black curtains—*the vanishing point.* I tell myself it's just a magic trick. That any minute now she'll spring up from some pew with a toothy smile, singing: "Surprise!"

But she doesn't. She is gone.

Flash.

"So little. So innocent. Do you think she even understands?" say hushed voices at the wake. *Yes, I am little,* I say in my head, *but I'm not deaf. And yes, I do understand that my mother is dead. Has killed herself.*

I pinch down hard on the backs of my legs, not allowing a single tear to escape. Instead stuffing half a moon cake in my mouth and enjoying how the sticky ashy-caramel lotus-seed paste clings to the roof of my mouth. The double yolk clogging in between my tiny, straight teeth. It tastes good. So good that I cram in the other half.

Flash.

My father walks over, disgraced at my greed, and slaps the fronts of my legs for all twelve mourners to see. And I cry.

I cry believing I will never stop. My mother now shoveled into a tan plastic urn.

Flash.

AND NOW SHAUN AND I ARE AT THE MOVIES. *TICK-TOCK.* A FAMILY-SIZE bucket of popcorn lodged between my thighs.

"You're quiet tonight. Everything okay?" he asks.

I place my finger to my lips and point at the screen, happy for an excuse not to talk. All the while thinking about the toys, the wardrobe of bribes, the broken pink rabbit—those batteries.

Groomers, Runner whispers, grabbing a fistful of popcorn, *what did you expect?*

My stomach flips.

Not this, I say.

9

Daniel Rosenstein

TELL ME ABOUT THE FOULS," I SAY.

"What do you want to know?"

"When they arrived. What purpose they serve."

She leans back in her chair. Gazes with listless inquiry at the oil painting. Her head tilting from side to side as if it might offer a different view of the cliffs. Another perspective.

"They make me do things," she says eventually, drawing her eyes to meet mine. "They make me hurt myself, then show up to scold or poke fun. They hate me. Us."

"Us?"

"The Flock." She smiles shyly.

"They're not part of the Flock too?"

She looks away.

"I've asked them to join us but they refuse."

"Why?" I ask.

"You tell me. You're the expert."

"First, I'm no expert," I say, "and secondly, we're in this together. It's not a Q&A."

She jolts back into herself, her earlier smile now gone. Then throws me a confused look.

"An expert requires no further learning," I continue. "I'd like us to make sense of the Voices together. This way you'll find a way to manage them and I'll find a way to guide."

She hesitates.

"They say I'm evil," she says, "rotten to the core."

"This quasi-religious evil . . . tell me, your father—was he a religious man?"

"No. He just preached a lot. Told me how lousy I was."

"Is it possible you've internalized his voice, created the Fouls to mirror your father?"

"You mean like self-punishment? Probably." She shrugs, answering her own question.

"Ever discuss this with Joseph?"

"Sometimes. But I was scared he'd see me for what I was."

"You feared his rejection?"

"Always."

"So you presented a false self?" I ask.

"There was a lot of that," she says.

"I see."

She raises her chin.

"Joseph had paintings in his consulting room too," she says, fixing her eyes on the cliffs. "There was one, a print, of a family. I think it was by Picasso. A mother and father with their four children. And a dog. A baby resting in the mother's lap. One of the children, I was never sure if it was a boy or a girl, stands, defiant. Their gaze is so fixed and penetrating. I hated it to begin with. The idea of family—it felt so alien. It was as if the painting was tormenting me. Waiting for me to leak all my badness into the room like some awful contagion—like somehow the idyllic portrait would set my evil and envious thoughts into actions. The Fouls used to tell me to destroy it. *Let him see how bad you really are,* they'd say."

"And how bad are you?" I ask.

She pauses.

I wait.

"How bad?" I repeat.

Her feet turn inward, a gentle wringing of hands. She shakes her head.

"I'm a good girl," she whispers quietly, "not like Alexa."

I note the switch.

"What did Alexa do?" I say.

"Last night"—she pauses, looks around, vigilant and patrolled—"she went to that icky place, Electra, with her friend Ella. I watched them from the Nest."

Bambi-eyed, she tucks her left foot beneath her thigh and bites her lip.

"You must be Dolly?" I venture playfully, noting the slight rise in my voice.

She nods.

"It's nice to meet you." I smile.

"You too," she says, rather too quickly.

I check the gold clock on my desk. Damn.

"Dolly," I say, "we have to finish now, but I hope you'll come back soon. I'd like us to talk some more. Maybe you can tell me about that icky place?"

She stands, her quick fingers tucking a wayward strand of hair behind her maimed ear. Feet still turned inward, she points at the door as if seeking license to leave, which I grant with a nod. When I turn the door handle she stretches into her former self. Her shoulders pulling back and rearing like a mustang as if to brace the outside once again. Seemingly given permission to take up more space in the world, Alexa smiles.

"Goodbye," she says.

I OPEN MY LAPTOP, CURIOSITY NOW HAVING GOTTEN THE BETTER OF me. A desire to know more about the icky place Alexa and Ella visited last night causing me strain.

An image of a girl with long red hair and heavily made-up eyes stares out, a mole above her glossed and slightly open mouth. I note how the pinch of her waist accentuates her large chest. A tight white tank top straining with the word ELECTRA in bright magenta printed across. My eyes travel to her string panties, a triangle of silk barely the size of a Dorito.

I slap the screen shut.

Attempting to steady myself for my next patient, I stand and gaze out the bay window, but an inescapable image of Alexa suddenly appears in my mind. She arrives at my office and morphs into a self-assured version of herself wearing red lipstick and heels. When I offer her a seat she scrambles into the far corner of my office like a wild animal, her eyes wide open and darting. Suddenly a child.

10

Alexa Wú

PASS ME THE LENS HOOD!" JACK ORDERS, HIS VOICE BARELY HEARD OVER the lobbying crowds.

A political rally.

Thousands marching to Downing Street demanding more cash for the National Health Service.

"Keep an eye out for anything interesting," he shouts again, "and stay close."

I scoot into Jack's side, our awareness and protection of each other evident by the proximity in which we move like armored side-walking crabs. I clench my own hand three times, the effect not nearly as reassuring as when Ella and I use our three-squeeze code.

It's okay, Oneiroi whispers, *we've got you. Don't panic.*

Rucksacks secured on our backs, Jack and I forge ahead, our hands free to protect our cameras and our eyes fixed on the marching men and women.

College suddenly seems like a far cry from working life. Work proving nothing like the safe environment of darkrooms and reading and lectures. Just three days in and already I'm starting to feel the burn, the rush. The thrill of being an *actual* photographer. I feel a wave of nausea—from either excitement or fear.

Excitement, Oneiroi champions.

Fear, the Fouls goad.

Why must you spoil everything?

They sneer.

I settle for excitement, then try on the feeling before deciding to speak the word out loud.

"This is exciting!" I cheer.

Jacks catches my eyes and smiles.

"You've got the bug," he shouts back.

"The bug?"

"It's infectious," he says. "In a good way."

I know that for a great, honest shot we'll need to move in closer, morph into part of the scene. Our cameras aimed at the lively health workers, activists, and pressure groups, their raised placards demanding we SAVE THE NHS. I focus on a man with a tan megaphone—part of the People's Assembly—*click*—his leadership addressing the marchers and stating the pressures to come. *Click. Click. Click.* Another tan megaphone follows his lead and momentum builds, their dual voices strengthening with each repeated protest.

An elbow finds its way to my chest, not intentional but all the same jolting the Body into submission.

"You okay?" Jack shouts.

I nod, twist my shoulder to fit the space where I can see a woman carrying a homemade placard: MY 15-YEAR-OLD DAUGHTER KILLED HERSELF, it reads. SAVE THE NHS.

Jack and I sidle up beside her. "Get her story," he whispers in my ear, "show her your ID."

I smile to test the waters. The woman notes my camera and nods.

"Pro or anti?" she asks.

"Pro," I say, showing her my news ID.

Her eyes start to fill.

"The NHS needs our help," she says. "My daughter killed herself after she was discharged from a psychiatric ward despite our plea that she be kept in hospital. We were told they needed the bed. We said she wasn't safe to leave."

"I'm sorry," I offer, my words feeling weak and insubstantial.

She grips the handle of her sign, her lower lip starting to quiver.

"She was really sick. Hallucinating and everything. Hearing voices through the walls, the TV. We didn't know what to do. Where else to go for help. We only had the NHS, we couldn't afford private health care."

Do something, Runner orders. *Help her.*

"May I?" I ask, offering my camera. "I can support your cause."

She agrees, anger and grief lining every angle of her face, loss pulling down like rain on her already slim shoulders. Raising my lens, I freeze momentarily, a slight hesitance to my *click,* thinking my camera's intrusion might cause her further distress. Suddenly she raises her sign, a swift gush of strength. A determination in her angry and grieving blue eyes. I feel my chest explode with pride and admiration. *Click. Click. Click. Click. Click.*

Good shot, I tell myself.

"Thank you," I say, moving on.

The mother lifts her head, pride and resilience forcing back tears.

"Fix it now! Fix it now! Fix it now!" the crowds chant.

Fix it now! Fix it now! Fix it now! the Flock mimic, their own protest going on inside the Body.

This feels good, Runner shouts, throwing a clenched fist in the air. *Let's do this!*

"Get the shot?" Jack shouts, joining the flow of revolt. His own camera aimed at a group of lobbying nurses.

"Yes."

Adrenaline drenches my entire body, a feeling not dissimilar to when I'd survived my father's wrath or had escaped his sly fists. A sense of empowerment mixed with relief surges through my chest. My camera now a mighty weapon.

I fill my lungs with air and push my body forward, eyes turned back and fixed on the grieving mother. The dense crowd's chant almost deafening.

This is no time to start feeling sentimental, Runner says. *Do you want me to take over for a while?*

No, I say, *I'm fine. I'm good.*

"Over there!" Jack points and I follow.

A group of nurses holding up a banner made of NHS bedsheets. We scoot up toward them, *click,* Jack suddenly kneeling to get a wide-angle shot of the nurses' linked arms. I join him. Chants ringing strong all around.

"This feels great," I say.

Jack smiles and points at my chest.

"That feeling there," he says, "it never goes away. Stand for something, and you'll never fall for shit that don't matter."

11

Daniel Rosenstein

Did you schedule an extra session with Alexa Wú?" the receptionist asks.

"No," I reply, "I'm heading out to my meeting. I just came in early to catch up on some notes before I meet with the governors this afternoon."

"Well, she's here."

"Give me a moment," I say, checking my diary. Memory immediately challenged.

"No," I repeat. "Nothing in my diary. Charlotte's due after lunch, then Emma. And then we have a team meeting at four P.M., before the governors meeting at six P.M."

"What would you like me to do? She's in the waiting room."

I check my clock—eight A.M.

"I'll come speak with her," I say.

Click.

Suddenly disoriented, even though I've checked my diary and know we never meet on Fridays because of my AA meeting, I surprise myself by not entirely trusting that I've got my timing right. I wonder about this, my countertransference experienced to be shaky and uncertain.

I check the diary again, run my finger down the list of today's patients and meetings. It's fine, I reassure myself. It's Friday. Alexa comes on Tuesdays and Thursdays. Eight A.M. Both days. I'm not mistaken.

SHE IS SEATED AND WAITING. YET ON SEEING ME APPROACH, SHE STANDS.

"Hello, Alexa."

She steps back.

"Have I done something wrong?" Her voice hushed and small.

"Wrong? Of course not."

"Your receptionist said I got the time wrong."

I notice her feet turn inward as she pulls down her sweater to cover her fists. A denim jacket worn on top. She suddenly averts her gaze, instead glancing at the Receptionist.

"It's okay," I say. "Take a seat for the moment."

"I prefer to stand," she quickly answers.

"I'm afraid I have to leave shortly," I explain.

"Leave?"

"Yes."

"So I did get the time wrong?"

"It's Friday," I say gently. "We meet on Tuesdays and Thursdays, remember?"

She nods, but I'm unsure if she really believes this to be true.

"Can I wait here for you?" she asks.

"I'm afraid not."

"Why?"

"I have to go to a meeting now, and then I have patients and other meetings for the rest of the day." I try to calm her apparent unease with a smile.

"So no time to see me at all?"

She picks at her cuticles nervously.

"Sadly not."

She inches farther away, her gaze trailing the floor, fists held tightly against her chest.

I check the waiting room clock, aware that I need to finish my notes and leave shortly, keen that this situation not escalate into something problematic. I turn around and face the Receptionist, who has one eye on her computer screen. She taps her watch discreetly and smiles.

"I'm sorry, Alexa," I say. "I'll see you next week, on Tuesday. Okay?"

She is still. Fixed. I watch her hands clench and unclench. She attempts an intake of breath, her gaze traveling up my body to meet my eyes. Suddenly her body jolts. She is striding toward me at speed.

"Well, thanks a fucking lot!" she yells. Her finger directed in my face.

I feel myself flinch, stumble backward.

"Useless piece of shit."

Stunned, I waver.

She sneers, sly. Turns and walks away.

12

Alexa Wú

I DIOT, THE FOULS SCORN.

I'm not an idiot, Dolly cries, *and stop being so mean.*

Alexa, sleepin' fuckin' beauty, is still out cold, so I muscle in and force the Fouls away.

Why didn't you wake me, Dolly? You're not supposed to come out alone, it's not safe. You know that.

I just thought I'd let you all rest. Don't be cross, Runner.

I'm not cross, I'm disappointed. You should have woken me up. It's not a lot of fun when you wake up and find yourself in this shithole faced with some bloke.

He's not just any *bloke, he helps us. He's nice,* Dolly says.

That useless piece of shit? Don't be fooled. Next time, wake me. Got it?

She starts to cry. Christ al-fuckin'-mighty.

Stop crying, come on. You're okay. I try to put my arm around her, but she pulls away.

I'm sorry, Runner, I was just trying to be helpful. We always come to Glendown at eight o'clock.

Didn't you hear what the doc said? It's Friday. F-R-I-D-A-Y. We come on Tuesdays and Thursdays, remember? Get it in your head.

She scoots into my side as I make my way down the white corridor. *Shall we wake Alexa?* she asks between sobs.

Not yet, she's tired and stressed. She's got a lot going on with work, the new shrink, and now Ella starting at the Electra. Just let her rest.

Dolly takes my hand, happy now that I've stopped yelling at her.

Runner, she says with a smile, *can we get breakfast? I'm soooooo hungry.*

Okay, I agree, reaching for a Lucky Strike, *what d'ya fancy?*

Eggs.

Eggs? I laugh. *Just eggs?*

Eggs and chips! With ketchup.

Oneiroi suddenly wakes up. *Where are we?* She yawns, stretching.

Glendown, I say.

Glendown?

Dolly thought she'd be all clever and bring us here.

Dolly!

I've already said sorry, Dolly says, irked.

Where are we going now? asks Oneiroi, rubbing sleep from her eyes.

To get some breakfast. Dolly wants eggs. We can wake Alexa in time for work.

I don't fancy eggs.

I don't care what you fancy.

I turn the corner. Dolly happy because she's got her own way, Oneiroi not so much. Approaching us are two girls. One fat. One thin. They stare. Smile. Stare some more.

"What the fuck are you staring at?" I yell.

Runner! Dolly says, covering her ears. *Don't be so horrid.*

"I'm sorry," I call out, amused, "I'm having a bad day. Forgive me. Come join us for eggs!" But already they are running toward the cafeteria at speed, their legs carrying them quicker than a friggin' freight train.

Attagirl, Oneiroi says, stepping out of the Nest, *you sure know how to make friends.*

13

Daniel Rosenstein

<u>Alexa Wú: September 21</u>

Today is Friday. Alexa arrived very confused. She believed
she'd done something "wrong," which I suspect is her trauma
history rearing its ugly head. When I informed her that
we don't meet on Fridays, she appeared ashamed and self-
conscious. She was clearly disoriented and I was aware of a
shift, a distinct switch, in her body language—becoming
childlike. Once I'd explained that we only meet on Tuesdays
and Thursdays, she became compliant, nodding and
pretending to understand.

I suspect Alexa was in a dissociative fugue, and that one
of her personalities, "Dolly," somehow made her way to
Glendown. Need to address the question of safety . . . ?

When I asked that she take a moment and have a seat, she
insisted on standing. My countertransference indicated she was
feeling immense shame, and that "getting something wrong"

made her undeserving of a seat, or kindness even. I sensed she felt incredibly exposed at this point.

When I told her I had no time to see her today, she then became incredibly hostile. She tried to intimidate me by pointing in my face and accusing me of being a "useless piece of shit." I suspect this was her "Runner" personality.

We should discuss this incident at our next session. But will bringing up her bizarre and aggressive behavior cause her further shame? Further anxiety? It is important to attempt integration by voicing what rogue personalities do whilst the host is in fugue, yet it can be beneficial if the personalities are left to discuss, raise, or reflect on their actions for themselves. Note: consider best course of action before next meeting.

Have I been neglectful? Unseeing and unalarmed? A bystander to her disorganized world? Should I have encouraged, or rather, insisted, that she stay . . . ? Demanded that her personalities explain the goings-on in her disordered mind?

Her condition is getting dangerous. Increasingly out of control.

14

Alexa Wú

Take off your clothes," he says in a low voice.

I tiptoe across the bathroom, bare feet kissing the cool tiles. Dropping whatever's left draped on my body to the floor. Outside, early evening light has turned to pink like candied marshmallow, everything hazy and soft and warm.

"Baby," he whispers. His hand cups between my thighs and I gently part them for him to hold. Heat surges through my insides like smoke, a flint of what's next. He kisses my breasts in turn, angling me to face the mirror. I watch him kiss my neck, a voyeur to my own intimacy.

He rests his hand on my dark triangle and I twist with zest, not quite knowing who has control of the Body, the way in which it finds rhythm and pleasure.

"Do that thing," he says, desire in his eyes.

My hand finds its place as we sink into each other, touch and timing as easy as breath, our fit something of a mystery.

"Shh," I say, my free hand muffling his filthy words, aware Anna is downstairs. The risk of being caught and punished adding intensity to my wetness. Part of me aches to be flogged, my mistake earlier today still causing me shame. The look on Runner's face when I eventually woke up and she told me Dolly had taken the Body to Glendown and Runner had woken up to witness her standing there, alone and small, begging Daniel to see us. I cringe, then slam myself harder against him, hoping he'll do the same. A grateful, deserving pain felt deep within me.

Runner hands me a tissue and turns away, relieved when the whole sordid event is finally over.

Why must you do that? Runner whispers. *It's too rough, Alexa.*

I deserve it, I say.

"What's the rush?" he asks, pulling me back—inked mermaids and monsters stretching as he draws me closer to his glistening chest.

I kiss his mouth, stirred from the depth of our sex.

Enough, Runner insists, *this feels wrong.*

For you, maybe, Oneiroi says, *but not for the rest of us.*

Oh, so now you like it rough too?

Sometimes, Oneiroi says.

Runner dials up the shower and pushes the Body toward the hot spray. Heat and steam swirling in the echoey box. Oneiroi stares with lust at Shaun's naked body, seemingly pleased, and reaches out to draw a fat heart on the steamed-up wall.

I'm going for a nap after our shower, she says, stretching. *Wake me up if Shaun fancies seconds.*

Twisting the knob left to right, Runner shoves the Body against the shower's wall.

Go cool off! she snaps.

WHEN I RETURN, SHAUN IS DRESSED AND CHECKING HIS PHONE.

"Navid wants me to work tonight," he says. "You okay with that?"

"Sure," I say, knowing I've agreed to have supper with Anna.

I realize Shaun must be thinking how cool and undemanding I am, because I'm thinking it too.

Thanks, I say to the Flock, not quite knowing who's responsible for my chill.

You're welcome. Oneiroi smiles. *Anytime.*

Shaun reaches for my waist, his body relaxed and horizontal. Post-sex pleasure pulling down on his watery eyes.

"I'd kill for a smoke," he says.

"How long's it been now?" I ask.

"Just over a month. I miss it after sex."

"After sex," I hiss.

"With *you*. I miss it after sex with *you*."

"Okay then," I huff.

He kisses my mouth, "Hey, I think we need to celebrate your first week at work." He shines.

"We already did," I flirt.

"My girlfriend, a photographer! First assistant to Mr. Jack Carra-squeiro." He smiles.

"So I'm your girlfriend now, am I? I kinda like that."

He winks.

"You're the only one for me. I'm so proud of you, baby." Then, more seriously, "He'd better not be good looking, this Jack guy."

"Mm, well—" I tease, raising my eyes. An attempt to keep Shaun on his toes.

He grabs me by the waist and pulls me into him. "I can't have my girl falling in love with her new boss."

He tickles my ribs, part of me knowing his little joke is not completely innocent. The dig of his thumbs just a little too firm on my skin. The pin of his eyes tightly in place.

I smile. My nerves hoping he's feeling possessive. Hoping he's not.

"So, you're cool about tonight?" he says, sitting up and casting me adrift.

I nod, withholding that I already have plans with Anna but wanting to score brownie points all the same.

"It might be a late night," he adds. "Some new girls are coming in."

"New girls?" I ask, trying my very best to steady my nerves.

But I know he senses it, is alert to my insecurity as he watches me clutch a pillow to my chest. I try to imagine what the girls might look like.

"If it's not too late, maybe you can come over when you're finished?" I say.

He shrugs. "Maybe."

Disappointment knees me in the chest, his own cool trumping mine.

"I'll be up anyway," I say.

A pause.

Shaun pulls me in closer, tosses the pillow protecting my chest.

"Navid thinks the club needs more girls, more choice."

"What do you think?" I ask.

He looks away. "Electra's changed a lot since I started work there."

"What do you mean?"

He doesn't answer.

"What?" I repeat.

Silence.

"Cassie has a brother," he says, "Tao. He lives in China. Says he has access to girls desperate for work. And Navid wants to branch out, you know, do more with the girls."

"More?" I ask.

He looks again at his phone.

"Porn," he says.

"I bet he does," I snap, knowing our matinee sex has loosened his tongue. "Is that what you think too?"

He wipes his mouth with the back of his hand. "I think I'd be a fool to cross him. That's what I think."

"Are you *scared* of him?" I challenge.

He tilts his head back, stares at the ceiling.

"Get dressed," he says, his mood turned low. "I need coffee."

He stands. Turns away. Presses the TV controls. One of the music channels leaking out some backbeat R&B. Two scantily clad girls dance across the screen circling a pool party before finally diving in among inflated pink flamingos and neon fruits. Their bodies surgically enhanced like manga characters with gigantic breasts and tiny waists, skin tanned and oiled. I look away. My carnal heart wishing he wouldn't stare like that. So fixed.

15

Daniel Rosenstein

THE OLD-TIMER LOOKS DOWN AT THE FLOOR, SUDDENLY OVERCOME. The room is silent. Still. Respectful of the words that he shared just moments ago, grieving his dead mother. He leans forward in his chair, struggling to find forgiveness for his father, whom he believes could have offered more patience and love—kissed her, held her, made her last few weeks more comfortable before the cancer eventually devoured her pancreas. "Destroying," he says, "a woman I barely recognized in the end."

He knows forgiveness will be the thing that heals, but today it's hard for him to reach. His anger and resentment sabotaging his recovery.

The Single Mother looks at him, uncrosses her legs. A tear slicing through any resistance she may have to let go. Her body responding to his grief.

"Last night, I wanted to drink," the Old-Timer says. "It caught me by surprise. I thought twenty years in I'd be safe, but apparently not. Apparently, addiction still wants to surface like some overflowing sewer. Persistent, this fucking disease."

One of the newcomers looks about the room, spooked. A certain panic setting in. Sensing his alarm, I attempt to catch his eyes—a codependent act, I realize—but as they meet I hold him steadily in my gaze. It's not unusual that significant loss can spark overwhelming feelings of despair, so much sometimes that relapse occurs, even for old-timers.

Clara suddenly sails into my mind, my own loss ignited. Remembering how I'd struggled with my addiction five years ago when her death became a constant companion to my waking day—preoccupation forcing me down, a little boy, into a deep well of sadness. I feel the loss lodge itself in the core of my chest, anxiety causing a rush of adrenaline. Dark and alone, I sense myself relieved the meeting has now ended. I look up at the Single Mother as she leaves. Her tears finally permitting the release of my own.

Hello, stranger."

"Hello."

"No friend today?"

"Unfortunately not. He's got a date."

I don't know why I say this; Mohsin does not have a date. Neither is he likely to have one until he completes the piece of research the Royal College of Psychiatrists has him working on day and night—this also being the reason I find myself alone, again, seated at our usual table, not speaking the truth. But I can't help myself. I'm a little liar.

"Someone he met at a reading group," I say.

Another lie.

"Well, I guess it beats internet dating." She laughs.

"Pfft." I snort. "I know what you mean."

I have no idea what she means. The one and only time I signed up for internet dating I met Monica. Mohsin's suggestion that I find a "companion" not something I'd wanted to even mildly entertain. But there were no bad experiences. I was instantly charmed by Monica's online profile on TopFlightSingles:

> Slim, bubbly and petite 35 yr. old Libran ISO fun, travel, and conversation. I am artistic, have left-leaning politics and a GSOH. I love mountains, trees, and challenges—I've cycled from Havana to Trinidad, climbed a glacier in the Andes, and I fancy Antarctica next. I enjoy being surrounded by white and silence (does that make me sound weird?). Is there a witty, dashingly good-looking Oscar Wilde or Ray Mears out there?

> I am someone who wants to make a difference in the world (I'm a doctor)—God, I sound like a beauty pageant queen! I hope that clarifies things . . . maybe not? . . . How about this? . . .

> I'm an ordinary girl striving to be extraordinary and I am amused by life's glorious absurdities. Laughter is important and a sense of humor a must. I love sunsets and fires, India and the Andes, sensuality and early morning dew . . . on cobwebs . . . ooh, and perhaps a stroll on the South Bank, a glass of vino, and a great deal of chatting. Finally, you must be an AL (Animal Lover!) although I have no pets.

A little voice in my head forced my hand. *Just give it a go,* it said, *she sounds funny and smart and lighthearted, what's the harm?* I was just a little naive, like a child posting a letter to Santa Claus. *Click.* And so we arranged to meet—at the South Bank for a glass of something, obviously not vino, and a great deal of chatting. I bought a new suit, new underpants, mildly relieved to no longer be hostage to the seven stages of grief. I was feeling again. An encore of senses. My manhood swelling and adolescent unruly. I was rekindled. Unchaste. And sad. But supposedly no longer alone.

THE PRETTY FRECKLED WAITRESS SHIFTS HER WEIGHT FROM LEFT TO right, a long, thin notepad in her hand.

"What can I get you?" She smiles.

"I'd like the shishito peppers to start," I point, finger trailing the menu, "followed by the salmon teriyaki."

I feel a wave of shame wash over my predictable choice and watch the Pretty Freckled Waitress write down my order. I'm sure she only does this to make me feel better, knowing I order the same thing every time.

"Anything to drink?"

"A bottle of—"

"Sparkling mineral water," she interrupts, "with lime cordial." Writes this down too. Cringe.

"That's all," I say, fingering the ceramic ginger jar. An attempt to mask my unease.

She underlines my order with a confident strike of her blue pen, then leans over to place a starched napkin across my lap. I note the trio of buttons casually left opened on her blouse, revealing the contours of her breasts. I look away, embarrassed.

"Okay then," she chirps, "back in a while."

"Crocodile!"

Oh sweet Jesus. *Crocodile?* My longing to appear light and quippy drags me into a further abyss of shame. Hopefully none of the other diners have heard. I look to the Zen garden, wincing, my fat friend the Buddha experiencing no such conflict, his laughing today, I imagine, aimed at my foolishness. I wish Mohsin were here to keep me company and help ease my embarrassment. My stony-faced friend, although rather jolly, isn't much of a talker.

A group of women opposite toast, for the fifth time. Clinking their champagne flutes while making exaggerated eye contact. Someone's birthday, I tell myself. One woman, whom it appears the celebration is for, starts to cry. Immediately manicured hands and reassurances are rushed in like cavalry from the two women sitting on either side of her. Instant gratification, I tell myself, likening them to a pair of slavish, pearl-clutching dimwits.

As my salmon teriyaki arrives, a tall man sits down at the table next to me with a young woman who I assume is his daughter. She throws her head back, revealing pretty white teeth, laughing at his goofy impression of whom, I'm not quite sure. The waiter joins in and hands them each a menu. It's not until I notice the girl's bare foot climb his leg like a tree that I realize they are lovers. Each of them enamored by their opposite. Age proving an attraction for both. The Electra complex, I tell myself, pulling back my shoulders and feeling somewhat envious of the man, his age close to mine. I throw Humbert Humbert a cold stare, painfully aware of my hypocrisy.

My mind wanders momentarily to Susannah and her much older beau. I wonder if either of them even know what the Electra complex is. Clara and I had hoped for someone who would be a match for Susannah's creativity. Someone of similar age. A man who was sensitive, kind, smart, and capable of intimacy and commitment. A man with courage. We'd even liked a couple of the guys she brought home whom she'd met through work at the gallery. But then five years ago when Clara's cancer raged, leaving us only three months to prepare for her death, Susannah met Toby.

She was sad. Vulnerable. In need of comfort, kindness, and a body—I imagine with unease—to hold her at night when she couldn't sleep. And he was only too willing to oblige. Even though he was married.

"Can we not be so quick to judge, Dad?" she'd said.

"He's married, for Christ's sake!" I'd yelled.

"Oh, Susie," Clara whispered, taking her hand, "are there children involved?"

Thankfully there are no children involved. Toby didn't quite graduate from dad school. And his itch of seven years to a woman I know only as "she" or "her" has now been scratched by my silly daughter and her romantic notions of the older man. Fifty-two years old to be precise, only three years younger than me.

I wonder if Susannah is searching for a replacement father figure. Whether Toby is he. What did I do that was so wrong that my only child settled for a man like him? I imagine her replacing the girl next to me; laughing, her bare foot resting against Humbert Humbert's thigh. I shake my head and quickly dismiss the entire sordid exchange.

I look up, my appetite killed. Opposite, the group of women are sawing lean meats and dipping rolls of rainbow sushi into soy sauce while the girl next to me opens her mouth like a bird, the tall man feeding her with his chopsticks.

Lunch left and unfinished, I decide not to leave a tip.

Come in, Charlotte," I say.

Earlier fatigue lingering somewhat, my eyes still appear blurred and tight. I notice loose change has fallen from my pocket onto the daybed, but rather than risk Charlotte see me reach over to collect it, I wait for her to sit, as is my habit.

Charlotte negotiates the side table and I note she is dressed rather eccentrically today: swaddled in bright-colored tie-dye, almost like a bandage, the colors fetching and optimistic compared to her usual uniform of blacks and grays. On one of her fingers I notice a ring that looks like it may have fallen from a Christmas cracker or one of those plastic eggs found in claw machines at fairgrounds. Charlotte regards me while I stare at the ring, then quickly places her hand beneath her thigh.

"I think Nurse Kennedy has a crush on me," she begins. "He sat with me. Helped me finish my jigsaw."

"A crush?" I say.

She looks down.

Silence.

Never work harder than the patient, let her come to you.

Nurse Kennedy, Peter, joined us six months ago, having worked on a psych ward somewhere in the north of England. I liked him, immediately finding his patience and engagement with the patients a refreshing change from the nurses currently here. He also has the most impressive heart-shaped hairline and piercing dark eyes—rather like a barn owl. This, for some reason, endears him to me. Not that I'm particularly keen on barn owls, or owls of any kind for that matter. Rather, that his looks posed little threat or competition.

I look up, Charlotte still in her head and preoccupied with the view outside.

My thoughts drift, picturing the waitress serving me salmon teriyaki. A dainty impression beneath her soft blouse. The afternoon light sends a glow from the glass roof bathing her strawberry hair, thick with curls. Her freckles like cinnamon dust. I ought to feel guilty, fantasizing this way, my commitment to Monica not even slightly denounced. *Dirty dog.*

Charlotte snaps her fingers, bringing me out of my reverie.

"Hello?" she barks, irritated.

I rearrange my face.

"You men. You're all the same."

"A rather sweeping statement, don't you think?"

"I know you sit there, bored, disinterested," she spits.

"You're projecting," I say, pinching my right leg.

She looks at me, scans my face for clues, but I'm giving nothing away. The pinch has me back on track. Focused.

Looking at my notes I clear my throat and slowly turn a page or two, buying some time.

"Last week we discussed how you felt dismissed by your father. How he ignored you. I wonder if something is being reenacted between us," I say.

Charlotte looks down at her feet, battles with a tear attempting to escape. I imagine her trying to push it back into her cage of pride, not wanting to allow me the experience of her vulnerability.

"Bastard projection," she says, "always fucks things up."

I feel my earlier fatigue melt. She has me now: compassionate and feeling.

"So it does." I smile.

Charlotte arrived at Glendown three years ago, clinically depressed and suicidal. Isolated, with limited contact with what remained of her family, she had a nonexistent desire for self-care, work, or any interests other than jigsaw puzzles. The emerging worlds from tiny cardboard pieces offering a regulating effect on her mind.

As a child, Charlotte lived on a quiet leafy street in Islington. Next door was a man named Tom, who lived alone with his three cats. The cats would roam from garden to garden, offering gifts such as mice and birds. Charlotte was very attached to the cats.

Slowly, Tom entered the lives of Charlotte and her family, offering to help out with the gardening, odd jobs, and, of course, babysitting. Tom was lovely. So friendly. The perfect neighbor. That is, until Charlotte refused to play his little game of musical chairs. Tom slipping his hand beneath and pulling at her underwear. Charlotte said no. And that was when things got nasty. If she didn't play, the cats would have to be punished, Tom said. She allowed his thick hand inside her.

Charlotte's parents called her a liar. An attention seeker. Tom was lovely, Tom could be trusted, what was she thinking? Her father ignored her. You're imagining things, Charlotte's mother dismissed. And Tom? Well, Tom eventually moved on, most likely to another quiet street, next door to another little girl. Lovely Tom.

What followed were a series of crimes where Charlotte fell victim to the abuse of those in power: a vicar who called on the house to "rid her of her lies," a teacher who insisted Charlotte stay behind to help tidy the store cupboard, and several unsavory employers. Each time her story was dismissed. She was deemed an attention seeker. A liar. So she turned to the words of poets, writers, and activists for sanctuary— those who found voice and language to cover paper with mighty words. Charlotte told me that she'd once written the names of these people on the soles of her shoes: Alice Walker, Audre Lorde, bell hooks, Andrea Dworkin, and Rosa Parks, to name a few. Then she'd push her feet inside and stand, wondering what it felt like to walk in the shoes of strong women. To have them march with her, refusing the torment of patriarchy. Women who fought back.

"Their names transport me to a world of empowerment," she said a year into our work.

"You're also empowered," I said.

She waved away my words of advocacy, looking down again at her feet.

I moved forward in my chair.

"The soles of your shoes deserve another name," I spoke softly.

She looked up.

"Charlotte Lakewood." I smiled.

Our session ended with me handing her a thick black marker while she paused, shoe in hand. Her thumb rubbing, repeatedly, its thin plastic sole.

"Go ahead," I encouraged, watching. A single tear traveling down her cheek.

And with that, she scrawled her name, large and proud. Excitement uplighting her damp face as she added, with zeal, an exclamation point.

"There," she said, embodied and firm. "That's me."

Her shoe offered steady like a gift, in both hands.

S HE LEANS FORWARD NOW IN HER CHAIR, STRETCHING BOTH TIE-DYED sleeves to hide her fists. "So this projection," she says, "how do I stop it? How do I *not* make you into my dad?"

"Good question," I answer softly. "First we acknowledge *our* relationship. Our attachment. I'm not your father. I'm nothing like him. We separate him and me. Men generally. Not all men will disappoint and dismiss you, Charlotte. We're not all the same."

16

Alexa Wú

EVENING. ANNA CLICKS ON THE RADIO, ADDING A LITTLE SWAY AND twist to her stand. She likes this song.

"Cheers!" she sings.

We clink glasses.

"So how's it going at work?"

"Great," I say. "I get my first paycheck next week."

"How exciting."

"I know, I'll take us out if you like?" I say, joining her jig.

"Let's do that," she allows. "So what does Ella think about your new job? Is she pleased for you?"

"Kinda. I think she's worried I'll forget about her."

Anna draws a deep breath. Her groove suddenly interrupted.

"What nonsense. Don't let her guilt-trip you, okay?"

She's right, Oneiroi adds.

I shrug, protective and accepting of Ella's insecurity in equal measure. A longing felt that she'll be pleased for me, eventually.

Anna leans against the kitchen sink. "So what hours are you working?"

"Ten till six. But Jack said I might need to be a little flexible, depending on the shoot."

Anna raises her glass and whispers, "I'm proud of you."

I take a moment to absorb her words, surprised and pleased, but also wishing they were my mother's words. That she was still alive to see me working my first real job. Resting my glass, I reach for my camera, its weight familiar and comforting in my hand.

"You look lovely tonight, by the way." I say. *Click. Click.*

"Stop that," Anna says, smiling into her shoulder. Palm outstretched in fey protest yet secretly enjoying the camera's attention. Her new highlights a little bolder than usual, a girlish bounce to her curls. I also note her choice of lipstick, a nod toward racy, a sly smear of kohl applied to the linings of her eyes.

"I'm having my friend Ray over later," she says, seemingly aware I've noticed the extra effort she put in. "We met at work. He manages electricals."

Click.

Anna has worked at a fragrance counter in a department store since I was thirteen. Before that she was a cocktail waitress in the West End.

"Can he get me a discount on a new camera?" I ask, resting mine now on the kitchen table.

"I don't see why not," she says, keeping her groove going with another glass of sauvignon.

Ask her to pour us another, Runner says, and I pass along the request: "Can I have a top-up?" I ask, handling my glass.

"Sure." Anna pours.

"Shall I stay out tonight?" I say. "So you and Ray—"

"That won't be necessary," Anna insists, throwing me a look. "We're just friends."

"*Friends?*" I tease.

She smiles, revealing neat white piano teeth. And I realize then that I haven't seen Anna this peppy for a long time. My father's abandonment of her spiking any desire for another man. Earlier self-worth collapsed like a deck of cards.

I remember how she sobbed when she found out. My father's choosing of a much younger woman branding, pummeling, and screwing with her head. She crumbled; of course she did. Her lack of trust passed down to me like torn, misshapen clothing. An uncomfortable fit forced over my head and worn like a noose while I waited. And waited. Expecting someone to come kick the stool.

Flash.

IT'S HOT. HIGH SUMMER.

The sound of lawns being mowed, hedges trimmed. Sprinklers are on. I'm lying in Ella's backyard. Grass warming itself between my sixteen-year-old thighs.

Flash.

Grace dances past me in a modest gingham two-piece, clutching a pink Beanie Baby, a pair of lime-green goggles strapped tight to her head.

She hands me a saltshaker. "Come on, Alexa," she says, tugging at my ice-pop-free hand, "I want to make a seaside in the paddling pool!" Shaker salt a little girl's dream when money won't stretch to a summer holiday. Ella is pumping up a dusty paddling pool with her bare foot. She bends down, shifts her red heart sunglasses to her head, and pulls on the green plastic hose. I watch it snake across the lawn.

My phone rings then.

"Hey, Anna," I say, a picture of the Wicked Witch of the West flashing up on the screen.

Anna is sobbing. "You have to come home."

I stand. "What's wrong?"

"Straightaway," she orders, frenzy tipping her voice. "It's your dad."

For a moment I wonder if my father has dropped down dead—had a heart attack, been struck by a car—but I know; I know in the pit of my gut what's happened. Why Anna is crazed.

Flash.

Our curtains have been drawn like defeated eyes. Anna is sitting at her kidney-shaped dressing table, staring at her reflection, crying. She doesn't seem to recognize the woman staring back and begins to do this strange wave, I guess to make sure it's her. Sure enough, the woman waves back. Kinda creepy.

She turns to face me, a pack of Xanax in one hand and a tumbler of vodka in the other.

"He's gone," she says.

A pause.

"Who is she?" I ask, rage raining down. "I'll hunt the bitch out."

"Someone from the casino. A croupier."

"A *what*?"

Anna doesn't bother to explain, instead throws two Xanax at the back of her throat and gags on the strength of the vodka.

"She's still in college," she cries, "a *college girl,* for Christ's sake."

I feel my dread reawaken while Anna scrunches her body up like a small child. She draws her knees tight to her chest. Abandoned. Unwanted. Slowly she rocks herself forward and back. For a moment I actually sense overwhelming warmth toward her. *Actual* warmth, without any of the bullshit, any of the pretense. Something about her thin, brittle body, her vulnerability, and my holding of her while she rocks making me feel more akin. But I know it won't last. Not the way I'd like it to, because I'm the kid she's been burdened with now that my father's shacked up with some fucking croupier.

She is in shock, I think.

Flash.

TICK-TOCK—

I, however, was not shocked. It made perfect sense to me. He had someone fresh. A *college girl,* for Christ's sake. Anna was no longer wanted and I was old news.

Tick-tock—

"Fancy another?" Anna says, holding up the bottle of sauvignon.

Say yes, Runner says.

Oneiroi steps into the Light, covers the glass with our hand, answering on everyone's behalf:

"No thanks," she says, "I've got my last shift at Chen's."

"Oh."

"And then Ella's picking me up."

"You girls doing anything fun?" Anna asks.

"Shaun's having a house party."

"Shaun? Shaun who?"

"Just some guy we met. I like him."

"Do I get to meet him?"

"I don't like him *that* much."

Anna grins, shrugging off Oneiroi's goofing around. "Want some food before you go? I've made—"

"No thanks, I've eaten. You need help with anything before Ray arrives?"

"No, nothing."

"Are you sure?"

"I'm sure. Just keep yourself safe, okay?"

"Don't worry," I say, taking back the Light, "if anyone tries anything I'll have them outnumbered."

This is a standard old multiples joke that I heard once on a TV chat show, usually good for a laugh, but tonight Anna just squeezes my shoulder, saying: "Off you go then, don't be making yourselves late now."

Mr. chen is cutting out a photograph of one of the queen's corgis from a glossy Sunday supplement. On reaching the corgi's tail he sticks out his tongue in fixed concentration, wielding his tiny scissors with precision.

"Hey," I say.

Mr. Chen looks up and smiles.

"Where's that one going?" I ask, noting another three corgis resting on the counter.

"Over there"—he points with his tiny scissors—"on the kitchen hatch."

"Why do you love the Queen so much?" I ask, realizing I've never asked before.

"She's a lady," he says, "and she's good for the country. There!" He holds the fourth corgi up to the light as if checking an X-ray. Pleased with his handiwork—his pack of posh dogs—he tosses the magazine into a large wicker basket behind the counter.

"So. Your last night here," he says, forcing the scissors down in his back pocket.

I nod.

"Thanks for everything," I say. "If you ever get stuck, need someone—"

"No. No more takeaway and washing dishes," he dismisses with a flick of his wrist. "You're a photographer now."

He hands me an envelope.

"For you," he says, "to buy a new camera."

"I can't—"

"Take it," he insists.

Stirred, I fling my arms around his back and squeeze. And while he remains composed, stiff as a board, I know Mr. Chen recognizes my thanks because the smile on his face widens. His eyes turning damp, the unsaid speaking: *I'll miss you.*

"Here, look," I say, unfolding a single sheet of newsprint and pointing. "I took that photograph."

"You?"

"Me," I say.

"It's very good."

"Thanks. This demonstrator was the focus. He's one of the London Black Revs"—I point—"and this here is the burger joint that was snaring their workers. Reporting them to the authorities and having them deported."

"Back home?"

I nod, noticing Mr. Chen's face turn somber. Homesick, I assume, for Xining. His story of immigration similar to that of my father, who also found himself in England with hopes for a better life.

My father's journey had involved two boat trips, an overnight sleeper, and a ride hitched with a man he didn't trust. When he finally reached the island of Thatcher, Duran Duran, and fish 'n' chips, my father continued on foot, garbage bags covering his feet, held tight with black gaffer tape. Money was tight and waterproof shoes were expensive. My mother told me she'd learned the tape was intended to keep out the weather but also to shape the plastic to look more like Western shoes. Not only were my father's feet dry when he arrived, but stylish too.

My father used to keep his shoes in stacked immaculate brown boxes beside his bed, and one of my tasks as a young girl was to spit-clean and polish them. A skill he'd taught me himself. Every Friday night the shoes were lined up outside the kitchen door like shiny black oversize beetles.

"Scrub harder, Xiǎo Wáwa," he'd say, checking for imperfections. "That's it. Then be a good girl and make a start on my shirts."

At the time I was pleased to have his approval, even if that meant being enslaved to a man who believed himself blameless and entitled. His words: *I can and I will,* notched up on his bedpost. A devious and tragic charm as he stood, smiling, watching, while I ironed and scrubbed.

ELLA IS STANDING ON THE OPPOSITE SIDE OF THE STREET, LEANING against her Fiat Punto.

"Ready?" I ask.

"I was born ready." She smiles, handing me her spliff.

We dial up the music and wind down the windows: our night world alive, alive. Stirred by the neat high, I glance over at Ella—blow-dried and dark browed, a drift of foreign musk perfume. I hardly recognize this new sharp version of herself. Her clothes too, all tight and designer, just like a model's. Spiky three-inch heels angling down on the clutch.

"New shoes?" I ask.

"Got them from the Electra," she says. "They were in the girls' wardrobe. There's so much great stuff in there. I can get you something if you want. New jacket maybe?"

"No thanks," I say, integrity holding me firm. "I wouldn't feel comfortable taking it."

I note a slight chill in the air. Our difference felt but not spoken. In my mind I try to make it not matter (too much) how at odds we are right now, and have a quiet word with myself not to judge (too much).

She's just enjoying the perks of the job, I soothe, *that's all.*

You're in denial, Runner says with a look of disdain.

I know, you're right, I confess. *If I'm honest I hate how fickle and easy she is.*

So tell her. Don't turn into some friggin' bystander like Anna. And make sure she knows this isn't okay.

Don't worry, I say, hanging my hand out the window to catch the night air. *I will. And soon.*

Ella and I top-body sway to the same song, yet I imagine we're thinking entirely different things. I catch this thought, reminded of how painful it used to feel when she and I had clashing tastes, thoughts, or ideas. But now I try to accept our differences, my hope that our love for each other overrides any slavish trust.

"Fuck, I'm totally wasted!" Ella cries, revving on the gas, a fiendish half smile. She crimps her eyes. And while my denial plays out, part of me secretly knows this could turn into something unsweet, our friendship in danger.

I CAN HEAR THE PARTY AS WE DRIVE UP THE SHOULDER OF BROADWAY Market, pulling in at Jackman Street. A sound system lodged on one of the windowsills of Shaun's warehouse apartment, filthy techno thumps while dozens of people pour onto the walkway. Crates of imported beer are piled on either side of the front door. A bowl of fresh limes balancing on top. I bite into one, a zing of zest waking my fried mouth.

Out back, slate rattan chairs and industrial chrome heaters are parked central to an impressive makeshift bar, where Shaun is pouring drinks in a tight white shirt, sleeves turned at his elbow. I resist running over and kissing his mouth.

Relax, Oneiroi says, *you've got all night.*

Fairy lights are strewn through tree branches and it almost looks like the sky has fallen down, stars resting just within reach. *Ahh, pretty,* Dolly purrs, eyes ablaze. I'm reminded of *Chicken Licken*—the folk story my mother would read to me at night, a flashlight beneath the sheets, voices given to the whole gang of clucking animals who believed their world about to end. My favorites were always Goosey Loosey and Turkey Lurkey.

"Hey!" Ella shouts, killing the memory.

"Hey!" Two girls call back. I recognize them immediately as the two members from my imagined girl band, still tanned, jeans just as tight. They must be working for the night, I tell myself. I also note one of them has a significantly larger chest than when we last met. *Where'd she get those?* Oneiroi asks. *Most likely Navid,* Runner says with a snort.

Wowser, Dolly says, eyes like plates, *they're massive!*

Shush now, Oneiroi interrupts, *back inside, Dolly, time for bed.*

No! Dolly shouts. *Stop bossing me around!*

Oneiroi strokes Dolly's hand, coaxing her back inside the Nest.

Come on, she says, *I'll read you a story, and tomorrow we'll let you have all morning in the Body. Isn't that right, Alexa?*

I look up. *Sure,* I agree; anything for a quiet life. This seems to help, Dolly heading back inside and climbing into the Nest with Oneiroi close behind.

"You okay?" Ella asks.

"Yeah, it's a bit noisy," I say, tapping the side of my head.

"Have you taken your meds?"

"Half," I say. "They're not a good idea if I'm drinking."

"Right. And stoned."

Our band members join us. A silver tray resting on each of their palms.

"Hey, how's it going?" the pretty one chimes. Then, not waiting for a reply, "Cocktail?"

"Definitely," Ella says, swiping two, handing me the largest.

"You look great, by the way," she says, rebalancing her tray, "love your hair."

"Thanks." Ella shines, smoothing the bob's sharp ends; its sleekness like drilled oil. "Paulo."

The girls share a look and suddenly I'm an interloper, an outsider, their world blackballing plain and flat-chested girls like me. I turn away—the runt—and stroke my well-behaved hair, assuming Paulo is a hairdresser they all visit. His blow-dry transforming the most ordinary of hair into heavenly manes.

"Isn't he the best? Shame he's gay, right?" our large-bosomed band member says.

"Yeah," Ella agrees, not caught on to the fact I'm cut from this conversation, my own hair not touched or teased for at least six months.

I stare down at my breasts, straightening my back, making them appear immediately less apologetic and dour. Runner digs me in the ribs, *Stop sticking your tits out like some weirdo. You've got enough tissue down there for all of us!*

Ella and I make our way over to the bar, where another couple of girls wait with silver trays, less flesh on show and lower heels. One of them throws Shaun a flirtatious wink but upon seeing me turns to her friend, pretending to turn chatty. I try not to show my jealousy and self-doubt, though I can't help but make a mental note to put her in my little book of girls not to trust.

"Hey, baby," Shaun says, kissing my mouth, "you look great. Drink?"

"Make one of those delicious rose gin slings," Ella jumps in, leaning across the bar and kissing Shaun's cheek, "the ones we had at the club the other night."

He smiles. Empties a previous drink from his shaker.

"I've missed you," he says.

I feel my breath halt, a horse in my chest. A flush rising in my cheeks.

"I've missed you too," I say, noticing Navid, Cassie, the redhead, and Sylvie on the other side of the decking.

I lean in closer. "What are they doing here?"

"Everyone's invited." He shrugs. "Open house."

He pours our drinks while Ella holds my gaze. Navid takes off his jacket, revealing an open fitted shirt, sleeves rolled. His body contending with Shaun's.

He places the dark linen jacket on the back of a rattan chair where he sits open-legged. Cassie joins him, followed by the Softee Sisters: their body-con dresses like poured mercury with an hourglass stretch. Navid fixes his gimlet eye on Ella and bids her come over.

"Come on," she says, tugging my cocktail-free hand, "just act sweet."

I look at Shaun, mouthing, *See you later*.

But already his back is turned, his hand reaching for a tall bottle of liqueur.

One of the Softee Sisters has been crying. A bloated red puff to her cheeks.

"She okay?" Ella asks.

Navid turns and the Softee Sister looks him straight in the eye, a post-cry shake to her barely covered chest. He tilts his head—waiting for what, I'm not quite sure—but when she looks down at the floor, I realize it's a standoff, Navid claiming power by staring her down. The other sister also looks south, shuffles her heel for distraction. An act of solidarity, I guess.

"Do you think it's possible," he says, turning to Ella, "that any girl could find a better—"

"I didn't say it was *better*," the Softee Sister interrupts, a jar to her voice.

Navid holds up his hand. "That any girl who wants to dance, feel pretty, protected, could find a *better* club to work than the Electra?"

Ella looks to me. "I guess not," she says.

I note Sylvie dig the redhead's side.

"You see," Navid says, "even our newest sister agrees. Right, Ella?"

Ella makes a face. "I guess," she says, turning to Navid. "Where—"

Navid raises both hands this time.

"*Where* and *who* are not important, Ella. What is important"—he turns again to face the now-crying Softee Sister—"is that you know I can set fire to your life any second."

Silence.

Navid smiles, too wide and too quickly.

"Got it?" he says tightly.

The Softee Sister looks away.

"GOT IT?" he shouts.

Bullying piece of shit! Runner shouts in my head.

"Yes," the Softee Sister chimes.

"Good. Right, I need a drink."

The Softee Sisters beckon our band members with their silver trays of chilled cocktails. Cassie handles one first. I note the berated sister is no longer wearing her delicate gold chain with its small key attached, and wonder if she's now been ostracized from her Electra Girl privileges.

"Join us," Navid says, staring at Ella, patting the rattan seat between them. His eyes locking with hers like she can't refuse. Like she's already his. I catch Sylvie and the redhead exchanging a glance.

I FIND MYSELF ON THE DANCE FLOOR. THREE ROSE GIN SLINGS AND several beers stirring in my head, the Body following instructions to move my hips and shake off anything to do with Navid. The fact that he can set fire to a girl's life at any second. I stare over at the bar, alert to Shaun and the redhead sharing a joke. She places a hand on his chest, hot with intrigue. Sylvie, awkward, in her sparkly dress, notes their intimacy and shakes her head.

One of the Softee Sisters joins me, dances close, her mood still set. The bloated puff of her cheeks visible but gladly fading.

"You okay?" I ask.

She nods, but I don't believe her, sensing tears ready to break.

"He's such an asshole," she spits, "humiliating me like that. In front of everyone."

A pause.

"How long have you worked for him?" I ask.

"Couple of years. But he likes Amy best."

"Amy?"

"My sister." She points. "I'm Annabelle."

We smile.

"How's it going with Shaun?" Annabelle asks.

"Good," I say, "you know him?"

"Sure, he's been around since Navid opened the club." She checks her purse and pops a pill. "I'd offer you one, but—"

She doesn't give a reason for her "but," so I just say, "I'm fine," making it easy for her.

The pill seems to calm her. A tilt and sway of her head and shoulders now eases in her dancing. The way she slows marking a letting-go. We settle. Me allowing the alcohol and earlier spliff to guide my mood, feeling somewhat free. Adrift. The music fading in and out.

Annabelle links her fingers with mine and I can sense her coming up. The rush of love causing her to lift our arms while her eyes roll. Her mouth wide and painted, with a touch of the lunatic. Two men sidle up beside us, moods aglow. The taller one releases his neck like he's waking from a ten-year sleep, his eyes closed but clearly blissed.

Annabelle pulls me in close. "Don't tell anyone," she whispers, giggling into her shoulder, "but I'm going to work at another club. In Soho. That'll show him."

"But—"

"He thinks he can control me like some limp-ass puppet. Amy knows, she told me not to do it. But I don't give two fucks." She sways. "Next thing he'll have us turning tricks and porned out. You wait and see."

"Really?"

"Really."

She moves in closer.

"He's really nice, my new boss. Russian." She catches herself, the trip loosening her tongue, and holds up her red manicured finger. "Bathroom," she says, "back in a minute."

I keep swaying and look around. Over by the bar I see Sylvie watching me. She smiles, tugs down her tight shimmering dress, and comes toward me.

"Hey," she says. "I'm Sylvie."

"Hey."

She lets out a puff of air, shoulders turning down.

"You okay?" I ask.

She shrugs. "Kinda. You?"

"I didn't enjoy watching that scene with Navid and the twins," I say.

"Me neither."

"Want a drink?"

"No, I'm fine," she answers, covering her glass with a palm.

Awkward, we dance. Silent.

"So I guess we're the girls on the outside." I smile, catching her eyes. "The ones looking in."

Sylvie pulls a face. "I guess," she says, a slow shrug into herself.

"Are you and Shaun dating?" she asks.

I nod. "I'm his girlfriend."

More silence.

Christ, talking to her is like pulling teeth, Runner huffs.

"I like your dress," I say.

"Borrowed it," she says, nodding back at the redhead. "Jane likes me to make an effort when we go out."

Jane? Plain Jane? The name jars, not quite computing in my already fried brain. The ordinariness of this sanguine creature's birth name ill-fitting somehow, like a fat ballerina, or a harmless pimp.

"How do you guys know each other?" I ask.

"We go way back. Since school."

"Nice."

"I'm not a threat to her. Not like some of the girls at the Electra," she says, eyes widening while scanning the room.

"Oh."

"Don't feel sorry for me. I like it that way," she insists. "It's the way it's always been. At least there's no pretense. We know our places."

"Sounds a little cold."

"Better that than having your heart broken. I've had too many friends pretend to be someone they're not. And I care about her. I care that she doesn't get hurt. Behind all that bravado is someone sweet and a bit naive. I don't always trust she'll make the right choices"—Sylvie looks me bang in the eye—"because not all girls stick together."

I clear my throat, the Flock's hackles starting to rise.

She's got a point, Oneiroi calls from the Nest.

Whatever, Runner spits.

I remember the times at school after gym class, painfully alert to the girls' half-naked nearness—their locker room banter, and how I'd longed to be part of their gang. I lacked trust and feared closeness, this causing me to scuttle off like a sap beetle, dull and infested with doubt. How I'd ached for a friend. Someone to hang out with, watch movies with, swap clothes and tell secrets with. A friend to engulf me with adolescent affection and fun. Back then I was blatant with need.

One time, a girl whose name I don't recall—possibly because she hurt me so much—became my friend for exactly three weeks. She was introduced by Mr. Stack as "the new girl" in class, and we were ordered to make her feel welcome, to show her around. I'd jumped at the chance. *A possible friend,* I thought. *A new girl* untainted by cruel rumors and classroom teasing. Someone who didn't know of my awkward relating, my distrust, too much insecurity and doubt carried around inside me like a peptic ulcer. I showed New Girl where to find the tuck shop, the bike yard, and the sports lockers; advised her which teachers to watch out for, the boys to avoid, the best time to line up in the cafeteria for fresh custard. We walked home together, shared lunch, had even gone to the cinema one weekend to watch *The Lion, the Witch and the Wardrobe.* And then she was gone. *Poof.* Just like that, with no word. Rumor had it her father returned and whisked New Girl and her mother back to where they'd come from. I tried to make her disappearance not matter in my mind. But my stomach, my imagined peptic ulcer, well, it felt something else.

Sylvie squeezes my arm.

"Anyway, good to meet you," she says, noting Jane slowly sauntering toward us. "See you around."

I hope so, but who knows, I say to myself. A familiar disbelief felt in my gut knowing I struggle to make and keep friends, but my longing still alive all the same.

What about Ella? Oneiroi says.

Let's wait and see, I reply. *She and I want different things now.*

Hot from highs and dancing bodies, I turn to search for Ella, who has moved away from Navid, and then spot her talking to Amy. They laugh, embrace, seemingly at ease with mild rapport before Ella finally makes her way over to me on the dance floor.

She pulls me toward her, smiles against my mouth, whispering, "Here, take this."

I look down at her hand.

"It's E," she says. "Don't worry, I've dropped one. It's good. Old-school, but really good."

Pleasured stares, hot rhythmic bodies, and a view of Shaun alone persuade me it's a good idea, so I pop the E on my tongue and swallow. A swell of excitement filling my entire body. I wait for the rush.

Still no sign of Annabelle. I scan the room, assuming that I'm now on what she's on. I feel a kind of urgency to share my up, as she did. All around me people are blissed out and loose.

"Who gave it to you?" I ask.

"Navid." Ella smiles.

Shaun starts to make his way to me through the crowd of raised arms and swaying asses. The smell of perfume and close bodies heightening my E'd love for everything and everyone. Nothing at all matters but this moment we're in.

I keep a cool but charged look on my face, not once letting Shaun's gaze escape. I wait for the chemical high to surge through me, willing it to dispatch. The soar that will take hold and release me. Nothing cuts me loose like music, I think. The thrill of beats repeated. Silky vocals bringing me up.

Up.

Up.

Up.

Shaun takes my waist, Ella now behind him. It would be a cliché to mention a sandwich. Shaun turns and nods, I imagine not wanting Ella to feel left out, but then darts his eyes back to mine, moving his body closer. As he approaches I smell his aftershave, then lift my arms and loop them around his neck, hanging off him like pearls. The sense he can hold me, take the full swing of my body, such a thrill.

Breathe.

What a cinch it is to be me right now, dancing.

Loved up. Free.

Up.

Up.

Up.

SHAUN'S BEDROOM IS AS YOU'D EXPECT FOR A TWENTY-EIGHT-YEAR-OLD guy. Vinyl. Sound system. Marshall speakers. A collection of incense burners and healing stones that I don't trust immediately but, knowing him as I do, accept is an attempt to touch the spiritual. Nudged up against the wall: a king-size bed with white cotton sheets, a faux leather head-board. At the end of his bed is a trunk, a folded blanket resting on top.

All three of us enter, giddy, a freshly rolled spliff tucked behind Shaun's ear. Grinning, we fall in. Shaun dives onto the bed, slides the joint from his ear, which unlike mine is capable of holding a fat smoke. He lights up, taking a rangy drag, and passes it around. After my third soak, I realize how wasted I am. Ella too. All three of us start to giggle. We know where this is heading.

Relax, Oneiroi says suddenly, joining us.

I feel Shaun's hand on my thigh, then turn to see him stroke Ella's—my desire to move toward her instinctive. My mouth searching to find her mouth. We eventually kiss. Our lips like the ebbing of petals, open and gentle. Awakening the taste of an earlier gin sling. Envy doesn't exist, I soon recognize. Our sharing of Shaun seemingly the most natural thing in the world.

Watching us, he rests his head. Runner climbs into the Nest. *I'm done for the night,* she says. *I'll see you tomorrow.*

Shaun gently tucks a wayward strand of hair behind my ear. I don't care that he notices its freakishness, his fingertips eventually finding my neck. A pretty stroke.

I pull my tank top over my head and unbutton Ella's blouse, unlatching her bra with a steady snap. Both of us at once naked.

I laugh then, I think out of shyness. Shaun slaps my ass, while Ella presses my palm against hers. My coyness fading like a distant song. At first his tongue is sensitive, traveling from my to Ella's lips. But then it lowers, circles my nipples. A wincing bite. The nip suddenly gets him going so he lifts his T-shirt, unzips his fly.

Slowly, I lower myself to Ella's waxed mound.

"Fuck me," my *Reason* whispers, her eyes fixed and slow.

A FTERWARD I SHOWER, MY HIGH WEARING OFF.

Hands not completely steady, I open the bathroom cabinet weighted with shaving balms and aftershaves. I listen for any mention of my name from the other side of the door, but there is nothing—just silence—so I relax.

Stashed and forced behind Shaun's laundry basket is a copy of *Asian Babes*. I sense a slight postsex sting between my legs. A thudding ache in my gut, I open the magazine.

Flash.

Oɪ. ᴋɪᴛᴄʜᴇɴ sɪɴᴋ. ɪs ɪᴛ ᴛʀᴜᴇ ʏᴏᴜ ʟᴏᴛ ᴄᴀɴ ꜰɪʀᴇ ᴘɪɴɢ-ᴘᴏɴɢ ʙᴀʟʟs outta your fannies?" Ross, the neighborhood bully, calls while balancing on his skateboard. "Well, is it?"

I ignore him and carry on walking. He sidles up beside me, a friend joining him. A racing bicycle this time.

Flash.

"—and that you lot shudder like Mount Fuji when you come?"

Both boys laugh. One pushing, one pedaling.

Flash.

I don't have the heart to tell the ugly little fuckface that Mount Fuji is in Japan—that I am Chinese. That Fuji hasn't erupted since 1707. *But we're all the same in your eyes, right? Chinese, Japanese, Thai, Filipino, Korean. All portrayed as submissive little dolls who enjoy folding our pants into perfect origami swans. The West's idea that Asian girls are only good for cooking, cleaning, and fucking, while you bigots attempt to force a subservience upon us—a cement necklace— pushing us under.*

I stop.

Flash.

"Bet your fanny's as smooth as an egg," Ross says. "Give us a look. We'll give you a fiver."

"Fuck you, fuckface," I say, my voice small and shaking.

"Oh, it speaks."

Flash.

Ella lets out an incredulous laugh.

Tick-tock—

—and I'm back. Paranoia finally seeking me out. Our earlier three-way now turned uncertain and cooled. *Tick-tock.* I stare down at Shaun's copy of *Asian Babes,* remembering the acne-faced boys, their cruelty. How I feared they'd wrestle me to the ground and discover my pancake chest, my fanny sprinkled with hair, this image forcing me to run and climb a fire escape on the next block. They eventually gave up, skated and cycled away, but on the way down I'd caught my foot. My sweater tangled with one of the railings on the third floor. At the time I hadn't felt any pain from the shock of the fall. Hadn't realized my right ear was hanging off, blood trickling down my face. Twenty-three stiches later I looked like one of those wild rabbits that had had its ear chewed off by a fox.

"I think it looks kinda hot," Ella said.

"Freak," I replied.

Three weeks later an envelope full of dog shit was posted through my mailbox. A little gift, I knew, from the two acne-faced boys. A fiver stapled to the corner.

I throw Shaun's copy of *Asian Babes* to the floor, suspicion in my gut that I might be satisfying some sort of Asian fetish. A simmering disquiet found in my eyes, green and watery, as I stare at the bathroom mirror. I organize his toiletries in alphabetic order to steady my nerves and hold up my hand, the one that just minutes ago had traced Ella's perfect breasts while the other released Shaun. I stare at it for what feels like an age. Is something supposed to feel different now? Am I meant to act like we're all just good friends?

No. Things are as they have always been. Same hand. Same girl.

Ella and I: best friends.

Shaun: the new guy.

Paranoia melting, I open the bathroom door, joining them again.

17

Daniel Rosenstein

Hey, what are you doing here?" I say, opening the door, nerves mildly rattled.

"I thought I'd surprise you." She smiles, handing me a square paper bag. Her eyes scanning the inside of my office.

I peek inside—the smell of warmed salt-beef bagel causing my mouth to water—and check the clock: 7:45.

My eyes widen. "Felicé's?"

She nods. "Your favorite. Extra pickles."

"You are sweet," I say.

I kiss her softly on the cheek. *How kind,* I think. Suddenly, my mother's voice fills my head: *A woman who surprises you is a woman hoping to catch you!*

I scrunch the paper bag closed.

"I have a patient," I say.

"I know. Alexa. Eight A.M."

"Monica! That's—"

"Confidential," she finishes, placing a single finger to her lips. "Don't worry."

She hands me my diary and kisses my mouth, but I pull away. Sharp and punishing.

"You left it at home. I thought you might need it. Anyway, it gave me an excuse to surprise you." She shines.

"Next time you decide to surprise me, please don't," I order.

I watch her face fall. I have hurt and humiliated her. Guilt yanks on my chest, the cruel bite of my words not dissimilar to my father's.

Just as Monica steps back, Alexa appears. Her eyes pinned on her phone. She looks up momentarily and heads for her usual seat in the waiting area.

"I have to work," I insist.

Monica notes my distraction and turns.

"Alexa?" she whispers.

My eyes remain fixed.

"She's pretty."

"Monica," I say severely, gesturing toward the door.

As Monica walks past Alexa, their eyes scan one another. Monica flicks her hair. Her walk, I notice, has a little more swagger to it, is a little more assertive than usual.

I close the door and settle myself for the next ten minutes, thoughts of my father cast to the front of my mind. I picture him: a man of few words, yet a bully all the same. Hands like spades, long delicate eyelashes. A mass of contradictions navigating the world as though he were two separate beings. At home he tipped his hat toward tyranny, moods swinging at such velocity that my mother and I would sneak around like cowed dogs, but in the community he wore a hat of pride, reeking of goodness and natural leadership. One Christmas, when I was nine years old, I was forced to go with him to our local community hall, my small nail-bitten hands clutching a damp cardboard box of toys. Old toys. Toys that were loved, cared for, and played with by me, yet my father had insisted I give them away to our less fortunate brothers and sisters. Among the toys was an Evel Knievel doll that I was particularly keen on at the time, but no—that had to go too, along with my collection of *Star Wars* figures and my cricket bat.

When we arrived I had cried, clutching the box to my chest.

"Stop that," my father ordered, his cheeks inflamed, "goddamn sissy."

Mostly absent during my childhood, my father had little concern that his generosity came at a cost to his own family, which collectively was me and my mother, Katherine, Kitty to those who knew her well. I now understand that what we believed to be selflessness was actually my father's fragile ego—university, after all, taught me something. His need to be loved verged on pathetic at times, his desire to fix, I suppose, not unlike my own. He was romantic, an idealist whose narcissism was disguised to look as if he cared, but really he reveled like a pig in shit when he felt needed and useful, and I suppose that was where my mother came in. She was adoring and lost. Unable to make decisions on her own. Without purpose, vulnerable, codependent, and therefore, in need of him. It had driven me up the wall for years.

"I'll just need to run it by your father, Daniel," she'd said.

"Well, okay, but I need an answer by tomorrow. It would make me very happy if you could both come."

My father never made it to my graduation. He was busy. A large company merger had sparked interest, and not trusting anyone else to finalize the negotiations, he had insisted on being around to seal the deal. My mother wasn't able to make it either, which I put down to flu and which she kindly agreed to, giving a tiny cough, congratulating me, then hanging up the phone.

It had been my father's hope that I would join the family business. Make him proud by becoming the natural successor to the white-goods sales empire he'd built with blood, sweat, and martyrdom. Instead, I elected for further education. Part of me wanted to fight him, reject him and his business by getting as far away as possible. Of course, he was furious when I told him, slamming the car door and leaving my mother sitting in the back, seat belt pressing against her burdened chest.

"Education is in the doing," he shouted, "actually working! Not in some sodding campus for jumped-up little twats who sleep till noon, wanking over grades. For Christ's sake, Daniel, grow a backbone."

I was silent, fear crawling around my intestines.

"Bourgeois and bloody useless." He huffed, his color rising.

The very idea of not having a backbone would implicate me as a flipperty-flopperty spineless man—a jellyfish, snail, tapeworm. My body unable to stand, let alone wank until noon.

I cleared my throat, intestines unraveling. "I take it I get your approval then?" my backbone dared.

"Not in this lifetime," my father said.

I chose clinical psychology. Not only did it sound good, but I was guaranteed to get laid. A predominantly female subject, with six girls to every boy as the average stat. I stocked up on Audre Lorde, Adrienne Rich, Gloria Steinem, Germaine Greer, and other salty feminists, hoping to snare the opposite sex. Often seen wandering the grounds of Cambridge University with a copy of *The Second Sex* tucked under my arm, I carried de Beauvoir's words around like a badge of honor, and to my surprise, it worked. Girls came and went, highlighting my fear of intimacy and the *real* reason I'd chosen psychology—I was completely fucked up.

ALEXA HESITATES. HER JADE-GREEN EYES DRIFTING ABOUT THE ROOM as if cast out at sea in search of a life raft. Finally they settle, on me, my eyes. She blinks.

Eye contact for more than eleven seconds, Daniel Stern says, indicates that two people will eventually make love, fall in love, or fight. I take a guess our eyes will fall away on the cusp of ten, avoiding any such territory.

Nine, ten—she looks away.

I note her silk dress skimming the top of her knee. It is a carefully considered length of modesty. A perfect proportion for her gazelle-like legs and slender calves. Around her neck is a rose quartz heart tied neatly with a slim edge of ribbon that, I remember, she wore to our first session. Hair sleeked back into a delicate French twist. A nonchalant elbow resting on the arm of the chair. For a moment, I wonder who she is today, this elegant young woman.

I contemplate gently steering the conversation to our last session, when Dolly paid a brief visit, and then sit back, aware not to hijack the moment on behalf of my own curiosities.

Silence.

"I had a dream," she finally says. "I know how you shrinks love a dream."

I clear my throat.

"Feel like sharing it?" I ask.

She gazes off, her eyes melting as if reentering the dream. I'm aware of wanting complete silence. Even the tick of the clock feeling invasive, a prickling of anticipation edging me forward in my chair.

"There's a child waiting in the shadows of a still village," she begins, placing her hands between her thighs. "She's lost, unable to find her mother. The Girl wonders where she can be and worries the river may have stolen her, taken her adrift to some other grassy bank. 'Mother, where are you?' the Girl calls out. Maybe the Tigers have her, she thinks. The Girl peekaboos but there is still no sign of her, or the Tigers. Abandoned and hungry, the Girl wanders over to the river, knowing its cool water could drown her in a second. She imagines holding large stones in both hands, her whole weight sinking among the circling tangerine fish. Then, removing her slip-on sneaker, she dips her toes and flicks. The river wobbling as she immerses herself. A sting of salt in her eyes. When she comes up for air, the Girl feels a tap on her shoulder from an orange paw. She turns, realizing it's the one who wishes to define her as a whore and a slave. 'My mother is gone,' the Girl says, 'and there's no food in my bowl.' The Tiger winds his muscular body in close.

"'Then work. Earn your keep,' he says. 'Get on your hands and knees.'

"The Girl lowers herself to the ground while more tigers surround her, watching. Fire in their eyes."

A pause.

"Bystanding bastards," she adds.

Alexa leans back, exhausted, it seems.

"Quite a dream," I say.

"I dream a lot," she says. "It's a gateway."

"To?"

"Old stories. New hopes. It depends."

"Any idea what it all means?"

She nods.

"We were at a party on Friday night," she says, crossing her legs, "at Shaun's house. Navid was there. Alexa needed to let her hair down."

I look at her quizzically, in desperate need of an explanation.

She smiles.

"Oh, I'm sorry," she says. "I'm Oneiroi, I should have explained when I came in."

Silence.

"Pleasure to meet you, Oneiroi," I finally say, my mind catching up.

Aware of my confusion, she waits for me to tailor my thinking: *I am now with another personality, Oneiroi, not Alexa.* I wonder then how often one of the Flock has to do this—wait for singletons like me to catch up when a switch has occurred, how irritating and time consuming it must be for them all.

"You too." She smiles.

"So who's Navid?" I ask.

"He runs the Electra. Nasty piece of work, if you ask me—has the girls in a complete spin, competing with each other, fighting for his attention. At the party he told one of the girls, Annabelle, that he could set fire to her life at any moment. All because she dared think about getting a job at another club. He's a complete psycho."

"This is very concerning. Is Ella aware it's not safe?"

"Kinda, she said she just needs enough cash so she can get her own place."

"Do you believe her?"

"I'm not sure. I'm afraid she'll get sucked in. It's hard to give up work when you get used to a certain lifestyle. But I'm also worried the Electra is having more of an impact on us than we realized."

"And this concern therefore finds its way to your dreams?"

"The royal road to consciousness."

"You read Freud?"

"Sometimes." She shrugs. "I got a few recommendations from Joseph."

"Ever read *The Interpretation of Dreams*?"

She nods.

"So," I ask, "what of the Tigers?"

"Perpetrators, aggressors."

I wait for her to elaborate, my hand encouraging her to be rigorous with herself.

"My father, and Navid."

"And the bystanding bastards?"

"Anna, probably."

A pause.

"You think Ella could get hurt as you were? That Navid could do as your father did?"

"Yes," she says, "and he'd enjoy it too. *Psycho*."

"A sadist?"

"I guess."

"Oneiroi," I say, locking eyes, "a thought occurred to me."

"Yes?"

"Does Navid know that Ella has a younger sister?"

Her face suddenly turns ashen. "I'm not sure," she says. "I don't think so."

Reluctantly I find myself imagining the worst-case scenario, my breath quickening, my palms moistening.

"I think you're in denial. Your friend couldn't have chosen a worse place to work if she tried," I say, "and you; you couldn't have chosen a boyfriend more unwisely. He works for a man who thinks it's okay to threaten someone's life. Do you understand? The Electra is not safe. You are not safe. I say this because I care, not because I want to scare you. But I can't be a bystander."

She pulls down on her silk dress, her body now stretching. A switch, I tell myself. She allows her legs to drop and gazes at the lithograph while moving her neck from side to side. The ribbon necklace falling into the well of her collarbones.

"Alexa?" I ask.

She nods.

I pause, attempting to gather myself yet again.

"There's a lot of switching today," I say.

"I know. I'm sorry."

"You don't need to be sorry. It's just an observation."

Silence.

"Do you want to feel safe?" I ask.

"I don't know."

"Why?"

"I may hate myself."

I wait.

"I always have. Well, part of me always has. Since I was a little girl."

"But you were not born feeling this way. Someone must have told you this or made you feel that way. And in turn you learned to believe it. Who was it?"

"My father."

"Tell me something about him I don't know already."

"I made him into a god."

I raise my eyebrows.

"He was the only person to give me any attention."

"Not all attention is good," I say. "He manipulated your attachment. A trauma bond."

She looks at me, registering what it is I've just said.

"He called me stupid. A worthless piece of shit. And then he made me his whore."

She looks away.

"So this man, your father," I continue, "who you believe holds a monopoly on your self-worth, told you these things and you believed him. He visited you at night looking for comfort in his nine-year-old daughter. He was a perpetrator. Your tiger. A pedophile. A man who believed it was his right, because he could."

"He told me he loved me."

"Was that before or after he raped you?"

Silence.

"I have to make you conscious of the things you don't see."

Her head drops, eyes filling with a lifetime's worth of tears.

"He was your father, but you were not his to own," I say softly. "You were a little girl who had just lost her mother. His words were manipulative. They silenced you. A child with no choice. You had to believe him, otherwise what else did you have? But you're no longer that little girl. You know the difference between right and wrong. And deep down you know you're not bad, or stupid. Or a worthless piece of shit."

Sermon over, I sit back.

Her shoulders start to shake; next, her chest. Violent and unwanted tears fought back.

"That was when it all started," she cries, hurt disrupting her voice, "leaving the Body, losing time, gathering the Flock. They helped me. They became my family and friends."

"When we first met, you talked about your family fighting a lot. You meant your personalities?"

"Yes."

Mouth dry, I swallow. "Are you still taking your medication?"

"Sometimes," she says, "but the Fouls hide it from us. I think they want me to turn mad."

"Part of *you* wants to go mad," I say.

"Part of me wants to go mad," she repeats, "a dark part."

"A saboteur," I say, "the part that self-harms, keeps company with potentially dangerous people. We agreed you'd reduce the medication slowly."

"I'm trying!"

She bends, wraps both arms around her waist. Rocks back and forth.

I wait for her to cry.

"I don't want to talk anymore," she says, looking up. Heavy arms surrendering, collapsing at her side. Her French twist falls around her shoulders.

"You are not mad, or bad," I say. "You are a fully rounded human being who has been subjected to the most appalling abuse by your father. You did nothing wrong. You were a child. It's important that you give time to these words. Digest them. Just for today, you will try your best to be the person you needed when you were young. Say them with me."

I gesture. "Just for today I am strong."

"Just for today I am strong," she repeats.

"Just for today, I will try my best to be the person I needed when I was young."

She clears her throat. "Just for today, I will try my best to be the person I needed when I was young."

"Good. Now say that five times and mean it."

She pulls up straight, her shoulders firm.

"Just for today I am strong. Just for today I will try my best to be the person I needed when I was young. Just for today I am strong. Just for today I will try my best to be the person I needed when I was young. Just for today I am strong. Just for today I will try my best to be the person I needed when I was young. Just for today I am strong. Just for today I will try my best to be the person I needed when I was young. Just for today I am strong. Just for today I will try my best to be the person I needed when I was young."

"Good."

"What now?"

"Now you digest."

"What if it doesn't work?"

"Is it difficult to believe me?"

She shrugs.

"Your father, you still search for him. Everywhere."

She nods.

"You prefer to believe your cruel, manipulative father?"

Alexa sits quietly, uncrosses her legs, her dress spilling between her thighs. The atmosphere between us now changed—from survival to empowerment. I feel my breath deepen, my senses alive. Intimacy has crept in and is quickly eroticized. I gather myself; press down hard with the soles of my feet. My internal supervisor keeping us safe.

"It's time," I say.

18

Alexa Wú

GRITTY AND REAL," JACK SAYS, POINTING AT THE DEMOLITION SITE. "Zoom in on the bulldozer and those local people we met earlier."

I aim my camera: a flare of possibility, a lodestar of hope. Sleek black edges, alloy chassis, lens as clear as the inventory it's about to take. As I twist the rubber-ridged focus, my right eye attempts to center on Borough Market, where buildings are being pulled down so commercial venues can be erected and sold at extortionate prices, making it near impossible for locals to stay where they've lived for most of their lives. *Click.* A captured moment of destruction.

Daniel's words from yesterday's session suddenly come flooding back: *Your father, you still search for him. Everywhere.* My witnessing of destruction conjuring up memories of my father's abuse.

Click, click.

Jack checks his phone.

"Take your time," he says, scrolling the screen. "The picture editor at the *Guardian* just messaged to say the story's going ahead, so make sure you get some solid shots. Something that'll make front page."

Click.

I stare down at my Converse—tired and battered—clearly dressed for the part as Jack and I manage a quick scan of the East London site. My camera focusing on the sponsored demolition panels where investors have advertised their new commercial venues and luxury apartments about to mushroom. An importance felt in my gut that I need to bring together this frightened community, and have it documented.

"Try getting a little heart into it," Jack says, and I nod, knowing exactly what he means. His suggestion that we get a shot that pulls on the heartstrings of London's mayor and the district council, supporting our cause, and the editor's wishes.

"I'm thinking local shop owner, community outreach worker, sad child on a swing," he adds, pointing at the local park. "Come on."

We push open the gate to the park, where local children are hanging off jungle gyms, others on swings. The younger ones balancing on playground spring rockers. Their mothers huddled together drinking takeaway coffee while keeping a close eye.

Click. Click.

Over the years, photography has allowed me to do what I did as a kid—record another world—that first camera given to me by my father a distant memory but most likely a muse. When you spend so much time obsessing over your past, photography is a gift. It cuts you loose from your ego. Sets you free from decline. It takes your very angry little heart, cupping it lightly, and speaks: *Let go, let go.* For me, the activity is so soothing I almost believe my life divided into two parts: before I took photographs, and after. The latter a salve for the preoccupation I had with some of the uglier aspects of my life.

"Good," Jack says. "Got it?"

"I think so," I say, "but I might hang around a while. I wanna get some shots of the local shop owners, and some of the families who've been forced out."

"Why not," he says, strolling toward the edge of the playground.

I take a moment and aim, like an arrow, at the pale blue sky. The movement is smooth: my arms raised, shoulders locked, fingers poised. A steady hold while the camera frames a view directly above me, capturing a rectangle of clouds, feral wood pigeons, and the movement of ancient green trees. *Click. That's so, so lovely.* Dolly sighs, her most favored pictures usually involving animals of any kind.

I feel a cool lick of breeze on my neck as I approach, I assume, a mother and son—matching smiles—conveniently on a swing.

"Hello," I say, "I'm covering a story for a national newspaper about the demolition of community homes over by Borough Market. Are you local?"

"For almost fifteen years. We live on the corner over there, just by the Hare and Hounds."

Ironic, Oneiroi scoffs.

"Where will you go?" I ask.

"Who knows? My son here just started grade school, and his two sisters just started nursery. I'm going to contact the council again, but that could mean a long wait for decent housing. I guess we'll have to take what's offered, which could be miles away. But we don't have much choice: If we refuse we go right to the bottom of the list. There's a points system. I'm Sandra, by the way."

I lean over, shake her cold hand. "Alexa."

"So go ahead, we don't mind. Do we, Billy?"

Billy shakes his head, avoids my eyes. Squealing happily as Sandra pushes harder. Her fingers tickling his navy puffer waist. *Click. Click. Click.*

"Thanks, Sandra. Billy," I say. "Good luck."

Take some more of Billy laughing, Dolly insists, jiggling on the spot, but then Runner seizes the Body and swings our attention toward a fit woman in tight leggings, running alongside her cocker spaniel. *Now there's a shot.* Runner smiles. *Click. Click.* Dolly quickly snatches the Body, aiming now at the spaniel. *My turn,* she insists. *Give it back.* But Runner nudges her hand, zooming in on the fit woman getting away. They tussle, and I imagine I must look like someone having a mild seizure. Dolly starts to cry. *Shhh,* I comfort, *Runner, let her take another shot.* Runner folds her arms, allowing Dolly to take hold of the camera. *Fiiine!* she says, rolling her eyes.

Squabble over, I scan my viewfinder, happy with my earlier shots. *Well, they're certainly gritty and real,* Oneiroi says. *Your mother would be so proud of you, Alexa.*

Affirmed by her words, I stroke my camera, delighted.

Approaching one of the park benches, I picture my sad, beautiful mother. How, when I learned of her death, I'd stared out of the kitchen window for what felt like days. Various birds nestling and balanced on the roof of the potting shed. The same potting shed where I, or rather Flo the Outcast, would later starve that poor guinea pig to death. At nine years old I still placed confidence in magical thinking: fat babies delivered by stem-legged storks, sugarplum tooth fairies, fluffy Easter bunnies, and Santa Claus. I also believed the birds perched outside carried with them my mother's soul, though this I thought less magical, more real. In my mind she was a passenger on board their flight, soaring above giant trees, their wild wings spread and warmed by the changing angle of the sun. There she was, her soul still alive, despite it all. Among birds.

Days passed. Seasons changed. Visits from my father worsened. But what remained was the company of birds. Their frequent return was somewhat of a pleasant mystery to me, yet each time they perched, my baffled heart felt grateful. Simple miracles.

I supposed the birds cared for my mother. Her soul touched by their absolute freedom, her own wings clipped and broken for most of her life.

Jack joins me on the park bench, a smoke in his hand.

"Happy?" he asks.

I pause.

"I'm not sure what that means," I reply softly.

He smiles crookedly. "Me neither. I don't know why I even asked you that."

His phone rings, so I busy myself, half listening to his conversation, half focusing on the mother and her son.

"East London," I hear him say while checking his watch. "Yeah, should be finished around six."

The little boy points at the sand pit, his mother now helping him down off the swing.

Jack coughs. "Whereabouts?"

She kneels down, searches for an instrument with which to dig the sand. Spots a polystyrene cup.

"I'm not sure I fancy a club tonight," he says, cigarette flicked to the ground.

The little boy jiggles his chubby arms as she scoops up the sand, shakes the cup. Then turns it upside down.

"The Electra?" Jack asks.

My chest tightens.

The mother pats the top of the polystyrene cup.

"It's not really my kinda thing," Jack says, nudging the cigarette butt with his foot.

"Ta-dah!" the mother sings.

The little boy claps.

Jack ends the call.

"Friend of mine fancies a night out," he says, lighting another cigarette.

"Oh," I say, voice low and soft.

"Some club called the Electra. Grim place by the sound of it. I never heard of it, d'ya know it?"

My heartbeat quickens. I shake my head.

Liar, the Fouls scold.

I feel my chest tighten and focus on the kids while I attempt to organize them in age order. The boy hanging from his knees like a monkey, I decide, being the eldest: *twelve, eleven, eleven, nine, eight and a half, seven, seven, six, six, six, six, five, four, four.* Next, their mothers: *thirty-seven, thirty-five, thirty-two-ish, thirty, thirty, twenty-eight, twenty-eight, twenty-five, eighteen, maybe nineteen.*

Nerves settling, I take out my phone and switch off the silencer, a chime suddenly alerting me that I have two missed calls. Two voice-mails.

I press the RETRIEVE button.

It's Ella.

"Where are you?" she'd asked. "You need to get over here. Right away."

19

Daniel Rosenstein

The man snatches his shopping bag from the cashier's hands, clearly vexed.

"I'll do the rest!" he barks.

Stunned, the cashier scans a family-size box of Cheerios, the man removing what she's already packed and reorganizing the groceries into neat towers as if playing *Tetris.*

Control freak, I tell myself.

The cashier's eyes turn low and I soon feel my hackles rise. Shame and public humiliation needling me in my gut.

"Bag!" He points.

The cashier attempts to unhook Mr. Control Freak another "Bag for Life"—her fingers alert and twitching—its handles quickly tangling.

"Christ," he says, rolling mean eyes.

I step forward, no longer able to bear it. "Hey. Go easy, man," I intervene.

He turns to face me.

"What's your problem?" he mocks.

"You," I say.

Silence.

She scans his last item: baby wipes; and for a moment I feel deep pity for the imagined child. A familiar dread rising in my chest whenever faced with male onslaught, particularly a father's.

He forces his bank card into the plastic slot, keys in a code, and stares at me while the cashier clears her throat, eventually handing over a receipt.

"Asshole," he mutters, then leaves.

I move toward the cashier and hand over cash for a bottle of champagne, a gift for Susannah, although I know she'll scold her addict dad for having bought it.

"Do you need a bag?" she asks.

"No thanks."

Tucking a wayward strand of hair behind her ear, she smiles, gently mouthing, *Thank you.*

CLOSE TO THE EXIT I SPOT MR. CONTROL FREAK BENDING OVER TO attend his numerous shopping bags. I consider booting his fat ass but as I pass instead slip the bottle of champagne into the remaining Bag for Life waiting in his trolley.

Without hesitation I approach the supermarket's security guard.

"Thought you should know; guy over there with the beard. He stole a bottle of champagne."

The security guard nods, no words, and advances. A confident stride, sensible boots, hands resting on his thick waist. I wait just long enough to observe the bottle of champagne pulled from his bag, Mr. Control Freak bewildered and recovering his receipt, the security guard guiding him back inside.

On my ride over to Susannah's I glance out the car window, traffic lights suddenly fixed on red. I turn up the music, smile to myself, and tap out a rhythm on the steering wheel. Serves him right, I think, imagining Mr. Control Freak sweating under interrogation. His fat ass kicked for thieving. If only my patients knew what I was capable of, the dark thoughts that pass through my mind. The malice. The revenge. Would they trust me? It is unlikely.

A father and his daughter, no older than ten, are awaiting the signal of the fluorescent green man and his panic-stricken beeps. The father takes his daughter's hand, but she pulls away—her twist like a revolving door—unconscious of the cold bite this will leave on his heart. Instead, she forces in earbuds and looks away. The father left to keep check on the traffic. A few moments later she scans her phone, studies it, taps on the screen.

Eventually, the green man flashes on and begins its countdown. I watch the father dither, wondering, I imagine, whether to attempt guidance of his daughter's steps. It is an uncomfortable moment of care: unwanted by the girl, needed by the man. Unsure, he looks at her and smiles. The girl smiles back and finally links arms with her father before stepping out onto the road. All is well.

I wonder about this, how one manages to let go of their daughter while still being present. How to guide without infantilizing, offer help without patronizing? How to be a good father when the mother is dead? My own daughter swears her autonomy is something not to be meddled with, her smarts making my care unnecessary and self-serving. My desire, she thinks, is misplaced. Believing my longing for Clara's living body has been projected into parental suffocation: unwanted by the girl, needed by the man. I smile to myself, thinking that's what happens when your daughter's recommended a good shrink.

Don't be overbearing tonight, I tell myself. *Relax. Let her breathe.*

But the moment I pull up and see her step out on the porch, waving her slim arms like a child—a short red dress—my good intentions fly out the window.

As I step out of the car, Susannah approaches and throws her arms around my waist, loosely, and kisses my cheek.

"Happy birthday, darling," I delight.

"Thanks, Dad," she says, now scanning the passenger seat, "but did you forget to bring dessert?"

I slap my forehead with my palm. "Damn it," I say, "forgot it. I'm sorry."

"That's okay." She smiles. "I forgive you."

20

Alexa Wú

You're grounded!" Ella shouts, a manicured finger pointed at Grace's darling chest.

"Pfft. You're not my mum!" she cries. "Your rules don't fly!"

I step in between them—a referee—Grace pulling back her shoulders and sucking her teeth.

I notice the maturing of her hips. Bee-stung lips. A tightening of her waist. Liquid liner applied to give a neat black flick at the edges of her eyes.

"Right now, I'm the closest thing you've got to a mum!" Ella says, grabbing the collar of Grace's denim bomber, only a couple of inches taller than her sister now. Her fists red with rage.

Grace stares at her, defiant.

"Go to your room, *stupid, stupid girl.*"

"Fuck you."

"Stop it!" I shout.

Ella releases her grip and steps back. Stuffs both shaking hands deep in the front pockets of her jeans.

"Steal anything else and I swear I'll—"

"*What?*" Grace goads.

"I'll—"

Ella's gaze remains fixed. Her breathing idle and jumpy.

"I *needed* them for school," Grace says, voice shaking at the edge. Face flushed and turning pink. "Mine are too small. All the other kids will laugh at me. I can't do gym in tracksuit bottoms that ride up my ass!"

For a moment I align with Grace. My arbitration of matters now informed by the memory of the cruel kids born to safe, steady homes. Providing parents. Home-cooked food. Sensible cars. How at thirteen years old—same age as Grace—I'd stenciled a Nike swoosh on a pair of cheapo generic-brand sneakers, a permanent black marker withstanding bad weather and humiliation.

"*Need* and *want* are two different things," Ella snaps.

"You *need* those new boots Navid bought you last week?"

"They were a gift."

"Show him your tits, did you?"

"Shut up! You don't know anything, *stupid*."

A standoff.

"Go to your room!" Ella points at the door.

Grace lunges past, knocking shoulders.

"Fucking bitch," Grace calls.

Ella slumps on the couch, defeated, head held in her hands. Her customarily neat bob ruffled and in need of a comb. "Thanks for coming. Can you believe this?"

"Go easy on her," I say. "She's just a kid."

Ella looks up momentarily, struggling to speak.

Silence.

It's not Grace's fault, Oneiroi whispers, *Ella taught her to steal in the first place.*

Yeah, Dolly agrees, *what about that leather jacket?*

Exactly, Oneiroi adds.

I take a moment to listen, thinking their voices might somehow give a clue to what I say next. Their jury about to impart penalty or judgment on Ella's mood.

She's such a freakin' hypocrite. Runner snorts.

"So, he bought you new boots?" I dare, a bite in my tone.

"So *what*?" Ella speaks to the floor.

"So, maybe you're giving Grace mixed messages," I say. "On the one hand, you want her to be honest and good, but she sees you taking gifts and nicking stuff yourself. It's confusing for her. Listen, I wasn't going to say anything, but I don't think you should be accepting gifts and money from Navid. It gives him the wrong idea and makes you look weak. Grace needs to look up to her big sister, and I need to respect my friend. And right now, neither is happening."

She throws me a black look. "Shut up, Alexa. You're supposed to be on my side."

I hear Grace hurl something. A crash. But not a break.

Ella shouts at Grace's door, "You'd better stop that right now!"

She throws herself back on the couch, stares at the ceiling. Eyes flooded.

I wait.

"Where's your mum?" I finally ask.

"Dunno." Ella shrugs. "She left a message. Something about needing to be out of town for a while, which probably involves a man."

Like mother, like daughter, Runner says.

Shhh, Oneiroi warns.

I settle myself beside her, my body pressing against the lumpy couch. Its cushions aged and bobbled, their stuffing sad and limp.

"Want me to talk to her? I can sleep over," I say, "give you a break?"

"Haven't you got therapy in the morning?" she asks.

"I can cancel," I say. "I'll get Anna to call."

"I'd like that." My *Reason* smiles, lowering her head. Teardrops escaping, fists removed from her jean pockets, laid flat now and resting on her thighs. Gently, she drops her head on my shoulder.

"They were on sale," she says, "the boots."

21

Daniel Rosenstein

I CHECK MY DIARY, NOTING A TWO-HOUR BREAK. ANNA WÚ'S EARLIER message left with my receptionist, adding yet another cancellation to my day. *I could have gone for a run,* I think, feeling irked, *or boiled an egg. Or maybe read the papers and stayed in bed, Monica's warm, slow breath sweeping across my back.*

Irritated, I make my way to the kitchenette and feed the French press four scoops of strong Colombian, wondering what to do with myself. Read? Catch up on my supervision notes? Call Mohsin?

Relax, I tell myself, *enjoy the time, some peace and quiet.*

Suddenly an image of Alexa—sick in bed—takes up space in my brain. I picture her asleep. Her leg resting on top of velvety sheets, toes painted red. White cotton pajamas? I wonder. Or a delicate silk slip? I quickly dismiss the scene from my mind.

Running the tap, I squeeze some dish soap inside the mugs, allowing them to soak before finally deciding to call Monica.

"I've had a cancellation," I say.

"Oh. Is that good?" she answers, voice laced with sleep.

"It's neither good or bad," I say, "I thought I'd just call you."

I imagine her stretching, a yawn. The cotton duvet pulled tight to her chest.

She clears her throat.

"Was it your eight A.M.?" she asks.

"Yes."

"Ah, the pretty one," she says.

"She called in sick, or rather, her stepmother did. Strange call. I imagined her more timid. Alexa's always painted her as a rather passive, quiet person. She thanked me for looking after Alexa, said that things at home had improved since she'd been coming to therapy. Rather assertive. Anyway, Alexa's ill, unable to make her session," I reveal, aware my confidentiality is in breach. My voice is sharp and defensive.

"So, she's in bed too," Monica adds.

A pause.

"Dinner tonight?" I distract, uncomfortable with Monica's suggestion. The image it re-creates.

"Why not?"

"I fancy a steak," I say.

"With mashed potato," she adds, her enthusiasm sent down the line.

"I'll be home around seven."

"Seven is good."

"Good. Good."

Silence.

"By the way," she whispers, "you're hopeless at disguising your thoughts. Just so you know."

I place the receiver in its cradle, exposed and embarrassed. The notion that Monica might think me unprofessional causing me to fret. I notice my palms moistening, a slight tremor in my chest. Did I not divert the conversation away smoothly enough to avoid this kind of disclosure? Personal. Ethical. Both equally suspect when it comes to discussing one's patients—particularly when they're pretty. I walk toward the now-boiled kettle and pour its contents into the French press. The thick, sludgy brown liquid pressed down hard with my palm. Contain it, I think. Don't let it percolate. Don't let it stir. Left for too long it might turn unpalatable.

22

Alexa Wú

A KIWI FRUIT AND A—" HE TURNS.

"—rose milk," I finish. "Extra pearls."

He smiles, locks his arms around my waist, possibly a little smug because I've just kissed him on the mouth. He strokes my neck, and a fleeting thought pops up: our three-way, Shaun, Ella, and I daisy-chaining while his party downstairs turned lively. I've wondered, in the past, about the lovesick kind of girls who have sex while their boy-friends watch. A window into the pleasure of soft bodies, curved and fitting. Shaun took us in; of course he did—like a drug—fucking us like he had something to prove. Our girl-on-girl action just a game for him. The sex something he believed he was controlling, our preference for each other too impossible for him to fathom.

The girl behind the counter writes down our order on a neon slice of notepaper, and then whips her blond ponytail around her shoulder.

I love Bubbleology, Dolly sings, her small fists clenched, *it's my favorite!*

She crosses her eyes and giggles, and it's hard not to eat her up, she's so adorable.

You can drink this, I say, *but then you've got to go back inside, okay? Oneiroi's waiting for you.*

Shaun hands me the bubble tea while Dolly takes the Light, sucking the chewy tapioca balls through a fat green straw. I'm not a fan of bubble tea, but Dolly, on the other hand, can't get enough of it. Absolutely loves it. When you're a multiple, different tastes can translate to different personalities. Take Marmite: Dolly and I love it, but Oneiroi hates it. Ask Runner to take a bite of toast with it on and she'd gag, preferring jam herself. And the Fouls, well, they don't really eat, choosing to watch and then scold us for our greed.

"Go easy!" Shaun says, knocking the straw out of Dolly's mouth.

Dolly tightens her grip around the plastic cup.

It's okay, I soothe, *take your time. No one's going to take it away from you.*

Dolly throws Shaun a dark look.

"*What?*" he says.

Behind us the door sounds. A polite *ting.* We turn.

Cassie approaches, Amy close behind with a preteen girl. She is small and thin, with long jet hair that a rushed hand appears to have tied into a messy ball, a black bomber similar to Grace's worn above laced-trimmed blue shorts. Her legs are pimpled with a late-October chill.

Who's that? Dolly asks, excited.

I'm not sure, I say, wondering if she's Cassie's daughter, but then decide their age difference would make it unlikely.

Maybe she's the daughter of one of the Electra Girls, Runner says.

Dolly shrugs.

I note the young girl is clutching one of the musical plush toys I'd seen downstairs in the club.

Can I go play with her? Dolly asks, still sucking on the straw.

Another time, Dolly, I argue. *It's late.*

Dolly makes a face, throws her empty cup in the trash.

You always say that! Why can't I stay up? I want to play and make some friends. You don't even let me play with Grace.

Runner moves forward and takes Dolly's arm, *Come on, back inside now,* she says. *We're your friends.*

Dolly and I switch, the aftertaste of rose milk bubble tea in my mouth not entirely unpleasant.

"Hurry up," Cassie snaps at the young girl, eyes fixed and ill tempered, "or no drink!"

It's clear the girl doesn't really care. Instead she stares vacantly until Amy turns back and pulls, a little too firmly, on her arm.

"Britney, nǐ zhè ge shǎ zi!" Cassie curses.

The young girl finally looks up, a gaze to try any heart. "I'm not a fool," she whispers, "and don't call me Britney. My name's Poi-Poi."

I wonder why Poi-Poi's dressed in shorts on such a cold night. Why Cassie is being so impatient and cruel. *Why isn't the girl in bed,* I think, *and who is her mother?*

I turn to Shaun and catch his eye. He looks away.

"Who's that?" I ask.

He shrugs. "Don't get involved, it's none of your business."

We step outside to the threat of imminent rain. A flickering streetlight overhead giving off a clement glow. I reach over to link Shaun's arm, but irritated, he pulls away, and I wonder whether it's Dolly's dark look or my curiosity that's annoyed him. His mood now cool and contemptuous, he begins to walk ahead.

"I'll come in the club for a while," I say, conscious of wanting to see Ella, "then I'll head back home."

He turns.

"Okay," he says, "whatever."

Jane and Ella are talking in reception.

Thrilled at seeing me, Ella steps from behind the black lacquered desk and flings her arms around my neck while Jane turns to hang two men's suit jackets on padded hangers.

"Another new skirt," I say playfully, pointing at Ella's legs.

"One of the girls gave it to me," she whispers, sliding both hands down the soft black leather. "It was too small for her."

For a moment, I'm envious. I look down at my jeans, their color faded, their cut not as fashionable as I'd like. My hair still hasn't been trimmed and styled for some time. And even though it's fleeting, the poisonous green feeling unnerves me because rivalry has been mostly absent from our friendship. A feeling both unfamiliar and biting.

You look great, I don't manage to say, *and I'm jealous. Forgive me.*

"How's things with Grace?" I ask, hoping our connection outside Electra will somehow make me feel close to her.

"Fine," she says. "A lot better. Thanks for talking to her."

"No problem."

I watch Jane leave through the glass double doors. A lick of red on the soles of her shoes like a siren. She pushes the door with both palms, gives her red hair a flick, determined strength in her upper arms. I cut a glance through to the club—Cassie and Amy talking beneath low-level lighting from the art deco lamps. Amy gesticulating, red faced and animated, while Cassie nods in acknowledgment.

"Fancy a movie tomorrow night?" Ella asks.

"Not sure. What about a game of pool instead?" I suggest.

Runner smiles, the suggestion taken in.

"Okay."

The glass doors fling open again. Amy suddenly bursts through, her gaze somewhat unsettled. She hands Ella a drink and whispers in her ear—*So rude!* Oneiroi says, gesturing toward Cassie with a raised hand.

"What was that all about?" I ask as Amy leaves.

"Annabelle."

"What about her?"

"She's walked out. Gone to work for the competition. The Russian."

"I know," I say.

"You *know*?"

"She told me at Shaun's party."

Ella steps forward, leans in close, and grips my arm.

"Ow."

"Don't mention this to anyone," she says, eyes flashing. Fear, anger—I'm not sure. "Or Navid will fuckin' flip."

"Let go of me," I say.

She doesn't. Not immediately. Her grip locked, fingers pinching. Gaze holding me accountable.

"You don't know what he's capable of, Alexa," she says, "you don't understand."

Two men enter and approach, their coats wet from the drizzle outside. Ella's hand finally falls to her side. A frenzied smile finds her lips.

"Hello," she says, mood pinging to something sweet, "how was your holiday?"

"Great," one of the men answers, his gray hair flat and dank. "How are you, Ella?"

"Good," she purrs, "I'm happy to see you both."

Pleased as cocks in a henhouse at the attention, they each slide Ella a crisp note.

Are they that stupid? Runner asks.

Clearly, Oneiroi says, *they hear what they want to hear.*

In return, Ella gives them each a disc. The word *Electra* elegantly engraved on one side in a swirled font. On the reverse: a letter *C* for the short gray-haired guy, and *D* for his friend. It's a slow night.

Another four men enter. Ella takes their jackets. Hands them discs up to *H*.

One of the men, with a full beard and sad eyes, places his disc in the breast pocket of his shirt. Like an excited, greedy school kid, he rubs his hands together. I imagine them to be clammy.

Runner takes the Light and reaches for Ella's drink, knocks it back in one swig. The man looks at me and makes a face.

What? Not ladylike enough for you? Runner shouts in my head. *Prefer her to sip her drink like a good girl? The gutter waits for girls like us, right? Well, the gutter only exists because of men like you!*

I FEEL MY MOOD DIP WATCHING ELLA AT WORK, ONE EYE ON THE DOOR, a rumble in my gut at the possibility of Jack walking in. I can't imagine he'd get off being in a place like this, he even said so himself, but what do I know? I barely know anything about him—his work: yes; the man: no. And who doesn't have kinks these days?

I touch the soft part of my arm, Ella's earlier grip leaving a tinge of red, thinking about the men who get off on the bodies of the Electra Girls, slipping used notes in their stockings. Patting the bows on their short black skirts. Something of an acceptance that this is just what men do, because they can.

I turn to Ella.

"I miss you," I say, my eyes cast down. Muscles knotted beneath my skin.

"Don't worry. Everything will be back to the way it was soon," she says, "promise. I just need to save a few grand so I can lay down a security deposit and have a couple months' rent. I saw this amazing apartment advertised last week, just off Broadway Market, but the landlord wanted six months' rent up front."

Noticing her drink is finished, she reaches in her purse. Pops a pill.

"Right," she says, "I'd better go. I'm on in five."

A pause.

"What do you mean," I say, "'on in five'?"

"I just told you. Annabelle's not here. But you knew that already, *right*?"

She drops a layer of clothing, exposing a sun-bed tan to rival the other two members in our girl band. The sound of tiny snaps on her blouse intimate in our moment of forced silence.

I take hold of her shoulders.

"You're going to strip, aren't you?"

"I have to," she says, sliding me a look. "I want to fit in. The other girls won't accept me if I don't do it."

"For fuck's sake, Ella!" I shout.

She turns away.

"I thought we talked about this," I continue. "You have to stop. Double-dealing, bribes. And now *stripping*? What about setting an example for Grace, what about—"

She mutes my mouth with her palm.

"Keep your voice down," she whispers, anger shaping her jawline. "You're becoming a complete drag, you know that? If you can't chill out I don't want you here."

I stare her square in the eye.

"Stop with all the judgment," she defends. "I have to do this. Grace doesn't have bills to pay. I do. And how am I going to ever get out of my mum's place?"

"But—"

"No. Back off, Alexa."

I drop a kiss on her forehead, aware of her need to be heard. And *accepted*. The Electra Girls now a conduit through which Ella might claim a place in the world, albeit one that feasts on false selves and longings.

"Don't do this," I say quietly. "Please."

THE LIGHTS TONE DOWN AND A CEASELESS BASS KICKS IN. SEVERAL girls, all in various stages of undress, are waiting small mirrored tables, placing drinks on paper napkins. Cassie watching them while seated at the bar. Shaun pours her a drink and catches me seated and alone, my fingers nervously picking at a zit on my chin. I beckon a waitress.

"Whiskey," I order, "neat."

More men have arrived. They gather like prowling tigers. Staring at the narrow, elongated stage, amber shots in their hands. On either side, lights resemble cat's eyes on a darkened highway. A shiny pole planted at the end with two blazing spotlights awaiting something divine, something wicked.

I gaze up at the stage.

The bass kicking harder, dread rattling in my chest.

She wears just a black PVC bra and matching thong. I hardly recognize her: heavy makeup, a shake 'n' go wig, and confidence so raw I divert my eyes. Ella parts her legs and licks her top lip, red and glossed. Teases the imposter hair, waist length and wavy. In her hand she harnesses a whip made of leather and light-catching crystal. It is delicate enough to hint at play yet hard enough to warn of domination. She cracks the whip before striding toward the men.

When she reaches the end she slut-drops. Her legs wide, both hands ordering the whip between clenched teeth. I feel my heart drop into a pit of despair.

I watch her eyes turn foggy and amiss, a lazy slant to the lids that has her looking like she's about to fall asleep or pass out. Skin shining like honey, she grabs and spins, gyrating to the music in three-inch heels.

No chance of running in those, Runner says, their shaping of the line of her legs ceremonious, making her appear taller, slimmer. Enhancers to men's celestial fantasies.

I wonder if the pill she popped earlier is alive. It being the very thing, along with the other girls' goading, that got her up there onstage.

She arches her back, turns and falls to her knees, and spreads her legs wide open. Longing to be fed.

With love.

Validation.

Acceptance.

A bedtime story.

But instead takes the money.

A man inches forward in his chair and wipes his hands down his thighs. I allow a single tear down my cheek.

You don't have to do this, I voice in my head.

Maybe she wants to, Oneiroi says, *maybe she likes it.*

Shut the fuck up! Runner yells. *No girl wants men lusting over her like dogs—it's not the fucking attention she wants. It's something else . . .*

I glance over at Shaun and Cassie, now joined by Amy—all three lost in Ella's striptease—feeling the encore of jealousy once again. Imagining Shaun masturbating alone in bed, picturing Ella, I drop the thought into a pit of self-punishment. The thrashing not kind but most likely true.

A group of men have edged nearer to the stage. Tiger paws waving notes like submission flags.

I surrender, Runner mimics, a tarred snarl to her lip. *Take me for the asshole I am.*

Ella drops on all fours and prowls closer to the men, guiding the cash to her slippery bra and thong. Two of the men stuff their bills rather aggressively while another appears a little more reserved. Woozy almost.

Why are you doing this? I scream.

I look around, suddenly noticing Navid leaning against one of the mirrored pillars next to the small, intimate stage. I watch him watching her, a glow in his eyes. Ella's intimacy with the pole seemingly pleasing him. Her performance revs up. Dropping her shoulders, she lets the straps of her bra fall like sin until she is free of it completely. The first man stands and with a doglike lusting reaches for the bra. With a turn on her spiked heel, Ella kicks it out of reach. She wags her finger, shakes her head, mouthing: *Naughty boy.*

Eyes fixed on her naked breasts, he hollers and whoops, checking behind him to see he has the leering support of the other men. A sheen of sweat glazed across his upper lip.

Ella stares out now, all at once childish. Lost. And with a half-teasing smile, her moves gradually slowing down.

I notice she is wearing a gold necklace. A dainty key hanging off its loose chain just like the one I've seen the other girls wearing. A gift from Navid?

Navid locks eyes with her, his paw raised, toasts her with a squat glass filled with dark liquid. She gyrates closer to him and fingers the necklace before cupping her breasts, then slides both hands between her thighs. And I know immediately the gift is from him.

A key to his heart? Runner mocks.

I close my eyes and try not to see any more.

I want to go home, Dolly says, awakened and rubbing her eyes. *I don't like it in here, Alexa. Not one bit.*

I look away. The churn in my gut too real, my throat tightening as I make my way through the glass double doors. *My best friend: a stripper.*

You knew this was coming, Runner says, stepping into the night. *I warned you.*

Not concerned with scoldings or *told you so*'s, I grab my coat and wait for Ella outside the club, knowing she'll come look for me. The night turning dark like my mood, and sure enough, Ella appears as Runner lights a second cigarette.

"Hey," she says, "can I have one?"

I nod, not trusting my voice enough to use it while Runner offers her a light.

Her eyes slip across my face to the ground.

Coward, I want to scream, but don't.

Hypocrite, the Fouls scold.

"I'm tired," she says. "I don't wanna get into anything right now. I'll call you tomorrow."

"Sure," I say, my nerves jangled, frustration forced down.

My *Reason* turns away and hails a cab, lifting her collar with both hands to shield her neck.

"For what it's worth, the girls thought I was pretty good tonight," she says, a look of green pride in her stride as she walks away, the night promising to accept what she's done.

I WALK UP THE SHOULDER OF THE STREET, MY WOOL COAT SMELLING OF wet dog. I blow on my fingers. The night has turned damp and icy. On the opposite side of the road I notice two figures, animated, bent over, then realize it's Amy and Annabelle. Confused, I make my way over to them.

I thought Annabelle wasn't working here anymore, Runner says. *She isn't,* I say. *She works at another club now, in Soho.*

Nearing the sisters, I notice both are crying. They are holding hands with an intensity that looks fraught and wild. When they see me, they startle. Annabelle is breathless, her makeup smudged. Hanging off her shoulders is an oversize black double-breasted coat—probably a man's—covering a tiny dress.

"It's our brother. He's been rushed to the hospital," Annabelle wails, edging closer. "Hit-and-run. It's all my fault."

Fear clangs at my gut. "So what are you doing *here?*" I ask.

"I came to get Amy. We're waiting for a cab."

I place my hand on her shoulder, trying to lock eyes. My fingers brushing away her wet, limp hair.

"Do you think—?" I dare.

All three of us are rooted to the spot. Amy takes my arm, her voice shaking at the edge:

"Yes," she says, "it's gotta be Navid."

Annabelle lets out a scream like a murder of crows. The streetlight ablaze and shining on her embossed temples, veins turning turquoise. A madness arisen.

23

Daniel Rosenstein

ALEXA FIDDLES WITH THE TIE ON HER SILK BLOUSE. HER DISCLOSURE of last night's events clearly weighing heavily on her mind.

"So how long do you plan on being away for?" she asks, eyeing the pile of premature holiday brochures on my desk, a look that, were it possible, might set them alight. Clumsy of me to leave them out, I think, insensitive.

"Two weeks," I say, writing down the dates on letterhead note-paper and handing it to her, "but it won't be until next month. Patients usually prefer to know well in advance."

She nods.

Silence.

"How do you feel about that," I ask, "under the circumstances?"

"What? You leaving?"

"Yes."

"We're used to it," she says, stuffing the note in her purse. "People leaving."

"Still, it's important to name it, acknowledge how you feel."

"I guess."

"Anyone inside want to say anything?" I probe.

I watch her attempt to speak, then stop herself. Unsure, I imagine, whether the Flock's words are worthy of acknowledgment, or if they'll be dismissed—causing shame.

She uncrosses her legs. Kicks the rug between us.

"We can look after ourselves," she snarls.

I note the switch. Runner, I think. "Are you sure about that?" I ask.

"Yes, smart-ass." She leans forward in her chair, rests both elbows on her knees. "Tell me something, Doc," she says with a look of disdain. "Do you always interrogate patients before you're about to abandon them?"

Definitely Runner—angry, enjoying it, and getting off on my attempts to catch up.

"I'm not abandoning you."

"Go fuck yourself. Don't pretend you give two shits."

"But I do give a shit," I say. "I also have to make you conscious of the things you don't see."

"Really? God, you're such an asshole."

"Asshole? Really?"

She looks away.

"You're angry, upset that I'm leaving."

She flashes me a look of pure hatefulness and folds her arms. I disgust her.

"I'm not leaving you," I continue, "but it makes sense why you're angry."

She rolls her eyes.

"Like it or not," I say, "I do care."

"Liar."

"Seems like it's painful for you to accept someone might care."

"Pfft, *care?* No one's ever cared, apart from Ella. And now she's got different priorities too, just like you."

Silence.

I leave some space for her to feel the bite. The burn.

"That's tough," I finally say.

"What would you know?"

"Well, I don't know how it feels for you," I say, "but I know what it feels like to miss someone."

She looks up, scans my face for clues, then tilts her head as if hoping gravity might hold back her tears.

"Sounds like you really miss Ella," I say, keeping an eye on the time, "like you're worried about her. The choices she's making."

I know this is the point when the Flock will finally cease the fight. We've done this merry dance enough times. I know the drill.

And sure enough, her tears fall. Mascara leaving a trail of deep hurt. Time slows down and my heart feels for her, this triggering my missing of Clara. Of our life. I check in with myself and breathe. The truth that we take our patients only as far as we've gone ourselves, Alexa's loss resonating with my own grief.

She crimps her eyes, shakes her head. "Sorry, how long did you say you'd be away for?" she asks again, confused.

I note the memory lapse.

"Two weeks," I repeat. "There's a note in your purse with the dates." I point.

She taps the side of her head.

"The Fouls are telling me you don't care."

"That's not true, Alexa."

"They're threatening to hide my medication while you're away."

"They want to sabotage our work."

"They're saying you think I'm needy, pathetic."

"Alexa, listen to me. They're trying to destroy all the work we've done. Hello! If you're listening, I'm telling you straight—Alexa needs her medication. Stop punishing her. Come out and talk."

A pause.

"They refuse," she answers on their behalf.

"It would be helpful to discuss why parts of you believe I would think you needy and pathetic, and why they wish to harm you," I say. "You need to keep taking it, Alexa. Certainly while I'm away."

A pause.

"Please don't go," she says, staring out the window. "Please stay."

I check the gold clock on my desk.

"I'm afraid it's time," I say.

She remains, her legs parted. Hands resting between her thighs. Her vulnerability exhibited in her large green eyes, clear and wide. Her cheekbones suddenly appearing openly defined, her skin strikingly awake and luminous. The light between us seems suddenly to melt. My breathing jolts, my chest slowly tightening. She stands, strokes the tie on her blouse, and walks toward me.

"Hold me," she whispers.

I pause. "There are certain boundaries we need to keep."

She moves closer.

I catch my breath and stare at the open button on her blouse, her waist now resting in line with my eyes. Her body giving off the fresh scent of citrus. I feel my hands wanting to reach for her, take her in my arms and stroke her hair, allow my mouth her mouth. I imagine the immediacy between our bodies, the heat it builds. The air between us thick, swirling, forming a vacuum of space and longing. Each of our losses instantly gratified. Swiftly, I steady myself. My internal supervisor eventually helping me rise from my chair. I walk over to the door, my head light and swimming. Suddenly imbued with reason.

"It's time," I say again. "You must leave now."

24

Alexa Wú

I AM LYING IN A STRANGE BED, STICKY WITH HEAT. BESIDE ME, A WOMAN with nut-brown skin is sleeping soundly, her waist-length hair silky soft and smelling of rose.

Earlier, I was walking through Shoreditch—alone—with every intention of going home, but then I stumbled on a bar. Live music. People dancing. I was tired and a little dour after work, Jack's uncharacteristic irritability and his insistence that we organize the entire studio affecting my day. The Fouls shooting their mouths and adding to my already low mood. *Just one drink.*

Suck it up, buttercup, the Fouls had sneered, their sarcasm biting me like some rabid dog.

As the night wore on and the bar filled up, I was beginning to feel mortified about my meeting this morning with Daniel, the Fouls kindly reminding me how I'd tried to seduce him. Confronting my shame with another drink, this time a shot.

Slut, the Fouls hissed.

Another shot. And another.

Mood dipping further, I then began wondering about Amy and Annabelle, their brother. I had terrible thoughts in my head. *Was his body broken? Could he walk?* I tried calling Ella, but there was no reply.

Just a familiar voice asking me to leave a message as if from some faraway planet. Unreachable. One huge sky between us darkening like a savage bruise.

Face it, the Fouls scorned, *she's moved on.*

Flash.

AND NOW I'M HERE. *TICK-TOCK.* NOT DRINKING, OR IN A BAR. MY clothes strewn across a parquet floor. A not unpleasant feeling between my legs.

I slowly peel the Body away from the woman beside me, immediately cooler and free. But as I do, she stirs. I note she is wearing an expensive wristwatch, a faint tattoo of a hummingbird inked across the curve of her ass. I have no idea what day it is, or whether day is actually night. The blinds pulled down and masking any sign of life. A hangover fills my head.

Where are we? I ask.

No one answers. I try again.

Who's that beside us, naked?

Dolly giggles into her hand and scuttles away.

Runner? Oneiroi? I demand.

Her name's Robin, Runner finally whispers. *We met her at the O Bar. I really fancied her.*

You were drunk, Oneiroi adds.

I slide my hand down the Egyptian cotton sheets—no knickers.

Runner! I scream.

She smiles: the cat with the cream.

What? she says. *I have to put up with you and that idiot Shaun.*

I reach for my phone: 6:48. Wednesday. Good. I've lost only a few hours. Not days. *Phew.* I don't panic and instead gather my thoughts and bearings. Covering up dissociation, a skill we've acquired over time. Now I just need to figure out how best to leave without appearing rude.

I notice a carafe of water beside the bed, a drinking glass turned upside down and balanced on top. Robin has one too. She must make a habit of one-night stands, I think.

Probably, Oneiroi says, *but Runner and her really hit it off. They had a great time.*

Dolly giggles into her hand, *And they kissed, a lot!* she says shyly.

I look around. Diptyque everywhere and still alight. Violet dressing the early morning air. A vague memory of our martini-stained lips— kissing—eyes overzealous and glittering. Our legs tangled on her soft leather couch until we finally fell into bed.

I enter the bathroom along the corridor. It is not hard to find, all the black walnut doors left ajar, revealing expansive rooms with low-level furniture and chrome uplights.

Classy. Runner smiles.

Get back inside, I snap. *You've got us in enough trouble.*

Trouble? she says. *You should try it sometime. Beats those lowlife men you choose to sleep with.*

I pause.

Maybe she's got a point, I think to myself, smiling at another memory of us dancing together closely.

I turn on the tap, debating whether to use the purple toothbrush resting in a clear beaker, and then open the mirrored cabinet above. A spare. Good. I split the perforated cardboard edge with my fingernail, staring at the array of beauty products, a skyline of orderly neurosis. I smile softly to myself.

She must be an older woman, I say, fingering an antiaging face cream, various procollagen heroes.

Fifty-three to be exact. Runner shines.

A little old, don't you think? Oneiroi scoffs. *She's older than Anna.*

I brush my teeth, ignoring their banter, quietly noting the list of daily affirmations tacked to the cabinet's mirror:

YOUR BODY IS REALLY RATHER BEAUTIFUL

WE CAN ESCAPE THE PLACES WE WERE BORN AND RAISED
WE'RE VERY NORMAL, CONSIDERING THE MADNESS
WE'VE FELT AND COMMITTED

WE COULD DISAPPEAR—
FOR A WHILE

WE CAN FEEL FEARLESS ABOUT AN ORDINARY LIFE
WE PERHAPS HAVE ONE GOOD FRIEND
JUST FOR TODAY WE ARE WARM
THERE'S ALWAYS SOMEONE SUFFERING JUST THE
WAY YOU ARE

WE CAN REINVENT OURSELVES—A LITTLE

OF COURSE,
WE COULDN'T HAVE KNOWN

When I return to the bedroom, Robin is gone. I don't know whether to climb back into bed or search for her in the labyrinth of illustrious white chic. I look around, noting a stack of slim poetry books, loved and well-thumbed, resting on a mirrored dresser; a Basquiat print, dozens of blush peonies in an antique vase. Hanging from an armoire is a long vintage kimono, wisteria and cranes hand-painted across the collar. The sound of footsteps interrupts my curiosity.

Robin appears at the door, a cream cashmere dressing gown wrapped around her lithe body, hands working its tie as we catch each other's eyes.

"Coffee?" she asks, walking toward me.

Be nice to her, Runner says, her voice slow and cool. *Just stay for a little while, get to know her.*

"Thanks," I say, catching Robin's hand, "I take it black."

"Sugar?"

"Please."

Robin kisses my mouth.

"But first—" She smiles, guiding my waist.

We glide toward the bed, part of me sensing Runner's libidinous joy, the flutter of her belly like roused butterflies.

Okay, I get it, I say, *you like her.*

Runner smiles from the Nest, heart slamming against her chest as she pops an angled leg out like a precious gift, a hint that I might do the same for Robin's touch.

Wake me up when you're done. Oneiroi yawns. *I'm not into the whole older-woman thing.*

I pause, wondering:

We can reinvent ourselves—a little.

ROBIN HANDS ME A CUP OF POSTSEX COFFEE, ITS SMELL FAMILIAR, sweet and intense. Resting her fingers on my belly, she lightly lowers her stroke to my thigh. Stirred, I edge closer. Her touch all at once attuned and thrilling, her gaze locked on my slow sips.

"Do you have a girlfriend?" Robin asks.

"No." I smile, noting Runner, in the Nest, smoking her second Lucky Strike.

"Would you like one?" Robin shines.

"Maybe," I flirt.

She laughs, her head tilted back. There is luxury in her demeanor, fifty-three years affording her ease in both conversation and sex. I note how relaxed she feels in her skin, how aware she is of her presence and zeal. My whole being starts to sing like an aria of hope.

I told you she's amazing, Runner whispers.

You're right, I agree.

I try to imagine myself, momentarily, in three decades' time. Whether I too could inhabit such confidence and allure when asking a woman half my age if she might like to date.

"I like being with you." Robin smiles. "I like how easy it feels."

"Same," I say, immediately realizing I've spoken too quickly. Like I haven't given her words time to settle, or the respect and tenderness they deserve.

I place my coffee on the nightstand and lean into Robin's shimmering collarbone. Her smooth skin smelling, not unpleasantly, of sleep and sex. I scout around for a sentence, words that will let her know how good it feels to be with her. Words that will mirror her words.

Get out of your head, Runner whispers. *Just tell her how you feel.*

A pause.

"I'm damaged goods," I risk, "but I like being with you too. Too much, maybe."

"Does that frighten you?" she asks.

"A little," I say.

She smiles.

"You know what? We're all out of whack," she says.

I feel the Body relax. My limbs heavy and satisfied, like they've been massaged and stretched. A grateful pain washes over me, offering the sharp truth of what intimacy and kindness really feel like. I wonder why I've been avoiding this kind of closeness. Why I've steered clear of female touch. Part of me—*That would be me,* Runner says with a smile—always knowing women to be tender, yet somehow fearing their power.

Not every woman will leave you, Runner says, her eyes turning damp. The smoke from her cigarette now climbing the sky, like a bird. For a moment, I picture my mother—no warning that she was about to end her life. She and I had been at the kitchen table, pressing wildflowers that we'd picked on our way home from school between thin pages of heavy books. A telephone directory for her, a Gideon's Bible for me.

Flash.

THIS ONE'S PRETTY," MAMA SAYS, HOLDING OUT A FRESH BUTTERCUP and placing it beneath my chin.

"I can see you like butter." She smiles.

"Let me," I say.

Handing me the tiny yellow flower, my mother tilts her face north.

"You too," I coo, happy to be just like her. A lemon glow cast against her skin.

Flash.

She takes my hands.

"Never forget what you like and who you are," she says.

"I don't understand," I reply.

She kisses both hands. Her eyes drifting as if an invisible line has pitched her gaze toward the dining room door, ajar.

"Your baba, he wants us to be a certain way, to like what he likes," she whispers.

"Like a good girl?" I say, pressing down hard, the buttercup hidden. Flat.

I watch a single tear leave and travel down her cheek.

"Mama?" I say.

Flash.

"You *are* good." She finally speaks, her gaze now returned. "You mustn't forget that either."

Flash.

Robin leans in and kisses my neck.

"If you don't call me, I'll understand," she says. "But if you do, be ready—for something amazing. Something real."

I look away, her words aflame. A bird rising inside me, scorched wings, fear ignited should it fly too close to the sun and whirl to its death.

25

Daniel Rosenstein

How much time did you lose?"

"Couple of hours," she says, straightening the rug between us, "four, five tops."

"Do you plan on meeting her again?"

"I'm not sure; maybe." She shrugs, staring at two squabbling patients outside. "But I guess Runner might."

"And what about you?" I ask.

"She was lovely." She shrugs again. "But—"

"But?" I stare at her intently.

"I don't know," she says, "it feels scary somehow."

"How so?"

Silent, she looks away. Refusing my curiosity.

Today she arrived fifteen minutes early. Caught me daydreaming with a fistful of beef jerky as I turned the corner to my office. Startled, I held the dried meat behind my back as if hiding something I shouldn't have. The reality of unusual junk food for breakfast not something I wish to share with anyone, especially my patients.

"I'm early!" Her voice glowed. "I'll just wait here until it's time. Boundaries!" Then winked.

I smiled.

"See you shortly," I said, closing the door.

HER HAIR IS LOOSE TODAY. A CASUAL SWEATER THROWN OVER HER shoulders, a tight denim miniskirt buttoned over knitted leggings below a pale blouse. Clacking on her arms: a stack of bangles and bracelets, all different colors and shapes. An eccentric look, I think. Strange. I wonder who dressed her this morning, then suppose more than one of her was at work, each personality undecided or fighting for a say. I picture them, the Flock, all jostling for power like feuding siblings playing dress-up.

We sit in silence while I tongue a stubborn piece of jerky lodged between two top teeth, wondering if Alexa realizes her fear of intimacy is tied up with her mother's suicide. If she understands that her night with Robin has thrown her off course, her feelings of longing too much to bear.

She shuffles in her chair, pulls down on her skirt.

"I'm sorry about our last session," she starts up again. Her gaze now returned.

A pause.

"For?"

"For standing so close to you. I was confused. Forgive me."

"Boundaries are important, they—"

"I know," she interrupts, her voice slow and steady. "You said before."

"They keep us safe," I finish.

She stares down at the rug, a lick of shame in her eyes.

"Any time anyone shows me they care," she says, "I mistake it for thinking I have to have sex with them."

"That you're obligated in some way?"

"I guess."

"Scraps," I say.

She looks to me, perplexed.

"Your father offered you scraps and you were grateful. Part of you believed you were obligated—sexually."

"Yes."

"You were not."

"I know." She smiles shyly.

Silence lingers between us.

"I'm sorry," I say, "I still have to make you conscious of the things you don't see."

"I just want to feel loved," she whispers. "You and I being close like that—it felt nice. I liked it. *I'm* sorry."

I imagine her turning herself inside out: heart worn on her sleeve.

"Often when two people feel safe, or intimate," I say, "the feeling gets eroticized."

She looks up, a hot stare.

"I sometimes miss out on the intimacy bit," she says, "and jump straight into downright fancying."

"Like you did with Shaun?" I ask.

She nods. "Runner does the whole intimacy thing. She likes it. Makes her feel, you know, whole."

"Like last night?"

She smiles. A different smile now, coquettish. "It felt different . . . tender."

I lean forward. "And safe," I offer.

"And safe," she returns. She licks her lips, lowers her eyes.

"We just, you know, talked. Robin made lychee martinis." She giggles. "We drank a lot."

"The alcohol? It loosened you up."

She stares and then pinches her mouth, seemingly displeased. My interpretation, I realize, too hasty. A fat slice of distance wedged now between us. Damn.

"No," she says, "it didn't *loosen* us up. It was nice. Fun. *Safe*."

I fear I've dampened her mood now. Shamed and exposed her in some way.

"I'm sorry," I say, attempting to claw back the moment, "it wasn't my intention to make assumptions."

"Okay," she allows. Suspicious.

"Sounds like you and Robin had a good time," I add playfully, realizing I haven't quite won her back yet.

"Mm."

"I'm sorry," I repeat.

"It's okay, Daniel. Really."

"What about the lychee martinis, any good?" I ask.

"Yeah." She shines, her mood dropped like a pebble in a lake, minor ripples now killed. "They were lethal!"

We laugh.

S OME TIME AGO I WORKED WITH A YOUNG WOMAN NAMED JOANNA, who shared how after our sessions she would buy a sweet pastry on her way home. I thought I was being terribly clever offering interpretations such as: "You feel the need to sweeten our sessions," or "The pastry offers comfort for your hurt." The work eventually became stuck. There was nowhere left to go. I was robbing her of any self-discovery. That is, until I discussed our work with Mohsin, who suggested I ease off. "Ask her what kind of pastry," he said. "More curiosity, less interpretation."

What followed was a rich exploration into the sweet pastries, what they represented, and why Joanna made certain choices on particular days. Why when she felt rejected she would choose strawberry tarts—a specialty of her mother's that were baked every Sunday after her father left one morning, never to return. When she was angry she chose truffles. "They can be scarfed—whole," she said, "and lots of them." On the days she felt melancholic, Joanna ate almond croissants. She would slowly peel away the fine layers of flaky pastry until the feeling finally left her, by which time she'd usually reached the gooey almond paste inside: a reward for getting through the melancholia.

In remembering this, I recognize my clumsy interpretation of Alexa's story as unhelpful, just as my work with Joanna was limited at first. *Ease off on her,* I tell myself, *don't presume to tell her what she's thinking, or feeling. It will choke her, and stunt the analysis.*

I LOVE LYCHEE," ALEXA CONTINUES. "YOU?"

"With ice cream," I say.

"Ooh, or what about crushed pistachio or syrup?"

"Sounds delicious."

"When I was small my father used to do this trick. He'd peel the top off the lychee and pop the whole thing out in one go," she says with a laugh, "pretend it was one of his eyes." She shakes her head.

"A fond memory?" I ask.

"He had his moments."

"Though few and far between, as I recall."

Silence.

"I refuse to let him spoil my mood today," she says brightly. "That's good, right?"

"Right."

"I must be getting better."

Silence.

"Right?" she persists.

Not wishing to gratify, I simply offer her my eyes.

She clears her throat.

"Just for today I am strong. Just for today I will try my best to be the person I needed when I was young."

"Good," I commend.

She stares at me, seemingly grateful for my gentle stroke.

"I fear I'm becoming too dependent on you," she says, voice shaking at the edge.

"Three months with someone, and you're dependent?"

"So it seems."

"Does this have something to do with my going away next month?"

She nods.

"It's important we spend some time on this," I say, "so you can tell me how you feel. How my going away might trigger previous separations, or losses. Your mother, maybe?"

"I tried to in our last session."

I think back, trying to lasso memories of what she said, thinking I'll check my notes, but then I suddenly remember her words: *Please don't go, please stay.*

"You asked me not to go," I speak gently, "to stay."

"I know. I'm ridiculous."

"I disagree. I think you were being honest."

"And ridiculous."

"Maybe a touch punitive."

She smiles.

"Fancy a little holiday here at Glendown?" she jokes.

"I'm not sure the weather's up to it," I say.

"I hear they make a mean margarita in that cafeteria of yours."

"Never been that keen on lime."

"Manhattan?"

"Or whiskey."

"Lychee mocktail?" She winks.

"Now you're talking." I laugh.

She stands, and this time a playful warmth swirls between our bodies. The cheeky little cocktail dance is both enjoyable and spontaneous, proving much different from our last session. I note her ease and my appreciation. Her play something to inspire any shrink, sustaining joy when we start to flag, sometimes unappreciated. A slow but steady disenchantment built from years of giving.

26

Alexa Wú

CLOSING TIME. UGLY LIGHTS. THE SCRAPE OF CHAIRS BEING PULLED, flipped, and rested on the small mirrored tables while the cleaning crew wipes away sin. Ella catches my unease. Our spat, her threat of freezing me out at the Electra last month not fully resolved.

Jane, unsteady on a barstool, turns to face us. Her eyes wet, bloodshot, and pinched. Sylvie is seated beside her, a look of concern on her face while she strokes her friend's hand. I note a bloodied scuff on Jane's beautiful collarbones. A violet bruise on her knee. She flinches as we approach—a twitching hare—while Shaun moves clean glasses to the top shelf of the bar.

"Hey," Ella says, resting her hand on Jane's shoulder, both of us now close enough to smell the sharp liquor on her breath. "What happened?"

Jane looks down at the floor.

"I'm fine," she says, nodding her head. Her hair, I can see, is matted and plastered to her skull.

"No, you're not," Sylvie whispers. "Tell her what happened."

Jane throws her a look. "Sylvie, please."

"Why do you keep protecting him? *Why?*"

Ella moves forward. "You don't look fine," she says.

"I *said* I'm fine."

Ella grabs a barstool, drags it close, and sits so their knees touch. "Looks like you could do with a drink?"

Jane creates some distance by resting her long arms on the bar. "Whiskey, then," she allows.

"Make that two," Sylvie adds.

I walk toward Shaun, knowing we've been drifting apart for a while, his eyes, I note, avoiding mine.

"She needs some whiskey," I say, waiting at the tail end of the bar.

"Here, take the bottle," he says, guardedly reaching over to kiss my mouth.

Bystanding bastard, Runner says.

I offer him my cheek. Not able to fully accept his fancy. An awful and prudent realization that he doesn't *really* want me, or care about me. Not really.

When I return, Jane is knocking knees with Ella, a small bowl of water cupped in her unstill hands. Sylvie takes a cotton ball, dips it in, and pats the crown of her friend's head—blood turning the cotton pink.

"We got into an argument," says Jane. "Navid found out it was me who introduced Annabelle to Viktor."

"Viktor?" Ella and I chime.

"The Russian," she says, irritated. "We used to date."

Sylvie dabs her head and its sticky wound, this time leaving the cotton a while longer. "It's the only place the bruises won't show," she says, shaking her head. "Apparently punters don't like to pay to see battered strippers. It spoils the fantasy."

Her words find my gut, giving it a sharp twist.

"All right, Sylvie!" Jane barks, pushing Sylvie's hand away.

"Do you need to go to the hospital?" I offer.

"No," she says, reaching for a cigarette, "I have to wait here. Navid wants the other girls to see me like this. I'm to be made an example of, apparently."

"That's fucked up," Ella says.

"You only just realized?"

Runner suddenly seizes the Light, spotting Navid through a chink of open door next to the bar.

"Cocksucking son of a bitch!" she shouts. "Who does he think he is?"

Jane's eyes widen, hysteria rising in her throat—a crazed laugh released that her hand mutes.

"Shh," she whispers, grabbing my arm, "he'll hear you."

I nudge Runner back inside the Body, inwardly warning her to cut it out.

What? she says, giving him the middle finger. *He is a cocksucking son of a bitch!*

Ella checks the open door. "You need to leave, Jane. Get away from here. From him." She speaks quietly, suddenly panicked.

"I've been telling her that for years," Sylvie adds.

"*Leave?* Are you for real? Look what happened to Annabelle's brother when *she* left." Jane scoffs. "Do you know she came back the day after he was knocked down? She's so terrified something will happen to her and Amy that she begged Navid to take her back."

"Are you for real?" Ella asks.

"Ask her yourself."

"We have to leave, Jane. All of us. We don't have a choice," Ella says.

Jane sighs, knocks back her drink. Seemingly exasperated.

"What if we go to the police?" Ella whispers.

"What, you think they'd help? We can't trust the police. Most of them are in here taking payoffs. They have no interest in helping whores like us."

"Speak for yourself," Ella sneers, hiding her rising fear.

Jane steps down from her barstool, locks eyes, and leans in.

"You think you're different? *Special?*" She pokes Ella's chest, trails her finger all the way up, and takes hold of her gold key necklace, pulling firmly. "See this?"

"What about it?" Ella says.

"It can be taken away anytime. Don't get too cocky, or too comfortable. You saw what he did to Annabelle."

I realize now that the key necklaces are a way for Navid to control the Electra Girls, a certain kind of branding, gifts to groom. Put one foot wrong and you're out. Or worse still, your brother's knocked down by a hit-and-run. I watch Ella's throat swallow, her necklace mirroring Jane's, her position of top dog both intimidating and tragic.

"I just meant I can leave anytime," Ella speaks softly.

Jane lets go of the necklace and jabs Ella's chest again. "You think so? And what about your kid sister?"

Ella looks up, suddenly crestfallen.

"You know how I know about her?" she says. "Navid told me. Said he saw a photo of her on your phone. How pretty she was in her pink polka dots."

"My *phone*? What the fuck's he doing going through my phone?"

"He has access to whatever he wants," Jane interrupts, then turns a sly smile in my direction. "Ask Shaun."

"But she's only thirteen," Ella spits.

I suddenly remember Daniel's words: *Does Navid know that Ella has a younger sister?*

A swollen rattle finds my chest.

"Jane!" Shaun shouts. "Navid wants you out back."

"I'm coming with you," Sylvie says.

Jane slings her handbag across her shoulder, leaving the bowl of bloodied water as a reminder, a poke at our naiveté. She wipes her eyes with the back of her wrist.

"Be careful," she says, "and don't trust anyone. Including me."

Flash.

Don't trust anyone," the pale girl says, a can of Coke half-drunk and resting in her palm. I am fourteen years old. She is three years older. I note the pudge of her soft belly behind her black Lycra miniskirt as she sways back and forth. A tight-fitting T-shirt several washes away from clean. Rumors say she and her friend turn tricks for twenty quid. Thirty if you want them both.

Flash.

"I don't trust no one. Never have," she says, checking over my shoulder. "Smoke?"

"No thanks," I say.

"What, don't your mummy let you?"

"My mummy's dead," I say. This shuts her up.

Flash.

Another girl from the neighborhood walks toward us. Tiny steps. Quick. Skittish. Eyes fried, hands wringing.

"Jez's looking for you," she says, "he's at the liquor store, with a john."

The pale girl throws down the red can, adjusts the strap of her handbag, and pulls it across her chest like a bandolier. Like she's going into battle. Her armor: snide Louis Vuitton.

"You coming, or what?" she says.

I shake my head no. "Gotta help my dad clean the house."

The pale girl jumps down from the swing.

"Whatever." She shrugs and walks off, pulling her knickers out from her ass.

"Later," she calls back, winking.

Flash.

I wondered what they'd buy with the thirty quid. makeup? More cigarettes? I seem to remember Jez and his lone gold tooth waiting for girls in a blacked-out Beemer. Offers of free vodka, a ride, or a kiss if they were lucky. A night out if he felt like telling them he was their boyfriend. He could sniff out the vulnerable ones a mile off. Feral, wide-eyed girls searching for some scrap of attention that was missing at home. I didn't understand why the girls did it. Why did they let Jez use them like that? And then I remembered my own longing, all swollen and fat. Settling for scraps. The birds resting on the potting shed my only real source of comfort.

There's always someone suffering just the way you are.

My mind suddenly wanders, momentarily, to my night with Robin. How nice it had felt. The memory a stark contrast to those of my lonely teenage years.

Why don't we call her, Runner suggests, *just to say hi?*

I can't right now, I say. *Maybe some other time. I've too much on my mind.*

But—

Not now, Runner, I say.

Runner throws me a look, disappointed it seems.

Maybe when I'm less stressed, I offer. *And anyway, Robin wouldn't want me to call until I can commit—until I'm ready.*

Fair point, she agrees.

Flash.

AND NOW WE'RE OUTSIDE. *TICK-TOCK*. SHAUN, ELLA, AND I. IN THE cold. Shaun walking ahead as usual. I picture Navid's fists crashing into Jane's head. A growl from his deeply unpleasant mouth. Jane crouches. Another swipe, his orange paws unable to stop, smothering her with his stripy mass. Roars of hate as she attempts no escape, her need for him far too great. The ominous necklace with its key held tenderly to her chest.

Ella blows into her hands, then wraps her arms around her body like a straitjacket, patting her back for warmth. November's tail end whipping our ears and cheeks.

Suddenly she stops. A pulse on the side of her neck pounding as she waits for Shaun to gain distance from us. She pulls me in close, her breathing raspy and quick.

"What?" I say, the Electra's neon sign casting a vermilion glow.

She looks me dead in the eye.

"We have to take the bastard down," she whispers, firmly holding my collar. "We don't have a choice. Get close to Shaun again; he knows everything about Navid. Do whatever it takes. Use him."

I take in her words. My *Reason*, I realize, suddenly making logical but terrifying sense.

27

Daniel Rosenstein

YOU CAN BREAK IT OFF ANYTIME YOU WANT," I SAY. "FROM MY UNDER-
standing you and Shaun haven't been getting along for a couple weeks
now."

"Ella doesn't think so, she thinks we should use him. She wants
me to get close to him again, find out as much as I can about Navid
so we can go to the police, take him down—if we have enough evidence,
we can do that. She has a plan."

"Ella's wrong."

She looks up, falling silent. Vexed that I've challenged their friendship. Again. I make a note of the splitting that's occurring between Ella
and me. Her best friend, her shrink. *Who will win?* I wonder.

"Is it time?" she asks.

I check the clock.

"Couple of minutes," I say.

"I have to take Grace to the dentist."

"How come?"

"Ella's busy. And their mum's still out of town."

She taps her foot, stretches her neck from side to side. I note she is
tired. Crusted sleep she hasn't bothered to wipe away. Her listless eyes
eventually landing on the oil painting above my head.

Her dismissiveness concerns me. A refusal to engage with the likely danger of their plan something she's barely acknowledged today. *This isn't some silly game,* I want to shout, *some TV drama where the bad guys get a good kicking.*

She stares at the painting, bored and beautiful. Crosses her arms over her chest.

What or *who* is she withholding from me? And why?

"Sometimes," she says, picking a zit on her chin, "this fucking therapy really sucks."

28

Alexa Wú

Y**OU CAN'T BREAK IT OFF WITH HIM," SHE INSISTS AS SHE WEAVES A** braid into Grace's hair. "Daniel's wrong. Shaun knows things. Things that will help us."

"I don't know, Ella, the thought of sleeping with him and—"

"Just imagine it's someone else. Close your eyes."

Grace covers her ears.

"I can't," I whisper, "I'll still know it's him."

Runner reaches in her purse for a cigarette. *Pretend it's Robin instead,* she says, stirred.

Time reveals things. Bad things. Like rotting fruit, curdled milk—a boyfriend who gorges on porn and believes stripping and sex work are choices made by women. "After all, if you've got a body like *that,* why wouldn't you?" he had said, pretending to wipe down the bar, ogling Amy and Annabelle, who'd returned the day after her brother was run over. "I mean, check these girls out—the way they earn cash, pfft, they put city boys to shame!"

"It's exploitation," I shouted, "modern slavery."

"Sex sells, baby." He had shrugged.

Time lets you know a person. It's a vandal.

Ella looks up at me, working Grace's bangs.

"You have to help me, *otherwise*"—she points down at Grace's crown—"we're fucked."

Grace turns to face Ella; turns back to face me.

"All done," Ella sings, dropping the hairbrush on the bed. "Now go do something. Anything! Leave me alone."

Grace breaks from her crossed legs and grabs her phone. Scrolls and double-taps.

"See you later, Alexa." She smiles, leaving.

"Bye, Grace." I smile back.

Ella flops down on the bed.

"What's wrong?"

She clears her throat and I sense she's gearing up for something. Like a racehorse with a sprint to win awaiting the sharp shot of a gun.

"There's this house," she begins, "in London Fields."

I wait.

"Some of the Electra Girls live there. Navid's been bringing in girls from overseas. He's been filming them. Shaun too."

"Porn?"

Ella nods. "Cassie's brother, Tao, he's bringing them here illegally. Girls from China, Laos, and Vietnam. Girls from poor families who sell them on for work."

I gasp. "Holy shit."

I'd heard about this kind of thing: modern-day slavery—millions of human beings trafficked each year, usually women and girls. I'd read about it, seen it on the news, sex trafficking among the world's fastest-growing criminal industries.

"Has Shaun said anything?" Ella asks.

"He mentioned some time back Navid wanting to make more *use* of the girls."

"We need to do something to stop it. Find enough proof so Navid gets arrested. We'll gather evidence that shows the girls are being exploited, lured by false promises and sold. Some of these girls are underage. We have to do this, Alexa, otherwise—"

"*Otherwise?* For fuck's sake, Ella, I cannot believe it. I told you *not* to do this. I told you not to work there. Now you've put us *all* in danger, including Grace. Just because you wanted to make some extra cash. You live like there's no fuckin' tomorrow and yesterday never happened!" I scream.

She looks behind her as if Grace's footsteps may have left an imprint. "I know," she says with meaning, "you're right. But we can make a difference, help the girls. Protect Grace. Please, Alexa, I need you."

Silence.

"You can be so fuckin' selfish," I say, not letting up.

The expression on Ella's face is low-spirited and heartbreaking.

Oh god, what a situation to be in. What are we going to do? the Flock question, suddenly alert to my mood.

I'm quickly grateful to have photography in my life, knowing it's kept me straight. Focused. Sane-*ish*. Like Ella, I could have taken risks, compromised myself, acted covertly to quell my pain. I could have lied, deceived, turned violent against those who didn't do what I asked of them. But unlike Ella, I've done my level best not to knock on dangerous doors thinking my sexuality could serve my greed.

Breathe, Oneiroi suggests, *you're getting yourself all worked up.*

Shoulders trembling, I try to stop myself from judging Ella, and fail. I turn away. The real reason I'm so angry is because I feel powerless and ignored, her refusal to listen and think beyond herself seemingly a trial. What I really want to do is shake her back to regular life. The hope that she might inhabit her body differently—no longer craving permission, looking to others (particularly men)—and find a solid place in the world.

Ella grabs the hairbrush off the bed, plucks at one of its plastic bristles.

"There's something else you should know," she says, her leg twitching like a captive hare. "Some of the girls in the house, they're even younger than Grace. Probably nine or ten."

I suddenly picture Poi-Poi. Her blue shorts with the lace trim. Her bare legs pimpled with cold—*I'm not stupid, and don't call me Britney.* I feel my head spin. A metal taste released and spreading in my mouth. I should have known this was coming, I think; *I'm* the stupid one.

Evening. I float through Ella's neighborhood in a stunned calm. My armpits drenched, head insistent that it reorganize itself to focus and accept our dire situation. I kick the tire of a car, half expecting an alarm to shriek. Nothing. Ella's words rattling around my skull: *But we can make a difference . . . Please, Alexa, I need you.*

This is really happening, I tell myself, crossing the street toward a swinging gate, a choke of hedges where a single blackbird is resting. I pause, leaving enough distance so as not to startle the hushed bird.

"Do you have my mother's soul with you today?" I ask.

The common blackbird stares. Its slim marigold beak and matching ringed eye unmoved.

"Because if you do," I say, "let her know I'll be fine. The Flock and I will be careful. I promise."

A mellow song suddenly beguiles the silenced street. The blackbird's tune faultless and falling gently on my ears, arousing calm. A bewitching wing raised as he balances—an exhibitionist—on the tiniest of twigs.

I value my garden more for being full of blackbirds than of cherries,
and very frankly give them fruit for their songs—

As a child I was not entirely comfortable with being seen. To be seen meant I had to engage with others and sometimes do things that I did not want to do. It meant people would have expectations of me, expectations I couldn't meet or didn't *want* to meet. A squirm of galling self-consciousness wriggling around inside me when mistakes were made, or when wrong words were spoken. Sometimes it meant I was considered amusing or desirable, and was touched inappropriately, and this, I think, was the worst way possible of being seen. Occasionally I'd try to make myself invisible, slinking off in the background and making quiet my voice, the truth of who I was and how I felt safely masked and protected by all the personalities I'd hidden inside.

Flash.

LET'S PLAY HIDE-AND-SEEK," MY MOTHER SAYS, TAKING MY HAND A little too firmly.

"I'll go first," she insists, a slight mania in her eyes.

Upstairs, I hear my father slam a door. We both flinch.

My mother smiles. "Count to twenty, then come find me," she whispers.

Flash.

I cover my eyes.

". . . eighteen, nineteen, twenty. Coming!" I shout.

Behind the dining room curtains, the coat rack; beneath the kitchen table; on the outside porch; behind the sofa—

"Found you!" I call.

My mother kisses my cheek. "Clever girl," she says, eyes fixed on the door.

"Now it's your turn," she says, "but this time you have to hide a little longer. Look, I've got *Chicken Licken* here for you to read. And here's Nelly. Now go hide. But you can't come out until I find you. Okay?"

"Okay," I agree. Unease yanking on my tummy.

Tick-tock—

Tick-tock—

When my mother returned, I'd fallen asleep at the bottom of my wardrobe. I watched her attempt to hide the violet bulge on her cheek. Her lip cracked and bleeding.

"There you are," she said, attempting to smile. "You clever girl."

Flash.

I THINK IT TAKES A LONG TIME TO BE TRULY SEEN IN THE PRESENCE OF others. I imagine it's one of the reasons why I turned the focus outward, my camera acting as a distraction to view anything other than me as I became an observer. I was someone who was invisible yet who saw everything. There was safety in not being seen back then, but I now realize it came at a cost, because if you are someone without a voice or someone who isn't seen, you are also easy prey.

29

Daniel Rosenstein

I WAIT MY TURN FOR THE ROWING MACHINE, A PATCH OF COOLED SWEAT blooming on my chest like a target, my heart pumping like a rhythmic ashiko drum. All around me, hot bodies are working hard to build muscle, stretch, strengthen, and strain—their faces alive with determination. I note that my energy feels good tonight. A grateful pain surging through my arms and legs from the weights I've pressed, the miles I've run, muscles slowly cooling down as I stand, waiting.

Taking a paper cone, I fill it with chilled water, drink, then disregard, the rower's sliding back and forth causing my concentration to drift. My breath gently slowing.

"Daniel!" I suddenly hear, and turn.

It takes me a moment to realize it's the Old-Timer.

"Hey, man," I say, noting my anxiety rise. Our compartmentalized worlds outside recovery now collided and momentarily awkward. "You a member here?"

"Joined last month," he says.

I take another cone—bend, fill, and drink.

"Thirsty?" he says.

"Hot," I say.

I note the tiny glistening beads of sweat across his forehead, a white towel worn casually like a scarf. His ebony skin pulled tightly across worked biceps, legs strong after squats, confidence leaking after years of ostentation and self-care. I breathe in and rest my hands on my thickening waist.

"I'm going for a steam, fancy it?" I ask.

"I'm heading home now," he says. "Another time, maybe?"

I nod, feeling a combination of relief and rejection as he wipes his palms down his fitted blue shorts. But the moment he turns and walks away I feel his slug of abandonment, familiar and braw, wishing he'd said yes.

In the steam room, three men are seated and discussing plans for the night, towels tucked loosely at their waists. *Gorillas in the mist.* One of the hairy men maneuvers his thick legs, making way for my arrival, nods, and then inhales with some effort the wet scent of minty-pine eucalyptus.

I lean back, worked muscles now loosening, the menthol heat opening up my chest. A lightness gradually felt in my head and causing a release of the day's events. My mind drifts to Clara. I picture her dancing on that first night we met, a puff of red taffeta in her wake, shoes flung in some distant corner of the community hall while both men and women watched in awe. And then that kiss, our first of many fine kisses—*I miss you, my love, we both do. Susannah thinks me a fool. A needy old fool. She believes she's in love—*

The door opens, mist clouding my sight before I finally realize the Old-Timer is standing beside me. Is close enough that I feel his leg graze my leg. He bends down, hands me a paper cone of chilled water.

"Have a good night." He smiles, stroking me lightly on the shoulder. "See you next week."

"See you." I smile, aware the men are watching and alert to our intimate and somewhat unexpected exchange.

When the door closes I drink the triangle of water, then scrunch the damp paper with my fist. I lower my eyes again, a puff of freshly released mist clouding my view and acting as a smoke screen to what I imagine to be male side glances and hushed words. The image of Clara in her red dress suitably alive in my mind.

30

Alexa Wú

FANTASTIC." JACK SMILES, HIS LEFT EYE RESTING ON A LOUPE ATOP A contact sheet of magnified black-and-white images, his right eye closed for added focus. He slides from his ear an old-school red grease pencil and circles his favorites, my heart jumping sideways with each mark. On the count of his five preferred snaps I have to look away, my flustered chest about to burst.

"*Really?*" I say, a little too meekly.

"Here." He points, handing me the loupe. "That's the one!"

His favored shot: Billy on a swing with enormous blue-gray eyes, red wellington boots, his mother, Sandra, pushing him from behind. Grimacing in the background are all the trappings of a controlled demolition site: bright yellow machines, abandoned brick walls, and men at work. The sky a blanket of moving black clouds.

The photograph, I'd hoped, would speak of people living on the margins. Individuals and communities operating against the wrinkle of greed. Fat cats getting fatter. Defenseless birds forced to take flight. The wreckage of the boy's village, no longer able to raise him the way it might if communities mattered in the slightest.

Jack smiles again.

"Great work, Alexa," he says, squeezing my shoulder. "Email it over to the news desk and CC me."

Yes, well done, Oneiroi adds, planting a delicate kiss on my cheek.

I settle at my computer and log into my account, Jack's praise causing emotion inside me to rear, pride swelling and alive like I'm winning. I've known for some time that after my mother killed herself, my longing for recognition was boundless—much like a tidal wave or some titanic tree without roots—my ache for validation overwhelming and vast.

I click on Jack's chosen shot.

"You know, you've adjusted so quickly," he speaks across his shoulder. "Some of my other assistants haven't been able to cope with the stress, you know, the obstacles that come with this kind of work: long hours, crowds, physical danger—but you've managed to juggle three or four things at once. Amazing." *If only you knew,* I think, the Flock overhearing and agreeing from the Nest.

I turn to Jack, who is still holding the A4 contact sheet of images, suggestive of a world askew; his concentration pinned on Borough Market's *gritty and real* outtakes, a pleased look on his face. I am suddenly stirred by his zeal, aware of the Flock also blushing with joy: Dolly's excitement to hug Jack's waist, Oneiroi's desire to kiss his mouth, Runner's cool high five, and the Fouls' slow, dismissive glare.

I eventually settle on a broad smile while keeping a strong hold on the Light, the Body seemingly delighted to have achieved something good, something that might make a difference to a little boy and his mother.

31

Daniel Rosenstein

THERE'S A PARCEL HERE FOR YOU," THE RECEPTIONIST SAYS.

"Can you bring it through, please?"

Outside, Nurse Veal is walking the stretch of early morning lawn, a pair of navy mittened fists clenched behind her back. Blades of grass frosted like they've been dipped in sugar. She approaches Charlotte, huddled in a lumpy wool overcoat, a tray resting on her lap that I suspect is holding an unfinished jigsaw puzzle. The border always completed first. They chat for a while, Charlotte blowing on her fingers. Her warm breath releasing a dense fog.

A knock on the door.

"Come in," I order.

The Receptionist approaches with a neat dash of efficiency and hands me the parcel. Her hair set free rather than in her usual twist.

"Thank you," I say.

She smiles.

"How's things? Your daughter settling into academic life?" I ask freely, knowing her daughter has recently left home. A bachelor's in history sweeping her north to Edinburgh University.

"Good, thanks," she says, yet I am not convinced. "Yes, *she's* doing great. Not so sure about me, though," she jokes, her voice shaking at the edge.

"Do you miss her?" I ask gently.

She nods, fingers the small gold clock on my desk, determined not to cry.

Silence.

"It's hard letting daughters go," she finally says.

"It is, but it's important that we do," I lie.

I picture Susannah at her birthday party, popping a champagne cork, her home bristling with attractive young people. Their love for her had felt like a shot in the arm. But as she smiled, I wasn't entirely convinced: her jaw just a little tight, her attention faltering and somewhat preoccupied. "Speech!" one of her friends called, causing Susannah to blush a hot pink that almost matched her dress. "Speeeech!"

Her mild discomfort had bothered me, so I immediately stepped forward, considering a speech on her behalf, wanting to relieve her of her squirm. But then *he* stepped in. Drunk and entitled. His arm clamped around Susannah's red waist.

THE RECEPTIONIST COLLECTS A STRAY TISSUE FROM THE FLOOR—probably Charlotte's—as if it's her responsibility, neither avoiding nor begrudging the balled evidence of hurt. As she leaves, I regard the tan parcel, turning it over in search of a return address, suspicious of anonymity. There isn't one. My address, however, is written in large cursive handwriting, rather like a child's. Cautiously, I slice open the paper and bubble wrap with Lucas's silver letter opener. Inside: a martini glass and a white paper bag bristling with fresh lychees. Around the stem of the glass is a small swing tag. On it, written in a slightly different hand:

Cheers!
Love, the Flock xx

A gift.

I bite the top off one of the rubbery lychees and pop the slippery flesh out whole, picturing Alexa, a little girl, laughing at her silly dad. The man who continues to live, rent free, in her head. Troubling her with his visits like some psychological squatter. I chew on the sweet fruit, spitting its smooth black pip in the metal waste bin beneath my desk. *Ping.*

I picture Alexa. Her hands stroking the loose tie on her blouse. Her waist a skyline for my greed. Jade-green eyes absorbing every flickering feeling she has aroused in me.

I take out my notebook.

Alexa Wú: November 29

I have received a parcel from the Flock: a bag of fresh lychees and a martini glass. This after a rather lively and playful session where Alexa tried to convince me to not go on vacation (see p. 123 of notes). A different hand was used to write on the envelope and the note attached. Her playfulness is indication that parts of her trust our relationship. I am interested by this, but also intrigued to think about the eroticization of her gift-giving—

I wonder, is this a gift that a girlfriend might send you . . . ?
Note countertransference: Zealous, aroused. Conflict.

32

Alexa Wú

A STERILE ZING OF MOUNTAIN PINE MIXED WITH STEAMED LOTUS ROOT invades my nostrils. Not an entirely unpleasant smell, I think.

Are you kiddin'? Runner says, masking our nose. *It stinks!*

And now Dolly joins in: *Yeah; it's real pongy, Alexa.*

I look around the unfamiliar kitchen, small and desperately clean. A square mountain of paper towels waiting next to a pair of pink rubber gloves that are hanging over the sink like some Dalíesque udder of a cow. On the windowsill: a white plastic lucky cat charged with sunlight, waving its paw up and down, up and down. Its slow smile teetering on menace.

Home is where we start from . . .

—a decorative sign reads, nailed above a tower of rice bowls stacked like the leaning tower of Pisa. The hum of the oven extractor so loud and cranky—like turbines of an airplane—that it feels like the kitchen walls are about to blow off at any second.

Cassie moves from wok to oven, oven to wok. Slow and meditative. A minor excursion to an oak chopping board where bok choy lies washed and limp, her hands wielding a precise steel chopper that would do well in the woods.

"We'll just stay for a while," Ella whispers. "I've promised I'll take Grace to see a movie later."

"Okay." I nod.

She knows I have mixed feelings about being here. Had checked in with the Flock before we arrived—Runner stepping out and saying, "We'll be okay," on our behalf.

Ella watches Cassie flip the wok—soy sauce added for salt—and wait for the right moment between the rise and dip of flames to taste. The smell of garlic and chili is so delicious I feel my tummy roll.

"Navid said you might need help setting up one of the rooms," Ella shouts over the oven extractor, "or with some of the girls. He mentioned them needing a little help with their English."

Cassie smiles. "One minute," she says, wringing the chopped bok choy, water leaking from the floppy dark green leaves like from a shaken umbrella. With an air of satisfaction she throws the greens on top of what I know to be pig's trotters, then adds a slather of honey, a scattering of sesame seeds. This was one of my father's favorite dishes. Suddenly, in a flash of remembrance, I picture my father, so alive he could be here right now, devouring the glistening, sweet flesh, his nose deep in the pot of suckling pig, the smell catapulting me back. His hair slicked back, a blaring-white shirt with its sleeves folded at his elbows.

Ella turns to me, then eyes three late-teen girls in various states of undress, their legs crossed, waiting around a low wooden table. Together they huddle around a ritual of green tea, four tiny cups. The most delicate cup set aside for Cassie, with a swirling orange dragon chasing its tail. One of the girls reaches for a set of chopsticks resting in a mug of disinfectant. She looks me up and down, stabs her sleek bun with one of the sticks.

"Tā mā de xiāngjiāo!" She snickers.

The three girls cackle like *Macbeth*'s weird sisters—

Fair is foul,

and foul is fair;

Hover through the fog and filthy air.

I don't respond, knowing not to show my bilingual hand just yet. Their internalized racism and self-loathing like an invisible dagger turned in upon themselves, and then out again at me. Their faces all twisted. I realize it is a learned behavior so entrenched that they can only hate.

Cassie bows her head close to the sticky pig's trotters and inhales, her nose almost touching the glazed succulent flesh. With her bok choy hand she spoons up the glistening aromatic liquid. Takes a slurp.

"Mm, good meat. Try some," she says, offering me her spoon.

I walk over. Bend down and taste.

"Mm. Nice," I say, the flavor reminding me of my father's world.

She pulls at the pork with pinched fingers, offering me the familiar flesh. "Builds strength, this meat. Hǎo bu hǎo?"

"Good." I nod.

"You speak Mandarin?" she asks.

I turn and face the three girls.

"Shì." I speak sharply. "Wǒ bùshì tā mā de xiāngjiāo!"

Cassie lets out a screeching laugh. Throws an unexpected tea towel at the three tea-sipping girls.

"Oh, she's smart!" she shouts. "And she's no xiāngjiāo!"

Cassie spoons me another taste. "Where are you from?"

"Here," I say. "But my dad's from Guihua Subdistrict."

"No!"

I nod. "Yep, he came over a long time ago."

"Still see him?"

"No."

She places her hand on my shoulder. "I'm from Xintangpo. Your dad would know this—Guihua, Xintangpo, and Daijialing were all part of the township before they got moved into the district." Laughing, she slaps my back, making me aware of her strength. "We're practically neighbors! Like family."

I fake-smile, joining in with her spirited joy. *Hahahahahahahaha.* I *will* gain her trust, I tell myself. *Hahahahahahahaha.* Shaun. Cassie. I will fool them both and get what we need to take that bastard Navid down. *Yeah,* Runner agrees, *we'll gather as much evidence as we can against them here and at the club—the illegal girls, the videos, the money laundering—then we'll take it to the police.*

I'll drain him dry as hay.
Sleep shall neither night nor day
Hang upon his penthouse lid.
He shall live a man forbid.

WHAT WAS THAT ALL ABOUT?" ELLA ASKS, HEADING UP THE SANDED wooden stairs to the second floor, me following with my portable fake smile.

"They called me a banana, a xiāngjiāo. Yellow on the outside, white on the inside."

"That's horrible!" she says, pulling a face like a child being forced to eat vegetables.

"I know," I say. "It hurts. Fucking bitches."

"Do you think those girls speak any English at all?"

"A little, maybe," I whisper. "Navid and Cassie will want them to know enough to follow directions and run errands, but not so much that they're *too* independent. That's probably why he's asked you to help them. What did he say?"

"Just that. To teach them the basics. Nothing else."

"Makes sense. If they're self-sufficient they might cause havoc."

You're right, Runner adds, *best way to control anyone is to have them feel as far away from home as possible. That includes not understanding the language where they live.*

I COUNT A TOTAL OF FIVE BEDROOMS IN THE GROOM HOUSE: THREE ON the top floor and two on the second. The walls are mostly bare, save for the occasional postcard or watermark. Cassie rears up behind us and points us into a small room with whitewashed walls just like the dressing rooms in the Electra. A red silk sarong hangs from a pole made of pine.

I steal a look in the room next door: two single beds nudged together, a king-size duvet to share. In the corner is a gigantic plush panda with huge jet glass eyes.

Looks stoned, Runner sniggers.

The panda reminds me of the toys seen at fairgrounds but rarely won, the lure of their size and cuteness always more appealing than the half-dead goldfish, which is more often the prize.

Cassie shifts a single mattress with her bare foot, knocking over a Hello Kitty alarm clock and a silver-framed photograph of Poi-Poi with two people I assume are her grandparents. The three of them are playing on the beach, sun beating down. I pick up the frame and place it on the pine dresser. A smiling Poi-Poi stares back at me, hair pigtailed, hands busy patting a blue plastic sand castle bucket. A yellow spade raised to the clear sky.

"These girls," Cassie warns, tapping the frame with a dismissive hand, "too stupid, too sentimental about home."

"Where is home?" I ask.

"All over," she says, pushing the old mattress against the wall. "Different girls, different homes."

The three of us drag the mattress out of the small box room, instructed by Cassie to lean it against the curving stair banister—a trail of crisp packets, melon drop candy wrappers, and an *Angelina Ballerina* magazine caught under the mattress's lumpy weight.

Opening the room's small window, Ella lets in the night breeze. Several dead flies lie scattered on the windowsill, legs in the air, wings weighted with dust. She aims and flicks each one. I imagine them landing beside the red bamboo plants below, their tiny insect bodies eventually freezing from the bitter cold. A picture of my mother's ending suddenly comes to mind, hers being quite the opposite of the flies'. A blowtorch swiftly worked on her broken body, a hot fire erasing her from my world.

"This room will be used for films now. Movie Room," Cassie says, manicured hands pressed against her wide hips. A sheen of sweat sliding across her upper lip.

"When do we need to have it ready by?" Ella asks.

"Next week. First, I need to buy a new bed. Make it look pretty," she says with a flicking gesture of hands. "Big clients with money want to watch our beautiful girls."

My stomach churns. An acidy, retching, thick-phlegmy, vile lurch.

"These girls," she continues, "so lucky. They have good lives. Good care. Plenty of money. Taken from poor homes to live here like princesses."

Liar! Runner shouts, causing me and the Body to jolt.

Cassie reaches for two large cardboard boxes stacked in the far corner of the room, sleek gaffer tape holding their edges.

With a penknife she slices the sticky tape. "Here," she says, handing Ella a boxed camcorder and me a tripod. "Take these."

She then recovers two webcams, a couple of hard drives, microphones, a DSLR, and a stream deck. Their instructions printed in Chinese. A mountain of clear, tiny-blistered bubble wrap spilling out on the floor like frogspawn.

"Tao, hǎo xiōngdì!" She shines.

"He lives in China, your brother?" I ask.

"Yes," she says, "for many years now."

She turns away.

Ella looks at me.

"You must miss him," I say.

"Must be difficult," Ella adds.

Cassie wipes her forehead with the back of her hand, the other attempting to flatten the box.

"Sometimes." She smiles, canines tinged with a treacherous brown like they've been dipped in tea. Payback for all the shit she talks.

I smile.

"I'll do this one," I say, grabbing the second box and emptying it of two more hard drives and cuddly stuffed animals, a smaller box inside filled with makeup and pastel sex toys.

"Thank you," she says, squeezing both my and Ella's arms like we're friends, "then we'll eat."

"Great," I say, stroking my belly. But as she turns I quickly slip a form labeled *Sender's Invoice* into my back pocket, Tao's address printed on the back. I pull out my phone.

Evidence #1

The Good Brother, Tao Wang, Pornographer/Trafficker.

Lives in mainland China.

Well done, Runner says.

I take a moment to think of the girls downstairs, trafficked under false pretenses. I think about the homes they were snatched away from, or the homes they never had. The pornography they'll be forced into by men who pay. I think about the webcams, the equipment. The hard drives. And their bodies: too young, too fragile, and still flowering.

And I think about the lies. The lies, most of all, are what haunt me most.

33

Daniel Rosenstein

A FEW DAYS AGO I TRIED HAVING A CONVERSATION WITH A BLACKBIRD," she says. "Do you think I'm mad?"

"Did it reply?"

She laughs. "Excellent diversion. And no, he didn't."

"It was a *he*?" I say.

"Most definitely."

"How do you know this?"

"Females are brown. Juveniles a reddish-brown. *He* was glossy black."

"So, you're an ornithologist."

She shrugs.

"Your talents are endless."

"Thank you," she allows.

A pause.

"I have this crazy idea that birds carry my mother's soul with them. It's been a way for me to keep her close. There will always be birds."

"Just like the Flock?"

"I guess they're an extension of her," she says, suddenly animated, "like family. You know, their personalities guiding me like a family might."

"Not all families get along," I offer.

"Quite," she says, crossing her legs. Her body slowly stretching. A switch? Possibly.

I take a sip of water, an eye on the time, making a mental note of my ongoing curiosities regarding mothers and fathers. For a moment I picture my parents, both still alive and rattling around their allotment. I feel relief they still have each other for company yet know one day this will not be the case, a guilty though honest hope that it will be my father who dies first.

Looking back, I believe my Oedipal complex was rampant as a child. I was not completely comfortable with sharing my mother with anyone—especially my father. She was my absolute world. I would orbit her, like Saturn; in the kitchen while she baked, in the bathroom as she applied cold cream to her neck, at the bottom of the garden as she pulled cabbages from the vegetable patch. I was constantly fearful she could be taken away at any moment, just like the time when I was six years old and witnessed her rushed to the hospital after her heart had shivered.

"Are you dying?" I asked my mother while I stood glancing at her flat body.

"I certainly hope not, Daniel. It's Christmas in two weeks."

My father told me that it was my fault my mother's heart was under attack.

"All your soddin' whining. That's what's done it." He spoke with stern resentment. He was sober at the time, no whiskey to take the edge off his barbed and misguided comment.

To give a child that much power has its repercussions. Naturally, I became petulant and precocious, omnipotent and almighty, believing that when it rained, I had caused it. That when a long-awaited bus arrived it was me my father should thank for the two available seats.

I understand now that this magical thinking was an attempt to gain agency while my mother lay in hospital, a desire so deep within me to reclaim control while feeling so utterly powerless.

Years later when Clara died, my worst fear came true. I was abandoned. Lost from the one whom I loved most in the world aside from my mother. My wife disappeared and would not be returning, however insistent my heart, however deluded my magical thinking.

I TAKE ANOTHER SIP OF WATER, MY REVERIE NOW SET ASIDE.

Alexa, or I'm pretty sure Oneiroi, touches the soft part of her neck.

"By the way, thank you for the lychee. They were a nice surprise," I say, a slice of guilt felt at recalling how I'd eroticized the gift, pictured her stroking the loose tie on her blouse.

"My pleasure," she says, fingering her collarbone. "Although I can't take full credit. It was Alexa's idea, but Dolly and Runner packaged them."

"Thank you. Everyone," I say.

She looks to the floor, shuffles in her seat, gently tugging at the hem of her skirt.

"So, by projecting your mother into living creatures—the birds—you preserve her somehow?"

"Her soul. I preserve her soul."

"I see."

"So, am I mad?" she asks.

"I'd say you're a thoughtful and sensitive observer." I smile. "Someone who misses her mother a great deal."

"You're very sweet." Oneiroi shines.

34

Alexa Wú

I RUSH TO POLISH ME PRETTY, ALREADY A HALF HOUR LATE. THE USUAL sugary *ting-a-ling* turning into an angry *dong* when I burst through the door.

"Sorry," I whisper, gritting my teeth, trying my very best to close the door quietly. Three girls look up in synchronicity and then return to their chattering. I spot Ella at the back of the salon deciding on a color, hand on hip. Hundreds of nail polish bottles lined up side by side like candy.

I creep up behind her.

"HAPPY BIRTHDAY!" I sing, squeezing her waist. A gift in my hand.

Startled, she turns.

"Fuck," she says, holding her heart like it's about to escape. "You scared me."

The three girls throw us a look, their nails baking under UV lights while they share a joke.

Ella flings her arms around my neck—an overexcited child—eyes ablaze from the new Fendi clutch I've blown a whole month's wages on.

"Like it?" I smile.

"*Like it?* I *love* it! I don't know what to say." My *Reason* sparkles with delight.

I blow on curled fingers, rub them against my collarbone, and wink.

"You're the best," she says, stroking the embellished clutch. "It's gorgeous!"

The feeling of getting something perfectly right lifts me, a feather, a cloud, floating amid bliss.

"Come on," I say, taking hold of her Fendi-free hand, "let's choose a color, then afterwards I wanna head into the West End. I need a new dress for tonight."

While we assess the tiny colorful bottles—me reorganizing and aligning the misplaced colors—the three girls all stand at once, each pulling down her skirt, and make their way to the door.

"I'm having this," Ella says. "You?"

"Mm. Dolly's got her eye on this one," I say, holding a glittery pink.

"And Runner?" Ella asks.

"The standard goth black."

"What about the Fouls?"

I look at her. "*Please*—"

"Oneiroi?"

"Natural or French."

"Boooring," Ella says, rolling her eyes.

Rude! Oneiroi shouts in my head.

"I can't decide." I sigh. Sometimes I paint each nail a different color just to avoid a headache, the Flock insisting they each have a choice—my hands a wiggling rainbow.

"Let's both have this!" Ella insists, forcing the bottle of deep red into my palm, and we head toward the chairs.

The nail bar is quiet. Just the sandy stroke of a nail file.

Seated in our pedicure chairs, we roll the legs of our jeans. Ella's a little more problematic because of their tightness.

"Gel or normal?" the technician asks.

"Normal," I say.

As soon as the word leaves my lips I feel a wave of *as if* crash against me. The sheer notion of a *normal* person causing me strain.

"Have you heard from Shaun?" Ella whispers.

"Yeah, he texted. Said he'd meet us tonight around ten."

"Right."

"To be honest, I really wanna end it. I know you said we need him, but—"

"I get it," she says.

Silence.

"*What?*" I say.

"Nothing."

"*Ella?*"

"It's just . . . A couple of the girls. They said he's been hanging out with Amy. I thought you should know."

The technician looks up at me and pulls a face that appears confused and concerned all at once.

"Right," I say.

See; told you he was a dick, Runner shouts, covering Dolly's ears.

Then Oneiroi jumps in: *You don't know for sure; ask him.*

Ask him?! Runner dismisses, flicking a cigarette outside the Nest. *He's a liar.*

"I will ask him, don't you worry!" I speak out loud, the technician now quietly nodding her head.

"You okay?" Ella asks.

"Yeah," I say, wiggling my toes, "I'm fine."

I take a moment to picture Amy and Shaun together, naked, trying on the idea of them laughing, fooling around. Their mouths kissing. I note my mild jealousy rising even though I don't want him anymore, but decide it has to be *me* who breaks it off, not *him*. The very idea of Shaun trading me in for another girl something insufferable, my competitiveness overbearing and foul.

When I look up my nails are already painted—*tick-tock*—a pink spongy toe separator wedged in between my tiny toes. The technician has moved and is bent over another girl's hands. Ella is flicking through a copy of *People*.

"You okay?" she asks. "You seem kinda quiet. Upset."

"I'm fine. Really," I say, dusting myself down. "So. What's the plan for tonight?"

"I thought we'd head to the O Bar—"

Runner suddenly sits up.

"—then, well, Navid's organized a small party at the club. I couldn't say no." She whispers with surrendering outstretched hands, "I know it's not the best idea, but we might as well go. Jane is going, and I'm sure Sylvie will too. What d'ya make of her?"

"Who, Sylvie?"

"Yeah."

"She's nice," I offer. "I think she's sweet. And much nicer than *Amy*."

"*Really?* I think she's weird," Ella says, missing my barbed comment. "Skulking around the club like some goody-two-shoes."

"Maybe she's looking out for Jane," I say, defense in my voice.

"I guess." Ella shrugs. "Also, there's a group of guys flying in from the Netherlands tonight. I'm pretty sure they've got something to do with what we unpacked the other night . . ."

She looks up, her words trailing off. Checking that no one can hear. Taking a deep breath, she admires her nails.

"I heard Navid on his phone talking to Tao," she says, lowering her voice further, "something about a shipment coming via Utrecht."

I close my eyes, imagining the night ahead. Shaun. Amy. Navid and the group of men flown in from the Netherlands—the idea of a new dress now seemingly wrong. I stand up. The pink sponge spreading my toes further. My heart suddenly waning. Hope starting to shrivel up.

A ring, Runner says, eyes ablaze. *He's organizing a trafficking ring.*

35

Daniel Rosenstein

A LEXA'S LATE. ALEXA IS NEVER LATE.

I rearrange my stapler and letter opener, aligning them with the small gold clock, then check my top drawer for chocolate. Nothing.

I decide to reevaluate my notes, our progress, or lack thereof. Alexa is still somewhat of a wildling, untamed and not unlike mist. Her core self not quite tangible, her personas complex and startling. Where is she? She's now twenty minutes late.

Alexa Wú: December 6

Today is a no-show. Alexa and I have now been working together for nearly four months. Although trust is emerging, it's proving difficult to integrate Alexa's personalities. I don't even know if this is the goal anymore. Maybe she needs to exist, or they need to exist, as separate parts of herself? I wonder if integration is even possible.

Alexa remains involved with the Electra, attempting to gain evidence against Navid (the club owner), using Ella, her best friend, as reason to stay entangled. I wonder if she is addicted to the thrill? The threat? Might she only feel alive amidst conflict and risk?

I need to be more rigorous, have her realize that her career as a photographer is far more important than acting as a snoop for her so-called friend. I will challenge her. Make her realize that her past is informing her present behavior.

Even though it's not my responsibility to engage with the drama, I question whether I'm being a bystander. Maybe I'm reenacting something from her past? Ignoring her ugly surroundings. By this, I have Dolly in mind. Is Dolly trying to warn me of something? Has part of me been refusing to listen?

I check my watch.

I'll wait another five minutes, I think, and then I'll call.

Through the window I observe two nurses, both thin in white coats, dash across the lawn like quick cigarettes, Charlotte clearly enjoying the chase. Eventually they catch up with her, each nurse taking an arm. Charlotte looks up at the sky. Her face strained, eyes like the sludgy puddles on Glendown's path.

Eight twenty-five A.M.

I pick up the phone and dial Alexa's number.

No answer.

I try again.

Still no answer.

Something's not right.

36

Alexa Wú

MY EYES FLIP OPEN—*TICK-TOCK*—PHONE OUT OF REACH AND RINGING off the hook.

Scrunched up beside me is a gold sequined dress, dirt dried along its hem, sequins escaped and scattered across the floor like glittering confetti.

I slowly stretch out an arm, noting a deep bruise on my wrist, sore and amethyst, my watch missing.

How careless of me to get my new dress so dirty, I voice in my head. *Careless and stupid.*

I close my eyes and try to focus.

What's happened? Why am I lying on my bedroom floor, naked?

The smell of rotting meat suddenly crawls inside my senses. A thud at my temples and a thirst in my throat.

Get up, the Fouls order.

Amazingly, the Body obeys.

Clearly I drank too much last night. Reorganizing myself, I stare down at my legs—pimpled and bare. *Wasn't I wearing stockings?*

I look about my room, but there is no sign of them. I attempt to sit up, noticing then the bruising on my other wrist. Frightened, I realize I have lost time. Lots of time.

I must have checked out, I think, knowing I lose time only when I am stressed, fatigued, frightened, or in denial. I tap my head, hoping it will shake something loose, or wake someone up. *Runner!* I shout. *Oneiroi!*

Nothing.

I stagger to the bathroom and collapse on the toilet. Bang the back of my head against the wall on purpose. As soon as I start to pee I realize I haven't lifted the toilet seat. But the act of standing again feels like too much effort, so I remain, warm piss streaming down the backs of my legs.

When I finally stand, I realize I'm still drunk—my balance un-settled as I bend to clean the dripping seat.

Look at you, the Fouls sneer, *you're a disgrace.*

Fuck you, I throw back.

I make my way over to the sink, running the hot water, its mist quickly filling the mirror above. With my palm, I rub away the fog in three swipes like a car windshield wiper. *Thudsqueeze. Thudsqueeze. Thudsqueeze.* My body jolts suddenly. A bruised girl stares back at me, a slice of violet already living across her neck. A small cut on her left cheek.

Is that me? Me, with all those bruises?

I quickly check the rest of my body for more hurt: the curve of my shoulder, I note, also grazed.

What happened? I ask again, desperate.

Silence.

The Fouls snicker.

Tell me, I scream.

Make us, they sneer, their smug and cruel faces turning away to form a putrid circle of rotting contempt.

I check inside for the others, but they are gone. Missing. The Nest now empty.

I'm sorry! I scream. *Where is everyone?*

I think I must have done something awful for the Flock to disappear, or maybe they're scared—maybe the Fouls' tyranny has forced them underground.

It's okay, Runner finally whispers, *everyone's safe. Don't worry.*

Relieved, I feel my chest settle.

Flash.

Aɴᴅ ɴᴏᴡ ɪ'ᴍ ɪɴ ᴛʜᴇ ʙᴀᴛʜ. *TICK-TOCK.* ᴇᴠᴇʀʏ ᴘᴏʀᴇ sᴛɪɴɢɪɴɢ ʟɪᴋᴇ ᴀ thousand paper cuts. My fingers grip the edges of the bath's enameled steel. Eyes crimping with pain, I wait for the Fouls' judgment, for mercy, for their sadistic permission to immerse my head under the water.

Who's a dirty girl? they snarl. *Clean yourself.*

I force my head under, tea tree oil swirling and burning the cuts on my face.

Me, I'm a dirty girl, I say. *Me, me, me, me, me.*

Tick-tock—

Tick-tock—

A knock on the door suddenly awakens me.

"Are you okay in there?" Anna shouts.

I check my surroundings. Bath. Mirror. Peach towels. Fizz bombs.

"I'm fine," I muster. "I'll be out in a sec."

"I'm just popping over to Ray's. I've left soup on the stove. Chicken, your favorite."

"Thanks," I say, disoriented and shivering. The bathwater now turned cold.

Wakey, wakey, the Fouls taunt, laughing.

I eventually manage to dress myself and make my way downstairs to the kitchen, checking my phone—12:17—and pour myself a bowl of Coco Pops, drenching them in Gold Top and wiping the creamed rim with my finger. The pops bob around like they're lost in a sea of chocolate milk. I spoon them down and drink the milk straight from the bowl. My mouth fried and throbbing.

Everything I do is experienced in slow motion. My mind and body filtering smells, tastes, and sounds like it's impossible to give them a life. I want to block out the entire day, and everything from the night before. *Oh please,* I think, then speak the words out loud for no one to hear—

"Please make it all go away."

The hum of the open refrigerator brings me out of my funk. A violent flashing red beep informing me the door is ajar. I slam it shut and a shooting pain splits through my vagina. I double over, grabbing hold of the kitchen counter, the Body now fully awake.

Sliding my fingers down into my clean underwear, I touch the hurt part of me, then pull them back out to smell. It is not as I imagine—my body isn't decomposing like some dead animal, some rotting meat left to fester in the corner of a grass field. There is no nasty smell, I think. I am still Alexa. I am still—

Alexa.

Alexa Wú. Born May 1994. Photographer. Best friend of Ella. Nest Builder to the Flock.

The phone rings.

"Hello?"

"Hey, it's me, Ella. Are you okay?"

"Did you call earlier?" I snap.

"No, why?"

"Someone called," I say, hearing grime breakbeats down the line.

"Not me," she says. "For fuck's sake, Grace, turn that music down. Sorry. Are you okay?"

"No," I say, staring at my wrists. "Something happened. Something horrible."

The beats disappear.

"I know. I was really worried about you, but you insisted on going home alone after I got you cleaned up."

"My face," I say, ignoring Ella, "it's all bruised."

"You just disappeared. Shaun and I looked everywhere. And then I found you in the girls' dressing room, passed out. Don't you remember?"

"No."

"God, Alexa, I can't believe you don't remember any of this. You got into some *thing* with Shaun and threw your drink over him. Then you started slamming tequilas—"

"What?!"

"—with that guy. Navid introduced you. I thought you were trying to find out about the Groom House. But as the night went on you seemed kinda into him."

"Into him?"

I close my eyes, a vague image of a man in a gray suit falling in the front of my mind.

"I think—"

Flash.

"I think I remember him."

"Well, he's nasty," Ella says, clearing her throat. "Annabelle said he's really rough with some of the girls."

I drop down on the kitchen floor, wedging the phone between my chin and shoulder, my wrists on autopilot and suddenly brought together.

Flash.

I am lying on the cold dressing room floor, unable to move. My wrists cuffed and forced behind my neck.

He pushes down hard on my chest with his knee.

I try to scream.

He covers my mouth.

Unzips his fly.

Flash.

"I think I was drugged and raped," I say. "Rohypnol. He spiked my drink."

"What? *Who?*"

"The Man in the Gray Suit."

"Oh my God, Alexa."

"I couldn't move, when he—"

"I'm coming over," my *Reason* says, "don't move. I'm on my way."

I put the phone down and throw up all over the kitchen floor.

You disgusting piece of shit, the Fouls sneer, forcing my hand to slap my face, hard.

37

Daniel Rosenstein

CHARLOTTE'S FATHER IS ON LINE THREE."

"Tell him I'm in a meeting," I say. "Take a number. Tell him I'll call him back."

"Pants on fire."

I smile, fancying the Receptionist's jest. The pain of separation from her daughter, it seems, slowly healing. I picture Susannah, a slideshow of postgraduation images suddenly appearing in my mind, remembering how pride had overridden my pining when she left home for York to study art history.

"Even mothers lie," I say. "It's in their job description."

The Receptionist laughs and ends the call.

I gaze out at the evening oak, its leaves fallen, bark gnarly and mossed. The crisp, curled wafers of foliage hoovered up by the handsome gardener and his greedy Flymo GardenVac. I linger on the view before checking my diary: *December 7, 5 p.m.—Alexa Wú.*

She'd seemed distracted when we finally spoke. Concerned that she'd missed her appointment. I suggested we reschedule our session. She agreed and admitted to loss of time and flashbacks. I hadn't wanted to get into it on the phone, but I felt her desire to talk, her voice shaking, concentration a little wild.

"Five P.M., then," I'd said, hoping her memory would hold.

You're a little early," I say, checking the gold clock on my desk.

She looks to me, confused. Eyes wide, hands wringing.

"I— Sorry, I—"

She turns to leave.

"Come in," I say, aware I'm in breach of our boundaries, but her disorientation bothers me so much that I fear asking her to leave or wait another thirty minutes might cause further anxiety.

I close the door, a mental note made of her disorganized arrival.

She smiles nervously. I'm aware of how young she appears. This evening, her hair is gathered up in a tight ponytail that swings from side to side like a cantering horse, revealing the olive skin of the back of her neck. Black round-toe slip-on sneakers and, pulled up over thick tights, a tiny pair of ripped denim cutoffs that are far too short, far too provocative. Especially for winter. She stretches the arms of her striped mohair sweater tightly over her fists and sits on them.

"I was worried," I say, leaning forward. "It's not like you to miss a session."

She doesn't answer. Instead, she sets free her hands from beneath her bottom, twirling now the long strands of her ponytail. I watch the gentle in-turn of her sneakered feet, a slight shake to her knee.

Dolly, I think.

She unties her laces and kicks off her shoes, then raises her legs, curling in the chair like a noiseless cat. Her eyes are like curious buttons, darting, scanning first my desk, the rug, then the oil painting before finally settling on me. With a vague expression, she pushes the arms of her striped sweater to her elbows.

There, no longer hidden by her sweater, are three-inch bruises violently circling her wrists.

38

Alexa Wú

DANIEL—MR. TALKY—IS STARING AT MY WRISTS. I TRY TO HIDE THEM but it's too late, he's already noticed that they're bruised and hurting. When I arrived he looked all surprised, like he forgot I was coming or something. But then I realized it was my fault because I arrived *way* too early. I smile and he smiles back.

"What happened to your wrists, Dolly?"

"I don't know."

"You don't remember?"

"Nope."

"They look very sore."

"They hurt."

"Do you have some cream for them?"

"I've got something called arnica. Alexa got it for me."

Tick-tock—

A minute ago I was curled up like a pussycat on the chair, but now I'm sitting on the floor with my legs crossed. I don't remember when I got down here.

Sometimes I don't like Daniel's chair because it feels all sticky, especially if I'm not wearing trousers or tights. It makes this really weird sucky sound when I move, just like when I drink bubble tea. So I come down onto the floor.

I use my finger to trace the pattern on the rug. *Across, across, across.* The purple and blue stripes reminding me of the sea.

The Owl and the Pussy-cat went to sea

I scratch my half ear and look up. It's dark outside. Daniel looks tired and a little bit worried now. I wonder if he's eaten anything or maybe had a drink. I had a cheese-and-tomato toastie and a glass of milk earlier. Oneiroi made it for me. I didn't like it very much but I didn't tell her that because she'd think me ungrateful, especially with so many other children worse off than me and dying in the world, as she is always saying. But the tomato made the bread go all soggy so I just ate around those bits and hid the rest under my napkin.

"Are you comfortable down there?" he asks.

"Yes, thank you. My wrists hurt a bit."

"You don't remember anything? How you did it—how someone else did it?"

"No, I'm like Mr. Forgetful today," I say.

"Seems that way, doesn't it. Why do you think that is?"

"Because my brain's not working."

"Oh, and why's that?" He smiles.

"Because Mr. Forgetful forgets stuff!" I laugh.

"Do you think Mr. Forgetful forgets stuff because he's not allowed to remember? Maybe he'll get into trouble if he does?"

"Not sure." *Across, across, across.*

My legs are starting to ache now from sitting on the floor, so I stand up and climb back into the sucky chair.

"Are you okay, Dolly?"

"Feeling sleepy," I say, not knowing why I feel so tired. We didn't even go to work today.

Tick-tock—

When I wake up there is a big woolly blanket covering me. Mr. Talky must have put it there. I'd like to drink a glass of water because I am very very hot and very very thirsty and my head hurts. Oneiroi says we should always drink water if our head hurts. I climb out of the blanket and sit up, then stare at my wrists. Those horrible bruises are still there.

"Why won't they go away? Can you make them go away?"

"I wish I could," he says.

My tummy feels all trembly and swirly like a washing machine. Just like the times when Baba would dress me up like a little doll. "Smile, Xiǎo Wáwa," he would say. So I did.

Now I can taste cheese and tomato in my mouth.

"I don't feel so good."

I used to feel this way when I first used to come here because Runner told me not to talk. *Button it, Dolly!* she used to say. Then she'd get real cross.

She thinks we shouldn't trust Daniel or any man, and gets all upset if I tell him our secrets.

You're gonna land us in deep, deep trouble, Dolly, she said. *Remember our rule, no one from the real world can enter the Nest, ever. If you tell Daniel our secrets he'll destroy our home, and us.*

She also said that we'll get locked up in prison with no keys and no food, or even worse, a hospital full of crazy people where they put big needles in your arms and only let you watch TV if you're extra, extra good. Runner doesn't like me to talk to anyone really, especially about our secrets, even though sometimes I can hear Alexa telling Ella our secrets. They don't know I can hear them, but I can, I can hear everything. I know what they're planning. That's why I came to visit Mr. Talky.

39

Daniel Rosenstein

I watch her leave—a divided self—noting her quick, petite steps. The striped mohair sweater once again pulled tightly over her fists. The woman I met last Tuesday now morphed into a little girl, a changeling, a human chameleon.

Head down and treading the corridor, she scuttles past Nurse Kennedy, then turns and waves at me with her striped stump. Wide eyes and gummy smile like an overanimated Studio Ghibli character.

I close the door and make my way to my desk. Sitting down, I pick up the phone.

This is the voicemail of Dr. Mohsin Patel. Unfortunately, I can't—
I hang up and reach for my notebook:

Alexa Wú: December 7

Dolly was here this evening. She arrived early and was disorganized and dissociated. There is bruising on her wrists. She claims not to know how this happened. Defenses are dissolving and her switching into alternate self-states is increasing, indicating her life has become high-risk—particularly as she has little memory of what happens when she checks out. Need to think about cognitive restructuring to aid memory—Alexa is not safe if she can't remember her actions.

I suspect one of the Flock knows why she missed her last session and what happened to her wrists. But it seems trust is still an issue. Many secrets. Discuss with Mohsin her extended regression and possible interventions. Do I need to visit the Electra and see what she's involved in?

I wonder: is she telling me the truth, or might the bruises be self-inflicted?

Mohsin's words flood back to me: *They're not straightforward—patients with dissociative identity disorder—dangerous in the wrong conditions.*

I put down my notebook and switch on the kettle, urging haste. It seems to take forever. Time has slowed down. *I* have slowed down.

I wait.

Who is she? What is she hiding? What is she scared of?

I run my fingers along the base of my spine until the kettle eventually reaches the boiling point. I pour the water and wait again. Be patient, I tell myself. She's not ready. Fear prevents her from letting me into her mind and the workings of the Nest. But it will come.

Doesn't it always?

40

Alexa Wú

THE LIVING ROOM SPARKLES.

"Ta-dah!" Anna sings. A Christmas tree dressed in wine-red and gold baubles, lights winking like they're holding a secret.

Preeeetty, Dolly purrs as I reach for the home-crafted fairy to place on top. She holds a five-pointed star wand. Tinsel for wings.

"I want you to make an effort tonight," Anna says, wiping her palms down her apron, "and if your moods decide to join us—tell *them* to make an effort too."

"I can't make any promises," I say, readjusting the fairy's full skirt, "but we'll do our best."

Anna fingers the cross-stitch holly on the apron's hem.

"You do that," she says, eyes staring, "because I really like him."

Ray, I've discovered, works in TV. That is, he sells them: high-spec and complicated with surround sound. Apparently he and Anna met on their lunch break. A chance encounter in the staff lift that led Ray, the next day, to purchase a bottle of cloying perfume for an "aunt."

"I know this great little Italian restaurant," he said, shuffling from left to right, "and I wondered whether you might—"

"Yes." Anna spoke a little too keenly. "I'd love to have dinner with you."

The fragrance counter, she told me, felt just a bit warmer afterward.

To date, I know the following things about Ray:

Second name: Homer (as in the legendary author and the bald yellow guy. D'oh!)

56 years old

Works on the fourth floor, in Electronics

Loves spaghetti carbonara

Recently split from his wife (overheard on phone)

Leaves soppy messages on the fridge, hearts dotting the i's (weird!)

No children (also overheard on phone)

Kind (got me a mega discount on my new camera)

Anna likes him

"Help me in the kitchen," Anna says.

I follow her swaying hips, entering a perfume cloud of beef Wellington and fresh horseradish. Roasted potatoes and a rainbow of vegetables coated in honey rest in tinfoil, while peach cobbler cools by an open window. Anna wipes her plucked brow, having spent the entire afternoon chopping and slicing while I lay in bed, having Oneiroi call in sick, citing the flu. Rather than admitting the truth of my wrists, I lied that I was running a temperature.

"Take the day off," Jack said in between lip-smacks of satisfaction, the rustle of a crisp packet heard down the line. "Come back Monday."

"Okay, thank you," I said with a faux cough, "see you Monday."

"Stir the horseradish," Anna instructs, pointing freshly French-manicured nails at the pan.

Pulling down my sleeves to cover my wrists, I stir, not wanting to admit to myself, or Anna, the ghastly events of the week.

"Slooowly," she says, grabbing the spoon, "like *this*."

I do as I'm told and stir. *Slooowly.*

She hugs me from behind. Forages her mouth against the nape of my neck like a mother cat about to carry her kitten off by the scruff of its neck.

"Thank you," she whispers.

I take a moment to acknowledge Anna's effort. A stark contrast to when my father left and evening meals became futile. Back then, her exotic tagines were replaced by quick salads, a plate covering their limp green edges with an egg thrown on top. I understood why. She was angry. And hurt. So I did my best to go unnoticed, making myself busy and eating elsewhere, usually at Ella's place or afterschool clubs. Anywhere that welcomed my teenage mooching.

A knock on the door.

"Go answer it," Anna orders, freeing herself of the apron. "And don't forget to thank him."

"What for?"

"The camera!"

I make my way to the front door and unlock the latch.

"Hi. Come in." I shine, my portable smile stretching.

Ray is flustered. A little nervous, I suspect, at meeting the new girlfriend's stepdaughter.

I notice his black hair is stiff with cold, hands protected by thick gray mittens. I think this rather strange: a grown man wearing mittens.

Man-child, Runner says.

For a moment I wonder whether there's a strand of wool threaded through his sleeves so that he doesn't lose them, a name tag sewn into the collar.

Portable smile still intact, I take his coat and hang it on the rack in the hallway, slyly checking for a string or name tag.

He's still a man-child. Runner snorts when I don't find any. *Look, sneakers!*

"Cold out there," Ray says, thrusting a small bouquet of pink roses to meet my flat chest. "I believe these are your favorites."

Touched by his effort, Dolly seizes the Light and flings her arms around Ray's bulk.

"Thank you," she says, holding on tight. "They're lovely. Oh, and thanks for the camera too."

Anna rushes through to Ray's rescue, discreetly prying Dolly from Ray's body.

"Comeincomein," she says, quickly closing the door I'd left hanging open.

Ray wipes his feet.

"You look stunning," he says, glancing at Anna's dress. Black and fitted. A thin snakeskin belt squeezing her waist. Her blond hair curled and boinging around her collarbones. Lips and cheeks dusted with rose. Heels elevating her fine stockinged calves.

"Thank you," she says, kissing his mouth, "you look great too."

I look away.

Dolly giggles.

Oneiroi lowers her eyes, offering a beguiling shoulder.

Runner observes vigilantly, her crabby lip curled, while the Fouls stare with hard red eyes. A watchful stillness to their black capes, delivering a veiled shiver to the warm room.

"I'll pop these in a vase," I say, navigating Dolly back inside the Body.

"Under the sink." Anna points.

Runner salutes and clicks her heels.

Ray's like some big, splendid peach! Dolly says, leaning back, legs dangling over the Nest.

Anna busies herself while Ray and I settle at the dining room table, a red poinsettia wilting in front of the panting oven. A white cotton tablecloth crinkled from the dryer covering years' worth of scratches and watermarks.

We take turns being polite, asking humdrum questions about the Christmas holidays, work, and what we've been doing all day.

Lying in bed, pretending to be sick, Runner says with a snort.

Dolly jumps down from the Nest, stamps her foot, and pushes past Runner and Oneiroi with stiff elbows.

Alexa is poorly! she says. *Look at her wrists. And it hurts between her legs.*

She deserved it, the Fouls hiss.

I look down at my wrists, *still there,* the violent bruising a reminder, and still sore. I pull down my sleeves again, this time securing both buttons.

Ray clears his throat.

"I've got some good news," he says, his chest puffing out like a fattened frigate. "I've been promoted. To area manager."

"Congratulations!" Anna sings, reaching over and kissing the top of his head. "I'm so proud of you."

See, man-chi—

All right, I shout, *I get it, Runner, now shut the fuck up!*

I'm aware of how Anna's words bite me, not a big wounding bite from some rabid dog, but a nip. In the heart. Anna rarely praising my work or me.

I feel a pang of jealousy grasp at my chest, which I instantly cut short with a sharp pinch to the back of my leg—old habits hard to kill.

Rome wasn't built in a day, Oneiroi offers, stroking my skin with her fingers.

Runner rolls her eyes. *Pfft,* she mocks, *you seriously are the queen of all clichés.*

I watch Anna glide around the kitchen like a figure skater. When she lays the banquet of beef on the table, Ray becomes jubilant. He stretches his belly against his purple shirt, tapping his jolly set bulge as if to notify it that something good is on its way.

"Wow, this looks amazing," Ray revels, tucking in before Anna and I have even picked up a fork.

"Please-please, start," Anna says, gently guiding her hair from her eyes.

"Delicious," Ray splutters, not caring his mouth is full—me getting a front-row view of chewed-up beef and pastry. A small dribble of brown leaking from his mouth. Anna leans over and wipes it for him. Runner throws me a look.

Eventually we move on to dessert. Peaches like the cheeks of babies, orbed and pink. A sprinkle of nutmeg like fine-grained freckles. Ray makes a sign for seconds while scraping his bowl, belly not quite content. His silly synthetic shirt slowly expanding, a gray tuft of hair peeking out from his chest.

"For you," he says, handing us gifts that he's had resting beneath the table.

"Thank you," Anna says.

I open mine in seconds, revealing a stunning leather camera bag. I lift it to my nose and smell the warm leather. Its smoothness a stark contrast to the canvas one I've been using for years.

Wow, the Flock shine.

"I love it, Ray." I smile.

Anna is also delighted with her gift—a brooch, which she immediately pins to the collar of her black dress.

"This is beautiful," she says, stroking the white enameled cat. "How did you know I like cats?"

"I didn't," he says, "I just saw it and thought of you. I think it's the eyes."

Anna smiles.

"Let's take a photo," she says, suddenly stirred, "put it on automatic."

I reach for my camera, currently resting beside the couch, and place it on the mantelpiece, all three of us smiling and awaiting the flash.

A warm glow fills my chest as I place my camera in its new leather home. A gratitude and contentment felt, so different from the Christmases we would spend with my father. Christmas was a time for drinking, and with that came hell, though I try my best to make these memories vague, like a dream.

Flash.

M Y FATHER THRUSTS A FOIL CRACKER AT ME. "PULL IT!" HE SAYS.

Inside: an orange paper crown, a thin little joke, and a tiny hand mirror. "Don't look," my father says, "it might crack!" *Hahahahahaha-haha.*

He drunkenly pulls me into his side. One hand picking at his teeth, the other sliding to catch my waist and forcing me onto his lap. Kisses repeated on both of my cheeks.

"Don't do that," Anna says, her runaway words sprinting before she's had time to rein them back in.

His eyes narrow.

"Fetch me more ice, girl!" he shouts, pushing me off his nylon-covered knee and waving his empty glass in my face.

Flash.

I stare at the bag full of ice—a line of chubby penguins dancing along the edge—smash it on the corner of the breakfast island, wishing it were my father's skull. *Thud. Thud. Thud.*

I hate you. My lips mime the words, yet they never leave my mouth.

Returned, I stare at the cold pork belly and devoured lobsters, not a turkey in sight, then drop a chunk of ice in his whiskey tumbler.

"More ice," he tuts, "so useless. So stupid. It's better to have geese than girls!"

He pokes at my belly.

"You get fat and no one will want you. Especially me." He laughs.

I stuff pork belly into my mouth and swallow. Defiant. A lump in my throat.

Flash.

They are drunk now. My father sporting the orange paper crown. Anna dancing to old Christmas songs.

Flash.

I climb into bed, alone.

Flash.

The sound of their bedroom door slamming.

Flash.

"Are you a little slut?" my father shouts on the other side of my bedroom wall. "Say it."

I cover Dolly's ears. Crimp my eyes tight. The headboard jacking against the wall.

"Say it!" my father shouts again, slurring.

Anna doesn't answer.

I imagine her mute, gagged or in shock. His rape of her something both feared and familiar.

Flash.

*T*ICK-TOCK—

I blink and the images are gone. But I remember how her silence and his words and the jack of their headboard echoed and churned in the pit of my stomach. How I'd blocked out my hurt by slicing my legs.

I clear the plates while Ray and Anna move across to our old lumpy couch. Bodies nourished. The Christmas tree lights casting a halo across their foreheads.

"I'll pop these in the dishwasher," I shout, leaning out of the kitchen. The stretch forces a shooting pain between my legs, triggering an image of the Man in the Gray Suit.

"Thank you," Anna says, magically transported behind me.

"Are you going out?" she whispers. "It's just—"

"Don't worry," I say, voice peaking on the last syllable. "Ella's picking me up in an hour."

"What have you girls got planned?"

"Not sure. Maybe a movie," I lie.

She reaches for a couple of round brandy glasses.

"Don't forget the Christmas presents under the tree. A headband for Grace and perfume for Ella."

"Got it," I say, "thanks."

"Is their mum back yet?"

"She got back a couple days ago."

"About time." She judges. "Just taking off like that, and leaving Ella to take care of Grace. So irresponsible."

Runner throws Anna a black look.

She's got some nerve, she says in my head.

Anna clears her throat and moves in a little closer to me. "Ray has to head off in an hour or so," she whispers.

"Okay, I get it," I say, loading the last dish and slapping the door shut. "I'll be upstairs in my room."

WE DRIVE. NO MUSIC. NIGHT SINKING DOWN. A SMATTERING OF DOG walkers and their leashed charges. Cyclists on a thin path cutting through the park.

"How are you feeling, you know, after what happened at the club? How are your wrists?" Ella asks with reserve, changing gear.

I exhale slowly. "Angry. Confused. Foolish."

It wasn't your fault, Oneiroi whispers, *you did nothing wrong.*

Nothing wrong? the Fouls dismiss. *She's a whore. A tramp.*

Don't listen to them, Oneiroi defends. *They're wrong.*

The Fouls look at me as I take hold of my wrist. I don't ever remember seeing them with such menace and savagery in their eyes.

Ella steps on the gas.

"Try to forget that night," she says.

"Easy for you to say," I dismiss in return. "You aren't the one who was *raped.*"

WE EMERGE ON THE EAST SIDE. ONCE-DERELICT HOUSES NOW RESTORED and gentrified. Potted palms, fast low cars, and majestic wisteria replacing what once might have been drooping fuchsia. We take a turn into rural quietness, where a baggy-jeaned kid runs alongside us as we park. He gives us the bird and sticks out his tongue. I return the gesture. He laughs and disappears into the early night, a six-pack of Bud—one missing—swinging from his fingers.

Obnoxious little toe-rag, Oneiroi mutters. Her nose in the air.

Ella kills the engine. I study the twitch of curtains like tired eyes on the face of the familiar Victorian terrace. *Groom Residence, how can I help you?* Its red door like an open mouth of something wild, waiting to be fed. A wolf, a lion. A tiger, maybe.

Navid appears at the window, smiling as we approach the iron gate. A cigarette hanging from his lip.

I follow Ella past the tall bamboo plants, as wilted as my desire to be here. We knock and an unfamiliar moonfaced girl with bee-stung cheeks and high ruler bangs opens the door. Her eyes swirling like the delicate hands of a clock. *Tick-tock.*

"Yeah?" she says, eyes suddenly paused before sliding down our bodies.

Another girl emerges behind us, breathless, all attitude and makeup. A large pack of paper towels and laundry detergent held to her chest.

"Let them in," I hear Navid call.

Ella's hand touches me lightly, then quickly disappears, so I hold hands with the air, wishing to God we hadn't gotten ourselves into this damn mess. All the while, resentment toward Ella slowly building in my chest.

Remember, it's for the greater good, Runner says.

Martyr, the Fouls sneer.

The girl with the detergent pushes past us and I realize then that she's the Banana Hater.

Just like Ray's synthetic-clothed belly, the Groom House is bursting when we enter: techno pumping from upstairs, *hmpf, hmpf, hmpf;* a gaggle of girls comparing nails in the kitchen; the Banana Hater feeding the washing machine with bath towels and bed linen; two girls in matching flip-flops exchanging whispers and giggling behind a porn mag, *Juggs.*

I spot Poi-Poi at the top of the stairs, undressing and re-dressing a Tiny Tears doll—a pair of four-sizes-too-big fluffy mule slippers dangling off her tiny feet. I wave to her but she doesn't wave back, seemingly disinterested, attention pinned on her doll instead. Watching Poi-Poi talk to her reminds me of my own juvenile conversations—a captive audience of teddy bears and rag dolls propped on my bed. They always spoke back, of course, agreeing with me. My father is evil. *He is.* Anna is weak. *She is.* I wish my mother were still alive. *Us too.* Shall we eat doughnuts? *Let's!*

Poi-Poi is acting as hairdresser now. Her small voice bossing Tiny Tears the way a mother might.

"Now sit still, here, that's it. Now don't get all silly! Shhhh. Ānjìng! Yes, quiet. Do what I say, okay? You're a big girl now."

She makes imagined scissors with her fingers. *Snip, snip.*

"There," she says, combing the doll's wiry blond hair, "wánshàn!"

I want to tell her: Don't concern yourself with being wánshàn. *Perfect* is a myth. And by the way, little girl, treasure grows from an ounce of *im*perfect breath.

Ella and I squeeze past a fresh delivery of boxes parked at the bottom of the stairs, which I align and straighten, their awkward lean causing my obsessive compulsions to quiver, and then head toward Navid. He is sitting on a chocolate leather couch, eyes pinned on a game show, a bowl of salted dried plums resting in his lap. The pale velvet curtains are drawn now. The room is cluttered with boxes of beauty products, clothes, various fans and blow heaters, and piles of magazines.

Navid looks at us both, chewing a prune, waves, then stares back at the line of excited contestants—fingers by buzzers, eyes locked on a bright flashing wheel.

Ella steps forward.

"Shaun said to give you this," she says. "This week's takings."

"Good girl," he answers, holding out his empty palm, his eyes fixed on the screen in front of him.

Ella places the manila envelope on his hand like a cake.

He counts the money and hands her a crisp fifty. Ella folds the bill and slides it into her purse with no pause or conflict. I, however, feel sick at her willingness, the ease with which she takes his payoff. Ella instantly catches my look of disapproval and turns away, the *zzziiiip* of her purse pulling Navid's gaze back toward us. He smiles like he knows how much she wants his money, then turns his focus on me. I pretend not to notice, instead choosing to dally with a make-believe something or other in my own purse. When I look up, his eyes are still on me, appearing to scan my wrists—I assume in search of the rohypnol's crimes. I stroke my wrists, wanting him to ask. Does he know what happened to me in the girls' dressing room? Did he discuss it with the Man in the Gray Suit? Did they laugh over it?

His glare makes me so angry I have to look away.

"Where's Cassie?" Ella asks.

He stuffs another prune in his mouth, then nods toward the ceiling. "Upstairs."

As we turn to leave, he stands. Reaches over and takes a firm hold of my arm.

"The other night," he says, pulling me close, "what happened? Did he hurt you?"

I don't answer.

He cocks his head like his neck's about to have bullets loaded. "I won't tolerate any of my girls getting hurt."

"I'm not one of *your* girls," I say, too quickly perhaps.

He drops his grip, strokes my heated cheek.

"You're here, aren't you?" he says, taking my waist. "That means you're one of *my* girls."

Ella squeezes my hand three times.

Play along, Runner whispers.

A pause.

I muster everything inside me and nod. Manage a smile.

"Good then," he says, again seated, "now go help Cassie."

The stoned moonfaced girl with the ruler bangs slides past us clutching a shawl around her body. A joint held in her free hand.

When I turn back I watch her curl into Navid's side like a pet. Her young, lithe body and perfect shoulders now free of the shawl. She looks up to him with her celestial cheeks and swirling eyes.

"You need anything?" she asks him.

"Maybe," he says, stroking her spine as if reading a thin line of Braille. His paws moving slowly across the terrain of her body. Eventually cupping her young *wánshàn* breasts.

I catch a whiff of expensive perfume curdled by hardworking sweat: Amy cleaning the windows, Annabelle fully back in the fold and hoovering the carpet while Cassie bends over a mattress forced against the wall and tucks in pink bedsheets. In the middle of the room a low table has been planted, a pretty tasseled lamp resting on top. I do the math:

5 bedrooms:
4 + 4 + 4 + 2 + 1 = 15 mattresses
A total of 15 girls; more if they share beds

"Hey!" I say.

Cassie turns, arm fat swinging like a flag.

"Nǐ hǎo!" She smiles back, flopping down on the mattress.

"More girls on their way. Should be here anytime," she says, picking at one of her toenails. "Tao said they're very good girls. Very pretty."

"How old are they?" I ask.

Be careful, Runner warns, *go easy on the questions.*

Cassie shrugs. "Not sure," she says, readjusting the furry koala currently on its back. "He didn't say. But they'll be *very* happy when they arrive. They come from bad homes."

"Oh," I say.

"*Veeeery* bad," she repeats.

"Bad how?"

"Their mamas and babas don't want them. So Tao gives them money. Here the girls have a better life. More school. More opportunity. More fun." She winks.

More danger. More violence. More abuse, Runner adds.

I sit down on the mattress opposite.

"Need some help?" I ask.

"The room next door needs bed linen," Cassie says, looking around. "Where did I put—?"

As if by magic, the Banana Hater appears, freshly laundered sheets piled high on her forearms.

"Ah. Good." Cassie gestures toward me. "You change the other beds?"

"Sure," I say.

The Banana Hater hands me the sheets.

"Nǐ xūyào bāngzhù ma?" she asks.

"No thanks," I say, hoping that speaking English will encourage her to do the same, give her a chance to practice. "We've got this."

"Okay, just tell me if you want me to help," she replies.

Meow.

There is something soft beside my feet.

A tiny gray kitten with watery eyes has wandered into the room and slinks around my ankles in a figure eight—*meeeeow*.

Cassie kicks it—*hissss*.

"In China we eat them!" She laughs.

Ella and I exchange a glance and head into the neighboring bedroom to change the sheets. Next to the bed: a table and a lamp mirroring next door's, four stuffed animals still with their tags, and a rack with no clothes, just several slightly bent hangers. A depressing sight. I plump up the pillows, trying to imagine who will sleep here. What kind of home they've *really* left. How much Tao paid for them—were there negotiations? Or threats?

"Take a photo," Ella whispers.

Quickly, I take out my phone. *Tap, tap.*

Evidence #2

One of the bedrooms where the trafficked girls sleep, many of them minors.

Tao Wang, accomplice and brother to Cassie Wang, is trafficking the girls and organizing their exit from "bad homes."

The girls are bought, amount paid currently unknown.

"Got it?" Ella whispers, stroking a stuffed rabbit.

I nod.

Poi-Poi appears in the doorway. "Have you seen my cat?"

The doll in her hand is naked, hair bunched on the top of her head like a pineapple.

"Yes," Ella says, "he was next door."

"It's a *she*!" she says, defiant. "Her name's Tinker Bell."

"As in Peter Pan?" Ella asks sweetly.

"As in the fairy. Stupid!"

Ella's mouth curls, but I sliver her a look not to get into anything, Poi-Poi's sass and strength of voice feeling uplifting, and necessary.

"Navid bought her for me," she says. "She's mine. No one else's."

"I saw her just a second ago." I squat down to her level. "She's very lovely."

Poi-Poi smiles. "I like it when you talk to me in English," she says. "It makes me feel not so stupid."

"Less stupid," I correct, catching the irony. "And you're not stupid."

"Less stupid," she repeats.

"It's important to try to speak the language where we live, right?"

"I guess," she answers. "I like to read in English too."

"Got a favorite book?" I ask.

"*Matilda*," she says, beaming, "and James with the peach."

"*Matilda* was one of my favorites too." I smile. "She's so smart."

"Smart?" she asks.

"Cōngmíng. Clever," I translate. "Now shall we go look for Tinker Bell?" I ask, taking her hand.

"Okay," she says.

Suddenly, Cassie bursts in, arms windmilling in the air.

"The girls are here! Run the shower, it'll wake them up."

I turn to Ella. "'Wake them up'?"

"He drugs them," Ella says. "If they're stoned they're easier to move around."

"Quick, shower!" Cassie shouts, clapping her hands.

"Why not just let them sleep?" I ask.

Cassie sighs, her hands now clasping her head in exasperation. "Because they have to work!" She taps her watch. "Webcam at twelve o'clock."

Poi-Poi skips out of the room.

"Tinker Bell," she calls, "nǐ zài nǎ? Where are you?"

She clicks down the stairs, narrow toes gripping the supersize fluffy mule slippers.

Click, clack.

Click, clack.

"Tinker Bell. Nǐ zài nǎ? It's not polite to hide. Our new friends are here. Hurry. We're going to make a movie. You can see how smart I am."

Click, clack.

Click, clack.

41

Daniel Rosenstein

CLOTHES HAVE BEEN APPOINTED POST-IT NOTES. ORANGE FOR BEACH-wear, yellow for daywear, green for evening and formal—the latter, the note states, to be packed neatly on top to "avoid creasing." A traffic light of orderly neurosis, I think, examining her handwriting for clues.

On first glance, I regard the letters: loose, pretty, and joined up, indicating openness and friendliness, but intuition tells me a tinge of passive domination lies beneath Monica's looped *g*'s and slanted *a*'s. I wonder who else color-codes their packing. And what the act might achieve or soothe psychologically.

Control, I conclude; when one feels out of control they will attempt to control others. I picture the time Monica taped handwritten labels to the entire contents of my fridge. "You need to keep a check on your expiry dates," she ordered. "No point getting sick."

This morning I was given more instructions as she slipped her slim, exercised legs into pale fitted jeans. A glimpse at her lace bra, the pearl buttons set free on her blouse.

"I've laid everything out on the bed," she said, hand hovering over her iPhone, "you just need to pack it, neatly, then change some cash and pick up the dry-cleaning. I'd do it myself but I've got this work thing."

Then she smiled, sliding her feet into tall black shoes. "You said you didn't mind."

"It's fine," I said, "I'll do it later."

So here I am. Doing it later. A green Post-it note in one hand and a pair of shriveled bollocks in the other. My backbone slowly crumbling as I gently place Monica's silk slips and flimsy evening dresses in our suitcase. I wonder if other women ask the same of their boyfriends. If when they reach customs, they lie, claiming they've packed their own luggage. A quick glance from the customs officer when he catches a subtle flare in their eyes.

I consider the times Monica has lied—once insisting she was going on a spa trip with friends, but I later discovered her ex-boyfriend had tagged along. Or the weekend she disappeared, claiming illness, even though she sounded perfectly fine on the telephone. Then there was the night I showed up at her apartment at two A.M. (admittedly a little suspicious) to find her out, gone. A text the following morning saying she'd stayed over at her sister's place. And then just last month, I saw an unknown number calling her phone in the early hours as she slept soundly beside me. The silencer switched on.

I sometimes wonder why we're still together. Fear of loneliness? Or laziness? The great sex? Fatigue at the prospect of having to start over with someone new? Or is it because I *also* lie? Acceptance permitted because I'd be a hypocrite, otherwise.

I think about lies a lot—about the lengths people go to in order to maintain duplicitous lives. The secrets, the hiding, the shame, the covert shenanigans. A memory of when I was drinking collapsing at the front of my mind and sending an uncomfortable icy chill down my pathetic spine. I imagine Monica engaged in an affair, suspicion slowly rearing in my gut as dissatisfaction propels her into the arms of another man. My fear of commitment suitably perverse and threatening.

Charged up, I reach for one of Monica's evening dresses and scrunch it into a tight ball, then stuff it at the bottom of our suitcase. Fear and spite forcing my hand. An orgy of resentments suddenly let loose in my mind.

42

Alexa Wú

D RINK?" CASSIE ASKS, WIPING DOWN THE BAR.

"No thanks," I say. "Heading off now."

"There's an apartment in Angel I wanna go check out," Ella adds, excited, while leaning across the bar with her elbows, eyes ablaze.

"You renting?" Cassie asks.

Ella nods. "I need my own place," she says.

"You live with your mama?"

"And my sister."

"This is good for you, yes?" Cassie smiles. "More independence. More fun."

"More commitment," I jeer, knowing Ella will need to make rent every month.

Cassie gives me a look. "Commitment is good. It requires focus. Determination."

Yeah, and a dependency on you and this place, Runner says.

I take a wad of tissue from my pocket and wipe a spot on the bar close to Ella's elbow.

"Missed a bit," I say, staring at Cassie.

She ignores me. "Tell you what," she says, leaning over the bar and squeezing Ella's shoulder, "I'll buy you a new sofa. A bed. Or a fridge. Whatever you want."

"Really?" Ella glows, eyebrows raised in surprise.

"Really."

Don't let her do it, Runner warns. *She can't be trusted.*

Or believed, Oneiroi adds.

But she'll need somewhere to sit, Dolly whispers, *won't she?*

Shhh, this is for grown-ups, Runners says. *Now go play.*

"That's so sweet," I intervene, squeezing Ella's hand three times, "but—"

"I insist!" Cassie says, her eyes locking first onto mine, then Ella's.

"Thank you." Ella shines.

More payoffs, Oneiroi laments.

Hearing sounds of laughter, I look behind me. Two familiar girls I remember from back at the Groom House goofing around on the nickel pole. One of them attempts a yogini, then box splits.

How come you know what those moves are called? Oneiroi asks.

I stare at Ella.

Right, sorry. I forgot.

Ella spins around on her stool, cups her hand around her mouth. "Those moves are too advanced for you!" she calls.

One of the girls gives Ella the finger.

"Don't get fresh with me!" Ella warns, suddenly on her feet.

"They don't know what you're saying," Cassie says, "they're stupid."

"Maybe you should teach them English, or send them to school," I say.

"Pfft. Waste of time. And money."

"Or maybe it suits you that way," I add, "them being *stupid*."

Ella turns back to face us. "Anyway," she says, cutting short my vex, "about the apartment. Do you think you could give me a reference? You know, for the landlord?"

Cassie keeps her gaze fixed on me, my face. No blinking.

"Sure I can. I like to look after all our girls," she says, aiming her comment at me. "It builds trust. And I can trust you, can't I?"

"Of course," I say, my palms turning damp.

"Because I'd hate to think there was a bad influence in here at the club. Or back at the house."

"What do you mean?" Ella asks.

Cassie sips her vodka, her eyes still pinned on me. "Well, I'd be disappointed to find it's just an act, that you're really here to cause trouble."

"What? *Me?*" I ask.

"You're privy to a lot of information. *A lot* of information."

I let go of Ella's hand, resting both palms on the bar to steady my nerve.

She's onto you, be careful, Oneiroi warns.

"What's your point?" I speak, an attempt to appear casual.

"Shaun said you don't approve of what we do here, or what we do back at the house. He said you thought it was wrong."

Little snitch, wait til—

"Shaun?" Ella interrupts. "Shaun can't be trusted. He was hanging out with Annabelle while she was working at that other club—even though Navid said none of us were meant to see her. Did you know that, Cassie?"

"How do you know this?" she snaps.

"Amy told me. They've been hanging out together, all three of them."

Cassie pauses, leans in closer. "Navid trusts him."

"Well, he would. He's a man!" I dismiss.

She lets out a cackle. "This is true," she says, lightness suddenly found in her voice. "But *your* mistake was thinking *you* were the only one."

"He said I was," I spit.

"He lied."

"Exactly!" I say, slapping the bar. "So what makes you think he's telling you the truth about *me* not approving of what *you* do? Have I ever given you cause to think otherwise, Cassie? Anything at all? It hurts to think you don't trust me, considering our paths and where we both come from. Like you said, we were neighbors. Like *family*. But instead you chose to believe some white boy."

Cassie pauses, stares at us both, and it's all I can do not to run. She waits, watching to see if we flinch, or stir. Trails her manicured hand through her alabaster-streaked hair.

"I believe you," she says, "but why would *he* lie?"

"Because he's moved on," Ella answers. "Because he's a dick."

Cassie snickers. "To Amy," she says.

"Exactly," I say, staring her straight in the eye.

"Drink?" she asks.

I pause.

"Why not? There's no rush, right?" I say, turning to Ella.

Ella smiles. "Vodka. On the rocks."

"Good girl," Cassie says. "Then you can be on your way. Go check out that new apartment of yours."

I hear the two girls behind me laughing, then suddenly a thud.

"Zhùshôu!" Cassie shouts.

Runner takes out a Lucky Strike, her Zippo. *Watch yourself,* she says. *Cassie; she's the smartest person in this joint.*

43

Daniel Rosenstein

HEY, MAN, IT'S JOHN."

John?

"From the meetings," the voice adds. "AA."

"John!" I explode. "How are you? Haven't seen you in a while. Are you still going to the gym?"

"I'm still a member, but you know how it is. Busy at work."

"Right," I agree.

"I hope you don't mind," John says, "I got your number from directory inquiries."

"Sure," I say, "everything okay?"

"Well." He pauses. "Not really. I'm struggling, Daniel."

"Your mum?" I ask.

Another pause.

"I can't seem to accept it, that she's gone. The finality of it all."

I suddenly realize John's call is an outreach.

I check my clock: 11:56 A.M.

"John," I say, mindful of Emma's arriving in less than five minutes, "I'm just about to meet with a patient."

"I wouldn't call, but—" he cuts in, clears his throat, "I'm desperate."

"Desperate how?" I ask, alarmed.

Silence.

"John?"

"Look, sorry to bother you, man, I shouldn't have—"

"Listen, it's fine. Really," I interrupt. "Can we speak later, say, around, six-ish?"

But already he is gone, our conversation killed. Shame, I imagine, pulling on his wrist to end the call. Damn.

With just a few minutes to spare until Emma arrives, I feel a rise of panic and irritation with myself for not taking the time to talk. But what could I do? I soothe, I have to prioritize my practice, my patients. I make a note to call John back after work to check that he's okay. Maybe I'll suggest we meet for coffee, or that we go to AA together sometime next week.

Poor guy. It wasn't long ago that I was in a similar place. How, soon after Clara passed away, I'd found it so difficult to seek help. Ironic, really, thinking now that John—the Old-Timer—had listened, checked on me, wiped me off the floor. His counsel at AA both consistent and sound. I hadn't realized at the time how deeply reliant I was on Clara, how codependent I'd become, and now that she was gone I was half the man and shaken to the core. *Finally,* I thought, *this is what alone feels like.* And I was scared.

A knock on the door.

I gather myself, catch a breath, and open my office door.

"Hello, Emma." I smile. "Come in."

Emma looks at me, ill at ease.

"Are you okay, Dr. Rosenstein?" she asks. "You look awfully pale."

44

Alexa Wú

THE TIGER STARES AT ME WITH SLIM SILKY EYES, HIS PAW PINNED ON A pale twitching hare—its throat torn and puce. A circle of blowflies compete for the sticky wound, the warm clot a bull's-eye, the flies speeding darts.

Run! a voice cries in my head, but I am unable—icebound—the Tiger striding closer to me at speed, the limp hare now clenched in his jaw.

He stops, amber eyes fixed on my shaking hands. His jet markings so confident that I fear they might leap out and blindfold me, demanding that I crouch and stoop and grovel while the other tigers watch. Cold savagery in their eyes.

I step toward him and stroke his orange paw to appease, yet secretly I think: *I will skin you; I will make you into a magnificent rug that covers my entire bedroom floor; I will remove my sneakers and cartwheel across your back with my small naked feet. Feet you wish to cripple and bind.*

I watch my dreaming feet suddenly narrowed and pinched, the Tiger's paw forcing me into high-heeled shoes. My mouth painted red.

Poi-Poi and Grace wave at me from the top of far-reaching stairs, a half-naked doll in each of their hands.

"Alexa, we're up here," they call.

"Wait there," I order, attempting to climb the impossible steps, my legs buckling beneath me like Bambi's.

Click-clack.

Click-clack.

Above me, crows circle in the air, their beady eyes locked on my attempts to reach Poi-Poi, but as I very nearly reach the top, I slip and collapse. The stairs now suddenly morphed into a slide.

A trail of laughter and the smell of rotting meat eventually rouse me from the dream, the Body splintering into a thousand tiny pieces, each fragment escaping my alternate world of big cats and small birds—

The eyes open, chinks of morning light sneaking in beneath my bedroom's stubborn blind.

Wake up, Oneiroi whispers.

You said dreaming people shouldn't be woken, Runner says.

It's all right if you do it gently; see—shake, shake—

The Body obeys, bolting upright, the chest, the neck, and the shoulders now suddenly alive. With care, I gather my one thousand pieces until I'm whole again. A small *me*-shaped space in the world, buckling under the weight of all the lives I live. Lives I've invented, lives I carry around inside me for company.

Oneiroi takes the Light and walks us to the bathroom, Anna's dressing gown snatched down from the back of the door.

"Brush your teeth," she says, squeezing the mint tube. "You have to be at Daniel's in an hour."

Do you always do the border first?" I ask, noticing a tray of tiny puzzle pieces resting on her lap.

The heavy blonde flinches. "Yes." An eccentric origami construction worn as a hat tilted on her head. "Are you going to swear at me again?"

"Swear at you?" I ask, baffled.

"Like in the corridor that time. When I was with Emma."

"I'm sorry; I don't know what you're talking about," I say, truly baffled.

"Oh, it's okay, I forget stuff too. You must have been having a bad day. Wanna try doing some jigsaw with me?"

"Sure," I say, still confused, then move across the waiting room to sit beside her. The radiators pumping out dry heat and catching my throat.

She hands me the puzzle's box lid.

"Van Gogh's sunflowers," I say, imagining myself splintering into one thousand tiny jigsaw pieces just like in the dream I had earlier.

Eyes riveted, she scratches her neck and scans the tray, I presume for the yellow top right corner piece.

"I hate it when I can't finish the border," she frets. "It really bothers me."

"Cut his own ear off," I say, rubbing my own.

"Pfft. The mad artist. Such a cliché. I'm Charlotte, by the way."

She holds out her hand: stiff and straight. Her welcoming formal yet adorable all the same.

"Alexa," I say, shaking it.

I join in the search for the yellow corner piece.

"I've never done a jigsaw before," I say.

Charlotte stops. Stares at me with pure disbelief.

"Are you kiddin' me?"

"Nope."

"Not even as a kid?"

"Can't remember. Probably not."

Charlotte closes her eyes, nods her head.

A little dramatic, don't you think? Runner snorts.

"I have over a hundred." She speaks with sparkling pride.

Runner pulls a face. *Whatever floats ya dinghy.*

"A *hundred*?" I say.

"Yep. Completed all of them, at least five or six times."

"So you're a compulsive too, then."

"You say 'compulsive,' I say 'creative.'"

Potato, potahto, tomato, tomahto. Let's call the whole thing off.

Daniel appears at the door.

"You missed your appointment, Charlotte," he says, beckoning me in. "Have reception reschedule another one, please."

"Okeydokey," she says, not bothering to look up. "Bye, Alexa."

I turn and wave then, pushing my hands deep into the back pockets of my jeans to feel the small and hard thing inside one of them. I walk on ahead with Daniel close behind and look down at my hand, confusion setting in—a yellow right-angled jigsaw piece.

Dirty little thief, the Fouls scold.

On entering the office I notice the suitcase, a neat leather tag tied to its handle. The elephant-suitcase in the room. I feel my heart clang— *Please stay, don't go.*

I choose not to comment on the suitcase, wondering if he's placed it there to get a rise out of me.

You're being silly and paranoid, Oneiroi mutters.

Even so, keeping my eyes locked on the oil painting, *I won't show my longing today.*

Daniel clears his throat. "Dolly was here for most of the session last week," he begins.

"I know. She told me."

"She couldn't remember what happened to your wrists."

I look away, a lick of shame in my chest.

"Maybe you can?" he probes.

"It's all a bit of a blur." I shrug. "The Fouls keep hiding my meds."

"Switching is exhausting," he says, stroking his freshly shaven chin, cuff links catching the light, "and your mind is doing its damnedest to protect you. Make you forget what happened. Like those amnesic barriers we've discussed."

"I see."

He stands. Walks over to his desk, takes a slim silver letter opener, and returns. "Concentrate on the tip of this letter opener," he says, moving the sliver of silver from left to right. "Focus on the tip."

Left to right; left to right; left to right.

"I want you to relax and feel your eyes get heavy. Focus. Left to right. Left to right."

I do as I'm told, sinking deeper into my chair.

"Now close your eyes. Listen to my voice. Only my voice matters right now. None of the others. Relax your body, Alexa."

I feel my throat swallow. Dolly yawns, setting off a chain reaction for the Flock.

Sleepy, she whispers in my head, her eyes eventually closing.

"Good," Daniel whispers, his voice faraway. "Now feel the weight of your limbs. Let go. Note where your feet are, and your hands. Relax."

I sink my feet into the thick carpet, my hands resting between my denim-clad thighs.

"I want you to track back to that night—"

I nod gently.

"—to the last thing you remember."

A drawn-out pause.

"Where are you, Alexa?"

"The Electra. Sitting at the bar. With Ella."

"Anyone else?"

"Shaun. Shaun's there. I'm so cross with him."

"Anyone else?"

Silence.

"Alexa?"

"A man."

"Who?"

"Don't know. Gray Suit."

"What else?"

"He's ordering drinks. Tequila."

"What now?"

"We're drinking. He's laughing—the Man in the Gray Suit. His hand is on my leg. Shaun's gone."

"Anything else?"

"More drinks. Gray Suit. Dizzy. Eyes won't focus."

"Where's Ella?"

"Dancing, with Amy and Navid."

"What's happening now?"

"Stairs. No. Get off me. You're hurting. Stop. Please. No!"

"Alexa, what's happening?"

"Make him stop. Please—"

Flash.

"Alexa, can you hear me?"

"He's got my wrists. NO. Stop! Can't move."

"Alexa!"

"Hurting. Can't move. Can't breathe."

300

"Alexa, come back. Okay, Alexa. When I count to three you will wake up. You will be back here in the leather armchair at Glendown, where you are safe. Now, come back, Alexa, one, two, three—"

Ping.

I open my eyes, grabbing the arms of the leather chair. I search, like a wild animal, for something familiar. Desk, purple-and-blue-striped rug, oil painting, bay window, Daniel.

Daniel.

Daniel's all blurry. He's coming toward me.

I try to focus.

He is standing in front of me now.

"Take this," he says.

He hands me a glass of what appears to be water. I take the glass, my hands shaking, while Daniel places the letter opener back on his desk.

Haven't you learned your lesson, stupid? the Fouls sneer.

I spit the water out. The spray reaching Daniel's waist. *Maybe the water's not safe, just like the tequila,* I think, wiping my mouth with the back of my hand. I try to hand the glass back.

You deserved everything you got that night. Whore! the Fouls scream.

Suddenly my mouth dries up. I can't get my words out—

Please

take

the

glass, please. Please. PLEASE.

With both hands I push the glass toward Daniel's chest. *Please. I don't want it. It's not safe. Take it. Take it. Take it away.*

I drop it on the floor, glass shattering everywhere.

"I'm so sorry, Daniel! Please, let me clean it up," I cry. "So clumsy of me, so stupid."

Silence.

The Fouls stare me dead in the eye: *Now look what you've gone and done, Stupid.*

Stupid. Stupid fucking crybaby.

45

Daniel Rosenstein

CAN YOU TALK?"

"Sure. Everything okay?"

I look over at the broken glass.

Silence.

"Daniel. What's happened?"

"Difficult session," I say, leaning across a stack of mail, looking for the letter opener.

"The DID patient?" Mohsin asks.

"Yes. She had a disturbing flashback."

"What to?"

"Something happened last month at the Electra. She had bruises on both of her wrists. I thought it might have been self-inflicted, so we engaged in hypnosis."

"What did you uncover?"

"I think she was raped." I speak quietly.

"Did she say that; in the hypnosis, I mean?"

"Her narrative was fragmented. I— I—"

"Slow down, Daniel. Take a breath."

Pausing, I stare at my desk. Momentarily distracted, convinced I put the letter opener right here. *Where is it?* "I think this case is getti—"

"Getting to you. I know. You need a holiday."

"Her regression's increasing and her memory's fading. I think the personalities are warring and blocking out each other's actions."

"Has she stopped taking her medication?"

"She's in and out with it; was adamant that she have some autonomy, so we agreed on a reduction, but I suspect some of the personalities are preventing her from taking it."

"What about her stepmother? Where's she in all this?"

"Anna?"

"Maybe she can get more involved. Encourage Alexa to keep up with her medication?"

"They don't have a great relationship."

"But they do *have* a relationship."

"Okay. I'll think about that."

"How did the session end?"

"I had one of the nurses administer antipsychotics. It seemed to help."

"Good. When do you leave?"

"Couple of hours," I say, my voice trembling at the edge.

Silence.

"I don't want to leave her, Mohsin," I say, eyeing my suitcase.

"You have to," he dismisses, "or you'll burn out. And anyway, you're not that powerful."

I sigh, knowing he's right.

"Give her my number. It'll ease your concern."

"Thank you."

I stare again at the glass.

"I've been having dreams," I say.

"What about?"

"Desiring her. Making love to her. I feel a certain guilt."

"Guilt is a waste of time—it's just resentment turned inward. But the desire needs to be addressed. And soon."

"I'll pass on your number," I say.

"Call me from the airport."

Click.

I walk toward the shards of glass scattered like fragments of the self: hiding and splintered beneath the chair. With a dustpan and brush I collect the pieces, carefully sweeping them to safety, mulling over Alexa's unsettling flashback. Who had control of the Body when the Man in the Gray Suit raped her?

I leave a note for the Receptionist to contact Alexa with Mohsin's number. Wheeling my overloaded suitcase toward my office door, I attempt a calm, steady soundtrack in my mind: *Everything will be fine, everything will be fine.*

46

Alexa Wú

I WALK THE GROUNDS OF GLENDOWN, SEDATED. MY TONGUE FRIED, MY pride lacerated. The residents gather like packs of zombies—shuffling, mumbling, and pulling at their clothes—curbed by the medication they've been given. Today I'm one of them. Chemically coshed. Mouth numb. Head like a freakin' hot-air balloon. Slashes of hysteria keen to remind me that I'm only two steps away from unbalance. I glance at the rose brick wall. A lone blackbird lifts a black wing.

I want to go home, Dolly whines, her tiny fingers fat and throbbing from the adult dose of medication.

Don't worry, I say, cutting across the lawn to the path, *we're heading back home now. Oneiroi will call Jack later and tell him we're sick again and we can stay in bed.*

Again? Oneiroi asks.

Again, I say.

You can't keep calling in sick, she demands, *or he'll fire you.*

Who cares? I say.

Glendown's windows feel like unsleeping eyes on me, vigilant and still, a sense of unease creeping up my back. I look at the menacing rain-filled clouds and exit the grounds.

A Tube ride.

A walk.

I am stalked all the way home by my *Stupid*.

Stupid.

Stupid-ness, like a shadow, until I finally turn the key to my front door—the Fouls insisting all the while that I climb the stairs. Reach under my bed. The blade already waiting for me.

I watch the familiar red slide out.

Deeper, the Fouls insist, adding the silver letter opener to my collection of strange weapons.

47

Daniel Rosenstein

Monica now settled in consumer heaven, I park myself on a gray plastic chair far away from excited crowds at Terminal 5, then take out my phone and dial the Receptionist.

"Daniel Rosenstein's office."

"It's me," I say. "I left you a note."

"I've got it. I left her a voicemail."

"Good. If she hasn't called back by the end of the day, chase her."

"Everything all right?"

I sigh. "Just about."

A pause.

"Oh, your daughter called. I told her you were on your way to the airport."

"Did she leave a message?"

"No."

"Daughters," I say.

"Daughters," she agrees.

I imagine the Receptionist's eyebrows raised, eyes rolling in their sockets.

"See you in a couple of weeks," I say.

"Have fun," she says.

Opposite me, a thin young man has arrived. He has slender pianist fingers that hold tightly to a white plastic bag full of magazines and bottled water. His face is kind, but beneath his eyes are dark half-moons. Exhaustion lines his cheeks. I note his jacket is slightly too small, his trousers too large at the waist.

He checks his watch—his knees pressed firmly together—then gazes at the overhead clock, followed by the check-in board. He then repeats the process.

Watch, clock, check-in board.

Watch, clock, check-in board.

I feel a paternal urge to calm his disquiet, remembering when I too was in my early twenties, my anxiety back then most likely the reason why I later turned to drink.

Before I was an alcoholic, I dabbled in the restriction of food. Mildly anorexic in my late teens, I would spend a significant portion of my day obsessing over counting delicious pastries neatly lined up in café windows, though I never allowed myself one to eat. I'd also weigh every portion of food I ate down to the last gram, flake, or sprinkle. Starving myself allowed me the control to resist any longing I felt. Drinking, however, meant submitting to it. This came later, after I eventually left home. The permission I gave myself to become completely intoxicated a paradoxical rebellion against the years of at-home deprivation. My desire to be loved something comparable to that of a feral animal, a low kick felt in my hindquarters every time my father rebuked my attempts at being his soft, sensitive boy, and what he termed my "girly ways." What to do when a feral animal growls after a good kicking? You give it another drink.

The anxious young man looks up and catches me watching his clasped knees. I quickly turn away—eyes focusing on a coffee carousel—not wanting to add to his anxiety. I wonder momentarily where he is traveling. Whether there is someone to meet him at the other end. If he has a good shrink.

I myself never traveled abroad until I was seventeen years old. Before then, family holidays were mostly packaged tours where all-weather clubhouses entertained us for the entire summer. I think now how unsophisticated we were as a family, convinced the evening entertainments of cabaret singers, magic acts, and buffets were the most glamorous things.

The clubhouse was where I'd usually find my father during the day, with the other men, drinking, talking, and playing darts. If I timed it right, usually around teatime, he'd have drunk enough for his cheeks to flush and his words to slur. "Here he is," he'd say, a sly look in his eyes as he punched me hard across my shoulder, "little wet wipe. Come to nose around for some more money?" Then he'd throw me a tenner while the other men laughed, joining in his cruelty. I despised my dad when he was drunk. But I often thought it worth being insulted if it meant I could escape for a while, using his money at the amusement arcades, the fairground, or on seaside candy. Misguided, I told myself: *I'll never be like him.*

L OST IN MY MEMORIES, I SUDDENLY THINK OF THE OLD-TIMER'S PHONE call. Feeling bad again about not speaking with him, I quickly decide I'll ring when I've had a chance to unwind and can give him my attention.

Instead, I reach for my phone and dial Susannah.

Hi. This is Susannah, I can't talk right now, but leave a message and I'll call you back. Beeeep.

"Hi, it's me. Just checking in. Mon and I are about to board. I'll try again when we get to the hotel. Love you."

Click.

When I look up, I see Monica coming toward me. She drops down beside me, seemingly exhausted but thrilled, a fistful of shopping bags plonked down by her feet. All of a sudden, I'm relieved by her smile, the simplicity of her presence.

"Let's go," she says, an excited child.

48

Alexa Wú

That's twice this month."

"I'm really sorry, I'll work overtime next week," Oneiroi says, speaking on our behalf. Phone lodged beneath the chin, pushed against a fresh zit.

"Have you seen a doctor?" Jack snaps, attempting to disguise how heated he is.

"Yes," she lies.

"And?"

"Tonsillitis," she says.

Silence.

"Listen. If this continues, you leave me no choice but to find another assistant. Someone reliable and ready to work. You've got real talent, but I can't be left hanging. It interferes with my deadlines. One more strike, Alexa, and you're out."

Click.

Oneiroi hands back the Body, the Light passed between us flickering momentarily, her annoyance at being asked to lie on my behalf—again—causing her to vex.

You'd better get your shit together, Runner snaps.

Otherwise you'll lose your job, Oneiroi adds.

Who cares, the Fouls scoff. *Right, Alexa?*

I do, I care, Dolly defends.

Panic rising inside me, I walk to the kitchen and reach inside the fridge. My finger swiping at a tub of hummus and nudging a tower of sad-looking leftover food in stacked Tupperware—Anna's attempt at being thrifty. Inside: a boiled egg still in its shell; a day-old turkey bagel, wilting spinach, half an avocado with its pip hollowed out, like an eye devoid of its pupil.

I touch the back of my left knee, this morning's wound now stinging and sore.

Oneiroi takes back the Light and pulls an ice cube from the freezer, sliding it across the tender spot, dried blood slowly vanishing.

We have to stop the Fouls from doing this, she says, recruiting the Flock as she dabs a tea towel to mop the melted ice. *All this self-harm and stress at the Groom House—it's wrong. We need to go to the police and be done with it.*

Runner steps forward. *We can't,* she says, *not yet. We need more proof.*

Proof? Oneiroi shouts. *At what cost? Christ, look at yourself. Look at what this is doing to us.*

Runner takes a hold of Oneiroi's collar. *Listen,* she shouts, *keep your eye on the prize, and stop being such a crybaby.*

Fuck you!

What d'ya think this is, some game? Navid is a dangerous man. A predator.

Oneiroi turns away.

You're losing your head. If we go now, Navid, Cassie, Tao, and whoever else will come after us and Ella. Then there's Grace. You wanna be responsible for what happens to her if we stop now, huh? What about that? What about us?

Get a grip. We're doing this. And that's final.

Quiet! I order. *Runner's right. We have to go through with the plan. And for that to happen we ALL need to get on board. It's done. Decided.*

Oneiroi dismisses our case, hands back the Body, and climbs into the Nest with Dolly. *Don't say I didn't warn you,* she snaps, a random twig poking in her side.

"Good, then," I say, militant as an ox.

T*ICK-TOCK*—

Outside, two sparrows are resting on my bedroom windowsill, the useless blind raised to reveal the brown husband and wife pecking at the birdseed I've placed in a small yellow cup. Even though Daniel left only yesterday, I've been aware of adding more feed than usual, in hope that it might entice more birds to settle my anxiety. I reach for my camera, resting on the oak dresser. *Click.*

Another bird joins in now, this time a finch. *Click. Click.* The loyal sparrows hop away, their commitment to each other far outweighing their desire for food. The finch pecks at the yellow cup alone, the plump sparrows now shuffling along the windowsill.

When I was younger I was fascinated to learn that certain species of birds mate for life. Swans, blue jays, albatrosses, barn owls, ospreys, red-tailed hawks, and scarlet macaws, to name just a few. I thought this very lovely. The strong bonds were nothing like the relationships I'd encountered, and I was thrilled by these solid unions. Having wondered myself about monogamy, I eventually made birds the poster children for commitment and alliance.

Some years later, though, I read that this idea of commitment in birds was not *completely* true. For me, monogamy is about remaining sexually, spiritually, and mentally devoted for one's entire life, but

315

this is not the same for birds. Monogamy for birds may last for only one nesting or breeding season—our fickle feathered friends not *entirely* devoid of affairs. I picture my father, remembering his affair with the college croupier, Anna sobbing, a pack of Xanax in her hand. Also Navid and Shaun, both men sleeping around and chasing skirt like two robotic lotharios, not a care for anyone's feelings but their own.

I look about my bedroom, suddenly stirred—people whom I've photographed these last few months blending in with the photographs of strangers already taped to my magnolia walls. Immediately my spirits lift. *More people to join us,* I think. Our community of defenders, fighters, champions, and mothers proudly displayed on the walls. I glance at the London Black Revs demonstrator; the grieving mother whose fifteen-year-old daughter was discharged, prematurely, from the psychiatric ward. Next: health workers, activists, pressure groups, and lobbying NHS nurses, arms linked in solidarity; Billy on a swing and his mother—a maternal tenderness in Sandra's eyes that I hope to feel someday.

I check my watch, realizing hours have passed somehow, the finch now flown, the pair of sparrows nowhere to be seen—*tick-tock*. I take out my phone and see two missed calls and two voicemails.

Hey, it's Ella, I've got a babysitter for Grace. Mum's gone AWOL, again. I'll pick you up around six. Love you—Click.

Hello, I'm phoning from Glendown on behalf of Daniel Rosenstein. Can you please call me as soon as—Delete.

Runner! I shout. *Why did you do that?*

Forget it, she says. *He's on holiday. Don't be fooled that he gives a shit.*

Too tired from the earlier medication to argue, I reclaim the Light and scroll through the photographs on my phone, creating an album called *Groom House,* and upload them to my iCloud. I imagine a bird of prey guarding the evidence that Ella and I have collected, and more that we will gather later tonight when she drives us back there.

I stare at the photographs: Tao's address, one of the bedrooms at the Groom House, and while knowing they're helpful quickly realize we'll need more. Maybe proof of the trafficking, withheld passports and the actual setup, and then we'll have a case?

We'll need more than that, Runner says. *What we really need is hard evidence that the girls are underage.*

Tick-tock—

Ella drops down on the bed, bored. I notice a Venetian three-way mirror has been planted on top of the pine dresser alongside a new head-board, erected in oyster velvet, its fabric the exact same as the barstools in the Electra. On the walls of the Movie Room are prints of sunsets and kittens and soft, naked bodies. A floor-to-ceiling mirror drilled and nailed to catch every angle of a girl's forced exploit. Tacky ivory satin sheets are draped across the bed, more stuffed animals, cushions that sparkle of girly innocence. *Santa Baby,* one reads in a leaning, peppy font.

The Banana Hater swipes at Tinker Bell with a pillow, and then tilts her head back and laughs.

Hissss.

"Stop it!" Poi-Poi shouts. "Tă mă de biâo zi!"

Hissss.

The Banana Hater approaches slowly and grabs a fistful of Poi-Poi's thick ponytail.

"Call me a bitch again," she warns, tugging hard, "and I'll chop its fucking tail off."

She makes a chopping gesture with her free hand and Poi-Poi starts to cry. I step in between them.

317

"Hey, come on," I say, my body a barrier, "let's go eat. Cassie's made food, niúròu miàn."

The Banana Hater thrusts her palm in my face and strides out while Poi-Poi attempts to fish Tinker Bell out from under the bed.

Together we kneel down and peek beneath the bed, Tinker Bell and her hovering green eyes crouching in the corner like a solitary specter from a previous life.

"Let's leave her," I say, "she'll come out when she's ready."

Standing behind Poi-Poi, Ella mouths something I don't quite understand, pointing at the pine dresser, a drawer carelessly left open.

Wait, I mouth back, my expression exaggerated and voiceless.

"Say, how long have you lived here, Poi-Poi?" I ask, trying my best to act dense.

"Since the summer," she says, reversing on all fours, "when Shaun came to get me."

"*Shaun?*" I say, my voice cracking on the question mark.

"The nice man who works at the nightclub. Amy's *boyfriend*." She giggles.

Ella and I catch each other's eyes. A pelvis-to-throat anger-envy surges through me like wildfire, remembering our last night spent together, six weeks ago. Shaun wearing a silk eye mask to rest his sly eyes and insisting we sleep top to tail: him yin, me yang. My face staring at his feet because he couldn't sleep, was hot, needed space. In other words, another man-child who feared intimacy. I'd been worried he'd kick me in the face, so I'd turned the other way—reversed, upside-down spoons—feeling abandoned after our sex, over quickly and, for me, orgasm free. How lonely and hollow I'd felt. Not sleepy in the slightest.

I'm done with this crock of shit, I voiced in my head—

Thank God! Runner smiled.

Just for today I am strong.

Just for today I will try my best to be the person I needed when I was young.

I take Poi-Poi's hand with energized determination. "Your mummy and daddy must miss you," I say.

Poi-Poi lowers her head and shakes it side to side. "They're dead," she says. "They got sick. But I have an older mummy and daddy—my grandmama and grandbaba."

Tinker Bell suddenly appears from beneath the satin theater curtain: a four-legged actress, dipping, humble for an encore.

"Tinker Bell," Poi-Poi sings, springing up and hugging her tightly.

Purrrpurrrpurrr—

I stroke Poi-Poi's ponytail—a maternal act—imagining it gives me far more pleasure than her.

"Do they ever visit, your grandparents?" I ask.

Poi-Poi shrugs. "They live in Hong Kong and they're old," she says, readjusting Tinker Bell's collar. "That's why Uncle Tao said he'd take care of me. With Auntie Cassie's help. I'm very lucky to be here."

I smile sadly, looking at Ella. My hand still not removed from her sleek hair.

"Shall we go and eat now?" I ask.

She nods. "I just need to wee-wee."

"I'll wait for you," I say.

Click-clack.

Ella pulls me toward her and points again. "Look."

Inside the drawer are five passports. I open one. A young girl with short black hair stares back at me.

SURNAME: Táng

GIVEN NAME: Huan

CITIZENSHIP: Chinese

DATE OF BIRTH: 28 May/2003

Huan? Christ, there's nothing *lucky* about this girl, I think. She is very *un*lucky, very *un*-huan indeed.

I flip open another.

SURNAME: Cheung

GIVEN NAME: Poi-Poi

CITIZENSHIP: Chinese

DATE OF BIRTH: 10 September/2007

I take out my phone—*tap, tap, tap, tap, tap*—and quickly photograph the five passports.

Evidence #3

Passports/visas of girls trafficked from China with diversions/transfers covering Macau, Taiwan, and Laos. Four girls arrived on December 7, 2018. Cheung Poi-Poi (alternate name: Britney) arrived in the summer of 2018 when Shaun Richards—a barman at the Electra Club—escorted her to the UK. She refers to Navid and Cassie as "uncle" and "auntie." Both of her parents are dead. Her grandparents, who she refers to as "grandmama" and "grandbaba," cared for Poi-Poi. Did they sell her on? Were they naive to Navid's intentions? She is 11 years old.

I finish typing my note. The air feels thick and lifeless.

Poi-Poi returns. A pearl comb with two shoots of dangling lotus added to the crown of her skull.

"Come on," I say, taking her hand—*Just for today I will try my best to be the person I needed when I was young*—and close the door to the Movie Room, where girls fight for survival and are made to feel lucky.

A room where dreams are killed and girls are forced to commit heinous crimes. Abused. Raped.

THE FOUR NEW GIRLS ARE SEATED IN THE KITCHEN AT THE LOW wooden table with the moonfaced girl. All five are cupping plastic bowls in their palms while chopsticks clack at the glistening beef noodles. The Banana Hater walks past Poi-Poi, gives her a push, and makes her way over to Jane, who fingers her vermilion hair.

Holding court with two other Electra Girls, Jane keeps them in line with a firm word or glance. I pick up on the pecking order as usual while she hands out makeup, magazines, and boxes of chocolates—gifts, bribes, and bait—the girls cooing and grabbing while Jane draws on their adoration in a cool, distanced manner.

On seeing Ella and me, she nods. An air of composure as she reaches for a fork, stabbing at the vat of noodles—pulling at them until they reach her mouth.

"Hey," I say.

"Hey," she throws back.

"How's Sylvie?"

"Fine. Why?"

"I haven't seen her for a while," I reply, "that's all."

She dismisses my curiosity and looks away, while Poi-Poi scoots into her side and points at the Banana Hater.

"She's been hurting Tinker Bell again," she whines.

"Snitch!" the Banana Hater shouts, an edge to her voice.

"Have you?" Jane asks, chewing.

The Banana Hater shrugs. "I don't like cats," she says, her eyes traveling down Jane's body and reaching the floor. "Especially that one. It shits everywhere!"

"No, she doesn't!" Poi-Poi screams.

"Yes, she does!"

"She shits on *your* stuff because you bully her. Bully, bully, big tits."

Jane raises her fork-free hand. "Enough," she orders. "You. Stop taunting the cat. And you. Stop being such a baby. No one likes a snitch. *Okay?*"

"Okay," Poi-Poi says, her head dipped.

"Here," Jane says, handing Poi-Poi a boiled corn on the cob, slathering on a knob of butter, and giving it a shake of salt. "Eat this. Then you can have some ice cream."

Jane turns to the Banana Hater with cold, flat eyes.

"I expect you to set an example for the younger girls. Not fight with them," she says, swiping back her earlier gift of a blush compact from the Banana Hater's hand, offering it now to one of the new girls and adding an insanely friendly smile.

The new girl smiles back.

"You're welcome," Jane says.

STANDING AT THE SINK, ONE OF THE GIRLS WASHES PLASTIC BOWLS while Jane braids Poi-Poi's loose ponytail. Ella reaches in her purse for a cigarette and lights it on the stove. Her black bob now grown out and swinging with her movements.

A rap at the front door.

"I'll get it," Poi-Poi sings.

"Sit. I haven't finished," Jane orders, winding an elastic band around her wrist and throwing the Banana Hater a fixed stare.

"Get that," she instructs, not quite having forgiven her and intent on keeping her in line.

The Banana Hater leaves to open the door, looking deflated.

Shaun and Amy appear, arms draped around each other's waist. He looks at me and nods.

Tosser, Runner shouts in my head.

"Shaun!" Poi-Poi cries, careful not to move her head and annoy Jane's braiding hand. "Did you remember to bring my Lelli Kellies? I left them at the club."

Shaun dangles an orange plastic carrier bag off two of his fingers. "Got 'em." He smiles.

"There," Jane says, resting her palms on Poi-Poi's shoulders, "done!"

Poi-Poi jumps down and hops toward Shaun, who releases Amy's waist and scoops Poi-Poi up like ice cream.

"Thank you," she says, hugging him hard, attentive as a sunflower. "Wanna come see what I've done with my room?"

"Later," he says dimly, looking up at Jane. "Is Navid here?"

"Not yet," Jane says.

Glancing at Shaun's hand on Poi-Poi's waist darkens my mood, knowing he was responsible for bringing her here, to be snared, groomed, and violated. How disgusting he is, and how dense I was—to fall, telling myself he was different, that he wanted to help the girls, not harm them. *I can change him,* I forced myself to believe. *He's just being friendly. And anyway, they shouldn't flirt so, sticking their chests out like that.* I ignored my suspicions, deluded.

Denial is king.

"Look!" Poi-Poi says, face bright, searching around at her audience, her feet slipped into sparkling Lelli Kellies. "Aren't they great?"

"Wow," I say, taking Poi-Poi's hand, "I love the sequined dolls on the toes. Let's go see if Tinker Bell is ready to play now."

I squeeze past Amy, who makes it just a little difficult for me to pass, then turn to Ella and smile.

"See you later." I wave.

"Okay." Ella nods, lighting another cigarette.

I take the opportunity to nose around the Movie Room more before Navid arrives. With Tinker Bell nowhere to be found, Poi-Poi decides to make a bed for her gang of stuffed animals.

"Now go to sleep and be nice, and remember, don't snitch on each other! There. A nice soft pillow."

I want to play, Dolly speaks in my head, clambering for the Light.

Just five minutes, I allow, adapting the Flock's rules, *then you have to come back inside the Body. Okay?*

Okay, she agrees.

Dolly takes the Light.

"Hello, Elephant. Hello, Squirrel. Hello, Tiger," Dolly says, smiling at Poi-Poi. "Come on, let's get them hot milk before they go to sleep."

"You sound funny," Poi-Poi says, staring at me, a mild look of curiosity alive in her eyes. Dolly now in control of the Body and pretending to boil a pan of milk. She places three imaginary cups beside the animals, ready for their bedtime drinks.

"Careful, it's hot," Dolly says, pretend-pouring the imaginary milk. Blowing on one of the make-believe cups.

Poi-Poi picks up one of the other imaginary cups and blows. "Hot," she whispers.

The three cuddly animals are each given their hot milk and settled down. The cotton blanket pulled higher to graze a trunk, a whisker, and an eye.

"There; all sleepy now," Dolly says happily.

Back inside now, Dolly, I say, taking back the Light.

Poi-Poi crosses her legs. "What do you do?" she asks.

I shrug back into myself, wondering if she means for work or generally. I answer the former. "I'm a photographer," I say.

"Cool, what kind of things do you photograph?"

"Lots of things, but mainly people. Sometimes, though, I like to photograph birds, or flowers. You know, nature."

"What about animals?"

"Those too," I say.

She smiles.

"Wanna photograph me?" she says, resting her chin, with both hands like an open book. Apple-size cheeks, a false and frenzied smile.

I stroke her hand. "I don't think—"

"What a good idea," Navid interrupts, suddenly appearing at the bedroom door. He sneers, locking his eyes on mine for what feels like a very long time. I keep my mouth shut and say nothing, the room suddenly spinning, an awful dread creeping into the pit of my belly.

49

Daniel Rosenstein

Nearly a hundred degrees and rising.

I reach for the SPF 50, squeeze, and apply it to the back of my sweltering neck while glancing at Monica, whose firm, perfectly bronzed body is looking more delicious by the day. A mix of envy and lust rises inside me, ambivalence felt at longing for her physique but not necessarily her mind. Part of me knowing it would be easier to leave her were she not so beautiful. I stare down at my bright pink belly clashing with red Ralph Lauren shorts—a gift from Monica (assigned an orange Post-it)—and breathe in. Last night a heat rash emerged while we lay together, naked, like Beauty and the Beast, my skin already starting to bubble. I have my mother to thank for this. It's her fault. Her pale, freckled skin and ginger hair both hand-me-down Irish traits that are certainly far prettier on women than on men.

I glance at Monica's side table: SPF 10 resting against a copy of *National Geographic* alongside a bottle of lavender mist that she enjoys spraying on her tanned skin as she ambles around the pool.

Overheated and uncomfortable, I turn onto my belly, conscious of my awkward body, wishing my skin were a little more accepting of the sun, my muscles a little firmer, abs a little tighter, all the while picturing the Old-Timer, toned and muscular. When I saw him last time, I envied how relaxed he seemed in his body. The casual white towel grazing his chest, the ease with which he'd rested his hand somewhere near his worked torso. I must call him, see that he's okay.

I pinch at my paunch, an inch of flesh caught in my hand.

You only have yourself to blame, a punitive little voice whispers in my head. *You should stop being so lazy and work out more.*

The tyranny of *should*s and *must*s.

I take a moment imagining what I would say to a patient who was thinking such things and begin a series of kindly mantras in my head:

A few parts of my body are rather fine.
Most of the 78 organs in my body have performed pretty well since
    the day I was born.
A few times, I really experienced what love felt like.
I can still enjoy how my body felt when I was young.
I can, with permission and on occasion, fantasize about someone I
    cannot have.
Without too much effort, I can order a burger and fries.
Just for today, my body can enjoy the sunshine.
I am not alone.

I feel my envy eventually melt.

Too hot to take any more sun, I stand. Monica stretches, revealing faint tan lines, and I feel a hardness grow inside my tight, wet shorts. Hesitant, I reach again for my sunscreen, waiting for my erection to die down, and cover up with a linen shirt.

"Fancy some lunch?" I ask.

"Sure. Why don't you choose?" She smiles, adjusting her bikini strap.

"Are you sure?" I ask, pointing at her tiny swimsuit triangle. "Maybe you've got some Post-it notes tucked down there with a suggestion or two."

She raises a single brow. "I'm on holiday, Daniel," she says, nose aimed in the air. "I have no need for such notes while on holiday."

Laughing, I kiss her fondly on her shoulder. Lavender filling my mouth.

"That said, maybe I'll have the crab dumplings or the flying fish." She grins, a twinkle in her eye.

I head toward the shady part of the restaurant, passing two girls in their early twenties with waist-length blond hair. One of them is swimming laps while the other, seated at the edge of the kidney-shaped pool, flicks water with an arched foot. Red-painted toenails. My mind unintentionally wanders to Alexa, an invisible thread of attachment leading me to wonder what she might be doing. I check my watch, imagining her at work, camera in her hand, or possibly involved with a late lunch. I wonder if she'll call Mohsin. And if she does, will she find him helpful? Charming? More charming than me? For a moment I consider phoning her to check if she's okay, and then quickly shut down the idea. Boundaries.

You're on holiday, for Christ's sake.

I take a seat at a table, shaded and cool, watching the two girls now splashing in the pool. Their youth, inhibition, and itsy-bitsy bikinis arousing within me a debauched flair.

I can still enjoy how my body felt when I was young.

I look away and focus on the menu placed in front of me.

A waitress appears, shortly followed by Monica, her wet honeycomb hair now piled high in a peach silk scarf. A white cotton sundress casually hanging off her shoulder, revealing a tanned slice of collar-bone, her neck and arms oiled for the gods.

"Let's be quick," she whispers slyly, "then we can go to bed."

She bites her lip. Slides her foot along my calf, which I catch with my hand. An excited fool.

"I won't be able to sleep." I smile, the two girls with their tiny bikinis and long blond hair caught in my peripheral vision. An imagined Alexa joins them to play, laughing, her red mouth matching the tiny dots on the girls' tiny toes.

I can, with permission and on occasion, fantasize about someone I can't have.

50

Alexa Wú

I SQUARE UP, DROP MY GOOD-GIRL ATTITUDE, AND DARE HIM TO SLAP ME.

"What d'ya want from me?" he shouts.

"An apology!"

"For *what*?"

"For sleeping with every other girl in here. For making me feel worthless. I know everything. Why did you lie to me?"

He doesn't slap me. So I wait, silently, secretly wishing he would. An excuse to slap him back. Because that's what I want, a fight. Physical, combative contact with the man whom, deep down, for inexplicable reasons, I want.

He looks away from me, too much to bear. Checks over his shoulder to see that no one except Cassie, whose head is buried in the till, is witness to our slipshod scene. I'm an embarrassment. A loose cannon. A raging banshee. *I'm sorry I'm hysterical because you treated me roughly,* I don't dare to speak.

Don't even think about apologizing; he's a complete asshole.

Okay, let's all calm down.

Stop patronizing me, I don't wanna calm down.

How can you accept what he's done?

Yeah, especially knowing it was he who brought Poi-Poi here?
Motherfucker.
And he's been filming the girls.
And he snitched on you to Cassie, what about that?
Maybe he can change?
Pfft; you're in complete denial.
This is not the time to get upset.
So shoot me!

Dolly covers her ears. *Please stop,* she cries.

The Fouls twist on their slim heels, satisfied smirks turned cruel.

Shaun unlocks his arms and draws closer to me like a moth in search of light.

"I didn't think you cared," he says, locking eyes. "I mean, one day you're all happy and hot for me, and the next you're completely weird and pissed off and telling me what a cu—"

I interrupt him with my hand, knowing he's referring to time spent with Oneiroi and Runner. I look away, licks of shame finding my insides and yanking like a fist working a chain. The reality of the Flock's varied and wildly different views a constant and stark reminder of our illness.

"For real," he says, looking me up and down, "it's like some fucked-up Jekyll and Hyde shit. One minute you're all sweet and kind, the next you're a complete madwoman."

Madwoman. There it is. If you're mad, you're not wanted. Act mad and no one is interested.

Ask anyone with multiple personalities why they're so conflicted and they'll tell you it's because they compartmentalize their feelings.

I wipe snot mingled with lip gloss with the back of my hand, still hoping Shaun will bend and say something kind.

Not able to help myself, I speak first. "Part of me does think you're a cunt."

He stares.

"I'm with Amy now." He speaks softly. And the words, even though known, still burn. There is pity in his eyes.

Runner suddenly jumps down from the Nest, strides forward, all elbows and tight jaw, and seizes the Light.

"Well, fuck *you*!" she screams. "We never wanted *you* in the first place, cocksucker!"

Shaun steps back, a shocked stumble that has his palms spread and raised.

"See what I mean, Alexa? You're all over the place," he says, hurt and defeated. "Look, whatever. Maybe you should get some help. Someday you'll realize I'm not such a bad guy."

He is gone—

I imagine in search of Amy, the sane, carefree girlfriend who doesn't throw insults and call him names. Her arms open and waiting for him and even more divine now I've shown my hysterical *madwoman* hand.

Cassie, hearing Runner's outburst, slaps the till shut with a *ching* and makes her way over. Places her thick arm around the curve of my jerking shoulder.

"You okay?" she asks, almost concerned.

"Yeah," I say, nudging Runner back inside and reaching for a barstool, "I'm fine."

"These men, they think they're men, but they're just *boys*." She rolls her eyes. "Immature little boys. They're not worth getting upset over, blah, blah."

"I know," I allow.

"They're ruled by their willies." She smiles, wiggling her raised pinkie. "You know that, right? We already talked about this."

I smile, momentarily humored.

332

Runner gives me an internal poke, *Don't let your guard down,* she warns. *Remember, she's smart.*

"I'm okay, Cassie, really," I say, brushing myself down. Aware I have an hour to kill before Ella's shift is over.

"Wanna call your mama?" she asks.

Her question startles me.

Don't tell her anything, Runner says.

"She's dead," I say.

Cassie's face turns suspiciously kind. She strokes my cheek.

Careful!

"Come." She smiles, taking my arm. "I need some help downstairs."

Navid's office is small. Claustrophobic. Stale smoke lingers in a grimy, noir kind of way, blending into the semidarkness except where a beryl-green desk lamp spotlights a copy of *Time* magazine. I scan the room, an abrupt rise in my breath as I realize this is my opportunity to gather the evidence. The sudden drench of my palms wiped down my jeans. A wad of receipts and a half-eaten croissant rest on a porn mag. On the whitewashed walls: posters of girls in neon G-strings, a vague look in their eyes that men interpret as seduction. I wonder about the kind of photographers who do this type of work, what it fulfills. What possible enjoyment they feel exploiting girls with dead eyes.

Isn't it obvious? Runner says. *They think the girls are vulnerable and submissive. You can bet your life they're almost all men who photograph them. These girls are slaves to their fantasies. Christ; just think of the metaphor: man, camera, zoom lens.*

I picture Modigliani's paintings. How he'd claimed to not paint a model's eyes until he'd witnessed her soul. Black ovals both alarming and creepy.

They don't believe girls have souls, Runner spits, *they're just collateral in their eye, meat.*

My body shudders, an image of Navid suddenly creeping into my mind. His insistence that I photograph Poi-Poi.

You need to take control, I berate myself, giving myself a sharp pinch to the back of my knee. *Don't lose sight of your career. All those years of hard work so you could become an assistant to someone like Jack. Focus, Alexa. Don't fuck it up.*

There are no windows in Navid's office, but the noise from lifted crates and clinking bottles indicates it backs onto an East End loading bay.

The floor is tiled—brick red—and looks like it hasn't been cleaned for months. Grime and cigarette ash peppered around the base of Navid's black leather swivel chair like somber confetti.

Cassie busies herself with receipts as I drop down on the chair, using my left foot to guide a side-to-side spin, reaching for the porn mag splayed across Navid's desk.

Inside, girls are reduced to two-dimensional objects. Voiceless, numb creatures impaled on the semigloss pages. One girl with large misty eyes and breasts the size of honeydew melons stares out with a look of vulnerability, a candy-pink nail resting on her glossed lip, unable to defend herself or strike back as she might in the real world. Even if she attempts a look of fierceness she is still imprisoned on the page. She can be insulted. Secretly hated. Called a whore. A slut. But still she remains compliant and will sometimes even smile back if you ask nicely. *She loves the fact she's got the power to stiff a dick in seconds,* they tell themselves. These men. She is aesthetically perfect and on tap for fantasy. Airbrushing has been applied, creating a smooth pussy; Photoshop has slimmed down her tummy and waist. There is not a single sign of cellulite. And in the rare case that she doesn't bring satisfaction, the page is turned. Another girl quickly replacing her. This girl is not a person at all. She is an object. A *thing*. Secretly loathed. Consumed and jerked over until their sticky come is thrown down on the page.

Cassie looks up.

"We need to take all the paperwork back to the house," she says, pointing at a black metal filing cabinet. "Can you help me empty out the whole lot?"

I walk over, sliding open the cabinet's top drawer, a fire-resistant safe parked by its side. Next to it, another large cabinet rests against the back wall.

"All of this?" I ask, taking out a stack of papers.

Cassie nods.

I offer her the manila files and dozens of loose sheets of lined paper covered in a green-inked scrawl: web addresses, notes on webcams, websites for escorts, and dark web accounts.

"Thanks," Cassie says, walking toward me. "Best to keep it at the house." She smiles, wiping a stray lash from her cheek. "It's safer there."

I take a manila file and open it.

"Who's this?" I ask, holding up a photo of a topless teen girl, skinny, with delicate breasts. A lunatic smile.

Cassie snickers.

"One of Navid's favorite girls," she says, a sly look stretching from me to a notebook pulled from another drawer. "Recognize her?"

"No. She works here?" I ask.

"It's Jane!" Cassie guffaws, stuffing a bunch of gray notebooks and receipts in a plastic carrier. "Before all the work and red hair dye!"

I join her laugh, colluding with her gibe. "She looks so different. He made her get the work done, right?" I goad, placing a manipulative hand on her shoulder.

She nods with raised eyebrows. "And he paid," she says, rubbing together her thumb and forefinger.

"How old is she here?" I ask, trailing the slim contours of Jane's face with my finger.

"Fifteen, sixteen?"

I open another file; inside, a list of names, phone numbers, and email addresses printed in a heavy font, some of the names ticked off in the same green ink.

Cassie leans over, points at the names with no ticks. "Navid's working on these ones."

"What for?"

"They haven't joined the live webcams yet, but they've shown interest."

"So, they pay to sign up?" I ask.

She nods. "But that's not why we want them to join." Pauses, then: "They're good for bribes. Men in positions of power. Police, lawyers, politicians—those types."

"I get it," I say, nodding back. "And these?"

She hesitates, swiping the sheet from my hand. "Navid better look after these. Dark web codes. For the very young girls." She looks at me knowingly. "Their babas make them do it."

She folds the paper in half, places it in the top drawer of Navid's desk, and locks it.

Shit! Runner whispers. *We need those codes.*

I clear my throat. "Shall I put the rest of this stuff in the carrier bags?"

"Yes, and these," she says, handing me two passports.

In the bottom drawer, I note a camera, a padlock, more porn magazines, and several small handbags: a clutch and a slim crocodile purse.

"And what about these, do you want me to move them?" I ask, recognizing Ella's purse.

"No. Leave those," she says, checking that the drawers are otherwise empty. "New rule: Navid said all the girls have to keep their things down here from now on. He insisted we make some changes after what happened with Annabelle. He even said we can only wear clothes that don't have pockets."

"Oh?"

"Pockets hide things," she says matter-of-factly.

I look at her with confusion as I reach into my coat pocket, not surprised to find another pilfered object—a screwdriver—surely Runner's idea.

"Extra tips, clothes, and gifts—apart from drugs—are also on hold, until he can trust again."

"How long will *that* take?" I smile.

"Depends." She shrugs. "But not too long; as long as there's some coke everything will be fine. He knows girls perform better if they're high." She taps the side of her nose.

"Oh, right," I say.

"He said I have to keep tabs on them too, you know, credit cards, receipts, men's business cards. That sort of thing."

Cassie leans the four plastic carrier bags against the wall. Files, notebooks, and paperwork stuffed inside.

"Keep an eye on these while I go grab a box from the closet upstairs," she says.

"Yep, no problem," I reply, careful that my voice doesn't shake.

I wait for a couple of seconds, then take out my phone: *tap, tap, tap, tap, tap.*

Quickly scanning the room for more evidence while watching the door and aiming my phone at the stash of black-market porn boxed in the far corner. *Tap, tap*—

My phone starts ringing: GRACE.

What can she want? I decline the call, switch the volume to silent.

Quick, Runner orders, *Cassie won't be long.*

Wraps of cocaine, two bottles of poppers, and a spliff stupidly left on the shelf. *Tap, tap.*

I pull on the top drawer again, knowing it's locked but trying all the same.

Shit.

Next, I scavenge through paperwork on Navid's desk, anything that might help our cause: the top copy of an offshore bank account statement and a memory stick quickly folded and stuffed in my jeans pocket. I see an unopened letter sealed with tape, and as I reach for it, knock over a mug of stale coffee. Outside, Cassie's footsteps are approaching.

Hurry, wipe it up!

I hear Cassie talking to one of the girls.

"Wǒ bìxū zuò suǒyǒu de shìqíng?" she shouts.

Runner looks at me. *What's she saying?*

There's a problem upstairs in the bar. She's bothered she has to take care of everything. Quick, help me clean this up.

"You okay?" Cassie says, looking in.

"Fine-fine," I say, wiping the spilled coffee with a bunch of tissues found on Navid's desk. "What's happening?"

"Some problem upstairs. I'll be back in a couple minutes."

I am breathing too fast. My mouth a pit of sand.

Get it together, Alexa.

"Need me to do anything?" I ask. "Shall I come with you?"

"No. Wait. Actually, okay."

I follow her outside the office, up the stairs to where Jane is waiting. "It's that weirdo from last week," she says. "The one who had a thing for Amy. He's refusing to pay for his drinks."

Cassie turns to me, hands me an empty box. "It's okay. Here; start filling this with all that stuff we pulled out," she orders. "Jane, get Shaun. Where is he anyway, who's working the bar?"

They disappear.

Evidence #4

Names, addresses, and phone numbers of men using the dark web—both those who watch and those who post their daughters online. Mostly minors. Cassie Wang and Navid Mahal have the codes. (Top drawer of Navid's desk, currently locked.)

Navid keeps track of the girls, demanding now that they leave their purses in his office while they work. He bribes them with drugs.

I quickly check I haven't missed anything in the cabinet drawers, then reach for Ella's leather purse, thinking I'll take it to her. But just as I'm about to place it on the desk, the Fouls order, *Open it.*

And I do. The act surprises me, my snooping like this. Though why should it? I've just spent the last hour doing exactly that, playing spy at the expense of our safety—only Runner truly on board.

Staring back at me and grinning behind a small plastic window of her wallet is a photograph of Navid—replacing the one of Ella and me.

Confused and stunned, I instinctively hurl the wallet and purse against one of the paper-thin walls. I kick the metal cabinet, causing a small dent.

Is she fucking him? Oneiroi asks.

Probably, Runner says, *wouldn't put it past her.*

Hold on a second, Oneiroi says, alarmed, *I imagine there's a reasonable explanation for this.*

Pfft, Runner dismisses, *get real, dream queen.*

Heavy with betrayal, I collect Ella's belongings and remove the photograph from the wallet, noticing the one of Ella and me tucked behind. Taken in Paris on my twenty-first birthday. Ella and I had spent the weekend as tourists. Both of us smiling at some dude whom she'd asked to photograph us as we held our arms up to the Eiffel Tower, a lit sky, the perspective making the Parisian icon a perfect hat.

The Fouls take the Light and tap the small plastic window with their long bony fingers, a smell of repugnant dead animal now alive in my nostrils.

Part of you has always known she's attracted to him and his power, they whisper, *we're just your subconscious, Alexa. We're only showing you what you choose to ignore.*

Maybe they're right, I think, crushed and loath to admit it—Ella's need to be loved beginning to outweigh any regard for her safety. Her longing potentially leading her to something so utterly destructive.

I claim back the Body and stare down at Ella's purse, tears filling my eyes. I am suddenly overwhelmed by how hateful I feel and how alone I am. And then a realization—hate is simply love turned angry.

51

Daniel Rosenstein

SHE SWIMS TOWARD ME. HER RED MOUTH UNTOUCHED BY THE POOL'S low and still water.

"Isn't it divine?" she sings, her voice calm and sweet. "So heavenly and warm. I will stay here forever."

Her words are dropped like cubes of sugar into unsweetened tea.

Stirred, I open my arms to catch her. My feet planted on the pool's tiled floor. She falls like rain into my reach, our bodies swaying, treading water, our breathing slow and free. I trace her skin, her hair, and the curve of her spine.

"Who are you?" I whisper in her ear.

She presses her mouth to meet mine. Runs her tongue along my lips. "I'm whoever you want me to be."

"*Alexa*," I say, "I want you to be Alexa."

Pulling me into her, she cradles my neck and hangs from it, then, with one swift move from her hips, she wraps her legs around my waist.

"If you surrender, I could drown you," she whispers, the wetness of her red mouth now pressed on my mouth. Her hand guiding the swell between my legs.

She closes her eyes, lets go, and dips her head beneath the trap of water, a playful tickle felt from the brush of her lissome thighs. I too dip beneath. And as we hold our breaths, both of us barely moving, I think to myself:

We are not alone.

Monica takes my waist.

"You were dreaming," she whispers, pulling my body closer.

A pause. A reorientation of my surroundings.

"What?" I say, confused.

"You were dreaming," she repeats, taking my damp cheeks in her hands, softly stroking my hair, our noses nearly touching.

Another pause.

"Daniel."

"Yes?"

"I want a baby."

52

Alexa Wú

So why's he in there?" I say, clearly vexed. "I mean, it's one thing acting the spy, but carrying a photograph of him in your purse like that—it's not right."

Ella pulls up the collar on her new sheepskin coat, her back facing Old Street Tube station. Her movements a little jerky, her eyes a little bloodshot. For a moment I wonder if Navid's slipped something in her purse, as Cassie suggested earlier. Ella's high the result of a slim wrap of coke left by him like a bone.

"I just did it to please him. It doesn't mean anything. Look," she says, pulling on her gold necklace, the dainty key hanging loose, "same as this. He gave it to me. I'm working on gaining his trust."

"You'll give him the wrong idea," I say. "You have to be careful."

"Alexa, I work for him. I'm already giving him the wrong idea."

"What do you mean?"

"He thinks all the girls want to sleep with him. I'm just playing along."

"So you're one of his 'girls' now?" I spit, taking hold of the chain around Ella's neck. "Key to his heart?" I snort, remembering Runner's previous comments. Sarcasm the lowest form of wit.

"I don't know what it's for, but maybe it unlocks something important," she defends.

Silence.

"Are you fucking him?" I ask.

My *Reason* throws me a look. "Are you *seriously* asking me that?"

"Well—"

"NO! I am NOT fucking him," my *Reason* shouts, grabbing my arms. "Look, we *both* agreed to do this. I'm keeping my side of the bargain. What about you? Are you gonna chicken out now?"

I realize I've peeled the potatoes but want to avoid their mash.

"No," I say, shaking my head in defense, "I just want to make sure you're safe. That's all."

Liar, the Fouls whisper. *Admit it, you don't believe her.*

We follow a woman in suede boots. A light dusting of snow evident on her heels as she clicks down the pavement before veering up the shoulder of Rufus Street. I look up at the unblemished winter sky, clear and starless, my eyes leaking from the cold as we dodge a loud stream of people heading along Old Street, dotted with Christmas lights and garlands. More than once my step falters, and I bump into a group of girls waiting outside a Spanish tapas bar, red wine in their hands.

"Want a smoke?" Ella says, showing me an open packet.

"No," I say, a little gruffly, "I want a drink."

We walk a while longer before Ella throws her cigarette to the curb. "Let's go in here." She points.

Two vodkas. on the rocks," ella says, inching her way to the bar.

A girl with a huge beehive smiles. Her Ramones T-shirt tight across her perky breasts. "Sure," she says.

Ella moves toward me, smoke on her breath. "What's going on? I feel like you don't trust me," she begins.

She's onto you, the Fouls snicker.

"It's not that I don't wanna do this anymore," I lie. "My work's suffering. All this snooping around, hanging out at the Electra and the Groom House—it's not how I wanna spend my time. It's not safe."

"You promised you'd help," she says, knocking back her drink.

I take a tissue from my purse and wipe the bar. Straighten the coasters. Wipe the bar again.

"I *am* helping," I defend, "but *Christ,* we need to get our lives back. You said you were only going to work there until you'd saved enough money for your own flat. Well, surely you've done that now? So leave."

"I will, stop buggin' me!" she shouts. "You know, I had to buy other stuff too."

"What? More boots? Clothes? Makeup? Guts to move forward with our plan?"

"All right!" she snaps. "I get it."

"Come on, we've got enough proof now," I argue, not letting up. "Names. Web accounts. Phone numbers. What more do we need? Let's just go to the police."

Ella orders two more vodkas from the Beehive, then shifts her eyes to my eyes.

"Navid told me you're gonna photograph Britney. Is that true?" she asks.

"*Poi-Poi,*" I correct her. "Not Britney, her name's Poi-Poi. And *she* asked me to—not him."

"How come?"

"She asked me what I did. Navid overheard us. It's a mess."

"So, will you? If we have photos of Britney, then we have proof he's using underage girls. *Then* we can go to the police. With all this evidence, they'll definitely have enough to arrest him."

Silence.

"And I can leave the Electra for good."

I look away.

"Please," she says, taking hold of my shoulder, staring at me with her mother's eyes.

"And how do you think that'll make *me* feel? It's hardly *Teen Vogue,* for fuck's sake."

"I'll do it with you," my *Reason* says. "You won't be on your own."

"I don't know, Ella, it's wrong. I don't think I can do it. We'd be colluding with his crime. Christ, she's only eleven years old. She's a *child*."

"Yes, but it's the sure way to get him arrested. With this, he'll go to prison for a long, long time."

"I'm scared," I whisper.

"I know, but we have to do it. We can finally put a stop to this. Help the other girls. Don't forget, some of these girls are even younger than Poi-Poi and Grace."

"That's a low blow," I say, casting my eyes down at the floor.

"But it's true."

I look around the bar at people smiling and dancing. All unaware of the scene less than a mile away. Girls crammed into a house like imported sardines; a room with pink beds like bars of soap; evil cameras; a red sarong and a pine pole; stuffed animals; a whirring fan; a wandering cat.

I am angry that the one thing I love, the one thing I'm *actually good at,* will now be used to incriminate a man in the ugliest of scenarios.

346

Is there not another way we can hold him accountable, another way that doesn't involve me photographing a vulnerable eleven-year-old girl?

A helpless panic finds my chest that I sometimes felt when I was at home alone with my father. How I'd hide in my closet, the bathroom, behind the curtains or beneath my bed. But he always found me eventually. He made it his business to know all of my hiding places.

You have to help her, Dolly whispers.

She's right, Runner adds.

A pause.

"Okay," I agree, "but that's it. Once we have the pictures, we go to the police."

Ella smiles and squeezes my hand.

"By the way," I say, "Grace left me a message. Said she hasn't been able to get ahold of you. You need to look out for her, Ella. Take care of her. Take her calls."

Ella rolls her eyes.

The Beehive collects our empty glasses.

"Two more," she orders.

53

Daniel Rosenstein

WE TILT OVER ANTIGUA'S BAY. ME BY THE WINDOW, MONICA UNFORTU-
nately in the middle, while some guy who appears to be hot and mildly
irritated marshals his bulky mass in the aisle seat. I notice his armrest is
raised. His thick legs leaking into her space like some consuming blob
in a low-budget movie.

Be kind, I tell myself, retrieving my copy of *New Psychotherapist*
from the holding net attached to the seat in front.

Monica releases her safety belt, twists her body while the guy
inches back, allowing her to pass. I dare him to notice her ass. *Go on,*
I goad in my mind. But he looks away, instead glancing at the queue
for the toilet snaking down the plane's narrow aisle, Monica falling
in at number six. I gaze out of the small oval window. The lights from
life below shimmering, long stretches of island roads shaping a fine
chain of luminous white.

I reach up and twist the cool air directly above Monica's seat, the
gentle squall of wind catching my shoulders, now cushioned by a red
Tempur-Pedic neck pillow. Removing my tan loafers, I notice a small
blister on my big toe. This the result of a long walk on the island

yesterday, Boxing Day—my mind largely preoccupied with Monica's admission that she wants to mother a child—both of us wandering, mostly silent, while fishermen hauled gigantic coral nets of barracuda and blackfin tuna. Part of me had longed for the sight of a sparkling Christmas tree, a turkey, cranberry sauce, and all the trimmings. Tradition needling me in the chest.

"Why don't you want another child?" she asked.

"I didn't say that," I answered.

"But you don't. I can tell."

We walked a little farther, more silence.

"I'm old," I eventually offered.

"You're scared," she snapped back.

"Maybe I am, maybe losing Clara and raising Susannah alone has been too much for me. Is that such a bad thing, that I'm scared? That I take seriously my role as a parent?"

"Susannah was already grown when Clara passed. This is about you feeling you weren't a good enough dad. And it's also about *your* dad."

"That was harsh," I say, irritation growing. "And what about my dad? What's your point?"

"My point is that you're constantly doing your best not to be him. Not to mess up as he did."

"*And?*" An edge to my voice now.

"*And* you're not him. You're *you*."

"But I'm flawed, just like him," I said. "And I'm tired. And old."

"And cynical," she spat.

I took her hand then, which she quickly withdrew.

"You know, if you're not open to having another baby," she warned, "this could be a deal breaker."

"I understand," I said.

Of COURSE SHE WANTS A BABY. WHY WOULDN'T SHE?

I imagine most women do at some point in their lives. The empower-ment of their bodies opening the door to possibly one of the most miraculous and uncharted moments in their life: the dazzling array of emotions on sight of a first child, no words entirely worthy, or strong enough, for that first mother-child gaze.

I smile softly to myself, remembering how simple it had felt to imagine children when I was a young man. How Clara had pinned me to a tree, hitched up her skirt, demanding I make her swell. There was optimism back then (and sexual zeal), as well as a hopeful willing that zips to the left side of your brain and has you believing love will afford anything. But my fifty-five years have slowed me down.

I close my eyes, trying to picture Monica, a new baby, and me flying as a trio. The baby crying, Monica pacing up and down the aisle; an hour later, exhausted and resentful, cutting me a look: time to swap duties. I strap on the baby sling—*click, pull*—and start walking. Secretly wishing I could stuff the baby in one of the overhead bins to drown out his or her screams so I could get back to reading *The New Yorker* or listening to the podcast I downloaded the night before.

It doesn't feel right, Monica and me becoming parents together. Even the idea of marriage gives me the feeling of having a pillow pressed down slowly over my mouth, chest cramping from its need for air. Panic takes some people to religion, volunteer work, drink, or despair. I settle on avoidance, the idea of additional loss or conflict not welcomed because I survived so much of it with Clara and my father. Clara as she lay in a hospital room, and gone from me. And my father as he took another pull of whiskey.

I casually flick through *New Psychotherapist,* packed with book reviews and ads for professional development, landing on a feature about transgenerational trauma. How unbelievably fitting. A man in his late fifties with pale skin and a carved jawline is holding a baby, the headline: LEGACIES OF LOSS: WHY DEALING WITH OUR PAST SHAPES THE FUTURE. The baby is fat and pink. A marshmallow chin with one solitary tooth. In his hand a yellow silicone teether. His father looks straight at me, and I wonder while flying closer to the gods whether the universe is conspiring to send me a message—older dad, legacy of loss—then hear Monica's words again: *This could be a deal breaker.*

Suddenly engulfed, I take a black marker from my jacket pocket and draw a mustache above the baby's heart-shaped lip, adding a beard. His face eventually littered with hateful, envious marks and scratches of ink. On his peach-fuzzy forehead I draw an upside-down cross— the mark of Satan—feeling an urge to deface him while remembering Clara. How she'd broken down after the miscarriage of our baby boy, already into her third trimester. A boy we agreed to name Joel. There were complications. A raging temperature. I found her trembling in cold sweat on the bathroom floor, howling. I'd looked down at her empty body, curled like a jellybean, forlorn and terrified.

She was never the same after his death. The loss of him carried around inside her and causing all manner of somatized pain. I blamed Clara's cancer on him, baby Joel, because he refused to fight for his life. I'd needed someone to charge. To blame. Someone to be angry with, so I made it him, baby Joel, because I am not a religious man and found it easier to direct my rage at someone who was dead.

Babies; I wish for no more.

MONICA RETURNS TO HER SEAT AND I HIDE MY SCRAWL, THE CHUBBY baby now disappeared. She adds a sweater to her shoulders. Next to her, the hot heavyset guy takes out a family pack of chili-flavored Doritos from a carrier bag stuffed under the seat in front of him. He opens the bag and daintily places a single orange triangle in his mouth, slowly crunching. He licks a finger, sticky with coral dust, and then offers Monica the scrunched foil packet.

"No, thank you." She smiles. "Just eaten." Then pats her tummy.

She looks at me, sad and longing. The desire of a giant. Her ache for a baby felt in my own belly as she swings her legs beside mine.

She attempts to kiss my mouth.

And I smile kindly, keeping my lips tightly sealed.

"Move over a little," I say, turning away and reaching for my eye mask. "I need a little space."

Monica stares at me. "Take all the space you need," she says, a bite to her tone. Her stricken face now turned away, the look of a woman soured and unloving.

54

Alexa Wú

So you'll be okay?" Jack asks, his bags resting by the studio door.

"Sure thing," I say, all breezy and excited that he trusts me again to take care of things for a week.

"There're no major shoots, just housework," he says. "I've left a folder on your desktop: invoices to pay, phone calls to make. Don't let me down, Alexa."

"Everything will be fine. Now *go!*"

Jack squeezes me hard, kisses my cheek, and smiles. *Whoa, go easy,* I think, but secretly I'm enjoying his affection, our intimacy.

"Call me if you need anything," he says, collecting his phone off the desk.

I throw him an *as if* look. "GO!" I order.

Once he's out the door, I click on the folder and check through the list of "Things to do while Jack's away." Fine, all good. No problem.

Pleased with myself, I feel almost tall in my chair. Proud and encouraged that I'm trusted enough to run the show after Jack's threat earlier this month—*One more strike, Alexa, and you're out.* Runner takes the Light and walks over to the sound system. She pumps out some Captain Beefheart, Oneiroi trying her best to muscle in with Mariah Carey's greatest hits. *Don't even think about it,* Runner grunts, turning up the volume. She pours herself a shot of the whiskey hidden away in Jack's filing cabinet and suddenly we're dancing. The Body cut loose and swaying, head dipped and whipping our hair. Feels good. Feels great. Another whiskey.

Go easy, I say, *we've still got work to do.*

Chill, Runner sings, her eyes closed, arms in the air. Laughing, I get on board, enjoying the freedom, Runner's unwinding. Her air guitar now in full flow, the Body kneeling and sliding across the studio floor.

"Let's call Robin!" she shouts.

"NO," I cry.

"You're no fun, Alexa." She smiles coyly and squeezes my cheeks. Another whiskey.

Runner noses around Jack's desk for something interesting: a black-and-white photograph of him and a pal kayaking, a stress ball, a couple CVs resting in his inbox. She flicks through them: the first one a recent graduate looking for unpaid work; the second Sam Driver, who's been working for three years on a national newspaper picture desk and is clearly ambitious, experienced, and keen to "branch out." "Mm," Runner says, "he's got drive, all right." She tosses the CVs in the bin. "But don't worry about it," she says.

Seated at my desk, I switch back into the Body, sync up my camera with the computer, and download the last couple of months' shots, noticing a file on the screen named *Us.*

What's that? Runner asks.

I click on the file. A distant and vague memory of Shaun and me messing around one night after work. A catalogue of images appear on the screen. Runner points at one and I click again. It is a picture of me, naked, a ribbon around my throat, legs spread open. Another whiskey. *Urrr,* my tolerance for neat liquor clearly nowhere near as matured as Runner's. I cover my mouth with my hand, but already Dolly has seen my shock. She turns away, Runner guiding her back to the Nest, Oneiroi slinking off in front. *Don't think we don't know this was you,* Runner shouts. Oneiroi's pace quickens. *Get back here,* Runner orders. *I know you did this for him.* I watch Runner grab hold of Oneiroi's shoulder, yank and pull her to face us. Runner grits her teeth, her breath fast and enraged. Oneiroi says nothing. Instead, she stares out at the image on-screen. Then she begins to cry.

I miss him, she confesses.

Miss him? He's a complete douche bag, Runner slurs.

You wouldn't understand.

Damn right.

Oneiroi takes the Body, swipes through dozens of shots. An intimate rectangle of our bodies damp with heat. A raised knee. An arched back. Fists clenching a pillow. Some of the pictures are unfamiliar, I note, but not all of them. These, I recognize, were of our early days spent together, when we were happy. It felt comforting to me, having someone close, someone other than Ella to take my hand; to hold and stroke and squeeze it. Sometimes I longed to be loved so badly I'd ache, but I saw it in him too. Both of us alive to our fears and hopes and past pains.

Oneiroi zooms in on a photograph of Shaun splayed across my bed laughing, a smoke in his hand.

I really miss him, she cries. *My body felt alive when I was with him.*

Runner stares, a look of defiance cast across her eyes. *You know what, I'm afraid for you.* She sneers. *You don't seem to grasp what's right and what's wrong. He will destroy you if you allow him. He will hurt you and leave you to rot.*

Don't patronize me.

Oh, please. And by the way, it's OUR body, she corrects. *OURS.*

"There's no such thing," Oneiroi speaks aloud. "But then, I don't expect you to understand that. Your words are not a warning, they're a curse. And just so you know, *you* are the one to thrust them against *us.*"

55

Daniel Rosenstein

Eight thirty-eight.

Sweating and desperate for the session to end, I risk a glance over at the gold clock, fearful she may catch me, my backbone giving a little yelp.

Eight thirty-nine. Eleven minutes to go.

Quick, eyes back before she catches you.

"What's the time, Mr. Wolf?" she asks.

"Mr. Wolf?"

"Never play that game at school?"

"No. Can't say I did."

"Then let me explain, Doc. Someone pretends they're the wolf. The other children have to creep up behind the wolf and ask, 'What's the time, Mr. Wolf?' The wolf chooses a time. Two o'clock, eight o'clock, et cetera, et cetera. When the wolf finally decides it's dinnertime, he or she pounces! Chases you. Gobbles you up. Fun, right?"

"Actually, I'm not sure it is."

She laughs.

Ten minutes. Christ, I struggle with this personality. She scares the shit out of me. Clinical theory encourages clinicians to find compassion and understanding for *all* personalities with a multiple, but this one tests me. I know she gets off on running rings around me like this, taking perverse pleasure in watching me sweat, squirm, and flounder.

I catch myself holding my breath. We sit in silence.

Seven minutes.

From inside her bomber jacket she takes out a neatly folded sheet of A4 paper. Reads it to herself and edges a half smile. But something stops her from speaking.

"Would you like to share that with me?" I ask, nodding at the page.

"All in good time, Mr. Wolf. All in good time." This she speaks in a deep, toneless voice. Almost metallic.

Her body appears strong today. Her denim legs wide open as she loafs—like a man. Her heavy trainers kicking the rug between us and causing a curl. I'm aware of my desire to straighten it, the angle making me twitch, but I resist bending down. Her body language warning me: *Bow down and I'll kick you in the head.*

When Dolly arrives, her legs and feet occasionally turn inward; with Oneiroi they are elegantly crossed while she works the exquisite arch of her instep with her thumb. As for the Fouls, I haven't had the pleasure of meeting them yet, their personality still an enigma, and if I'm completely honest, I'm a little apprehensive of encountering them.

She digs out something from one of her teeth with her nail, then rests her chin on a clenched fist and leans forward. A standoff. Stalemate.

For a moment I picture her running around both our chairs, chest pulled back, trainers set alight like a flint. We suddenly burst into flames. The two of us caught in a swirl of inferno above the Nest, awaiting rain. Anger comes like a sudden flight of birds. *Why must you set fire to our work? Why do you wish to destroy it?*

A saboteur.

Five more minutes. Excruciating.

She wipes her nose with the back of her hand.

"Tell me, Doc, do you think it's good practice to leave your patients when they're so vulnerable?" she asks.

"You're upset about the break."

"Upset. *Please.*"

"And angry."

"I'm angry when I see you checking the clock every five minutes, angry that you jet off thinking everyone will be fine. Don't forget, Doc, I see everything."

"So it seems."

Four minutes.

"See all those lunatics out there pacing up and down, talking to themselves?" She points at the bay window. "They're incapable of telling you how negligent you are. Fuck, some of them can hardly speak!"

"You believe I should *never* take a break, is that it?"

She shrugs.

"A little unreasonable, don't you think?" I say, palms turning damp.

I adjust my collar. A phlegmy racket escaping my throat.

Maybe I'm coming down with something—a virus caught on the plane while traveling back home? Or possibly the lack of sleep after another argument with Monica.

"Hot, Mr. Wolf?" She snorts.

I gather myself, resentment brewing. "Why do you sabotage our work?" I ask.

A pause.

She takes the A4 sheet of paper and scrunches it into a tight ball.

"Catch!" she shouts.

The hurl has me off guard. The paper ball lands in my lap. I feel my temper rising.

"What is this?" I try not to shout, but do.

"A gift from the Fouls," she says, leaning back, resting a calf on her knee. "It's a list."

"*A list?! A list of what?*" I hiss, imagining snakes alive on my skull.

"Of ten ways they want to hurt you."

I open the scrunched ball of paper.

"They said to tell you number five is their preferred choice."

She stands, already knowing we're at time, and leaves.

I walk over to my desk, burying my face in my hands. For the first time I note my grave fear, not of Alexa, but of the trauma within her. The distinct madness. The pain.

I take out my notebook to record what's just happened but put it down, instead pick up the phone.

"Hello, this is Dr. Patel speaking."

"It's me."

"Hey, welcome back. How was your holiday?"

I close my eyes. "Okay. How's the research going?" I answer, fatigued.

"Oh, that good, eh?"

"It could have been worse. I guess."

Mohsin clears his throat. "Well, research has made me a mad person." He laughs.

"Is there not pleasure in being a mad person, which none but mad-men know?" I say.

"Ha! So today you're a poet."

"And mad, apparently. Selfish too."

"Ouch. Problems with Monica?"

"Monica wants a baby," I say, my mood turned low, "*and* I've just had a visit from Alexa's gatekeeper."

"I'm not sure I'm comfortable with you naming your partner and a patient in the same breath."

"Well, there it is," I say, surrendering, suddenly exposed.

"You okay?" he asks.

"Sure. You know how I get after a holiday."

"Cynical?"

"Disenchanted."

"What was she like, the gatekeeper?"

"Fierce."

"Of course she is. She's protecting Alexa from potential threat. She'll be doing anything to ensure there's no repeat of abuse."

"She and her foul sidekicks want to hurt me."

"So potentially violent?"

"You don't say."

"She's frightened, Daniel. You have to earn her trust. It takes time."

"And in the mean*time* she's left to run amok and terrorize me?"

"You're being dramatic. She's just testing you, waiting for you to slip up."

"She's a man-hater."

"Can you blame her?" he defends. "Does she have a name, this man-hater?"

"Runner."

"Runner?"

"Likes to run rings around people, gets off on it. Enjoys the power."

"Is there a part that Runner cares about, possibly loves?"

I consider this. "Dolly. The youngest."

"Makes sense. So the key might be to bond with Runner through Dolly."

"I'll try."

A muted sneeze in my earpiece.

"Bless you," I say.

"Thank you," he allows, sniffing just a little bit. "Remember the multiple I worked with last year?"

"Jessica?" I say.

"That's the one. She'd send me emails, sometimes five or six from the same address. Her gatekeeper would send me threats under the name of Felix, a male part, remember?"

"How did you manage her? Him?"

"It wasn't about managing him, it was about gaining trust. Felix appeared after Jessica was assaulted one night in her own bed. Two neighbors—brothers—crowbarred their way into her home. Felix swore nothing like that would ever happen again. You need to listen to your countertransference. One foot in the ditch—"

"And one foot out," I add.

"Exactly. And try not to let her flood you."

I end the call and reach for the scrunched-up sheet of paper, ironing it out with my palm. I stare down at the Fouls' list:

5. Pour bleach down your throat.

56

Alexa Wú

Our bodies collide like head-on traffic. A sudden blow to my chest. The man's phone crashing to the ground.

He tosses his morning coffee, catches my fall. "I'm so sorry," he frets, "are you okay?"

Shocked, I don't answer. Our collision causing my balance to lurch.

I find my breath, my brain adrift. Eyes amiss and blurred as they try to focus on the corner pavement, a graffitied white wall. Soho Square opposite: a vague mass of swaying trees.

I reach out both of my hands to touch the wall, something concrete to steady my shake.

"I'm so sorry." His soft words repeated. "I wasn't looking where I was going," he adds.

The man, blond and slim with a tie, moves closer. Takes hold of my arm, bends and collects his phone. A crack across the screen.

"Shit," he curses. Rubs the phone along the sleeve of his gray suit jacket.

I reel backward.

Flash.

Rᴏʙᴇʀᴛ.

Tequilas.

Flash.

"Get away from me," I scream, shaking loose the man's grip. Forcing him away.

Breath racing. Legs shaking. *Help.*

Stunned, he steps back. Palms raised.

"It's okay," he whispers. A dazed look in his eyes.

Flash.

Flash.

I ᴀᴍ ʟʏɪɴɢ ᴏɴ ᴛʜᴇ ꜰʟᴏᴏʀ. ʙᴏᴅʏ ʜᴇᴀᴠɪɴɢ, ᴡʀɪsᴛs ʙʀᴜɪsᴇᴅ. ʜᴇᴀᴅ ᴛᴏ one side and legs unnaturally wide. A pair of twisted black knickers somewhere close to my foot. A sequined dress scrunched at my waist.

I dare not sit up. Fearful I may enrage him further. This man. Slightly overweight and balding—a middle-aged cliché. He throws an expensive gray suit jacket across his thick shoulder and looks far too pleased with himself. He has drugged me. Slipped rohypnol into my drink.

I have a clear memory of talking to him in the bar, slamming tequilas. He works in PR. Name is Robert. Fifty-one years old. Has no children and is divorced—an expensive and messy affair, though he still wears a platinum wedding band. Robert likes to holiday in the spring—usually in the South of France—because the months of July and August are too warm for his pale skin.

Robert also likes to handcuff women and rape them.

When he finally leaves, he throws a sleek twenty next to where I lie unmoving, surviving.

Flash.

THE MAN CHECKS HIS CRACKED PHONE AGAIN—DEAD IN HIS HAND—while I focus on the graffitied wall, my head full, mind wandering back to Robert in the Gray Suit—my amnesic barriers now melting. The flashback even clearer—

THE GIRLS' DRESSING ROOM WAS COOL AND DAMP. TWELVE MISSHAPEN wire hangers dangling from the clothes rack in the far right corner. I heard the door slam shut, Robert now disappeared. His gray suit jacket slung over his shoulder as he left like he was about to head out for ice cream. *Sprinkles with your raspberry ripple, sir?*

Motherfucker, Runner hissed, the rohypnol still chasing our veins.

Try to move the Body, coaxed Oneiroi.

What d'ya think I'm trying to do? Runner challenged.

I'm just saying; we need—

Don't tell me what we need. Just shut the fuck up.

You deserved this, the Fouls sneered.

Dolly started to cry. *Please don't say that,* she begged.

I saw Ella's leather jacket hanging among others, a BIRTHDAY GIRL badge pinned to its collar. A thumping bass could be heard from upstairs, the Electra Girls serving drinks from silver trays and allowing their bottoms to be patted and stroked.

I suddenly felt cold, wishing I hadn't thrown my drink over Shaun and that I could reach Ella's jacket. I wanted to rest it around my naked shoulders to warn off the floor's frigid edge. Eventually, the Body roused, my feelings slowly handed back.

"Oh my God, what's happened?" Ella said, bursting through the door.

I still couldn't move, not much. Robert's drug still in my veins.

Hysteria found her eyes. They were wild and fearful and stared into the pit of all my misery. It was a subhuman part, extraterrestrial, not human at all. *A worthless piece of shit. A tramp. A whore who got what she deserved and then got paid for it.*

Ella pushed my legs together gently and pulled down my dress, dirt drying along its hem. I felt the soft part between my pelvis come alive, the service station where he'd emptied his manhood and refueled on my aching need.

Head pounding, vision blurred, I tried to stand and failed.

"I'm losing my mind," I said, searching for my twist of underwear. "The Voices. They're getting louder," I cried.

Ella helped me up, pain surging through my vagina like a hot knife.

"Let's get you cleaned up," she said. "Then we have to go find Navid. Tell him what's happened."

"No," I warned. "No. I don't trust him."

We didn't speak as she led me to the women's bathroom. I guess there was a part of her that blamed herself. A part that felt shame because she'd gotten us involved. Amateur spies. Clueless fools. Both of us in denial of the *real* danger we were putting ourselves in. Ella reached for my abandoned black underwear and handed them to me, unwanted and soiled. I told myself that if I hid them, scrunched them into a tiny tight ball, they would disappear. Make what had just happened go away. *Take me,* I thought. *Incarcerate me. Punish me. I deserve it.*

Finally, she gets it, the Fouls jeered.

Standing before the trio of mirrors, I did not recognize the Girl staring back, the bruise on her cheek. Grazes on her wrists turning coal colored.

I blinked and the Girl blinked back.

Widening my eyes, I watched her do the same.

Then I frowned and she copied.

I pulled at my bangs and she did too.

I pulled and I pulled and I pulled—even harder at the skull.

Hateful and violent.

Large chunks of hair fell away in my hands and the Girl opposite began crying, wailing. I watched her clenched fists pounding the mirror, not caring if it shattered. Next, she clawed at her skin. Her neck. Her chest. A scrawl of blood leaking down the length of her arm.

Ella stepped in then. Took hold of my hands. Bound me to her. "Please stop," she pleaded.

I picked up my hair, in clumps on the floor, believing I could stick it all back. That it would attach like fuzzy felt, or a magnet—and simply carry on growing like before.

A moment of madness.

"Let's get you dressed," Ella said.

But I refused to move. Instead I waited for Ella to dress me. I thought it was the least she could do.

"Stop!" I screamed, touching the soft part of me. "I'm still bleeding." Flash.

CAN I DO SOMETHING?" THE MAN ASKS, LOOSENING HIS TIE.

I shake my head. He tilts his, and attempts to take my arm again. I pull free.

"Here"—he points—"sit down for a second."

Cautious, he nods at a wooden bench a short distance away. My head catches up. The flashback slowly ebbs. *Focus*, I tell myself. *Concentrate.*

He chooses to stand while I sit. Frowns. Runs his phone-free hand across his blond head.

"Just leave me alone," I say.

"Are you sure? I can—"

"*Go,*" I insist. Fatigue pressing down hard on my bones.

He walks away, shakes his head, and forces his useless phone in his back trouser pocket. I aim my recovering eyes at his back, his gray suit jacket. A fantasized knife suddenly pictured in my hand—steely and curved—now forced deep into Robert's spine.

57

Daniel Rosenstein

I'M CONSIDERING A SABBATICAL," I SAY.

"Really?"

"Really."

"It's not a total surprise," he says, "considering how you've been struggling."

"It took Monica to intervene, point out how stressed and rotten I've been. I'm not sleeping. Dreaming a lot, but not sleeping."

I blow my nose. I sense a cold emerging. My throat already raw from a night's worth of dry coughing.

"I'm sorry," Mohsin says, scanning the room. "Let's order. Then we'll talk."

In pursuit of the Pretty Freckled Waitress I too glance around the room, but it appears she is not here today. Maybe she's got the day off, I think, picturing her on the back of some boyfriend's motorbike, her strawberry curls catching the wind.

"I can't get up in the mornings," I begin.

"That's not like you."

"Find myself making all manner of excuses not to go to work. Just like when Clara died."

"I see."

A pause.

"So maybe it's nothing to do with your practice," he says, fingering his tie—a Windsor knot. "Maybe it's you. What's going on, Daniel?"

"I wanted to drink last week," I say.

"Sorry," he says firmly. "Not an option."

A waitress finally arrives at our table. Pretty, but not freckled.

"Large bottle of sparkling mineral water, please. Two glasses. Thank you," Mohsin orders.

The waitress nods and walks away.

"Were I to refer Alexa on, what would be the protocol?"

"Just Alexa?"

"I feel she needs specific analysis."

He squints at me, notes a flicker in my lower lip.

"What's *really* troubling you?"

"I just don't feel equipped."

"Go on."

"I should let someone else take care of her. I'm too involved. Too attached. Part of me wants to go to the Electra and—"

He sighs. "So now you're some vigilante shrink?"

"I should refer her on to someone else, probably a woman."

"That's not the answer."

"I feel impotent."

"Literally? Or metaphorically?"

"The latter. And just with her, I might add. I have fifteen patients, most of them steady and improved. But with Alexa, it's different. This crippling disorder of hers, it's too much."

"It could be harmful if you give up on her now."

"Really?"

"Yes. You're more than equipped to do this piece of work. You're tired. She's traumatized. What's happening with your countertransference?"

"I feel both powerless, ineffective, and without agency."

"That's three."

"Sorry?"

"You said both, then gave three."

"Oh. Well, mostly powerless."

"Which is how Alexa feels, only a hundred times more. Listen to your countertransference. It's the best tool you have, apart from that big brain of yours. Remember, we can read as much as we like and consider ourselves incredibly clever with interpretations and insight, but in the end it's authentic feeling and countertransference that informs the work. A direct result, a window into the patient's unconsciousness."

A pause.

"Look. Alexa's inability to control her desire and the course of her life is a moral problem. One might say her pathology is political. You need to make her aware of this."

The waitress arrives with our water. Lands two glasses and pours.

"What would you like?" she asks, taking out her notepad and pen.

"The crab," Mohsin answers. "Times two."

"Very good," she says, turning on her heel.

"You were saying?" I ask.

"You need to make her aware of her pathology."

"I agree. But it's when I'm faced with Dolly, her youngest personality, that I unravel. She's so vulnerable."

"And what does that say about you? *Your inner boy?* Maybe there are some things *you* need to work through?"

I nod, agreeing.

"I miss Clara and I barely see my mother," I say, a swell of sadness finding my throat. "And now Monica wants a baby."

"Quite a trio."

I nod again, sipping the bubbly water.

Mohsin places his palm on my wrist.

"You're overwhelmed. Flooded."

I feel myself wanting to cry but hold back, fearful Mohsin will become exasperated with me. Instead I reach for my briefcase, the distraction soothing my hurt.

"Alexa left these at reception for me, just before my holiday," I say, offering him the manila envelope.

To Mr. Talky,
I drew these for you. Love, Dolly

Mohsin smiles.

The first picture is of an orangutan. A large, scrawly but immensely accurate line drawing. Its markings with an amber-colored pencil capturing the swinging ape almost perfectly. Long hair blowing, the orangutan hangs from two beetling vines. I note the intense concentration that has gone into its face, particularly the eyes. The second picture is of a gibbon, again drawn with tremendous detail. Its sinewy arm stretched toward what appears to be a thick rope. The third is of a rhesus and her baby—mother and child—both resting with the aid of hunched legs and open palms, their arms clinging protectively. While it's not as accurate as the orangutan and the gibbon, I favor this one most, which I imagine is due to my respect for psychologist Harry Harlow and his observations of the wire-monkey mothers, his discoveries changing how we understand early attachment.

"She's talented, this younger part. Creative." Mohsin smiles, placing mother and child on top of the other two.

"The drawings are representative of her loss," I say, "her mother in particular."

"I see. And what about her stepmother, Anna?"

"I suggested Alexa ask her for help with her medication, which she was open to."

"Good. You could even schedule a call with Anna, maybe."

"Really? Might that not jeopardize trust between Alexa and me?"

"Mm, possibly. Have it as a backup plan, then."

I picture Alexa clinging to a surrogate wire monkey mother, realizing she was instead thrown to wolves.

"Look, no one said this work is easy," he says, handing back the manila envelope.

"I know."

"And there are certainly easier ways to earn a living."

"So it seems."

Mohsin loosens his tie and leans back.

"Intervention is needed," he says. "Clear your mind. Sooner or later you need to make some decisions. All this conflict with Monica—it's impinging on your work and well-being. If you don't want another child, tell her. If you do, then great. But try to level out. Visit your mother. Figure out what you want. Regarding Alexa: You've been colluding with her neurosis, allowing her to act out with little challenge. All this evidence gathering and risky behavior—it has to stop. She's repeating a pattern of abuse and needs to extricate herself from that club and anyone who's associated with it. While she continues to be involved she remains in trauma time, not *real* time. Encourage her to cut contact. And quick."

I pause. "So more intervention."

"Precisely."

58

Alexa Wú

I'M SO HAPPY YOU'RE BACK," I PURR.

He clears his throat.

"Runner wasn't," he says, looking at the small hole in my stocking above my knee. "Neither were the Fouls. They gave me a list of ways they'd like to hurt me."

"I know," I say, crossing my legs, shame needling in, "I was watching from the Nest."

He stares. Scanning, I imagine, for clues to who I am today, or perhaps whether Runner is close by.

"You were *watching*?" he says.

I nod.

"Runner made me rest with a headache. But I didn't know she was going to be so mean to you. I'm sorry."

He waits. "Does that happen a lot, you acting as a bystander?"

His challenge surprises me.

"It's not that simple, Daniel," I defend. "Sometimes I'm just too exhausted or stressed to do anything. All the switching makes my head hurt. And your going away really upset me, so the Flock had to take over."

"I see."

Silence.

"So how have you been?" he asks.

I yawn quietly. "Tired," I say.

"Trouble sleeping?"

"A little," I add, stroking the rose quartz pendant at my throat, Oneiroi, although fatigued, longing to take over the Body. "I've been waking around three, unable to get back to sleep."

I've missed him most, Oneiroi pleads. *Let me out.*

"Sounds like insomnia," Daniel says.

I pause.

"We missed you," I eventually say.

"'We'?"

"All of us," I say, glancing at Oneiroi's crossed arms.

"That's nice," he says.

"I'm really sorry about the list," I say. "I feel terrible."

He leaves me hanging. I guess wanting me to take responsibility for the Flock's actions. I stare down at the rug.

"Thank you for *your* apology," he says, "although it might mean more if it came from the Fouls, or Runner."

"That will never happen."

"Why?"

"Because they don't believe they have anything to apologize for."

"They threatened me."

"They're hateful."

"I think they're scared too," he says.

I sense his hurt and try smiling, but he remains, tanned and handsome and buttoned up. His bronzed face in desperate need of an explanation or apology. I imagine him sunbathing on his holiday: the sea holding his weight as he drifts on his back, the feel of soft waves.

"I had another dream," I whisper, allowing Oneiroi out to fully claim the Light.

Go sleep, Alexa, she says. *I can take over for a while.*

Okay, I surrender, climbing into the Nest.

Daniel smiles at me, finally; eyes like the lapping cool sea, part of me longing to dive in, naked. I imagine lust waits for me there, his hands reaching for my shoulders and cupping the curves of my breasts. I fancy myself walking toward him and dropping my past on the sand. Slowly, I open up my arms to him. *Take me,* I ache to speak.

"A dream? Please," he says, inching forward.

"It started, again, with the Tiger—running down a deer. I was watching him through my binoculars, not my camera, as he chased her. I quickly realized the Tiger was my father."

I clear my throat.

"The deer swerved, the Tiger close behind. When the deer eventually fell, the Tiger landed his jaws around her neck. His body suffocating her. I lowered my binoculars, thinking I was the Tiger's daughter, which surely meant I was just like him."

I wait, head suddenly throbbing.

"Alexa?"

Massaging my temples, I say, "It's my head. It's pounding. Just give me a second—"

He waits.

"'Come with me, Xiǎo Wáwa,' the Tiger said. But I refused, and instead walked over very calmly to collect the deer—my arms covered in her blood. I stroked the backs of her bloody, maimed legs. I had to save her."

I look Daniel square in the eye. "I had to save her."

Eyes glazing over, a single tear escapes.

"A startling dream," he says quietly. "Who's Xiǎo Wáwa?"

Silence.

I step back, encouraging Dolly now to take the Light.

Come on, Dolly, I say, *tell him.*

"Who's Xiǎo Wáwa?" he repeats.

"Little Doll," I sing, happy to be back in the Body.

"Little Doll?" Mr. Talky says.

"Dolly! Me, silly."

The rapid switching makes my head go all light and fuzzy and hot.

Mr. Talky smiles.

"Hello, Dolly," he says.

"Hello." I smile.

"Dolly, maybe you can help me out."

"I'll try my best," I say, stretching my neck, proud at the idea of being helpful.

"I think Alexa or Oneiroi was just here. And then she just disappeared. *Poof.* Do you know why she left?"

"Oh, they're tired, especially Alexa. She's hardly slept, you see. But she and Oneiroi wanted to tell you about a dream we had."

"I see."

"Between you and me," I whisper, giggling behind my hand, "Oneiroi's been thinking about you an awful lot."

Stop it, Dolly, Oneiroi orders. *Right now. You're embarrassing me.*

"Is that right?" Mr. Talky says.

"Yup. But don't tell," I say, holding a finger to my mouth.

He smiles.

"So how have *you* been?"

"Good. I have a new hobby," I say, clapping my hands. "Drawing monkeys. Do you like monkeys?"

"Err, not particularly. But I don't dislike them."

"I think they're the best. I left you some to look at just before your holiday. Did you get them?"

"I did, thank you."

"There was a gibbon, a rhesus, and an orangutan."

"Yes, I thought they were excellent, Dolly."

I kick off my shoes and sit cross-legged in the chair.

"What is it that you like about them—the monkeys?" he asks.

"They're funny," I say. My hands shake with excitement.

"They are rather, aren't they," he agrees, "but they're also very clever animals. Their feelings can change if they are stressed or confused, just like humans. And if they feel frightened they cling to one another."

"I cling to Runner when I'm scared."

"Why Runner?" he asks gently.

"Well, she's strong, and sensible. And . . ."

"And?" he says, like he's trying to be helpful.

I hold up clenched fists. "She can box and kick and chop!" I roar, aping a superhero, and making him laugh.

"When you were on holiday, Runner had to protect me when I was at the Groom House."

"You *came out* at the Groom House?" he says, worried.

"Yep, and I made a new friend—Poi-Poi. Runner and Alexa kept watch while we played, though, because it's not always very safe there."

"What do you mean, Dolly?"

"Well, you know that man Navid who does bad things to the girls. Some of us think Alexa's best friend Ella loves him, we're not too sure yet. But Alexa really hates him, she thinks he's dangerous and cruel."

"Where is this house, Dolly?" he asks.

"Dolly?"

My knees start to shake like I've done something wrong.

"Dolly?!"

Runner knocks me out of the way, her eyes sly and mean. "Don't pretend you give a rat's ass about us," she warns, suddenly standing. "And stop interrogating Dolly."

He jolts.

"You'd better watch yourself, *capisce*? Don't forget, Doc. I see everything."

59

Daniel Rosenstein

<u>Alexa Wú: January 8</u>

I have just completed a session with Alexa. Secondary traumatic stress is upon me. Work with her is proving complex and disturbing. After our discussion today, I feel ill, like I've been slung around at great speed, my head feeling like it might implode. There was so much switching. Three alters were here today: Oneiroi, Dolly, and Runner. When Runner was in control, she claimed that she "sees everything." She believes I am interrogating Dolly and threatened me. Her contempt was shocking.

The switching of personalities is speeding up and it's difficult to know exactly what might fly at me, hence my secondary traumatic stress. I have become fearful for my safety, as well as Alexa's.

While dissociative fugue is diminishing, loss of time is still a factor. But it seems the personalities are coming out now at such speed that I suspect Alexa is losing control over her personas along with their actions. I also noticed a dissociative trance in Alexa's face today (like her eyes were dead) that worried me greatly. It seems as though there's a dehumanization to her at times, like she doesn't feel anything, lacking emotion and empathy. This is disconcerting. Mostly because she is close to acting on her rage—just like Runner did today, who incidentally was vile.

Rethink: Containment for Alexa (especially Dolly), safety and possible intervention. Do I need to increase her medication . . . ? Involve Anna, her stepmother, as Mohsin suggested?

Or does she need to be committed?

To switch from a regular personality to seductress to killer within minutes is terrifying. Neither of us is safe.

60

Alexa Wú

I PLACE MY CAMERA ON TOP OF THE PINE DRESSER.

"Why don't you both go sit on the bed?" he says, his eyes fixed and stark.

I take Poi-Poi's hand and squeeze it, catching Navid stealing a glimpse at Ella's white T-shirt—worn tighter than usual, no bra—the heels on her shoes lifting her a couple of inches higher than they might have six months ago. Ella flicks her kinked hair and bends down to adjust the strap on her shoe, her skirt riding like a raised flag, alerting him to her delicious danger and knowing how much he likes it. He smiles and strokes Ella's cheek.

"I like your shoes." Poi-Poi smiles.

"Thanks," Ella says, "they're new."

"Turn that down a little." Navid points to a shoddy plastic CD player, its sound homegrown and tinny.

Eyes on Ella as she twists down the music, he paws at the camera's tripod—unscrewing and lengthening its legs so its height matches the bed. Ella fingers a lonely strand of hair. Is she flirting? Did he catch her nervous laugh earlier, the twitch of her upper lip that I know to mean she's stirred, or fearful? An arch in her back hinting at sex. Is she acting? Or does she mean it?

Navid rests his hands on his hips, concentration fixed. His tongue curled at the edge of his lip. Poi-Poi bounces up and down on the bed.

"I want new shoes too," she demands.

Nobody answers.

I start to wonder how putting a lens between myself and the world has been a protection against more than physical danger. It has shielded me, offered opportunity to combat illness, and protected me from terrible things: demonstrators, grieving mothers, and families forced to leave their homes. For a moment I worry that the very thing that has helped balm my struggles will now be used against me.

Navid wipes his forehead with the back of his hand.

"There," he says evenly. "We're good to go."

Ella smiles.

We're good to go.

Go slow.

Go? No.

Yes, go.

Go. Go. Go.

Leave.

Run—

I can't leave, I say, the Flock watching from the Nest.

Navid finds an edge on the bed and glazes over, I think with either anticipation or thrill—it's hard to tell.

"You're so pretty," he says, catching Poi-Poi's free hand. "Isn't she pretty?"

Ella and I turn away.

"Thank you," she says. "Is Shaun coming to watch too?"

"Not today, baby," Navid says.

I stand, the Body needing to orient itself. Steady its shake. My feet fixed firmly on the floor.

The music, now low, takes a turn from dance to R&B. Poi-Poi begins to swing both my and Navid's arms in time to the rhythm. A swaying back and forth of our hands not unlike a mother and father walking their little girl to school.

Urgh. Go. Go. Go. Leave. Run—

Dolly is ordered to stay inside the Nest while Oneiroi keeps watch. Runner waiting by the Light, just in case. I stare down at Poi-Poi, hating myself for what I'm about to do.

Navid turns to Ella. "Here," he says, handing her a bundle of clothes and suddenly standing. "Take her next door and help her get ready."

SITTING CROSS-LEGGED ON THE FLOOR, THE BANANA HATER CUTS ME A glance. I note a tasseled lamp has been planted in the center of the room, along with posters of Justin Bieber, Katy Perry, and Chinese pop stars whose names I don't know. In the far corner a thirteenth birthday party balloon sits deflated.

There is a girl slumped on the pink mattress.

"Don't mind her," the Banana Hater says with a dismissive hand, "she's wasted. Had enough K to blow a mule."

K? I voice in my head.

Special K, Runner informs me, *ketamine. Horse sedative: completely knocks you out cold.*

"She'll come back around soon enough," the Banana Hater says, turning the page of a gossip magazine. "Shaun said to let her sleep it off."

A shudder runs through my body.

I stroke the arm of the wasted girl. A white tag around her wrist like on a newborn baby: *Liang. 14?* written in green ink.

With her age unknown, I wonder if she was ever held in her mother's arms. Or if her assumed fourteen years have been lived in motherless fear. Did her mother sell her out? Or was the woman seduced by Tao's money and lies that spoke of taking care of her baby girl, *more opportunity, more fun?*

She stirs.

Get the photographs over with, then we leave and go straight to the police, Runner says.

Momentarily calmed, knowing this will be our last time here, I drop down on the mattress, Poi-Poi at my side.

"See you later," the Banana Hater says, magazine now rolled and held like a baton. "I need food."

I sense Ella hesitate as she unfolds the bundle of clothes—a white pleated gym skirt, a tank top, bobby socks, and pumps. Two hair baubles meant for two pigtails. A cheerleader.

"I'll dress myself," Poi-Poi sings, "I do it all the time."

My heart snags on shame, then shrivels to the size of a nut.

What are we doing? Oneiroi shouts.

Quiet, Runner orders, pointing. *Keep watch of Dolly.*

Both asleep—the wasted girl on the pink bed and Dolly in the Nest—I feel my envy rise at their lack of witness to this sordid event.

Focus, Runner says, digging me in my rib, *buck up.*

Nodding, I shrug back into myself and take out my phone, my focus on the wasted girl's name tag.

Tap, tap.

"What are you doing?" Poi-Poi asks.

"Just practicing before I photograph you," I say, turning away, tears slowly releasing.

Stupid fucking crybaby, the Fouls scoff.

Navid is sitting on the satin sheet waiting for us.

"She needs more makeup," he says, spinning Poi-Poi like a prima ballerina on pointe. "And her hair—it's too limp. Curl it."

I make a face and reach in my pocket, feeling for whatever weapon Runner has hidden. This time brass knuckles.

"What's wrong?" he asks, confused.

I don't answer.

"*I said,* what's wrong?"

I shrug.

He stares.

"Time of the month?" He snickers.

Silence.

"Hey!" he demands, a little too aggressively.

"Nothing," I answer. Quick and sharp.

"For fuck's sake. You girls: moods like fucking yo-yos."

I throw him a black look.

"I'm fine," I say.

"No, you're not," he spits, "one minute you're all happy and 'Oh, I'll help you, Navid,' next, you've got a face like fuckin' thunder. Snap out of it."

Attempting calm, Ella steps in.

"Come on," she sweetens, placing her hand on Navid's shoulder, "let's do this."

Navid nods his head, exasperated.

"That's more like it," he says, taking Ella's waist before turning to me.

I force a smile.

Ella finds a set of curlers in the bathroom and plugs them into the wall while Poi-Poi shakes the fat red pom-poms.

"Look!" she says, waving them high, forming an X with her body. "I'm a cheer girl!"

"Yes, you are, Britney," Navid says. "Can you cartwheel? Do a split?"

Not a split, not a split.

Poi-Poi doesn't correct him with regard to her name. She is too high and too fizzy from all the attention. She drops down and slides. Legs wide open. Cheer girl scissors.

"Can Tinker Bell come in the photograph with me?" She sparkles.

"Sure, baby," he says, turning to me, "that'll be cute, right?"

Silence.

"Right?!" he shouts.

"Right," I say.

NAVID POSITIONS POI-POI ON THE BED. HAIR FRESHLY CURLED. LIPS fully glossed. Cheerleader costume in place. A wandering cat.

Senses alive, I make my way across the room. Gut in knots. Everything in my periphery heightened in sound, color, and smell. Joss sticks. Whitewashed walls, satin sheets, red pom-poms. An R&B loop. My mind attempting to *focus, buck up.*

"Ready?" Navid says.

"Ready!" Poi-Poi sings.

I reach for my camera, the heat from the overhead light burning my neck. Ella catches my eyes, fear plain in hers.

Focus, buck up, camera. Camera button. Light burning my neck. Light burning my neck.

Burning. My. Neck.

"Let's go," Navid says.

Focus, buck up, camera. Camera button.

Press.

Flash.

H<small>E TRACES HIS HANDS DOWN THE LENGTH OF MY BODY AND PULLS UP</small> my nightdress, fingers stroking the humble puppy fat on my nine-year-old thighs. I pretend to be asleep and pull Nelly closer. Her cuddly trunk resting beneath my chin.

Crying, I turn away.

"Shhhh, Xiǎo Wáwa. Be a good girl," my father says. "This is what all daddies do when mummies go to heaven."

Flash.

I silence my mouth, imagining it stitched up with wool. This the first of many silences. Mini deaths. Jabbing strikes of fever cut through my vagina, my eyes watering with each thrust. I scramble behind my bedroom wallpaper, hundreds of tiny printed balloons. Why is he doing this? Is this really what all daddies do when mummies go to heaven? I don't know.

The question rolls over and over and over in my mind until the words become one: *Isthisreallywhatalldaddiesdowhenmummiesgotoheaven?* Now the question makes no sense at all.

Flash.

His release comes quickly, the sticky mess pouring down my non-virginal thighs.

Suddenly, another little girl joins me. She smiles and straightaway I can see she looks just like me. Same eyes, same hair, same nose. Same face shape.

I'm Dolly, she says, stroking my head, tucking Nelly tighter beneath my chin. *Don't cry, it'll be over soon. Promise. Just close your eyes.*

I do as Dolly says and squeeze my eyes tight.

Flash.

My stomach cramps from the size of him, my face wet with shock. Finally, he gets up to leave as quickly as he arrived, not bothering to wipe away his crime. And like a shadow, a dark mysterious force committing the worst act imaginable to any little girl, he abandons my young, burdened body. The stench of rotting meat drifting from my bed like plague. *Please stay,* I whisper as he closes the door behind him.

Flash.

Flash.

Flash.

TICK-TOCK-TICK-TOCK-TICK-TOCK—

I step back from the tripod, my hands shaking.

Navid takes my hand.

"Well done," he says, stroking my cheek. "You did it. Welcome to our little family."

61

Daniel Rosenstein

It's time," I say, rattled from our session.

She pauses, places a lone finger to her lips, and hands me a pink note. On it: an address written in a childlike cursive hand.

"Shh," she whispers, her forehead resting in her palm, "don't tell Runner."

I wonder if I'm being tricked—Runner waiting in the wings and ready to seize the Body and pounce. *Don't forget, Doc. I see everything.*

I hesitate, suspicious, but Mohsin's words find their way into my mind: *She's frightened, Daniel. You have to earn her trust. It takes time.*

She smiles and turns her feet inward. Hands nervous and wringing.

I quickly place the pink note in my pocket.

"The Groom House?" I whisper.

Dolly nods.

Thank you, I mouth.

She stands and gathers her red satchel and pale blue mittens. Takes her time to hang the strap diagonally, then pushes her hands through thick knitted wool. I also stand. My internal supervisor preventing me from running over our boundaried fifty minutes regardless of my desire to hear more about last night's espionage involving a photo shoot.

"Maybe you can ask Runner to come next time," I speak loudly.

"I'll try," she says, rubbing together her mittens, "but she doesn't like it here very much."

"I know. She thinks I ask too many questions. She wants to protect you."

Dolly glances down at the rug between us.

"I guess," she says, eyes fixed on her feet. A nervous lean. "Oh, I forgot to tell you; the Flock keep traveling back in time, just like *Doctor Who*. It's not nice. It feels scary."

"You mean like a flashback?"

She shrugs.

"It's okay," I say, walking her to the door, "we'll figure it out, Dolly."

"Bye-bye, Mr. Talky." She waves.

I sit down at my desk, hoping that penning some notes will ease my surging disquiet. I place the pink note in my top drawer along with a bunch of unopened letters and take out my notebook, a mild shake to my hand:

Alexa Wú: January 10

Dolly has disclosed the Flock's dangerous and compromised "evidence gathering" at the Groom House (address to be confirmed). She claims to have "woken up" and witnessed Alexa taking photographs of Poy-Poy and Britney. (Explore this, very confusing narrative. Are they the same person?) She also alludes to an increase in headaches, flashbacks, loss of time, and mood swings.

391

Today I observed her switching into alternate self-states at great speed, again, and have written a script for additional risperidone and quetiapine—twice daily. I have also suggested she ask Anna to help her remember her medication, and she was not averse to the idea.

It seems Alexa's personalities are warring for autonomy and power. It is now much clearer how Alexa (and her dissociated parts) functions, detailing her behaviors when engaging in specific situations (e.g., at work, when faced with conflict, and in relationships) and we are discovering how adaptive these action tendencies can be.

Oneiroi (I think) cited that Runner is keen for the Flock to uncover the trafficking ring and expose Navid (*the Recruiter*).

Tow, or Tao (*the Transporter*), is operating from mainland China, where the girls are coerced, purchased, and trafficked via Myanmar, Laos, and Malaysia in small groups or individually. From my understanding, they have come from poor families or parents who believe their daughters will be offered a better life. Tow/Tao's sister—Cassie (*the Middleman/ Harborwoman*)—is responsible for live pornographic streaming of underage girls, of whom there are approximately fifteen, all being held at the Groom House, where Cassie lives. She acts as "mother," madam, carer, discipliner, enforcer, and the main link to buyers—mostly men.

I have warned the Flock about the potential danger they are in, suggesting that one of them—preferably Alexa? or Oneiroi—contact the police as soon as possible. If she is unable to do this, then I will need to report these crimes to the authorities myself.

I am left wondering about Alexa's role in all of this. Is she acting as negotiator for all of her personalities? Or is she a conduit? A body? A hostage?

For a moment my confidence is lost, my mind turning blank—too tired to think—white noise replacing any prognosis. "I need coffee," I speak out loud, and then as if from nowhere a voice—low, mean, and vindictive—whispers in my ear: *Just one little drink, no one would ever know.*

62

Alexa Wú

I'VE MADE ELLA A SURPRISE LEMON MERINGUE PIE. HER FAVORITE. A kind of twisted celebration now that we've gathered enough evidence to go to the police and Ella's decided to leave the Electra. To mark new beginnings.

I picture Ella and me at the police station: a white boxy room with unflattering fluorescent lights, a cup of sweet tea offered in a white polystyrene cup. Our hands in our laps, feet flat on the floor. We'll dismantle our lives for the past six months and explain how we were too afraid to leave in case Navid harmed us, or Grace, and how I was forced to photograph Poi-Poi. The sickness and fear I'd felt as Navid stood behind me giving instructions. His hand touching my back, Ella touching Poi-Poi's cheek for necessary comfort. We'll hand over the incriminating facts and photographs: email accounts, Tao's address and his accomplices, the girls' passports, Cassie's offshore bank account statements, and a memory stick of photographs posted on the dark web. *We need to get Annabelle and Amy's brother's medical notes too if we can,* Runner suggests.

"Annabelle might agree to it, but not Amy," I say out loud. "Now that she's Shaun's girlfriend."

I gaze down at the pie. I've added a hint of mint glitter to the whisked meringue that I now hold above my head, like a hat. Testing for stiffness. *Voilà, parfait!*

I wash my hands seven times (better), bleach the linoleum kitchen floor (cleaner), check that the windows are locked (good), count the knives in the cutlery drawer (twelve), then pour a large bowl of Coco Pops, adding milk.

Take your medication, Alexa; it's three A.M., for Christ's sake! Oneiroi orders, *You haven't slept for two days straight.*

I'm fine, I say, spooning the candied pops in my mouth, *stop fussing!*

You're not fine, and you lied to Daniel. You said you'd ask Anna for help.

Oneiroi shakes her head and leaves. A puff of exasperation to her cheeks.

You try talking to her, she says, addressing the others.

The Fouls take the Light and slap my face. It stings just a little.

Your so-called friend's not interested in pie, they snicker. *She wants Navid.*

*T*ICK-TOCK, TICK-TOCK—

It's close to five o'clock when we eventually venture out in the cold to deliver the lemon meringue pie. My head is thick with slumber and I feel foggy and disoriented from the Nytol Oneiroi forced me to take.

It's okay, Oneiroi soothed, *you needed to rest. You've been asleep for most of the day.*

Tick-tock, tick-tock—

When I finally arrive on the corner of Ella's street, Runner steps out and checks my phone to make sure the photographs I took at the Groom House have been uploaded to the cloud, then hands back the Body. Head still a little hazy from the Nytol, I note the front curtains drawn at Ella's flat. I make my way across the driveway, crunching the gravel, a spill of engine oil leaked and smelling. Next door's cat paws its way toward the leak and sniffs its black goo, sneezes, then, spotting me, quickly sprints off.

Ahhh, look at the kitty. Dolly points.

"Cute, isn't she?" I speak out loud.

Balancing the pie on my palm, I press the doorbell and wait.

No answer.

Again.

No answer.

There's nobody in.

Told you she's not interested in pie, stupid.

Quiet!

Christ, my head hurts.

Just leave it on the doorstep.

No, someone will steal it.

Don't be ridiculous, who'd nick a pie?

Where's the kitty gone?

Maybe check the back door.

Good idea.

I walk around to the side of her flat and open the back gate, the loud sound of grime breakbeats coming from an open window. Grace must be home, I think, no surprise they couldn't hear me ringing the doorbell. I look down at the wooden slat table parked on the garden lawn, noticing a recent cigarette stubbed out in a glass ashtray, smoke still drifting. A pack of Marlboro Reds resting on its side.

Who smokes Marlboro Reds? Runner asks.

"I'm not sure." I speak out loud. "Shaun used to, but he quit, remember?"

Something doesn't feel right, Oneiroi says as I approach the back of the flat. *You should walk away right now.*

Ignoring her warning, I step up to the window and—

I stop breathing. The pie slips from my hand.

There, on the couch, kissing Ella's naked breasts, is Navid.

I try to look away and fail.

My *Reason* sways with pleasure, her eyes gently sealed, her mouth easy and open. Luxury moves her further toward him as he takes hold of her ass. Navid working over her nakedness like a predatory cat. Charged and confident, she edges closer and arches her back. My disgust mixed with just enough envy has me suddenly feeling like I need to leave the Body immediately.

How could she, I say, dampness creeping beneath my arms.

With Grace at home too? Oneiroi adds.

You absolute fools, the Fouls sneer.

Reaching to kiss Navid's neck, Ella opens her eyes and—

I stumble backward. She screams. Jolts. Stands and pushes him away. But it's too late. I've already seen her. And him. Together.

*T*ICK-TOCK—

I do not remember fleeing or how I came to be here, wherever this is, outside in the cold. No pie. I light a cigarette and check my watch, noting I've lost at least two hours, my head throbbing with pain. It's as though someone has whacked my skull with immense force. Nervous, I touch it, checking for blood—but there is none. Sweat creeping up the back of my neck, I force my eyes to blink.

The image of Ella and Navid suddenly returns.

We need to check on Grace, Runner says.

We can't go in there, Oneiroi orders.

All I can think about is the desire in her half-closed eyes. The memory now branded in my mind and unlikely to fade.

You liar, you whore, you disgust me. I want to scream, but don't.

Pathetic, the Fouls scold.

Were I to take her lying, treacherous words—*It'll be the last thing, I promise. Then we'll go to the police and I can leave the Electra for good*—and drag them across my legs, they'd cut far deeper than any knife. How could I have been so dense? So foolish? Clinging on to memories of when we were younger and how there was an innocence to our friendship like to a life raft. We knew our bodies were blooming but we didn't know the power they held, the sex that was inside us. Teenagers, we practiced fun and fashion, swooned over boy bands and exercised ways to clear zits, unaware of the consequences our naiveté held. So silly we were. And stupid.

Stupid.

Stupid.

Stupid.

Stupid.

Stupid, the Fouls mock.

Tick-tock—

The rattling from a closing garage door startles me. I search for my phone to call someone, anyone, needing to hear the kindness of another's voice, but then realize there is no one.

Anna, call Anna, Oneiroi says, panicked.

I look up, the sound of a car's engine fast approaching; its music bleeding into the onset of night.

I scroll through my contact numbers, pausing on *Anna W.* before moving on to *Daniel R.* I check the time—7:58 P.M.—and dial.

Deeply ashamed that the only person I feel able to call is my shrink, I force my hand down my leggings and drag my nails along my inner thigh. Immediately any numbness reawakens.

The call goes directly to voicemail.

Convinced Daniel is ignoring me, I run my nails a second time. Blood appearing like the scrawl of something wild.

63

Daniel Rosenstein

A BRUNETTE WITH A ROUND FACE AND HIGH BANGS HAS REPLACED THE previous redhead.

She rests herself against a pine dresser, a caramel Stetson perched on top of her head. In the background, a thin red curtain casts a crimson glow across her collarbones, fledgling and slight, as she stares out from the screen of my laptop; heavily made-up eyes like pits of smoke, one hand resting on her slim waist. Her other hand turned into an imaginary gun as she blows.

Scroll down, the screen instructs.

I reach her denim cutoffs, worn beneath a holster containing a faux gun. Then another message appears: Fantasy Friday! Come and meet all of our beautiful entertainers in your favorite wear. I feel an awkward strain between my legs.

Above me, Monica's footsteps pad across the bathroom floor, a rose oil bath run by me earlier hoping it might soften her mood—and buy me some time to research the Electra.

I try, unsuccessfully, to picture Monica's face morphed on the screen. *Monica Cowgirl*. The brunette's brown eyes replaced with

Monica's blue. But her presence is too powerful to be recouped by another, so she remains—eyes lingering with silent inquiry. Her smile large, wide and perfect.

Vibrating in my front pocket I feel the insistence of my phone. I reach inside. Hardness grazing my hand.

Alexa Wú.

I feel a sharp sense of alarm.

"Hello."

"Mr. Talky?"

"Dolly?"

I stand, eyes still locked on the screen. The cowgirl still insisting on my attention.

"Dolly, is that you?"

I hear the shrill in my voice. *Stay calm,* I tell myself, erection now wilted.

"We caught Ella with the Bad Man. Doing Bad Things. Grace is in the house too. Alexa's very upset. She's going to hurt herself."

"Dolly, listen to me. You have to call out Runner," I order, Mohsin's words, *Intervention is needed,* ringing in my ears.

A pause.

"I'm frightened," she whispers. "Alexa wants to run in front of a car."

"Where's Runner, Dolly?"

"Not sure. All confused. My stomach hurts. Alexa is going crazy in her head."

I gather myself.

"Dolly, you need to be brave and call out Runner. Show her the Light. Tell her she needs to take control."

"Be brave. Call out Runner. Take control," she repeats.

The cowgirl hasn't moved. Her face suddenly appears to me like it is sealed and fixed. A digitalized mannequin of compliance, disdain in her eyes.

"Dolly?"

Silence.

"Dolly, are you there?" I speak louder.

"Yes."

"Are you safe?"

Silence.

"Dolly. Alexa. Are you safe? DOLLY!"

"Relax, Doc. We're all safe, for fuck's sake."

Just like that, the phone call is ended. A flatlining silence filling my right ear.

Relieved at Runner's intervention, I feel my eyes close. My breath searching for a slow and steady rhythm.

It's not until I hear Monica enter my office that I realize I have my head in my hands, my elbows resting before my laptop. Legs clenched together at the knee, my ankles cramped. A strained contortion of pain shooting up my shins before finally reaching my thighs.

I eventually turn.

Swaddled in a white terry-cloth robe and smelling of rose, Monica stares at me, at my laptop—the cowgirl still there, hand resting on her slim waist. Her contempt filling the entire screen.

Monica's eyes narrow, their blue turning green. "What are you doing?" she asks.

"Research" is the best I can muster.

She exhales. "I'm leaving. Too many deal breakers. Don't come after me."

I do not wait to watch the door or go after her, part of me knowing she had already left anyway.

Forlorn, I finally let go. My inner boy surrendering as I cradle my body with self-parenting arms. The same relief drenching my whole shape as when my mother would rock me at night when I was unable to sleep. Her cotton nightdress damp with my night terrors.

64

Alexa Wú

Eᴌᴌᴀ's ᴇʏᴇs ᴀʀᴇ sᴡᴏᴌᴌᴇɴ. ʙᴜʟɢɪɴɢ ʟɪᴋᴇ ᴇɢɢs. ʜᴇʀ ᴍᴀsᴄᴀʀᴀ sᴘᴏɴɢᴇᴅ away but still detectable by the slight tinge of coal above her cheeks.

"Thanks for meeting me," she says. "I didn't think you'd come."

I am silent. Waiting, I suppose, for her to feel something, as I have for the past two days, willing myself not to immediately try to make it all better and have us talking like nothing has changed.

She catches my eyes. Early light casting an eerie haze through the West End café's blinds. A block of morning shade hovering above our beige Formica table and across our hands. Ella guides a spray of loose sugar into a neat pile, then flicks it away.

"Nice café, didn't realize you worked so central."

"That's because you've never asked."

She nods. "You been here long?"

"Long enough," I say. "I'm actually meeting someone here in half an hour, so let's get this over with, shall we?"

A pause.

"I'm so sorry," my *Reason* finally says, resting her hand on top of mine.

Though stirred, I am instantly suspicious. Untrusting. Still vexed. And betrayed.

I pull my hand away to punish. "What were you thinking?" I say. "He's a fucking pimp."

Ella pokes nervously in her purse, retrieving first a cheapo lighter, then a cigarette that she holds by its tan tip. Her nails chipped and bitten down.

Our silence is uncomfortable until our waitress appears and sets down a mug of dark tea for Ella, then slides an early breakfast of sausage, scrambled eggs, and beans toward me. I pepper the eggs and saw at the sausage, then pile up my fork. But the moment I open my mouth my stomach protests. I push the plate away.

"Not hungry?" Ella asks, her mug held like a begging cup in both hands.

"Not particularly."

"Not like you."

"How would you know? What I like, what I don't like. What's *like* me or not?" I snap. "Do we even know each other anymore?"

"I get it," she says, putting down the mug, "you hate me."

I look away. Tears loading up in my eyes like bullets.

I search my pocket for tissues, feeling a sudden urge to wipe down the table, realizing I have none.

Ella clears her throat. Retrieves a cotton handkerchief from her purse, offers it to me.

"How long are you going to punish me?" she asks in a small voice.

"For as long as it takes to sink in," I say, leaning over my food, my chest an umbrella, and wiping the tabletop. "You slept with the pimp we were trying to whistleblow. Are you insane?"

She is silent.

"Are you *in love* with him?" I ask.

"No!" she defends.

"Look at me!" I hiss. "*Why? Why* did you sleep with him?"

Ella lowers her eyes, now half-mast and pinned on my chest. Contempt breathes between us, something that might identify as hatred.

She looks up. "Because I could. Because it's the one thing I can do better than you. Attract men."

I look at her, nerves jangled. Heart low in my chest. Her envy-fueled attack on me undoing our bond.

"So this is what we've become," I say. "Rivals."

A pause.

"No. I—"

"You did this," I spit, eyes ablaze. "You made me someone to compete with. I'm your best friend. *Why* did you do this to us?"

"I was jealous," she says, her voice low and controlled. "Look at you. You've got everything: a great job, a future doing something you love, a stepmom who's not running in and out of your life, a shrink who actually cares. And then there was Shaun. I was even jealous of him." She snorts, rolling her eyes. "When we slept together that night, part of me wanted to make you jealous. Show you what it felt like; punish you by letting you see he wanted me too. But it didn't work. You seemed to enjoy it."

"Of course it didn't work," I say, the control of her tone tempering mine. "You've always meant more to me than some random guy. Always."

She starts to cry. And I allow her this, at least.

"Nothing's changed," she finally says. "I still want justice, to take Navid down. I lost my head. He just showed up at my house and we got into something. I regret it now."

"Grace was in the house," I say, shaming her further. "You have a responsibility to look after her. Keep her safe."

She looks away.

"You do know he sleeps with every girl in the Groom House, and the club?" I say. "He doesn't even care how old they are."

Ella's eyes slide down into her mug of tea. "That's sick," she says.

"*You* fucked him," I spit, a forgotten headache now returned. The cruelty found in my voice not altogether comfortable.

A pause.

"I shouldn't have lied to you," she says, pitching her words with care. "I'm sorry."

Silence.

Runner steps out. Collects the knife and fork and nudges the sea of beans around my plate. She jabs at the eggs and squashes the beans, stabbing at them over and over with no intention of eating, and then, like a frustrated teen, throws the knife and fork down on the table.

Ella leans forward, tears filling her eyes with regret, and takes hold of my angry fists. Runner turns on her heel and hands back the Body.

You deal with her, she orders, huffing off.

This is my best friend, I remind myself.

This known fact is far more important than anything else, Oneiroi says.

Ella squeezes my hand three times, no words, then looks up. "He hit me," she says.

I look up, Oneiroi, Runner, and Dolly peering over the Nest, awaiting my response. For once I applaud their silence.

"*What?*" I say, firmness in my voice.

"Across the head."

"*When?*"

"The first time was—"

"The *first* time?" I interrupt, forcing myself to delete any impatience in my voice and throwing my hands in the air.

"Please," Ella says, taking my palms, squeezing again, "let me finish."
I lower my hands.

"The first time," she continues, "was after you caught us. I knew how upset you'd be, so I got dressed to come find you. He hit me when I tried to leave. Told me I was being pathetic, a stupid little girl."

She breaks down. Rocks back and forth on the café's white plastic chair. "I was scared."

This time I place my hand on top of hers. "Why did you go back to him, after he hit you?" I ask, again attempting patience.

"I guess I convinced myself it was a one-off. A blip. And after he calmed down I believed him when he said he was sorry, that it wouldn't happen again, that he loved me. I missed you and I was lonely. You've been so busy with work. And I figured you wouldn't want anything to do with me after you knew I'd slept with him. The next day I caught him in bed with Jane, even though he said they were over and promised he only wanted me."

She clears her throat.

"And by the way," she continues, "you were right about Sylvie, she is sweet. I bumped into her at Planet Organic before Christmas. We went for a coffee. She said she'd never go back to Electra again, after the way Navid's treated Jane. She tried to get Jane to leave. I don't think they really see each other anymore."

"That's what Shaun said to me too: that I was the only one. They're born liars, both of them. And that's a shame about Sylvie and Jane."

I take a breath, thinking of our own friendship. "So now what?"

"Now I want revenge."

"You should have wanted that months ago." I judge, again.

For a moment I consider reading her the riot act. Reminding her of the times we've talked about girls who end up with violent men. The kind of girls we said we'd never be. We sneered at girls like this, the ones you'd see yapping at the ankles of shitty men. Later drinking, drugging, or having sex with another man just to numb the pain of their rejection. We called them weak. Pathetic. But of course we are, and have been, this kind of girl. Both of us. Fatherless, and looking for a man to put right the wrongs done to us. Repeating madness, hoping for a different outcome.

Just for today I am strong. Just for today, I will try my best to be the person I needed when I was young.

"You know, I haven't been able to forget what happened in the girls' dressing room." I touch my wrists. "What that monster did to me. I can't shake it. Forcing himself on me like that. What kind of man handcuffs and rapes a woman who can't move?"

"A complete sicko, that's who."

"Every time I see a man in a gray suit I flinch. I should've done something about it. We should have never gone back after that."

The waitress appears and stares at the breakfast carnage on my plate.

I attempt a smile, hoping it's enough to let her know it's nothing personal. That my hunger has lapsed because my best friend has just told me she's been hit and now that I have this piece of information I don't quite know what to do with it. Or what to say. My appetite now gone.

I wanted that, Runner says, glancing the waitress's thick back, carrying away our mangled breakfast.

Me too! Dolly joins in.

Runner shrugs, *Meh,* and then rummages around the Nest for a smoke.

You need to eat something, Oneiroi adds.

Yeah, go get the eggs back.

Where the hell are my cigarettes?

Settle down.

Go on, before she throws it away.

Don't bother; you could do with losing some weight. Worthless piece of shit.

Please stop this.

Worthless—

I'm tired.

Piece—

Go home.

Of—

Where are those goddamn cigarettes?

SHIT—

Please, I wanna go home.

"QUIET!" I scream.

I am standing.

Everyone in the café turns: their mugs held in the air, forks fixed midbite. I glance around, my breath heavy and exposed. Ella places her hand on my waist.

"I have to go," I say, standing.

Ella tugs on my sweater. "Sit down, Alexa," she whispers.

"The Voices . . ." My sentence tails off.

"What about them?"

"They've gotten so loud. All the time now."

"It's okay. Tell everyone inside things are gonna be okay."

I sit down and rap the side of my head with my fist.

Ella takes my scarlet face in her hands and moves in closer. "Look, I've got a plan. Wanna hear it?" my *Reason* whispers, fingering the dainty key on her gold necklace.

I nod yes.

"Every Monday, Cassie goes to the bank with the week's takings. But if she can't go for whatever reason, Shaun goes instead. They keep note slips and coin bags in that top drawer where the dark web codes are, right?"

"Okay . . ."

"So next Monday I'm going to distract Cassie, make up some problem that she *has* to sort out at the club—I don't know: I'll block a toilet or have the girls lose something, clothes or their makeup. Something. I'll figure it out—so Shaun will have to go to the bank. Then I'll get the key off Cassie and offer to help Shaun bag up the takings. But I won't lock the drawer, I'll leave it open so you can go down there later and get the codes and all the other men's contact details. Then we hand them in to the police. Once and for all. The codes, as well as the photographs of Poi-Poi."

"But we have enough proof. Christ, Ella. Haven't we both put ourselves in enough danger?"

She takes my hand, squeezes it three times. "Please trust me, Alexa," she whispers.

For a moment I have trouble wresting my eyes from her necklace, but I manage to nod again before she gathers her things to leave.

Ella smiles. "I love you."

65

Daniel Rosenstein

I KNOW I SHOULD LEAVE BUT I DON'T.

Psychiatry regulations would have my guts if they knew, my license withdrawn, but I decide to risk it and remain. Seated in the corner, I watch Alexa drink her coffee, both hands wrapped around the mug protectively while she blows. Across from her, a man in a black leather jacket. They talk quietly. He leans forward, she lowers her eyes. Their conversation intense and still. The rules say that should I, the shrink, enter a public space to find one of my patients there, I must leave immediately. But I don't. I remain. A snoop. Unable to take my eyes off her.

Thinking I'd grab a coffee in the West End on my way to my AA meeting, I was shocked to look up and find her seated at a table across the room. I was curious, charged, a hit of adrenaline surging through me that I knew wasn't from coffee. I felt a craving to watch and observe. A voyeur.

I've already decided that should she recognize me I'll pretend I haven't seen her, feign reading. I've pulled out my clinical notes from my leather briefcase in preparation. I've even got my response down:

"Alexa, hello." Surprised face. "What a coincidence. Look, I'd better be on my way." She'll understand, respecting my boundaries and considering my exit both ethical and safe.

I wonder who the man is. Could this be Shaun? Navid? Jack? Someone she's been keeping secret from me? I scan my memory of the descriptions she's given of all three men. He could be any of them.

The man stands and heads for the bathroom and I note he is cleanly shaved, handsome, casually dressed but smart. *Navid?* Maybe. I feel my breath escalate thinking about the Groom House, the Electra, and the girls. Alexa's wild and dangerous involvement with each and her entanglement with Poi-Poi and the photo shoot. The risks and exposure she's taken now mirroring my own as I sit here, waiting.

Alexa takes out a lipstick and compact mirror, applies and pouts. A tug on her bangs. Or maybe it's Shaun? Maybe she's trying to win him back?

She moves her face from side to side, checking, I imagine, her profile. Runs her finger slowly along the edge of her mouth and presses together her rouged lips. Who does she see staring back? Who is she right now? Oneiroi? *Runner?* Unlikely.

I look down at my notes, pausing on January 8:

To switch from a regular personality to seductress to killer within minutes is terrifying. Neither of us is safe.

I wonder if she's scheming. Planning her next move, seducing Shaun, or possibly even Navid, so she can seal the deal—bring their whole operation down. Why would she be with Navid, unless Ella put her up to it? Is she planning another photo shoot, further espionage? Christ, no.

A metal taste in my mouth.

A jolt in my chest; a racehorse; a gunshot start.

My father's voice all of a sudden in my head without warning: *Where's your backbone, you little wet wipe? Why are you being such a coward? Such a lily-livered bystander?* And now Mohsin's words also flood back: *Intervention is needed. Clear your mind. Sooner or later you need to make some decisions.*

My temples start to pulsate at speed. A matching heartbeat. *What if this were Susannah? What would you do then?* I ask. *Would you let some man control her? Put her in danger?* I picture Toby, his ugly teeth and flashy dress sense, remembering how smoothly he'd moved in on Susannah, such easy prey after Clara's death. How I'd known after meeting him just once that he was a prize prick. What kind of father am I? I should have protected her, loved her. Made her feel safe. It won't happen again.

Forcing my notes back inside my briefcase, I stand. Rushing to gain distance. Alexa snaps shut her compact mirror, pulls out her phone.

I imagine grabbing her wrist, dragging her away and forcing him, the unknown man, down in his seat. *Leave her the fuck alone!* I try out in my head, my heart suddenly racing. *What kind of monster are you?* I scan the men's bathroom door. Where is he? *Get out here, you piece of shit.* The rush has me surging forward, no care that I could lose my license. My livelihood.

Suddenly another man pushes past me and sits down beside Alexa. She smiles, but only slightly.

What's going on?

I stop.

Who is this one? Is that Shaun? Navid? Who's in the bathroom?

Two against one. I'm outnumbered. What if I take them both on? What if I get Alexa away before the other man returns?

Wait. Think.

What am I doing?

The bathroom door opens. The man returns to his seat. Alexa and the two men now returning to their coffee, their conversation.

Attempting control, I catch my breath, reaching for an abandoned mug resting on the table next to me, ready to hurl.

Put it down, you fool, a voice orders in my head, and I retreat.

66

Alexa Wú

FEELING RATHER FAMISHED, MY EARLIER ATTEMPT AT BREAKFAST WITH Ella a disaster, I tap my foot, wishing he'd get to the point of our meeting.

"I fancy a pastry with this." He points at his mug of coffee. "You?"

"Why not," I say, with relief. "Danish would be great. Thanks."

He takes another sip of his coffee, glancing around for the waitress. "So, you're aware of how busy we've gotten lately?" he begins.

I nod.

"Well, I need extra help, and that's why I've asked Sam to join us. This way I won't have to worry about being without an assistant or missing any deadlines. I've decided you guys will work together, at least for the next few months. Alexa, you'll be my first assistant. Sam, you'll be second."

I warned you about taking time off work, Oneiroi says, miffed.

I worry now that my flakiness has brought this upon me. Jack's decision to hire a new assistant causing me to sweat.

Jack, still not spotting the waitress, gets up and heads to the counter.

"This is going to be great, right?" Sam says. The sparky new boy.

"Right," I reply.

I check my phone, desperate for a distraction, and sure enough, there are two messages from Ella.

Sorry I lied to you (all). Love you xxx
I meant what I said about my plan. Tell everyone inside I miss
them. We can do this, can't we? xxx

Ok, I write. Clean and simple.
No kisses? Oneiroi asks.
Christ.

I think about our morning together. How I'd been meaner than I needed to be. A certain satisfaction felt that I'd called her out, hurt her, forced her to apologize and take ownership of her sex crime with Navid. How when she threw her arms around my waist and kissed me with her eyes wide open I'd turned away. Our once juvenile sweetness turned tart. I imagine her proposed heist, Ella blocking a toilet or hiding the girls' clothes, anything to jeopardize a night's takings and cause Cassie to panic. I shudder at my cruelty but delight at Ella's revenge and decide to text her again, a jolt of forgiveness suddenly pulsing inside me.

Yes, we can do this xxx

Happy?
Oneiroi nods.
Jack returns, landing three pastries.
"I'll go grab some waters," says Sam, standing up.
I clench my jaw and reach inside the pocket of my fleece, Runner having placed a Stanley knife with a retractable blade there. I trace my thumb along the switch, feeling a certain comfort from the clicking plastic.

Why do you keep putting these in our pockets? I ask. *It's like every day, a different weapon.*

For safety, Runner snaps.

Jack clears his throat.

"You've been a little preoccupied lately, Alexa. It seems you've had more sick days than workdays the past couple weeks."

"That's a slight exaggeration," I interrupt.

Jack stares at me, sips again.

"Sorry," I say, "carry on."

He continues. "Sam's a good kid. Bags of ideas, bags of energy. And he has great references."

"Are you trying to tell me something?"

"I am."

He pauses.

"I really like you, Alexa, you've got a great eye," he says. "But if you don't get it together, you're fired. I can't have my work suffer because of your unreliability."

I stare at him in disbelief.

"I'm sorry," I say, unable to contain my hurt, Sam now heading back toward us, waters in hand. "It won't happen again."

"Make sure it doesn't. I don't want to have to lose you, but you'll leave me no choice."

67

Daniel Rosenstein

I ARRIVE LATE, THE MEETING ALREADY STARTED. THE SINGLE MOTHER smiles, revealing new veneered teeth, and uncrosses her legs. Smiles again. A friendly gesture, I tell myself to ease any feelings I may be having—lateness often and understandably frowned upon.

I scan the room for familiar faces, immediately noting that the Old-Timer is missing. I suddenly feel a pang of guilt, remembering I never returned his call. That was slack of me, I think, negligent. His absence viscerally sensed, I check the door and comfort myself with the idea that he's simply running late as well. Is either stuck on the Tube or waiting for a bus. That he'll be here shortly.

A newcomer shares how she's about to leave her fiancé of three years.

"Still no wedding band," she says, raising her left hand, "and now he's relapsed."

She breaks down. I want to tell her it's not about the ring, but the commitment. But then realize his relapse is testament to that.

The room is silent except for her sobbing.

I check the door.

"My partner caught me looking at a strip club's website," I say, surprising myself. "She hates me."

The room is silent except for my sobbing.

OUTSIDE, I CALL MOHSIN, READY TO SHARE THAT I'VE BROKEN MY ethical code while playing snoop on Alexa. No answer. I call Susannah instead.

"Hi, Dad, feeling any better?"

She's referring to the cold I've had for the last week, but one would think I'd been struck down with a terrible virus.

"Much," I say.

"So we're still on for supper?"

"Of course."

"You sure?"

"Susannah."

"Great. Let's go to Sheekey's. I'm in need of comfort food."

"How so?"

A pause.

"It's nothing, Dad. Really."

I know this Susannah, the one who puts on a brave face, battling away her struggles in order to protect her widowed father. The Caretaking Child. The one who puts others' needs before her own to avoid upset. A memory of her in hospital clinging to her parents as though her *own* life depended on it, telling us over and over:

"Everything will be fine, I know it will. It has to be."

In that moment, the Caretaking Child was born into a bleached-out room with the stench of imminent death. If Clara had still been alive, there would have been phone calls, putting right whatever it was bothering our baby girl, me catching up later when either of them decided to share their conversations.

"I'll book a table for eight o'clock," I say.

"Great. I'll be on my own. Toby's got some crazy deadline at work."

"Oh, that's a shame."

"Daaaad!"

"What?"

"I'll see you later. Love you," she sings.

My smart cookie, my daughter who doesn't miss a beat. She knows I don't give two shits about Toby. I know she knows it, and she knows I know she knows. But both of us refuse to name it. He's an ass-hat. An entitled, stupid idiot with little integrity and an ugly set of teeth who apparently has to sleep facing a window while listening to the sound of whales. She could have had her pick. But no, she chose him. Toby the investment banker. Toby the divorcé with his fake, nervous laugh, confessional self-deprecations, and false humility. Toby has a fragile ego. And I don't like the idea of my daughter loving a man with ugly teeth and a weak ego. He also has a thicker head of hair than mine. Thick hair, shallow mind.

68

Alexa Wú

I HAVE NO IDEA WHAT TYPE OF CLOTHES A GIRL SHOULD WEAR FOR SUCH an assignment. Dark jeans? Black hoodie? A balaclava? A weapon of some kind, should things get nasty? I glance over at Runner, who's nodding.

Sensing my anxiety, she steps into the Body and hands me a pair of black leggings, a hoodie, trainers, and my vintage eighties CHOOSE LIFE T-shirt, me pegging her attempt at irony as a little on the nose.

I don't have time for your satire, I say, her dark twist on humor not helpful in the slightest.

She shrugs and hands back the Body. *Only trying to help.* She grins.

I look in the mirror, scraping back my hair and securing it in a top-knot, my bangs now fully grown out. My arms, I notice, appear thinner and have the look of someone who's quit their medication. In fact, it's not just my arms—my whole body appears slightly drawn. My skin a little loose on its bones, chest even flatter than usual.

Oneiroi suddenly steps out, takes a pale lip gloss—a gift from Shaun—and with three strokes covers my lips.

Really? Runner dismisses, pulling Oneiroi back inside, then wipes the gloss away with the back of her hand, Dolly now watching them squabble.

The switching makes my head spin.

"Stop!" I order. "Give me my body back. Now."

The Flock suddenly stop and stare. *OUR body!* they demand.

Suddenly overcome with guilt, I hug my chest—

Just for today, I will try my best to be the person I needed when I was young.

I'm sorry, I say. "You do know how much I appreciate you all, don't you?" I speak out loud.

As soon as the words leave my mouth, I realize how mad I must appear, staring at myself, talking to the reflected me opposite. A marionette with no puppet master. A talking head.

That's okay, Dolly offers kindly, *you're stressed.*

"I am," I say. "I'm worried about tonight."

Do you know what will happen to Poi-Poi? she asks, her concern and frustration shown as she socks the Nest with her kid-size fist.

"Don't worry," I say, not entirely trusting my words, "everything will be fine."

Runner unclenches Dolly's fist and strokes her head. A tender and maternal act.

Yeah, everything will be fine, Runner says.

And it's strange, because for once, her words seem more viable than mine.

DOWNSTAIRS, ANNA IS PARKED OPEN-LEGGED IN FRONT OF THE TV, halfway down a cigarette, wearing faded cotton pajamas and watching QVC—a credit card in one hand, her mobile phone in the other. An attractive woman with a mousey blow-dry and a perfect French mani-cure holds up a tub of "miracle cream" for a close-up and unscrews its shiny lid. She smears the white cream on the back of her hand, giving testament to how "silky and nourishing" it feels.

I bounce down beside her and the lumpy couch sinks. Preoccupied with the miracle cream and what it promises, Anna says, "For you, sorry it's late," and hands me a gift.

"You okay?" I ask, noticing her mood is low and distant.

Anna shrugs. "Ray and I broke up."

"I'm sorry," I say. "You really liked him."

Her eyes stay locked on the TV, wet and wide open. Not blinking.

Open it, she mouths.

I open the New Year's gift, a ritual Anna and I have had since my father left. Inside: a mother-of-pearl-effect picture frame, a photograph of us both in Chinese traditional dress. I look to be around eleven years old.

Same age as Poi-Poi, Dolly says.

I smile.

"Thank you," I say, kissing her lightly on her cheek. "I'm sorry it didn't work out with Ray."

"Shh," she says again, pointing at the TV, "let me just order this."

"Okay. But I gotta go," I say.

She waves, mouthing a *See you later,* and then turns back to the TV.

I pull down my CHOOSE LIFE T-shirt over my sinking leggings and take a gulp of what I assume is wine, *Yep, very cheap wine,* before kissing the top of Anna's head. The smell of tea tree oil or some other hair remedy oozing from her scalp.

The wine, or maybe the act of drinking the wine, has a calming effect, and for a moment I wonder if I should tell Anna that I'm going to the Electra, just in case, but then decide I don't have time. Already running late, I wave goodbye, collect Runner's denim rucksack, and head out, closing the front door behind me.

I BREATHE IN THE EARLY EVENING AIR. RELIEF OPENING MY CHEST. Each step along the graveled path feeling increasingly alive. I sense myself surge forward—adrenaline rushing in the knowledge that tonight the police will have all the evidence they need to make sure Navid is arrested. That Ella has finally seen sense, her revenge no bad thing.

Keep Dolly inside, Runner instructs Oneiroi. *We've got this—Alexa and I.*

Oneiroi lets off a nervous smile while Dolly gives me two tiny thumbs up.

Good luck, they chime.

The Fouls suddenly appear.

Come to help? Runner asks.

But they don't answer and simply stare without a word. Their eyes like slits of night, mouths petulant and unmoving. Dramatically they drape cloaks of self-loathing across their shoulders, the smell of rotting meat surrounding their vigil. Farther back they go, into my mind, their voices gently whispering of no such alliance.

"Right. Let's go," Runner says.

WALKING ALONG GREAT EASTERN STREET I WATCH THE NIGHT UNFOLD. Restaurants and cafés swamped and bristling with life. Bars swell with overenthusiastic dancers: rushing, pie-eyed, and loose, their happy chemically induced smiles tuned to the music.

I feel an uneasy funk inside me remembering Shaun's house party. How I'd danced: high, carefree, loved up, and thrilled from the night filled with sex. I am suddenly overcome; an unwanted missing of him quickly pushed away with a firm and clear head while my heart feels something else.

For Christ's sake, Alexa, Runner says, exasperated. *Get a grip!*

I cross the road, dodging the close wind of cars, then reach into my coat pocket to feel the coolness of the silver letter opener, reassuring in my hand.

Music behind me now and thumping like some ferocious soundtrack in my mind, I look up at the Electra's neon light for the last time.

Ella has already arrived and comes to meet me at the door, squeezing my hand three times with a smile.

"Hey." She winks. "Drink?"

"No. What's he doing here?" I whisper, nodding toward Shaun behind the bar. "He's meant to be at the bank. What's going on?"

Shaun heads out back, leaving the towel he was using to dry glasses.

Asshole, Runner snarls.

"Change of plan. Cassie needed to get a manicure, so she said she'd stop at the bank herself," she says. "Don't worry. Have a drink."

"I don't want a drink," I say. "Let's just get the codes and go."

"You need to calm down," she says firmly.

I take a deep breath, locking my eyes on hers.

"Okay?"

"Okay," I say. "Where's Navid?"

"At the Groom House. Apparently there was a problem."

"What kinda problem?" I ask.

"Some psycho followed one of the girls back there. He's been leaving her gifts, blah, blah, blah. And tried to crowbar his way into the house."

"Are the girls okay?"

Ella shrugs. "Not sure, I guess," she says, indifferent. "Anyway, where's your rucksack?"

Annoyed at her lack of concern, I swing my shoulder around so she can see it.

Ella takes my arm and rubs her palms along the hips of her jeans, her eyes a little wider than when I first arrived.

"Are you high?" I say.

"Just a little. For the nerves."

I notice her movements get a little sharper now she's named it. Her senses alert to any sound or movement. Eyes feral. Alley-cat wild.

She leans in, sensitive and vigilant. "Here," she whispers, placing her gold necklace with the dainty key in my palm. "I think it might open the top drawer of Navid's desk."

"So why haven't you tried it already?" I ask.

"Cassie's only just left. And I didn't want Shaun to suspect anything. Just try the key," she insists. "If it works, you'll be able to get the codes for the dark web." She closes my fingers. I feel the heat in my palm like a forest fire.

THE BANANA HATER AND AMY PASS ME ON THE STAIRS, BLACK SKIRTS worn even shorter than before. No pockets.

Amy grabs onto the handrail as we walk by, avoiding eyes, adjusts the bow on her ass, and wipes her nose. High as a kite. She glances back at me.

"What?" I say.

Amy sways on the step.

"I never had a problem with you," she says. "You should know that."

MOUTH TURNED STALE, NERVES ALIVE, I ENTER NAVID'S OFFICE. I stare at his desk, the incriminating top drawer. The key in my hand pressed so tightly in my damp palm that it leaves a clear imprint.

Do it, the Flock call.

The key slides in, but as I try to turn, it sticks. I wiggle it around, my wrists shaking, heart jacked up, but it refuses to twist. I pull it out and try again. Nothing. I blow on it, wipe it down the thigh of my leggings, and try again.

Shit.

My chest thumping, my head turns light with fear. The sound of clattering bottle crates makes me jump. I pause. Listening to the sounds of men's gruff voices on the other sides of the rice-paper-thin walls.

Ella was supposed to deal with this, I say. *Dammit.*

I scan Navid's desk for a sharp object to pry open the drawer. Nothing but pens and porn and receipts. An ashtray. A stapler.

I check the shelves, rising up on my tiptoes and running my hand the length of the top one. But there's nothing.

"Think," I speak out loud, rapping my fist on the side of my head.

Check your pocket, Runner orders.

Of course. Daniel's letter opener.

I slide it in the gap between the drawer and the frame and try wrenching it up and down.

Let me, Runner says, seizing the Body.

She rams harder with her fist, her whole weight pulling up and down on the drawer.

Wait, I say.

Outside, the sound of girls' voices near the door.

Runner flinches.

Quick, I shout.

Twice more and the drawer finally bursts open.

"We're in," Runner says, sweating.

I take over. Inside are passports, note slips, coin bags, a Moleskine notebook, a page of phone numbers. I open the notebook and see hundreds of webcam addresses. *Bingo.* I quickly stuff it in my rucksack. Next: a folder of invoices, beneath that a letter addressed to Navid written in pink ink. I quickly scan it, the words *pregnant* and *kill myself* jumping out in the second paragraph. The last line stating how much she loves him.

Put those in too, Runner orders.

At the bottom of the drawer is a slim black binder.

Open it, Alexa.

That's it! Runner shouts, the dark web codes listed on the single sheet of paper I'd seen Cassie place in the drawer. On a separate sheet of paper: descriptions, ages, and names written alongside photographs of the young, naked girls.

Holding my breath, I scan the next page.

The girls are no older than nine or ten and are sitting on the knee of a man whose head has been conveniently cropped off. One girl holds the hand of an out-of-focus woman wearing a jade bangle.

Cassie, Runner says.

I note she is also cropped, just above the waist. Avoiding any chance of recognition.

I turn the page.

There, staring back at me, is Poi-Poi. A white pleated gym skirt, tank top, bobby socks and pumps. Two hair baubles meant for two pigtails. A miniature cheerleader.

I throw up.

Quick and violently.

All across Navid's desk.

I take a deep breath and wipe my mouth. Steadying myself, I move the rucksack away from the heave of my tummy. The weight of evidence now dropped to the floor.

Then, as if waiting for the perfect opportunity, Anna steps out, seizing the Light.

"Oh my goodness," she speaks out loud, staring down at the photographs. "What on earth have you gotten yourself involved in?"

69

Daniel Rosenstein

I DRIVE TOWARD SOHO'S PAY-AND-DISPLAY AT SPEED, SEETHING. MY back wheel scraping against one of the yellow bumper curbs. I wouldn't mind but she's so goddamn childish; leaving my belongings in black garbage bags outside my front door. A message attached in an angry scrawl: *DON'T CALL ME.* So unreasonable and unnecessary. Cruel. Anyone could have stolen them, mistaken them for rubbish. *Call her?* She's out of her mind. Good riddance, I think.

I step out of the car and feel light snowflakes landing on my cheek as I set out toward Old Compton Street. My hope that nightlife and a short walk among civility might ease my rising disquiet. Walking slowly, I check the road for traffic and enter a liquor store—twenty Camel Lights dancing in my mind—my conscience reminding me that I gave up smoking twelve months ago.

A plump man with a kind smile who appears to be wearing his son's T-shirt looks up from a copy of *Men's Health*.

"Twenty Camel Lights," I say, "and a lighter."

"Cold out there," he says, handing me the requested items.

"Winter," I reply.

Outside, I take the hit, not having smoked for at least a year. My addiction sliding over to smokes instead of liquor. The nicotine's reward floods my brain as I walk. The kind smile of the man behind the counter softening my mood.

Walking toward me, two laughing girls are being held up by an equally happy guy. They push past me, knocking my cigarette to the ground, ash scraping one of the girls' suede jacket.

"Watch it," the girl warns, her chipper spirit now turned tart. She throws me a bitter look. "Idiot."

I inch across the road to a bar I used to know, the nicotine hit killed by the girl's irritation. My poor mood returns, bringing me to think again of Monica.

Why don't we just call it a day? she'd shouted at me last week. *You're obviously still in love with your dead wife.*

Cruel, I decide. Cruel and unnecessary.

Without thinking, I head inside and take a stool at the bar.

"Diet Coke," I say, the monkey on my back ordering a Jack Daniel's.

Two seats down, an attractive woman with blond highlights and ridiculously long legs catches my eye.

She smiles. Twists her body toward me while the barman pours my drink.

Smooth as a fox, I move across to the next stool, catching a whiff of her inexpensive perfume. Spoiled at the edges by smoke.

"Teetotal?" she asks, glancing at my glass.

"A little early for me," I say.

She smiles again, her gaze like someone with a secret. "I'm Chloé," she says, offering her hand.

"David," I lie, shaking it.

"Good to meet you, David."

I move in closer, immediately recognizing Chloé is stoned. Eyes bright, gaze fried.

We chat. Politely. Made-up answers, none of them true. Our bodies inching closer all the time.

"Fancy a rum in that Coke?" she asks, a knee gently grazing my thigh.

Chloé has turned into the mind-reading chimp on my back.

"Or I've got a little something else," she says, tapping her delicate nose. "Want some?"

Chloé steps down from her stool. Beckons me to follow her to the bathroom. I watch the barman reach for a bottle of tonic water, his back to us.

Follow her, Danny Boy, the monkey beguiles.

I stand, Chloé awaiting pursuit.

Then leave.

The streetlights kindle my way back to Soho's pay-and-display. A panic rising in my chest. I need to get to a meeting, I think, and quick. I rest my head in my hands, unsure how to free myself from grief, to unshackle the demons now clinging to my heels. Shaking off the wet from my boots, I key the ignition. A warm hum from the engine, a quick blast from the heater. The silver mist on my window eventually gone. All the while, the monkey, cunning, baffling, and powerful, telling me to go back to the bar and to Chloé.

Just one line, it whispers, *you've got enough clean time now. You won't get hooked. You're not even an addict anymore.*

I turn on my GPS, forcing the monkey into the back seat of my car and slapping his monkey face a half-dozen times.

"Buckle up," I order him, Dolly's handwritten note taken from my jacket pocket. The Groom House address keyed into the GPS.

Why are we going? the monkey asks. *What do you think we'll achieve?*

"Justice," I say.

After all, I think, a man needs a backbone.

70

Alexa Wú

Anna lowers her head in disapproval.

"Alexa, this is—" She casts her eyes down at the slim black binder, appalled and unable to find words to describe the heinous crimes against the young girls *For Sale.*

She picks up the binder from the floor and turns the page—

More girls, more codes.

Then turns another—

More girls, more codes.

"Why didn't you tell me?" she speaks out loud, stomach heaving from the sour smell of vomit.

I stare out from the Nest, part of me relieved that Anna is finally aware of our situation, another part fighting the urge to pull her back inside the Body in case she messes things up.

I thought you'd try to stop me going to the police, I say.

"Since when have *I* been able to stop *you* from doing anything?" she says.

Since I made you into my stepmother, I reply.

I stay seated in the Nest while Anna continues to page through the binder, a tight clench to her jaw. I do not recognize some of the girls and wonder where they are now. Another house? Another country? Are they still alive?

One girl with painted red lips, I note, is particularly young. Her eyes are sad, her eyebrows drawn in fine pencil. She's been dressed in a black silk skirt with slits on either side. A matching low-cut top slashed across her soft, unformed shoulders. She is seated uncomfortably, cut adrift from a life where unicorns fly and daydreams are wild, where butterflies land on freckled hands, the fizz of cherry-ade tickling the hairs on her nostrils.

Flash.

I AM SITTING ON MY BED DRESSED IN A RED MANDARIN DRESS, A HELLO Kitty toy forced in my hand.

"Smile, Xiǎo Wáwa," he says, a camera directed toward me, "it's your birthday!"

Flash.

Balloons are raised in the corner. Ten, to match my years.

My red mouth instructed to perform heinous crimes.

Flash.

He leaves. The door silently closed behind him. The Body afloat. Cast, like an eleventh balloon.

Flash.

TICK-TOCK—

Wake up, Runner shouts, *I need your help.*

I watch Anna slap closed the black binder.

"I suggest that whatever it is you've got us all involved in stops right now."

Quick, get her back inside, Runner orders, *she could screw up everything.*

I do as I'm told, forcing Anna back inside the Body and enlisting Runner for help, who is only too keen to assist, giving Anna a quick shove. Her dislike for Anna because she believes her a bystander.

Over the years, I've tried to explain to the Flock that we needed some kind of mother to care for us, but also to make more bearable what had passed between my father and me—the Body believing it was older when Anna took the Light and allowing my nine-year-old self to dissociate. It was just more manageable this way. I guess because part of me needed someone to rebel against, someone to blame, and let's face it, stepmothers are such an easy target. Look at Cinderella and Snow White. But the terrifying reality of my having knitted myself a mother figure hits me. A certain and unescapable realization that Anna wasn't, isn't, and never will be my *real* mother.

I'll never have one.

Because my mother is dead.

71

Daniel Rosenstein

*Y*OU *HAVEN'T THOUGHT THIS THROUGH PROPERLY,* THE MONKEY SAYS, his thick prickly tail coiled tightly around my throat.

"Shh," I order, yanking him off.

You should turn back, Danny Boy.

"What, so I can get stoned with Chloé?"

Beats losing your license. Imagine that: Dr. Rosenstein loses medical license after he breaks ethical code and batters human trafficker to a bloody pulp.

"There will be no violence," I say.

The monkey gives me a dubious look.

"There will be no violence!" I shout again, stepping on the gas. My throat, all the while, craving a Jack Daniel's. On the rocks.

72

Alexa Wú

I REST BOTH PALMS ON NAVID'S DESK AND CATCH MY BREATH. THE whirring fan at the back of the room cools my mood, its sound adding further distraction.

Right, do we have everything? Runner asks. *Just make sure, but be quick. We've got to get a move on.*

I scan the room.

What about his pockets? Runner points, Navid's suit jacket hanging on the back of the door. I quickly check but there is nothing. Just a handful of toothpicks and two sticks of gum.

You need to stop all of this and get us away from here, Anna says.

Quiet, Runner orders.

You be quiet, Anna argues. *You should have protected Alexa from this.*

Runner ignores her, pointing to the back of the office. *Check the cabinet, Alexa.*

I open the doors and find inside a huge plasma TV, a DVD player, and a library of catalogued DVDs—

Abbie. Abbie. Amy. Amy&Annabelle. Amy&Annabelle. Amy&Annabelle. Amy&Annabelle. Becky. Becky. Becky. Bella. Bella. Bella&AmyXXX. Bella&Amy. Beth. Beth. Britney. Britney. Britney. Britney. BritneyXXX—

My stomach flips—

Candi&Amy&AnnabelleXXX. Candi. Candi. Candi. Chantel.
Chantel. Chantel. Chloé. Chloé. Chloé. Chloé&Annabelle. Charlize.
Charlize. Charlize. Dana. Dana. Dana. Dana. Danielle. Danielle.
Deena. Deena. Eleanor. Eleanor. Eleanor. Elisa. Elisa. Ella. Ella. Ella.
Ella&Shaun&JaneXXX—

Ella?

Ella&Shaun&JaneXXX?

I pull out the case, retrieve the disc, and place it in the DVD player.

We need to go, Runner says. *There's no time.*

Let her watch it, the Fouls insist.

The moment I press PLAY on the remote control, I feel myself leave the Body—fear completely taken over.

I STARE AT THE SCREEN.

The back of a girl's head.

A shiny black bob.

Tanned jutting shoulder blades.

I know those shoulders; I've placed my arms around them enough times in moments of comfort, and happiness, fun and despair.

The camera pans out slowly to show a dark room. My *Reason* lying on a double bed.

Her slim waist and perfect bottom are defined by gentle lighting. A slow soundtrack heavy on the chords. I recognize the shape of her body and the way it moves, the familiarity of the curve of her back, seen so many times as we were growing up—swapping clothes, skinny-dipping, showering after gym class.

The camera closes in on her black G-string, stockings, and three-inch heels—a pornographic cliché. Smooth in its glide, it follows in another girl with long red hair. *Jane,* Oneiroi says.

The camera pulls back. Slides around so that Ella's body fills the entire screen, her face out of view. She touches herself and the camera zooms in: first on the circling of her hand, and then on her thighs. Jane leans against a dresser made of pine that I immediately recognize as the one back at the Groom House. There, she watches Ella pleasure herself. Jane, the voyeur.

A man enters—

Alexa, we need to go, Runner warns.

"Wait," I shout from the ceiling, the Body still standing in front of the huge plasma TV.

—and walks across to the bed. I look away for a moment. The reality of what Ella's been doing for the last six months feeling like an axe splitting open my chest. The man drops his trousers and enters her while Jane watches. Ella drives her ass high in the air, a panned-out shot of one of her red-heeled shoes, while he tilts his head back and slaps her, hard. All the while pulling tightly on her hair.

"Good girl," I hear Shaun say.

Ella releases a moan.

"You like that?" he whispers. "You like me fucking you?"

Another moan.

"Turn around, baby, come and suck me," he says. "That's it. Let me see your beautiful face."

Ella releases Shaun, and as she turns, still on her hands and knees—I drop the TV controls.

There, staring back on the forty-nine-inch screen, I realize, is me.

73

Daniel Rosenstein

Pᴀʀᴋᴇᴅ, ɪ sᴛᴀʀᴇ ᴜɴʙʟɪɴᴋɪɴɢ ᴀᴛ ᴛʜᴇ ɢʀᴏᴏᴍ ʜᴏᴜsᴇ. ᴛʜᴇ sᴛʀᴇᴇᴛ-lights burning low on urban night life.

Seriously, you haven't thought this through. It could be the end of you, the monkey grunts.

It's true, I don't have a plan, exactly, but I've got a good idea of what to say to whoever opens the door. Especially Navid.

My phone rings—

Monica.

I slide the switch to silent, forcing the phone into my coat pocket. She's probably calling to apologize after speaking with Susannah, I think. Her earlier message, *DON'T CALL ME,* now void. She's like a child, wanting what she wants when she wants. At some point we'll need to have a conversation, but not yet. Not tonight. Relationships are for people who don't mind disruption or change. It's for those who are willing to compromise and trust again. But babies, babies are for those who are committed to a complete and honest life together when the lustful heart has cooled. And I am not that man, I will have to say. Eventually.

Because Monica's right, I am still in love with my dead wife. Clara and I were good at loving each other. We were smart in love, and by that I mean we were realistic and understanding of our limitations of the love we could offer and accept. We knew when to avoid each other and when to stick around, were attuned and sensitive to our worlds together and our worlds apart.

I SILENCE THE ENGINE AND FOR A MOMENT DEBATE WHETHER I SHOULD take a weapon of some kind, thinking of the metal toolbox in the boot of my car. Screwdriver? Wrench? Drill? I think, unable to decide, and then attempt to calm myself by putting on a baseball cap.

Heading down the path, I gaze up at the Groom House's windows, alive with dimmed light. Night creeping in. I shudder theatrically.

Clenching my right hand, I rap on the door, and wait.

Someone on the opposite side turns a lock and secures a chain.

"Hi," I say to a girl locked behind a gold safety chain, "I'm sorry to bother you. But I've broken down and my mobile is out of charge."

I point at a random car parked on the street.

I recognize her immediately as the cowgirl on Electra's website. No gun or Stetson this time, but instead one serious attitude.

She stares me up and down. Pulls her dressing gown tightly across her chest.

"So?" she sneers.

"So I was wondering if I could use your phone?"

"No," she says. "Go away."

"It won't take a—"

"No!" she shouts.

I wedge my foot in the door opening, the gold chain straining against my force.

"Then you'd better give Navid Mahal a message from me," I whisper, leaning in close, "tell him we're watching him. Tell him we know what he's doing and it won't be a secret for much longer."

74

Alexa Wú

THE BODY FEELS A MILLION MILES AWAY.

Tick-tock—
Tap-tap—
Click-click—
Flash-flash—

I WATCH THE STARTLED *ME* BELOW STARING AT THE TV, HER WET GREEN eyes wide open and flashing. She reaches, with one hand, for Navid's desk, a corner to steady her shake, the other hand outstretched and clutching air.

Pushing both palms against her ears, she drops to her knees. The sound she makes akin to a rabid animal, a howling baby. Too much to bear.

THE DOOR OPENS.

Shaun appears. A drink in his hand.

"What the hell are you doing in here?" he asks, taking in the video playing and stinking odor of vomit.

Get back in the Body, Runner warns.

"Turn that off," Shaun says, setting the glass on Navid's desk. "What the—"

"That's *me*? Doing *that*?" She points.

"Why are you watching this? You know it upsets you." He locates the remote, kills the TV power.

"*Me?*" she repeats.

I force myself down from the ceiling and reenter the Body.

Shaun inches forward and stares at me, bewildered. "What's going on, Ella?" he says. "Did you take too much?"

I do not answer him.

Runner seizes the Body at once, aware of my shake.

"Get the fuck away from me," she screams, wielding Daniel's letter opener.

Shaun steps back. Palms outstretched and raised.

"What the fuck?" he speaks quietly.

Runner picks up the glass and launches it at the wall.

Shaun inches farther back.

"What the fuck is wrong with you?" he screams. "You're acting like a fucking lunatic! I don't even know who you are anymore. You've become a total nut job."

His words penetrate. The truth of my multiplicity clear and stark. His observations and knowing of me fair and blunt.

Grabbing the rucksack, Runner heads for the door. The letter opener held out in front of our chest for protection. No longer able to trust what she might do, she backs out of Navid's office, a trickle of warm pee sliding down our legs. Head filling up with dread like a tank about to capsize.

RUN, the Flock calls.

$T_{ICK-TOCK}$—

I wander the streets, my CHOOSE LIFE T-shirt ripped, my sagging leggings soaked and stinking. I light a cigarette, not minding who watches me, what I look like, if anyone cares—I am already disappeared. The Mad Girl walking mad streets. The Vagrant. The Whore. The Rented Womb. The Industrial Cunt. Miserable and cheap.

My body was never home to any of you—to pierce and puncture. You were not even my guest. You were not invited.

I throw my cigarette to the curb and hail a black cab. My mind already made up.

The cabbie nods and turns off his light.

"Archway," I order.

WITH BALLED FISTS I PRESS ON BOTH TEMPLES, THE VOICES JOSTLING for power and growing fierce—the kind of bedlam one really ought to fear.

You should have asked me for help, Anna scolds.

You? Help? Get real! Runner shouts.

Oh right, because you've done such a great job, Runner, getting everyone involved and acting like some halfwit mole. Your stupidity and selfishness are appalling.

Shut up. SHUT UP.

I won't shut up, who do you think you are?

Both of you, be quiet, Oneiroi orders firmly. *This isn't helping.*

A distant sob heard now from Dolly.

I STARE STRAIGHT AHEAD AS WE RIDE ACROSS CAMDEN TOWN. WALKERS, cyclists, and cars scooting at our side. Trucks barreling along as they shoulder up onto offshoot streets.

I attempt to focus, the Flock's switching forcing a rise of pressure in my head.

I am breathing too fast, I think. My heart racing.

No best friend, no stepmother—just voices, I say to myself, aware the cabdriver is watching me through his rearview mirror. *It's all me.*

I feel a depressive slide take hold, nothing but the awful truth falling at the front of my mind. *I created them all.*

Runner, Oneiroi, Dolly, the Fouls, Flo the Outcast, Anna, Ella, and Grace.

Where earlier sun streamed over the city, clouds have emerged. Birds are no longer singing. The imminent outbreak of rain threatening to crack. Shining with sweat, I take hold of the cab's door handle and squeeze. Something to hold on to. Something to make this nightmare feel real; spasms of denial like my mornings spent unremembering night terrors: tigers tearing at flesh, clowns with filthy neck ruffles, a giant knife chasing a child. The earlier rejections of truth a balm for my reality.

But now everything is returned to me.

The sound of a small key unlocking my self-slaughter that hangs on a hinge. Nowhere to go. I force my hands down my stinking leggings— *Quick, stop her,* tries Oneiroi—and drag my nails along my thighs. *Too late,* Dolly cries.

A DOWNPOUR OF RAIN HAMMERS ON THE ROOF LIKE A DOZEN ANGRY fists. Windshield wipers screech. I think of the stolen leather jacket, the Electra's pink neon light, the watery blue of Ella's eyes—wondering if mine are still green. I check the cab's rearview mirror.

Yes.

I lower my damp green eyes and pull long-lived-with Ella—the part of me I've most wished to escape—tightly toward my body. I submit to her, accepting her heart-racing existence. The Body shaking in forced recognition.

We will be as one. But it will be short-lived, I say.

Ella nods, compliant.

Alone, I feel sick. Dizzy.

I touch my hair, bangs outgrown but its length familiar. And now my cheekbones: still high and soft. When I catch my reflection in the rain-drenched window—eyes shot, mouth downturned and trembling—I look away.

"Who knew?" I hear myself speak.

A traffic light flashes red and the cab slows to a stop.

In his rearview mirror, the driver stares at me. Hard and fixed.

I fold my arms to cover my chest: no longer flat, but mature and plump like bedroom pillows. My *real* breasts nothing like the dysmorphic prepubescent acorns I've imagined.

Who knew?

I look out the window at a mother and daughter preparing to make their way through the rain. A tender, protective arm laced behind the child's waterproof back. I hate them both.

Our eyes meet.

Worthless piece of shit, the mother mouths.

Whore, the little girl adds.

They laugh and smile and skip over the crosswalk, an umbrella held high enough to protect their hurried march. I force down the dripping window and scream something primal, no words, just noise. Something akin to a rabid wildling. The mother and daughter jump, startled. When the mother turns back to inquire, her loving arm is momentarily dropped, and I am slightly less green because of their separation.

"I have no one!" I scream. "I'm all alone."

And again, that noise.

Rabid and crazed and hurting.

The mother turns back, holds her child tightly once more, and rushes her across the street. A look of bewilderment wide and alive in her eyes. I have scared them both and I am satisfied.

Baba would relish the fruits of his sadism, Oneiroi says, rocking back and forth against the cab's leather seat.

Please d-d-don't let him win, Dolly stammers.

Silence.

"He's already won." I cry.

Flash.

Flash.

Flash.

"Thisiswhatalldaddiesdowhenmummiesgotoheaven."

Flash.

A PRESUICIDE HIGH FORCES MY HEAD AGAINST THE WINDOW GLASS. Again. Harder. Pain spearing the backs of my eyes. Harder. Travels to meet my skull, my nerves. Harder. A choke in my throat.

The cab halts.

"Out!" the driver orders.

Harder.

Harder.

Harder.

We struggle. A grabbing arm and fist. I feel my weight land on the wet, frigid asphalt. A graze to my cheek.

The cabdriver comes in close. "Crazy bitch," he says, wiping his mouth with the back of his hand, a glob of phlegm spat down at my face.

Who knew? the Fouls belittle, laughing.

I lift my head to the rain, my senses alive, the night's smell increased. The Body feeling like it could run a marathon. A taste of used coins in my mouth. I stand up, adrenaline like a shot in the arm, and call up my shame, directing a sharp slap to my cheek.

Again.

Again.

Again.

The mind is an unfathomable thing, I realize.

I CUT ACROSS ST. JOHN'S WAY TOWARD ARCHWAY ROAD, NOT BOTHERING to wipe away the cabdriver's spit, traffic barreling along beside me. My pace quickens, the earlier sense I could run a marathon now picked up and gaining speed in the pissing rain. Archway Park; Waterlow Road; Hornsey Lane; Jumpers Bridge now in plain sight. I slow down as I approach the vast linear railings, like soldiers guarding the road, the Body now drenched and exhausted.

Several dark bushes act as bookends for the stretch at Jumpers Bridge. I imagine the countless suicides committed here. How unloved and unwanted they each must have felt. Men and women, boys and girls who believed their worlds too brutal, existing as though underwater— never truly living, simply existing—the people around them casting dark shadows and unreachable. I imagine the insanity of the jump. Bodies slammed by fast-approached asphalt, cars swerving furiously. Limbs broken and scorned. Their defeated, busted bodies forming the same mutilated shape as my own mother's. Blood trickling out. Eyes still open when the ambulance arrives.

As I edge closer, I hear Daniel's voice in my head: *Just for today I am strong* . . . But the words are quickly drowned out by my own: *Strong? Never. End it now.*

THE VOICES DRIFT IN AND OUT. LIKE FLU. WEATHER. WEEKEND SHAGS. I picture Ella—me—on the huge plasma TV. Then Navid, Shaun, and Cassie. The Electra Girls. The club and the Groom House and my existence in both. The New Girl—Ella in the club—who slotted in like some perfect puzzle piece providing a common value. I think about Navid—the man who took me under his paws and was everything all at once, changing to fit whatever I might need him to be: father, lover, employer, higher power. Perpetrator.

He said it thrilled him to watch me as I took on the shape of a stripper. So I entered a world where I allowed the ghosts of my childhood back in, performing pleasure for others as I had for my father. And in some dark, buried part of my soul was a tiny frightened child, in hiding, crouching, scared by the depth at which there lingered something wild.

Tick-tock—

Tick-tock—

Tick-tock—

And now comes the presuicide calm that I've read about in books.

A swelling of time and space. All the stars have aligned, and I am nothing; nothing but a small speck of dust. One blow, and I'll be gone.

No one ever lacks a good reason for suicide. My mother's was my father, and her father before. I wonder what it must have felt like for her to have that much power. To have the final say. Her suicide attempt holding the grand rites of femininity where women are supposed to lose in order to win—tragically outwitting or rejecting her feminine role at the only price possible: her death.

I climb over the railings and look down, the delicate gold chain and its key still in my hand. Beneath me: the backup, close to a mile, crawling under my feet—snaking the strip—my eyes crimping from their blaring white lights.

Your mother is waiting for you, the Fouls whisper, pointing to the sky.

I crane my neck in search of birds, my mother's soul not immediately sensed. Where are they? Where have they gone? Each one a story, a truth, a testament against forgetting, against pain, against the loss of my beloved mother. I close my eyes tightly and try to picture one of the many species I've photographed over the years, hoping memory will somehow conjure a bird in flight—a slideshow of images flipping at speed through my mind.

The Mind finally settles on a phoenix, although I have obviously never met one in real life. I imagine it's a sign sent down from my mother, the phoenix filling my mind with freedom like an orchestra filling a concert hall with symphony, sounding of love.

Don't keep her waiting, the Fouls say.

Numb, forlorn, grief drenching my empty body, I loosen my hands. The Voices whispering softly in my ear: *Jump, you fucking crybaby.*

75

The Solitary Goose

—DU FU

孤雁不饮啄

飞鸣声念群

谁联一片影

相失万重云

望尽似犹见

哀多如更闻

野鸭无意绪

鸣噪亦纷纷

gū yàn bù yǐn zhuó

fēi míng shēng niàn qún

shuí líng yī piàn yǐng

xiāng shī wàn chóng yún

wàng jìn sì yóu jiàn

āi duō rú gèng wén

yě yā wú yì xù

míng zào yì fēn fēn

The solitary goose does not drink or eat,
It flies about and calls, missing the flock.
No one now remembers this one shadow,
They've lost each other in the myriad layers of cloud.
It looks into the distance: seems to see,
It's so distressed; it thinks that it can hear.
Unconsciously, the wild ducks start to call,
Cries of birds are everywhere confused.

76

Daniel Rosenstein

Jennifer said I might find you here," I say.

"Jennifer?"

"Jennifer, Jen. From the meetings."

John lifts his glass and sips, not caring to meet my eyes; his are defeated and lost, his focus gone.

The bartender approaches. "What'll you have?" he asks.

"Diet Coke," I say.

"Make that two," the Old-Timer adds. "But throw a whiskey in mine while you're at it."

I sit, not bothering to remove my overcoat. "A little early, don't you think?"

"Depends what you call *early*."

I check the clock overhead: eleven A.M. A difficult and guilt-ridden decision made yesterday to clear a window in my schedule so I could hunt down John. A huntsman, a hawker, a friend.

"So. Is this how it's going to be?" I challenge.

"Certainly looks that way, Daniel."

We both sip our drinks in silence. I imagine my monkey colluding with the drunk one clinging to the Old-Timer's back, now set free to do as it damn well pleases.

"Another whiskey," he shouts, slamming his palm on the bar. "Make it a double."

"Come back," I say, "there's a meeting in a couple hours. We can go together."

The Old-Timer clinks my glass.

"No can do," he says, eyes fixed on his drink.

"No such thing," I reply.

He turns to me, rests his palm on my thigh, swaying a little. "You know, I thought I'd cracked it. Just one drink, I told myself. Just to take the edge off things. I thought I was safe. Then one drink became a bottle. Then a phone call. A score. A hit. And quicker than you'd believe, I was right back into it. Deep."

He holds out his hand. Proof of the shakes.

I place my arm around him, remembering the times we've sat together and shared our war stories, shame melting because we were not alone in the struggle.

"I'm sorry I didn't call you back, John," I say, suddenly crestfallen. "It's no excuse, but I've had some things on my mind. I split up with my partner."

"Sorry to hear that."

Over the years we've talked each other down off a cliff regarding our significant losses. For the most part, he was a beacon of the AA Big Book directive, his recovery steadfast and tight. A man with immense integrity whose bridge to normal living was both staunch and unyielding.

"Your monkey try and convince you that you're no longer an addict?" I ask.

"Something like that," he says, reaching for a smoke.

"One drink is never enough," I say. "Your monkey's a liar."

The Old-Timer stares into my eyes and nods. "Well, you'd know all about that, right, Daniel?"

"Touché, John," I say, standing. "Touché."

He looks over at a couple ordering brunch. "Go," he says. "I wanna be alone, Daniel."

As I leave I turn back, reluctantly, and see John order another drink. He lurches on the barstool, no concern for my exit. His stoop not dissimilar from my father's, content at the bar, shelling peanuts, a TV overhead blasting out talk shows and sports news. A glaze falling over his sad, lonely eyes.

The door now closed behind me, I recall my first and only relapse. I was twelve months sober and a week away from collecting my chip when the monkey on my back forced my desire sky high. I didn't want to succeed, I wanted to get wasted, have sex. Sabotage all the hard work of the last twelve months because someone looked at me the wrong way. The look turned into defeat; I told myself no one cared. Clara was long gone, work was a drag. *Just one drink,* the monkey said. *It'll take the edge off things.*

Like John said, one drink turned into a bottle, or three. Next, a cab ride to Soho. Cocaine in a bar, girls, more drinks, a hooker.

A shiver falls upon me. "I won't allow John to give up," I speak out loud, reminded of how he's had my back, talking me off a ledge after that messy relapse when all I could think about was getting loaded after Clara's death. How he had helped me find a sponsor. His grit was much greater than mine, his fight both determined and needed. "I will do the same for him."

I spin around on my heel, burst back into the bar, and grab John by the collar.

"I'm taking you to rehab. I'll be back in a couple of hours. Leave, and I'll come find you. Stay, and we've got ourselves a fight."

John breaks down, slings his arms around my back, and holds on for his life. Purpose and survival forcing our spines to realign.

456

Outside, I race to my car, knowing I need to get to work by midday, pulling out my phone. I see I have two missed calls and a voicemail. Rattled, I press PLAY.

"Dr. Rosenstein," my receptionist says, "you need to come into the office immediately. Something terrible has happened. It's Alexa Wú."

77

Alexa Wú

ALEXA," HE WHISPERS.

I attempt to focus my eyes.

A blurry Daniel and two vaguely familiar nurses wearing white tunics are standing beside me. One holding a big fuck-off needle that only moments ago was injected into my left arm.

My useless eyes slide around the alabaster room. Placed by the window next to me, violet ranunculus sit in a turquoise vase, their scent a sweet perfume. Outside, Glendown's residents wander the lawn. Hats and scarves covering soft parts of their bodies. A woman sits on the bench and stares at the sky, awaiting its weather or wildlife. The hazy view caught like an impressionist painting. Thin and visible brushstrokes accentuating the passage of time.

Daniel leans closer and places his hand on my shoulder, adjusts a scratchy smock covering the Body.

I am fatigued. *Battle fatigued.* I hear him order one of the nurses to fetch another blanket, and my brain, very slowly, realizes it is Nurse Veal. The stern nurse who gave me the medication after I'd smashed the glass in Daniel's office.

She returns with a white cellular blanket and swaddles it around my chest as if I'm a baby. In the distance I hear Dolly's cries fade, the medication already taking effect. Its liquid entering my thin, reluctant veins. The swell of drugs races to greet my brain, shooing away the Flock like a scarecrow.

Please let them stay. I need them.

Thrashing the Body is useless. Soon I will lose control of the Body, the Flock. And as much as I want to think I'm fighting the numbing medication, opposing its controlling force, I know it will always win in the end.

The Body lets go. Curling up like a coral shrimp.

Daniel smiles, an unblemished jawline smelling of expensive scent, clean and woody. He rests his hand on my cheek, and my eyes pull down like two garage doors. My mouth dribbling out a warm, dewy moisture. Eyes half-open, I glimpse Charlotte standing at the door, her stunned mouth covered by her chubby hand.

"Bring her to my office when she wakes up," Daniel says, his words giving way like forgotten snow. "I have to talk to the police now."

78

Daniel Rosenstein

I SLUMP IN MY CHAIR, MY CONFIDENCE LOST.

This could have been avoided, I think.

I should have had her committed and not have colluded, turning a blind eye to her attempts to bring Navid down. It was too much for her. I should have intervened.

The tyranny of shoulds *and* musts.

I glance at my clock, awaiting the police. PC Keith Chandler wishing to return to question me further about my work with Alexa Wú. I of course have trust on my side. The offering up of information about a patient deemed unethical in the eyes of mental health law unless patients have disclosed terrorism or murderous intention. I've already decided I will not disclose to PC Chandler that I visited the Groom House. I am irrelevant in all of this. But it's safe to say the Flock gathered enough evidence against Navid Mahal to bring him down.

PC Chandler was only too happy to escort Alexa here for treatment after he'd gently persuaded her down from the bridge and questioned her. Where else would she go? Here she is safe. The medication has likely sent her along a royal road of consciousness, allowing in dreams. There, the inner child will prevail.

A child needs as much time as possible for knowing everything, remembering everything, about herself, even if it takes forever. Why should it matter if things are delayed?

A pause.

A pause.

A pause.

And if some days the mountain proves too brutal to climb, a landslide occasionally sending her off piste, she will get back up. She will rise. Because nothing is more important or more significant than knowing oneself.

The phone rings.

"PC Keith Chandler is here to see you," the Receptionist says, efficient and quick.

"Send him in," I say.

79

Alexa Wú

PAPER TIGERS ARE CIRCLING ME.

Knowing I'm lost, they release a roar, their thick bodies twisting.

Where are my sneakers? I wonder, noticing my soiled feet covered in brick-colored dust.

The Paper Tigers move closer. Starvation in their eyes.

With no gods to play witness to the Tigers' carnage, I fear I'm alone. I watch a glob of one Tiger's phlegm fall and land in the dust, leaving a patch of congealed goo. A sickness emerges inside me.

Another Tiger approaches. Larger. More muscular. His orange paper neck as thick as my waist. I recognize him as the paternal one who lowered his hand across my mouth.

"Why?" I ask.

"Because I could, Xiǎo Wáwa."

The Tiger speaks truth.

I look away.

It is not until I hear the crack in the sky—a flock of pink-footed geese rattled and taking flight from the strike of light—that I realize the gods have not in fact left. They have been here all along. The sky, dark and relentless, finally opening. With another flash of light, the weather unleashes on the origami tigers. Paper eventually buckling under the rain's falling weight.

I open my arms, grateful for spring. The Paper Tigers' markings disappearing slowly—drip, drip, dripping black stripes smudging and smearing across neat folds before they eventually collapse.

A mound of wet mush.

Releasing held breath, I walk over and grind my bare heels into the orange pulp. A paper tail. A claw.

The Paper Tigers are gone now. Stricken snarls lowered in their paws.

All around me: the sound of honking and cackling geese.

I kneel before them, a chosen bow of the head. Words escaping my mouth and speaking to the sky, where I imagine us flying together. A Flock.

Suddenly, I hear my father's words in my head: *It's better to have geese than girls,* which I quickly replace with the beginning of a new song.

A song to oppose, the Swan Song.

A song that celebrates life.

When I awake, Oneiroi is waiting for me.

She smiles, eases my numb feet into hospital slippers, waffled and white. Still stoned under Glendown's chemical cosh, my head is thick, my tongue a little fried.

Nurse Veal approaches, takes my arm; careful to make sure the white blanket covers the opening on the back of my loosely tied smock.

"Come with me," she says.

DANIEL IS SEATED OPPOSITE ME.

I lift my head, attempting a smile that unfortunately doesn't materialize. The muscles in my face not yet up to speed with my brain. Should I find it in me to smile, there is every possibility my mood might improve, but as bad luck has it, I cannot. I am a dribbling fool.

The stagnant dream is still with me, the Paper Tigers clear in my mind: flat and destroyed. Their orange mush now hallucinated and sinking into the blue and purple stripes between us.

Daniel reaches down and adjusts the rug—its corner curled—an orange paw oscillating back and forth into the morphing hand of a man. He looks up eventually to see me blinking.

"How are you feeling?" he finally asks, his voice soft and low.

"Like crap," I muster, "you?"

He smiles, his head tipping to the side just a little. "That was some protest back there," he says.

"And that was some heavy shit you had Nurse Veal stick in my arm."

A pause.

"I'm sorry," he says.

I give my body permission to slump while another warm dribble of phlegm escapes my awkward mouth. I imagine I must look how I feel: god-awful. But I don't care too much, given my current state. My eyes strain to reach the small gold clock.

I turn my attention to Daniel, trying to recall the fateful night's events: the DVD, the bridge, the police car, and the questioning. I feel Runner rousing, her arms wrapped tightly around Dolly's waist.

Go back to sleep, I say.

Medication wearing off, I clear my throat.

"How long have I been here?" I ask.

"Two days," Daniel says, uncrossing his legs. "One of the other personalities must have taken over the Body after questioning. We had to sedate you."

"We agreed that I would reduce my medication. *Remember?*" I say.

"You entered a psychotic episode. You needed more, Alexa. You were very confused."

"You pride yourself on being a man of your word, *yes?*" I challenge.

"I do."

"You failed," I say.

He falls silent and leans forward, tears casting a glaze across his eyes. "You tried to jump off a bridge," he says.

His words spike the air and swirl, like birds.

I reach out my arm like the branch of a tree, my hand and its palm facing the floor. Each word landing to rest:

You—a goose
Tried—a starling
To—a nightingale
Jump—a skylark
Off—a sparrow
A—a phoenix
Bridge—a blackbird

Daniel looks at me, puzzled, noticing my floating arm and unaware that his words are landed there and resting.

"Alexa?"

I lean toward my wafting arm and blow. His words slowly soaring toward the veil of drooping wisteria outside and scattering across the dew-coated lawn. The promise of morning about to break captured among apple trees, soon to be home for clattering birds and their song.

80

Daniel Rosenstein

SHE CLOSES HER EYES, HER ARM STILL RAISED IN THE AIR. A SINGLE tear traveling down her cheek.

For a second time, she blows on her hand, and I think this a spontaneous act but then wonder if she's hallucinating. Or simply releasing her feelings? Her breath a way of exhaling Monday night's sordid events.

As I wait, my heart starts jackhammering. *Breathe, Daniel,* I tell myself. *Breathe.*

A lingering silence.

She opens her jade-green eyes. They are softened and fatigued.

"Why didn't you tell me Anna and Ella and Grace are part of the Flock?" I speak quietly.

She blinks. "I needed to feel I had some control over who I brought here and who I kept away."

"I don't think that's entirely true, Alexa," I challenge. "You had no control over Ella. You cast her out just like Flo, the personality who killed that guinea pig, remember, when you were sixteen years old."

She looks away, hurt. "You're right. It was just like Flo," she allows. "I cast out both of them because I despised their behavior. Flo was

466

violent and Ella was weak. I felt ashamed of Ella's greed, and yes, I know greed comes from deprivation, but still. She was so sexualized and needy, but it was her lack of integrity I hated most. I completely exiled her from the Body, which she'd enter when I was in complete denial or had checked out. My other personalities didn't dare to challenge or tell me, just like the time they didn't expose Flo. I think they must have thought I'd banish them too."

"I don't understand," I say. "You had me believe Ella was your best friend?"

"She is. Was. But as we got older things changed. She started to use the Body to manipulate. I didn't like it. It scared me."

"You mean you didn't accept these qualities in yourself?"

She hesitates. "Yes."

"You know, one of my tasks is to encourage the reclamation of all your exiled parts. That includes Flo and Ella."

She looks at me, her gaze steady.

"And my task?" she asks.

"To stay alive in the process."

She presses on her chest with the palm of her hand, I think to calm her fast heart.

"And what about Anna?" I say.

She shrugs.

"So long as I came to therapy she didn't care much for coming herself. I was happy with that too. Part of me wanted to try to forget what passed between my father and me, and I was worried that if I brought Anna here you'd analyze the extent of the abuse and why she was created. That bothered me."

She removes her palm, rests it now on her knee.

"Part of you didn't trust me," I say. "If you had, you might have realized I would do only what was best for you—and the Flock."

"Some of us thought you'd try and muscle in on my plan," she adds, "or convince me to stop gathering evidence against Navid. I couldn't have that. I had to make sure he didn't hurt any more girls."

"I understand," I say. "Your revenge might seem justified after all your years of hurting. This is not to dismiss Navid's sordid crimes, but it's unlikely you would have found yourself involved with the Electra had you not suffered at the hands of your father."

She takes a sip of water. "I just couldn't face who I *really* was, what Anna, Ella, or I were doing—or had done—with my father, or Navid, the club, everything . . ."

Her sentence trails off, too much to bear.

"You're Alexa," I finally say, "ornithologist to the Flock. Someone who has done her absolute best to nurture parts of herself under heinous circumstances. Someone who knitted a family of personalities to survive. Your past doesn't have to define who you are, Alexa, but it can inform who you might wish to be. With time."

We look at each other.

"Do you still think you are mad?" I ask.

She smiles slowly, wearing the face of a girl who survived the Jump.

"I'd say I'm someone who has suffered a great deal and misses her mother terribly," she says. "Someone who is strong, with fight at her core. The kind of person I needed when I was younger."

I DIDN'T HEAR THE POLICE CAR EDGE UP BEHIND ME. SOMEONE STEP-ping out.

A man appeared, spoke to me real simple, and eventually had it all make sense. His voice was gentle and considered. Rivaling those in my head, particularly the Fouls—*Jump, you fucking crybaby.*

Finally coaxed down from the ledge, I was driven in the pouring rain to a police station, PC Keith Chandler taking his time, swerving around blips in the road. Going easy on the clutch. He was careful to speak softly, noticing my bloodshot eyes, a tremble in my limbs. My leggings still wet and reeking of urine.

IN A SQUARE FLUORESCENT-LIT ROOM AT THE POLICE STATION, A female officer with a half smile joined us at an oblong table. I suspected her to be just a little judgmental. A slight flicker to her eyes when Runner emptied the rucksack of its entire contents.

She stared at me: an alternate personality destroying a criminal underworld from the inside.

Suddenly overcome, I gave a statement. Well, Oneiroi did, with Ella's help. I stepped back into the Body, thinking she might articulate better the sequence of events. I was tired.

Four hours later I was committed.

Glendown is home now for a while. At least until the Flock are con-sidered safe enough for flight. Daniel believes my dissociated identities are what saved me. That without them I might not have survived the club or the Groom House, and even though his administering medication mutes their voices, we're figuring it out, together—the Fouls, of course, remaining our biggest challenge. It's our hope that one day I'll integrate a little more—*us, we,* and *them* taking on the curious shape of an *I.*

Because *I* can mean any one of the eight personalities—nine, including me—that I've gathered over the years. *I,* the Nest Builder. But in this, I have not lost sight of the girl who was born and named, the one growing and learning person I know as Alexa Wú.

THE ELECTRA, ALONG WITH THE GROOM HOUSE, EVENTUALLY SLIPPED off the front pages of local newspapers. Then, when the arrests were made, hacks wrote hyped headlines: HUMAN TRAFFICKERS ARRESTED IN THE EAST END: 15 WOMEN RESCUED.

They got the "women" part wrong. Most of them were girls.

Another claimed: POLICE ARREST 11 PEOPLE INVOLVED IN PEDOPHILE RING AS SEX WORKER TIPS OFF LOCAL POLICE.

The subheading named Navid Mahal and Cassie Wang as the ringleaders, the story accompanied by a black-and-white photograph of Navid, Cassie, and Shaun, handcuffed, outside the Electra. Its pink neon light killed. Each had been taken in a separate police car, the crowns of their fallen heads forced down further as they stepped inside. In the end, Navid had shown his vulgarity by turning around and giving his fame the middle finger, a nasty curl to his lip. A week later there were more photographs. Of Annabelle and Amy and their brother, who gave testimony to Navid's hit-and-run. Of Jane—though no Sylvie—with a new hairstyle, no longer red but blond. They all still wore their gold necklaces, a key dangling from each—their longing and childhood wounds heartbreakingly and infuriatingly unresolved. I wondered if the authorities caught up with Tao Wang and what had become of Poi-Poi. Had she been sent back to China?

That was five weeks ago, when I believed myself destined for Jumpers Bridge or a life of crime. The Flock splintering into warring parts as protection against our pain. Who knew how much trouble we'd get ourselves in? The risks we would take. How justice and revenge would take over like some rabid beast, those helpless girls reminding me of all the times I too had my voice silenced. Unheard. A sense of powerlessness felt for so long.

So few people tell you there are other choices. That you can change the story. That we're not a fixed product of our past. That there's a way to reclaim the many frightened, exiled parts of ourselves. That we're not worthless, or stupid; or; or; or.

Instead they gaslight.

And lie.

And shark.

And groom.

But they're wrong.

We will triumph.

ACKNOWLEDGMENTS

My gratitude to all those who helped build a village during the delightfully long and sometimes lonely development of *The Eighth Girl*. To everyone at William Morrow and HarperCollins, especially my editor, Liz Stein, who got it, got me, enchanted me with her bull's-eye edits, and made this story wildly better.

To Bill Clegg, my dazzling agent, who has my eternal adoration and respect, and without whom this novel would surely not exist.

To Eugenie Furniss, who believed in my very early words and patiently walked beside me as more and more words followed.

And to Molly Gendell at William Morrow and Laura Cherkas, whose assistance and final editing was nothing short of amazing.

My family: Yvonne and John Prendeville, and in particular my brothers, Martyn Chung and Mark Mak. I thank you for both your love and divine sense of humor.

To my wonderful friends, champions, and readers, whom I neglected when writing took over, especially Dr. Kirsty Rowan and Toni Horton. Also: Chi Chi Izundu, Charlotte Henson, Carolyn Roberts, Christine Blake, Greg Horton, Susannah Nwaka, Violet Nwaka, Harriet Tyce, Louise Hare, Ann Russell, and Andy Darley—all of whom encouraged me by offering fair and just insight and unshakable friendship.

To Cosmo Landesman, whose zeal inspired me to cut loose my reins of funk and suggested I find a way, any way, to write. To David Matthews, who kept me sane by reminding me gently that the personal is *always* political. And my dear friend and guide Joanna Briscoe for our time spent together at the Faber Academy—kidnapping characters.

Also to my patients, past and present, who show up and are curious and questioning of their lives and with immense generosity share their stories with me. You are all fierce and gentle, brave and committed, and the heroes and heroines of my every day. Thank you, I am still learning.

My clinical supervisor, Judy Yellin, whose generosity of spirit and razor-sharp analysis enabled me to practice effectively while I ventured into a fictional world of dissociation and held me throughout.

And my beautiful son, Dexter Landesman, who was just nine years old when this all began and now as a teenager rightly earns the accolade of *portrait of a young man with most patience.*

Finally, thank you to Joe, comrade and tender giant from whom I learn most things and who dared me to struggle and dared me to win, and then asked . . . *If not now, when?*

1. Is there one of Alexa's "flock" you admire or relate to the most? Why is that?

2. The novel alternates between Alexa's point of view and that of Daniel, her therapist. What did you think of Maxine Mei-Fung Chung's portrayal of their relationship, and how it changed over the course of the novel?

3. Daniel writes in his notes that "it's proving difficult to integrate Alexa's personalities. I don't even know if this is the goal anymore". Do you think that integration and "curing" should be the goal in cases such as Alexa's? Could there be some positive side effects to Alexa's multiple personalities?

4. How important is Alexa's mother to the person she becomes?

5. What does Alexa's choice of career as a photographer say about how she sees the world?

6. Much of the novel takes place in and around the strip club where Ella goes to work. What did you make of this setting and the people who worked there?

7. What does the novel suggest about the treatment of women of Asian heritage in British society?

8. What did you think of Maxine Mei-Fung Chung's portrayal of a neurodivergent woman? How did it compare to other depictions of mental illness you might have seen in film, TV and other books?

AVAILABLE AND COMING SOON
FROM PUSHKIN VERTIGO

Jonathan Ames

You Were Never Really Here

A Man Named Doll

Olivier Barde-Cabuçon

The Inspector of Strange and Unexplained Deaths

Sarah Blau

The Others

Maxine Mei-Fung Chung

The Eighth Girl

Amy Suiter Clarke

Girl, 11

Candas Jane Dorsey

The Adventures of Isabel

Martin Holmén

Clinch

Down for the Count

Slugger

Elizabeth Little

Pretty as a Picture

Louise Mey

The Second Woman

Joyce Carol Oates (ed.)

Cutting Edge

John Kåre Raake

The Ice

RV Raman

A Will to Kill

Tiffany Tsao

The Majesties

John Vercher

Three-Fifths

Emma Viskic

Resurrection Bay

And Fire Came Down

Darkness for Light

Those Who Perish

Yulia Yakovleva

Punishment of a Hunter